LULLABY GIRL

ALY SIDGWICK

BLACK & WHITE PUBLISHING

First published 2015
by Black & White Publishing Ltd
29 Ocean Drive, Edinburgh EH6 6JL

1 3 5 7 9 10 8 6 4 2   15 16 17 18

ISBN   978 1 84502 950 0

CREATIVE SCOTLAND

ALBA | CHRUTHACHAIL

Typeset by RefineCatch Limited, Bungay, Suffolk
Printed and bound by Nørhaven, Denmark

For Sim

PROLOGUE

Two hands, splayed softly on the stones. They relay secrets, like poison sucked through roots. Of a larger place than this. Grand skies, bleached pale. Faces. An' a pain that tastes like salt.

Overhead, a darkness. Foam strokes in, pushin' sand into clouds. A moment of chaos. A swirl. Then it curls over an' the hands drain back. In circles, this goes on. I watch the frothin' edge. Goin' in. Out. In. Out.

Cold burns like acid. Dark specks stick on. Flounce off.

Another rush. Close my eyes too late. Cough water out. Lay my head down, an' then I see the beach. Stretchin' away through murky veils of rain. Rocks stand guard, as wet an' dull as my nerves. I am part of this picture. I don't understand. I don't remember. I can only look, an' shiver.

In time, I realise that the hands are mine.

1

The man's coat is red. He jumps round my head. Scary shoutin'. Big eyes, like he's gunna cry. Thur's a dog. Runnin' round, *woof woofin'*.

Sea comes back, *whooooosh*. Hurts like fire.

'—ame?'

Won't keep still.

'Wake up! Stay with me!'

Want him off me.

'What's your name?'

Hurts. Head hurts. So cold.

Wait . . .

I move, jus' a bit. I look.

What . . .

Sand, all round. Sea whooshin' up my legs.

Shells. Pain. A tree, far back, blown sideways.

Try to move. Heavy.

More men. Runnin' close. Pebbles flyin'. Big feet slippin'. Hands. I'm scared. All shoutin' fast an' noisy. Grab me, move me. Now I'm high up, lookin' down. Legs upside down all runnin'. My head hurts an' my legs an' my hands, an' I see sand. Then mud. Then stone. I'm sleepy. They put me down. An old man with a bag. Kneelin', plastic trousers, red face. Pulls my eyes open. Cold metal.

Growly noises. Like sea, but diff'rent.

3

'Stay awake,' someone says, a lot. An' I think, *I don't know what my name is.*

Down down down. Shoutin' stops an' iss warm. Warm. Iss okay.

Bleep-beep, bleep-beep, bleep-beep.

#

This place is Invercraig. I heard the doctor say it. Him an' the men that come here. They look at me. They talk about me lots. I don't like 'em. They don't know I'm lis'nin'. They said I'm prob'ly dumb.

I remember the beach. Cold an' dark. Lyin' there alone, before the shoutin' an' the men an' the questions. I liked the quiet better. Questions hurt my head.

'Who did this to you?' They say that all the time. They make me look in the mirror. They point at my purple nose. At the squashy bits under my eyes. The black bits on my legs, the cuts an' the bits under the bandages. 'Who did that?' they ask. 'Were you with someone? Did you fall off a boat?' I don't like those men. They talk too loud, an' they're here too much, an' they won't let me be alone.

This is the doctor's house. They put on my bandages here. But now I'm upstairs. My bed's in the slanty bit under the roof. I've got a nightie made of paper an' a jumper that's too big. The men sit downstairs all day. Thur's noise an' cars. Thur's a van outside, with a dish on top an' black wires comin' out. Men come with cam'ras, an' a fancy lady talks at 'em with her finger in her ear. I listen through the window. She sounds sad, an' mad too. At night the men talk lots.

One day they show me a telly. Thur's words goin' fast at the bottom, an' a long number: *Loch Oscaig Girl Hotline.*

4

Thur's a man in a black-an'-white hat, talkin'. Then the fancy lady from outside comes on. She talks for a bit, all sadmad. Then the men turn off the telly. Iss the same men as before, an' they ask the same questions. One time they put a pencil in my hand. They wait, but nothin' happens. One man gets mad an' shakes my arms. Then the doctor shouts an' makes 'em go.

#

I wake up an' thur's a lady here. I've never seen her before. She's not the telly lady. Her hair's ginger. She smiles, an' iss a nice smile.

'Hello, my name is Rhona,' says the lady.

Her voice is quiet. I don't feel scared.

'You're going to live with me for a while,' she says. 'It's a special house in the country, for people just like you. Would you like that?'

Downstairs, I hear men. I look at the door.

'You'll be safe there,' says the Rhona lady. 'There's a big fence, and we only let nice people in. Does that sound good?'

I look at her. Thur's some lines round her eyes, but not so much as the doctor.

'All right,' she says. 'Let's get you dressed.' She opens a bag an' takes out stuff. A jumper with a flower on it. A long, soft skirt. Pants. Socks. Wellies. The wellies are too big. 'That's okay,' she says. 'We're not walking far.'

The doctor says byebye. Men stand round us, with hats like the man on telly. Rhona puts her coat on my head. We open the door. Thur's shoutin'. Lights flash. Loud an' bright. Rhona holds my hand. We run. I fall down. The hat men go in front. I see their legs. The shoutin' gets louder. We get

5

through. Round the corner. Thur's a car. We get in. Rhona's laughin'.

'Elvis Presley, eat your heart out!' she says. I don't know what that means.

She drives the car. Thur's one white car in front of us an' one white car behind us. We go past fields, an' ev'rythin's brown an' green. It rains. I see a cow. We go up a hill.

Rhona clicks somethin', an' a voice starts talkin'.

'—will not release a photograph at this time. We have reason to believe her injuries were sustained *before* she went into the loch, and until we learn more we're taking every precaution to protect her identity.'

'Can you tell us more about the area? Loch Oscaig is tidal, is it not?'

'Yes, it's the sixth-largest sea loch in Scotland, and its tidal currents are notoriously strong. The area is sparsely populated, due to the mountainous terrain, and there's no public transport for a twenty-mile radius. In fact, the north shore has no vehicular access whatsoever. We're talking about one of the last great wildernesses here.'

'So it's unlikely that the victim came to the area by car?'

'Unlikely, but not impossible. A B-road follows the south shore for several miles, but no abandoned vehicles have been found.'

'So where do you think the woman came from?'

'Personally, I believe it's a boat we're looking for. We've shifted our search to the water but, frankly, we haven't turned up much. There's forty-odd miles of coastline to comb, and the weather has not been ideal.'

'Have you had much response from the public?'

'Well, it's still early days. We're working closely with the Missing Persons Bureau, and there's a *Crimewatch* special going out tonight. Hopefully that will throw up more leads. The sooner we find out who this woman is, the sooner we can help her. Right now that is our number-one priority.'

'Has she told you her name since regaining consciousness?'

'Well, this is one of the things we're trying to determine. She has not spoken at all, and—'

'You're saying she is mute?'

'It's . . . certainly a possibility. We'll know more after her psychiatric evaluation.'

'So it's true she was moved to an institution this afternoon?'

'Yes, that is correct.'

'Detective Gordon Fraser there, of the West Highland police force, who spoke to our correspondent earlier today. Once again, here's the number to call if—'

Rhona makes a noise with her teeth. She puts out her hand an' the voices stop talkin'.

The rain is loud. The sky gets black. Rhona gets out the car, an' gets back in. We go through gates. Thur's a big white house, an' iss windy an' cold. My hair gets wet. Rhona takes me in. We go upstairs. Thur's voices. The room is dark. I get in the bed, an' Rhona brings me tea. Thur's a dark-green stripe on the cup. I hear rain. Iss hard to hold the cup through the bandages.

'This is Gille Dubh Lodge,' Rhona says. 'It's your new home. And this is your room. No one can come in here without your say-so. Only I can come in, because I'm your case worker. So you're safe. Okay?'

I look at Rhona. She looks sad.

'I can't begin to imagine what you've been through, sweets. But things will be better now. We're all here to help you.'

7

My hands are sore. I look at them. Rhona hugs me. I don't like that.

#

'Little Miss Famous.'

I'm in a room an' iss light outside. Iss a big room. Big windows, an' thur's people.

'What happened to your face?'

A girl's talkin'. Curly hair. Standin' close. All eyes. Lookin'.

'Another Mary on our hands.'

Curly girl waves her arms. I look at her.

'Hell-o? Hell-ooooo?'

'See? Hey, Mary! You've got a twin!'

Thur's a quiet girl behind the door. Her face goes red. People laugh.

'No fun. Come on, Jess.'

Paper hats. Laughin'. Thur's a cake an' the curly girl blows on it. Songs. Music. Quiet girl's lookin'. I look. She smiles. Her hair's very long.

I'm sweaty. I sit in a chair next to Rhona. A lady with white hair sits down. I move away from her. They look at me funny.

'It's only me, dear,' says the lady, an' Rhona says, 'It's only Mrs Laird.'

I look at the floor. Their voices get mixed up.

You've met her loads of times. Don't you remember? I'm your psychiatrist, dear.

I keep lookin' at the floor. From here I can see the lady's shoes. Green. Bashed up but shiny. I've seen those shoes before, when the voice was talkin'. I don't like the voice. It says things like *po-straw-matic* an' *hip-no-regreshun*.

Rhona puts a spoon in my mouth. Iss sweet. I eat, but jus'

8

a bit. Things get noisy, so I get up an' go away. I come to a room with a see-through roof. Thur's tables an' chairs, an' a big window. I go to the window an' look out. Hills. Water. Sky. Iss quiet here. Thur's a tree outside. I like that. I sit down an' look at the tree. My mouth tastes sug'ry, an' it makes me feel funny. I shut my eyes. *Swish swoosh* goes the tree. *Swish swoosh oooooosh.* When I look again, thur's a lady there. I don't like her face. She's a diff'rent lady, with red glasses. Her hair's all hard-lookin'.

'*There* she is,' says the lady, like she's talkin' to someone. But thur's no one. Jus' me an' her. She holds my arm, an' her fingers stick in hard. She pulls me up. It hurts. She starts to walk, an' her hand drags me too. We go back to the noisy room.

#

Rhona takes me outside. We walk round. She points her finger. 'That's Loch Ghlas,' she says, 'and that's the perimeter fence.'

I look down the hill. The fence looks tiny. Wind blows on my face. I close my eyes an' breathe. Rhona keeps talkin'.

'I suppose some folks might feel trapped by a fence. But it's actually a nice thing, because it means no bad people can bother us. We're safe and cosy in here, and you can walk around the grounds without having to . . .'

Rhona's coat swooshes. Quiet. She talks again. Slower.

'You like it out here, don't you? Well, we'll be coming out here a lot more. We can come out every day if you like.'

That smell . . . I know it. Where do I know it from?

I . . .

I open my eyes an' see the sea. Far off. Grey. Iss further than the perimeter fence. But somehow the sea is all I can see. Suddenly I feel funny, like I can't breathe. In my head, a picture of waves. Cold. Heavy. A blackness under me, an' no place to put my feet. Iss the sea I smell. An' . . . I've been closer to it than this. Much closer. Not jus' on the beach, when the men came. I was *in* it . . . Far out . . . In the dark . . .

The funny feelin' grows. I breathe out an' can't breathe back in. My heart goin' *bump bump bump*. Rhona's mouth is movin'. Can't hear her now. I go backwards. I gasp. The sky goes massive. All white, in my eyes. My ears are screamin' an' I can't breathe. I can't breathe . . . I . . .

Music plunging hard. I'm on the floor, pressed flat as possible. Dust in my mouth, in the deepest darkest animal trap, and above my head the screams keep coming. On and on and I can't stand it and Katty I can't I can't . . . Katty! His face bathed in red and the words moving out of him . . . Slowww his hand comes up they will get me and I know then I know I am done for . . . . . .

. . . .

. . . .

. . .

Fallin'. Dark shapes. Hands round mine. Pressed on my belly, too tight. I feel sick. The sky slams down, knockin' a yell out of my mouth. I'm on my side. Grass in my face. An' a voice, a noise, a song, all around. Iss comin' from me. I'm makin' it. I can't stop. Rhona is sideways. Eyes in circles. She doesn't move.

Solen er så rød, mor
og skoven bli'r så sort
Nu er solen død, mor
og dagen gået bort.

10

Ræven går derude, mor
vi låser vores gang.
Kom, sæt dig ved min side, mor
og syng en lille sang . . .

#

Iss quiet when I wake up, an' I'm lyin' on somethin' soft. My throat hurts. I stare into the dark, tryin' to understand. What's that smell? Flowers? I think of the sea, an' shiver. No . . . I roll sideways an' put my arms round myself. There. That's better.

What's that sound? Breathin'? I hold my breath an' listen. The sound keeps goin'. *Hnnnnngh . . . Pfff . . . Hnnnnngh . . . Pfff . . .*

How long have I been here? My bones ache. In my head I see pictures of myself, standin' in front of people. They smile slightly. The old ones clappin' their hands. At the back, I notice four faces. A blonde lady, the white-haired lady, the lady with red glasses, an' Rhona. They stand together an' nod an' whisper. For some time Rhona stands in front of me. She holds my arms. Talks at me. Tries to take me away. But in the pictures I won't go with her. I want to stay in the big room. Singin' an' singin' an' singin'.

Hnnnnngh . . . Pfff . . . Hnnnnngh . . . Pfff . . .

Carefully, I sit up. Bed. Of course. I'm in bed. I put my legs out into cold air. Below my feet, thur's carpet.

I've been dreamin' . . .

Arms out, I start to walk. Iss so black I can't see myself. *Bang* goes my knee, into somethin' hard. The breathin' noise stops. A pause. A *swoosh*. Then brightness pings on. I see Rhona, squintin' up. We're in a small pink room. Not the room she said was mine.

11

'Hey, sweets. What's wrong?' Rhona says. She gets up.

I stand where I am. Lookin' at the two single beds, an' the shuttered window an' the bolted door. Tears come to my eyes. Thur's so much I don't know, but I know this room. The 'crisis room', Rhona called it.

'Come on. Let's get you back in bed.'

Rhona puts her hands on my arms. I look up, an' see her for what feels like the first time.

'You're freezing,' she sighs. 'Come on, sweets. Back to bed.'

Katty.

Her hands jump. We look at each other.

'Did you just . . . ?'

'Katty,' I repeat, so quietly I hardly hear it, an' for a moment my feet seem incredibly far away from me. I look at 'em, my heart beatin' fatly. *Boomboomjaggaboomboombooom* all over the place. So messy an' zigzaggy an' mixed up I'd understand if one little word got lost in there. My ears whistle. I wonder if I spoke at all. If the word didn't really come out. But it must have, cos Rhona's actin' diff'rent. She ducks her head down close, an' her eyes whizz round my face.

'Ka— Is that your name? Katty? Your name is Katty?'

I look at her. That clear, kind, familiar face. Suddenly, I know iss true. I look her right in the eye, an' I take a breath, an' I nod. Rhona's face changes again. She opens her mouth a bit. We look at each other. Then she stands back an' puts out her hand. I've never seen her smile like that. Her eyes are alive.

'Well,' she says. 'It's a pleasure to meet you. I knew you'd show up sooner or later.'

\#

'Katty? Katty. You remember Vera, don't you, Katty?'

I look at the blonde lady who's talkin'. We're in a whitish room. A pale-green sofa, like before, an' I'm sittin' on it.

'My . . . name . . . is . . . *Car-o-line,*' says the blonde-haired lady, all loud. She points at me an' says, 'Your . . . name . . . is . . . Katt-ee.' She points at the white-haired lady an' says, 'This . . . is . . . Vee-ra.'

Why's she sayin' *Vera*? Rhona said the white-haired lady is Mrs Laird.

I look at Mrs Laird. Thur's lots of paper on her knees. My head hurts, like iss squashed. I close my eyes an' put my hand on my eyes. That helps. My hand is sweaty-hot. Caroline's started sayin' *Katty* a lot. They all have, since me an' Rhona were in the pink room. I don't know how long ago that was. That day's jumbled up with the rest an' iss hard to work out what came first.

Mrs Laird's the one who always talks at me. I don't know why Caroline's here too. I think they want me to talk back. Sometimes I open my mouth an' see 'em waitin'. Then my head starts hurtin' an' I have to close my eyes. My knees itch in the place where the scabs are. I wish Rhona would take me outside more. My head feels better out there.

Caroline an' Mrs Laird look at the papers. They whisper. Caroline leans forward, holdin' a bit of paper, an' says, 'Katt-ee. Verstehst du mich?'

They wait. Caroline's lookin' at me all super careful. I bend to scratch my leg, an' her eyes whizz after me.

Caroline looks at her paper. 'Singen sie gerne?'

Mrs Laird shakes her head. Whispers to Caroline. They look at the paper again. I don't know what's goin' on.

'Er du dansk, Katt-ee? Forstår du mig nu?'

A pain goes through my head. Like someone whacked me

13

from behind. I stand up, fast, an' get my legs muddled up. Suddenly Caroline is in front of me. Her eyes are excited. I back away, grabbin' my head, an' before I know what's what I'm on the floor. What's hap'nin'? Why can't I breathe right? Those words *did* somethin'. Iss like a magic spell. I start singin', to make the bad feelin' go away.

'Danish,' says Mrs Laird.

When I've stopped bein' scared they put me back on the sofa. They talk at me for a long time, but now they jus' talk with the funny words. Readin' out stuff. Waitin'. Writin' stuff down. When they talk about me they don't whisper. Iss like they think I can't hear 'em any more.

'I don't know,' says Mrs Laird. 'I'm still not convinced she understands.'

'Come on! That's the biggest reaction we've seen in a month.'

'We're close, I'll give you that. But no . . . I don't know. I think the truth's more subtle. That lassie's British. You mark my words.'

'She hasn't uttered a word of English.'

'Call it a gut feeling . . .'

Mrs Laird puts her chin on her fist. My scabs itch. I look at the window.

#

I wake up to twilight an' the sound of a bell. Far away, for ages, the bell tinkles. *Chingle-ingle-ing, chingle-ingle-ing, chingle-ingle-ing.*

Sometimes the bell stops, an' voices fill the silence. Other times it keeps goin'. I fall in an' out of sleep. The voices I hear get angrier. At some point I hear shoutin'. Crashin' noises, stompin', an' a door slammin'. For a while after that iss quiet. But later on the bells come more an' more. When I wake up prop'ly, the room is bright. Rhona sits in the chair by the bed. I watch her for a while. Her face is frownin', even though she's asleep. The bell rings, jus' then, an' her eyes open.

'Morning,' she says when she sees me. 'Or should I say goddag?'

She looks an' sounds exhausted, an' she doesn't smile. In the background, the bell keeps goin'.

'That's the phone,' says Rhona, without breakin' eye contact. 'The newspapers have gone bananas for you.'

Chingle-ingle-ing, chingle-ingle . . .

'Shut *up*!' yells a voice, from somewhere close by.

'Why?' I whisper. A short silence. One corner of Rhona's mouth curves up.

'I *knew* it,' she murmurs. 'Your song, I'm afraid. One of the cooks filmed you and sold the video to the *Daily Post*. Now everyone and their dog's calling up to tell us you're Danish.'

I frown.

'I'm sorry, sweets. She filmed it on her phone. We sacked her this morning.'

'The . . . cook.'

'Yes.'

I try to understand what this means. Iss hard. I don't remember seein' any cook. When my eyes open again, Rhona's lookin'.

'Why do you sing a lullaby, Katty? Why a *Danish* lullaby?'

I look at her, an' frown.

'Katherine,' I say.

Rhona's mouth opens a bit. Then she closes it.

'You're not Danish, are you?' she says.

I look at her, an' wonder about this. Am I?

15

'I . . . don't . . .'

'But you understand me, now, don't you? Your first language is English?'

'Mmmmgh,' I say, an' hold my head. I'm not used to mixin' my thoughts with someone else's. Iss like bein' forced to do maths. Unfinished problems, with a tickin' clock an' jus' one right answer.

Rhona smiles, in a sad sort of way. 'Sorry, hon,' she sighs. 'Overload, huh?' She frowns at the floor for a while. 'It's a long road,' she murmurs.

I look round the room an' see a clock on the wall. I never noticed it before. A quarter to eleven, it says. The quick hand's gone round once by the time Rhona talks again.

'This . . . newspaper. They've got a picture of you now. No one was meant to have that. They printed it with a fuzzy patch on your face, but still . . .' She puts her hand on her head, the same way I do, an' goes quiet for a minute. Then she says, 'They started a sort of fan club for you, a fortnight ago. People give money to help you, and they've been sending it all to Gille Dubh. You're quite popular, you know. Since this video turned up they're calling you Lullaby Girl.'

'Lullaby . . .'

'It's a lullaby. The song you sing. Don't you know that?'

She stares me out. Tears come to my eyes.

'No,' I say.

Rhona holds her head. She keeps lookin', but her eyes have gone tired.

'Well,' she says, softly. 'You're the only one in Britain who doesn't.'

2

MmhorGDRegP89/10
Name: 'Katherine'
Gender: F
DOB: Unknown. (Est. age 30)
Date of session: 20/04/2006
Duration: 15min
T: Therapist, P: Patient

[Note: Patient is now in a hypnotic trance and has just visualised stepping through a door . . .]
T: What do you see?
P: Too bright. White.
T: Can you hear anything?
P: Birds.
T: Can you hear any voices?
P: Not sure. No. Hear self breathing.
T: Is it still bright?
P: Can make out shapes.
T: Let your eyes adjust to it and then you can tell me when you start to make things out.
P: Sitting on something hard. A suitcase. Snow. Outside. Lots of snow.
T: Look around you. What else can you see?

P: A street. Wooden houses. Yellow. Red. Green. Candles in ice.

T: Are there any people in the street?

P: No.

T: What can you see in front of you?

P: A house. Curtains closed. I want someone to come to the window. Want them to let me in. It's so cold.

T: Is it daytime?

P: Yes.

T: How long have you been sitting here?

P: Not sure. Came on a bus.

T: Do you live in the wooden house?

P: No. Came a long way. It's very cold. Too cold. Scared will die. Fingers. Freeze.

T: What did the bus look like?

P: High up. Dark. Travelled in night.

T: Can you see the front of the bus? Can you see the name of the destination?

P: Not sure. Looks wrong. Funny words.

T: Who do you want to come to the window?

[No answer. Patient sobs.]

T: Can you see their face?

P: Yes.

T: Can you describe this person?

P: Handsome. He is smiling. Lines around eyes. But he is not old.

T: Do you know this man?

P: [Pause.] Yes.

T: Why does this man upset you?

P: [Long pause.] My fingers hurt.

T: Do you know the man's name?

18

P: [Sobbing. No answer.]
[Patient is brought out of hypnotic trance.]
Session ends

#

Breakfast goes on in the dinin' room. I don't like it down here, with all the people. I've been here every day, I think, but I didn't really notice till now. Like my body was here without me inside it. I sit close to the door. Heart bumpin'. Tryin' to eat. Thur's people all round. It feels like thur's hundreds of 'em, but now I know thur's jus' fourteen. Fifteen includin' me. All women. I try not to look at their faces. I don't like this room. Not by myself. I want to get out.

Where's Rhona? She said *See you at breakfast*. Why's she not here? I want her to be here.

I see somethin' bright, an' risk a peek. Iss a doorway on the other side of the room. Oh. I've been through that before. Iss the room with the glass roof. My legs are shakin'. I should jus' go upstairs. But the glass room is callin' me. I remember the tree, an' decide I need to look at it.

I stand up, put my head down, an' walk quickly at the light. Someone laughs, from somewhere.

'Hey Katty, gizza song!'

Other voices. I feel eyes on me. Then the doorway comes up, an' I'm through it. Away. Under the glass. No one is out here. Jus' me. I breathe an' feel much better. Thur's tables an' chairs, like the dinin' room. I walk right forward, to the end of the room, an' sit down. Here, I can't see into the dinin' room, an' they can't see me. The tree is right through the glass. Iss like I'm outside, without Rhona. But it doesn't feel scary. Iss lovely.

19

'Katherine,' I say, quietly. Testin' my voice out, an' that word. The name that I know is mine now. Katherine. Kathy. Katty. All three of 'em are inside me. It feels funny to have so many. Rhona said the people over the fence made up lots of 'em. She said they know I'm Katherine now, but they're hangin' on to the names they made up. Lullaby Girl. Lock-oss-ki Girl. Viking Girl. An' more I can't remember. Rhona says they like Lullaby Girl best.

Outside, the moor fills most of the window. Iss greyish purple, runnin' all the way down to the sea. I can see for miles. Past the perimeter fence. Across to the dark-brown mountains. Wind blasts the heather. Clouds the size of countries cross the sky.

Jus' then, somethin' twists against the purple, an' a thin shape unfolds from the ground. I jump an' move back. Iss her! The quiet girl. She hasn't seen me yet, cos her eyes are pointed down. She walks forwards, gettin' battered by the wind.

Rhona said the girl's called Mary, an' that she doesn't talk at all. She used to talk, long ago, but some bad stuff happened, an' after that she jus' stopped. Her mum an' dad stuck her in here, but they never come to visit. *Poor Mary* Rhona always says. She says her dad's a priest.

Mary's reached the gravel now. Her eyes come up, towards the glass room, an' without thinkin' I take a step back. Mary's eyes go straight to me. I gasp. Both of us go still.

For a second, nothin'. I don't move an' neither does she. Wind makes her hair whirl round. I can see her face better from here, an' she looks real sad. We look at each other some more. Then she lifts her hand. Sends a tiny wave.

I wave back.

A big *whoosh* hits the window, an' thur's a *splat* above my head. I look up. The tree's dumped a clump of leaves. Narrow. Silv'ry brown.

I look back at the gravel, but Mary's gone. Rain starts pattin' down. Soft at first. Then the clouds come down low, so I can't see the moor any more, an' the roof comes alive with noise.

I sit where I am, lookin' up. It feels great to be out here without gettin' wet. Like I'm cheatin'. The clouds get lower an' blacker. When I can't see the moor any more, I come inside. The dinin' room is dark, an' thur's no one in it.

Iss taken me a while to find my way round the house. Even now, I don't always remember where stuff is. I'll walk left at the bottom of the stairs instead of right, an' end up down the wrong corridor, or in the toilet instead of the dinin' room. Usually this happens in the mornin', when my head's still fuzzy. Rhona's office is easiest to find, along the long, straight corridor that's painted blue. The blue corridor's where all the important rooms are. Rhona's office, Joyce's office, Mrs Laird's office an' private sittin' room . . . When that doctor lady came here, she sat with me in Joyce's office. I didn't like it in there. It was the wrong colour, an' it smelled funny. Caroline doesn't have an office. I sometimes think she might be mad about that. But the computer room's sort of hers. I've never seen any other staff in there.

I walk through the hall an' stop at the bottom of the stairs. Iss darker in here, cos no one's bothered to put the lights on. The ceilin' has wooden panels with pictures carved on 'em, an' iss higher than the other ceilin's in the house. The stairs are made from the same wood as the ceilin'. Dark an' shiny, with smooth oval hollows in the middle of each step. Like a heavy person walked up 'em once an' left footprints. Above me is the landin', which leads to the corridor where the

21

bedrooms are. On each wall of the downstairs hall thur's a doorway. One leadin' to the day room, one to the offices, one to the dinin' room, an' one to the outside. The dinin'-room corridor has a bump halfway along, with a glass door. Through that is the back porch.

Where is ev'ryone? I don't want to be with 'em, an' I don't want to talk to 'em, but I want to know where they are.

A noise comes from my right, so I go through that doorway. This is the way to the day room. Another noise, now. A voice. Music. I edge along the corridor an' peek through the day-room door. There they are. All sittin' down on chairs. I can't see what they're doin', an' I kinda want to know, but thur's no way I'm goin' in. That's the place where I used to sing. If I go in, they might make me do it again. Then ev'ryone would laugh.

No chance . . .

I creep away from the door.

Wait though. Wait. What's *that*?

I stop. At the end of the corridor, thur's somethin' I never noticed. A little door at the top of three steps. *Library*, it says. Have I been in there before? I can't remember.

I look back into the day room. No one's lookin' this way, so I sneak past an' climb the three steps. The door at the top has a handle with a six-pointed star. I go in.

Books, of course. They're everywhere. The room's not much bigger than my bedroom, but iss packed tight with novels an' manuals an' picture books. Shelves from floor to ceilin', saggin' in places. I sit cross-legged on the floor an' grab a book called *Native Woodland of the British Isles*. In it, thur's a drawin' of a tree that looks like the one outside. *Common ash*, it says. (*Fraxinus excelsior*.) Thur's two more drawings beside it. One of green leaves, an' one of the brown things that dropped on the roof. They're not leaves at all, it says. They're called keys.

I like the library room very much. I sit in it for a long time. At one point I hear voices, but nobody comes in here.

#

Some men ring the bell at the perimeter gate, an' Mrs Laird lets 'em in. They're news men, from a paper called the *Western Courier*. When I see their faces, I know they've been here before. I don't know when or how many times. That whole time is fuzzy in my head. But I remember them bein' here, drinkin' tea. Specially the biscuit man. I remember him sayin' *Any wee treats?* an' Mrs Laird bringin' the chocolate biscuits out. Then he ate half the tin, an' there weren't enough left to go round.

The men are old an' they smell like tobacco. All of 'em wear pullovers an' these stretchy band things round the arms of their shirts. Biscuit man's teeth click when he eats, an' his hair looks funny, like iss slidin' off the front of his head.

I watch 'em write with the blue biros. Watchin' me all close. Waitin' for me to say somethin', or cry, or do somethin' they can put on the front page. But I don't say anythin'. I jus' sit here, squashed between Rhona an' Mrs Laird. Mrs Laird does all the talkin'. The worst bit comes when they try to take my photo. A man stands up, without askin', an' sticks a cam'ra in my face. 'Smile!' he says. Rhona puts her hand in the way.

'We already told you, no!' she says.

'We can blur it afterwards. It's really no big—'

'Then why bother?'

23

Photo man sighs. The man with the blue biro gives him a look.

'*You* don't mind if I take one, do you, Kathy?' says photo man. 'Pretty girl like you.' He reaches out. A big, red, hairy hand. I watch it comin', in slow motion. All the way to my face. Closer. Closer.

Somethin' electric goes through me. Suddenly I'm movin'. My chair goes over, knockin' a mug off the table. It smashes. Tea goes everywhere. Over their shoes, into my socks, over the cam'ra, under the sofa. People suck in breath. I stand behind Rhona, shakin'.

'I wouldn't try that again, if I were you,' Rhona snaps. Silence rings out. The man blushes.

'All right, gents. I believe that's enough for today,' says Mrs Laird. She takes 'em away.

Later, I tell Rhona I won't see any more newspaper men.

'Oh, I don't know,' she says. 'I think it might good for you.'

I glare.

'Meeting folk is good for your recovery.' she says. 'The *Western Courier* guys are a bit annoying, but—'

'I won't do it again,' I growl. 'I'll run away.'

Rhona puts her hands down flat.

'Where would you run to?' she asks quietly.

I look at her. I can't work out if she's angry. She stares back. But the moment passes.

'You know, running away never solves anything,' says Rhona. 'You can't spend your whole life in the conservatory. We're here to help you. Mrs Laird, Caroline, Joyce . . .'

I make a face. Joyce is the lady with red glasses.

'Then there's Dr Harrison, who was here last week. You remember the woman who made you go to sleep?'

I glare at Rhona.

'Don't need any of you,' I say, though I know that's not true. I need Rhona quite a lot.

'Hon, it's not good for you to be isolated. Now that you're talking, it's important to keep moving forwards. *Up*wards. And that means increasing your social circle. When you finally go home to your family, you'll want to be able to talk to them.'

I gasp. Tears come into my eyes.

Home. I've never told her how much that word scares me. How can I go back to a place that doesn't exist?

'I . . . don't have . . . family,' I say.

Rhona sits forward in her chair. 'Everyone's got family, Kathy. It's just that you've forgotten who yours is.'

'They'd've come to get me.'

'Oh, hon . . . There could be all kinds of reasons for them not getting in touch. Remember, no one out there has seen your face properly. The papers aren't allowed to—'

'They'd still *know*! They'd know I'm *gone*!'

Rhona looks at me for a long time. Her face is sad, but she doesn't say anythin'. In the end I turn over, pullin' my bedspread with me, an' lie with my back to her. Through the window, the sky is black. I can see myself in the glass, like iss a mirror. Over my shoulder, Rhona's head is in her hands.

#

Dark dreams follow me through the night. Movin' in circles. Chased by tears. Afterwards, I only remember one.

A man stands tall against a blackened sky. Shinin' pale, with his back to me. Snow swirls down an' lands in our hair. At our feet, hundreds of jellyfish lie dead.

Help me, I say. *Help me.*

Thin hands hang by his sides. One clutched tight. The other creased and limp. I reach for the second one, but my hands drift right through. Suddenly I see I am barefoot.

Help me . . .

The man's back quakes. Like laughter, emptied of sound. I claw at his hands. The silence grows. Shoals of stars buffet us. He will never turn around.

#

Breakfast time. I look through the mugs to find the one with the green stripe. At first I don't see it, so I almost don't have tea at all. But iss there at the back. I take it to the hot drink machine, put it under the tap, an' press *Tea*. Then I put in three sugarcubes an' carry it with me to the conservat'ry. I feel a bit sick today, so I don't get any food. Thur's only three people in the dinin' room, an' none of 'em stare. I look at their faces as I go past. They're all old. One is Mrs Bell an' one is Mrs Shaw. I know the third one's face but not her name. Prob'ly another *Mrs*. Only the staff call the oldies by their first names. I get the feelin' they'd clip the rest of us round the ear if we tried. *Mrs* is safer. I don't want to talk to 'em anyway. I don't like talkin' to anyone besides Rhona.

In the conservat'ry, I start to feel better. The sky is pale, with hardly any clouds. Across the moor, the mountains are solid-lookin'. Rich, hot-chocolate brown. I sip my tea an' look at 'em. Outside, the tree is perfectly still. It must have been windy in the night, cos thur's lots more keys on the roof today. They cast a muddy shadow over the room, with little gaps of sky shinin' through. It feels nice. Like I'm in a nest. This is the closest I get to goin' outside alone. I'm allowed out without Rhona, of course. The fence is there, so they trust me to walk round the grounds. But I don't want to. Iss big out there, under the sky, an' I still can't face it by myself. That's okay, though, cos Rhona always says she'll come with me. I think she even thinks iss her idea.

The world over the fence terrifies me, though I know I've been out there before. Folk say the sea washed me up, an' I know that that bit's true. I remember the pain an' exhaustion. Kickin' in darkness. Thinkin' *I will die now*. But my life before that stuff's a myst'ry. Ev'ryone thinks I'm from a country across the sea. Or, well, they *say* that, but they say it in a way that sounds like they don't believe it. I don't know what the truth is. Sometimes when I wake up my head has little pictures in it, of things an' places an' people I don't know. But they never stay clear for long, an' I'm never able to piece them together.

My song is the strangest part of all. I can reel off those funny-soundin' words as easy as the ABC. But when it comes to their *meanin'*, I'm stuck. Even when Rhona showed me what the words meant in English, I couldn't understand. Iss jus' about foxes an' the sun an' stuff. Why would I bother to learn *that* by heart? Iss part of me, like a dead plant rooted deep inside my head, an' I don't think I'll ever dig all of it out. But I won't sing it any more. How could I do that, before, in front of ev'ryone? What a clown. The song has started to scare me, cos iss a bridge to a part of myself I don't know. I want to stay on this side, with Rhona an' the conservat'ry an' the tree. Things are simple here. I need things to stay the same.

Voices drift through from the dinin' room. Louder for a while. Then nothin'. I reach for my mug an' iss gone cold. I drink the tea anyway. Nice an' sweet.

3

Saturday is music therapy day. Iss somethin' I've stayed away
from, cos I know now that that's where I used to sing my
song. But Rhona gets cross today when I say I won't go. She
says I'll get no treats if I don't start joinin' in. I scowl.

'I'll be next to you the whole time,' Rhona says.

I grab her arm. We go down the stairs an' follow the others
into the day room. Thur's a man at the front with a little
white bit on his neck. 'That's the vicar, Mr Duff,' says Rhona.
He has a green guitar on a strap an' he hugs it to his chest as
he chats to Mrs Laird. Ev'ryone comes in an' finds a chair.

'Ready?' says Mr Duff when ev'ryone's sat down. He has a
deep, boomy voice. Caroline comes round with bits of paper
an' shoves one in my hand. For a few minutes, ev'ryone talks
at once. Then Mr Duff plays a note on his guitar, an' they go
quiet.

'Page four,' whispers Rhona. She opens the leaflet in my
hands. 'Amazing Grace', it says. Ev'ryone starts to sing, an'
actually they don't sound bad. The older ladies are the
loudest – all warbly *tra-la-la* – an' Rhona whispers iss cos
they used to be in the village choir. When the song's over
Rhona says, 'Well done,' even though I didn't join in. No one
else looks at me, an' that is good. They sing one more song,
an' another, an' another. At the end they sing 'Somewhere
Over the Rainbow', an' I'm so surprised to hear it that I sing
along with 'em. Rhona smiles at me, an' I smile back. Maybe

this isn't so bad after all. When the singin' is over, Mr Duff reads some words out from a little book. Ev'ryone puts their faces down. 'Amen,' says Mr Duff. Then he goes out of the room. People start talkin'.

'It's dancing time now,' says Rhona, an' helps me to my feet. Mrs Laird wheels in a gramophone on a wooden trolley an' fiddles with it while Caroline moves the chairs into the corner. People start dancin' to the music, but no matter how much Rhona nags me I won't join in. She sits with me a while, watchin' the others whirl round the room. Then Joyce comes in, sayin' thur's a telephone call, an' they both disappear. The Mary girl whirls over, lookin' happier than I've ever seen, an' grabs my hand without askin'. I don't want to hurt her feelin's, so I dance with her an' it ends up bein' tons of fun. We fall over a lot an' bump into people an' jump over chairs that've been knocked over. By the time Mrs Laird turns off the music, I'm out of breath.

'That's right, Kathy!' calls Mrs Laird. 'Shake a leg!'

When I see Rhona later, I tell her I had fun at music therapy. I'd thought that'd make her happy, but instead she hardly looks at me. Her eyes an' nose are all pink-lookin'.

'Are you sad?' I ask.

'My mother is very sick,' she tells me, after a pause. Then tears come out of her eyes, an' she goes across the room for some tissues. I tell her I like dancin' now, an' she says, 'Oh that's nice.' She doesn't say more about her mother, an I'm glad about that. I don't like Rhona bein' sad. When she wipes her eyes I look the other way.

'I danced with Mary,' I say.

'Oh? That's nice, that you two should make friends. Being the youngest and all.'

'Mary's the youngest?'

'Well . . . She was until you showed up. But we still don't know for sure how old *you* are. So, you see, you're both competing for the crown.'

'How old's Mary?'

'Twenty-eight.'

'So . . . I'm twenty-eight too?'

'No, hon. I just told you. We've got to guess. The doctor said he thought you were thirty years old.'

I think about this. Thirty is a terribly big number. It doesn't seem fair.

'Why do I have to be thirty?'

'Well, there were several factors to consider. Your skin, your hair, the state of your tee—'

'I want to be twenty-eight!'

Rhona sighs a big sigh. Stuffs her tissue up her sleeve.

'Well, who knows, sweets. Maybe you'll get to be. All you've got to do is remember.'

I scowl. Rhona tries to pat my arm, but I hop off the bed an' move to the window. For a while, she doesn't speak. Then, right when I don't expect it, she says, '*Have* you remembered anything?'

I turn an' look at her.

'If I do . . . you'll send me away. Won't you?'

'You'll get to go home.'

'Hmm.'

'So have you? Remembered anything?'

My mind is full of fuzzy shapes. Iss been like that for a while, but there *is* one new thing. One very big, very scary new thing, an' that is the man from my dreams. I've never seen his face, an' he hasn't popped up much, but I know he's important. Somehow, deep down in my heart, I've come to

30

know the dream man's really out there. He's real, an' he knows who I am. Thur's a badness round him that scares me. I don't think anyone could protect me from badness that big.

'No!' I say, louder than I meant to. I think Rhona gets a shock. Her eyes go big for a second.

'Sure?'

'Yes.'

Rhona's eyes shrink an' go back to bein' puffy. She stands up from her chair.

'Well,' she says, 'when you do . . . I'll be here.'

That night I dream of the man again. When I wake up the bed is full of sweat. Thur's a warm cup of tea by my side, but I'm the only one in the room.

#

Tuesday is my day for havin' Mrs Laird talk at me. She's the brain doctor, Rhona said, an' ev'ryone has to see her once a week. I don't like tellin' her stuff, cos I know iss not really private, in the end. Rhona always finds out what me an' Mrs Laird said, an' she tries to sneak it in when we're talkin'. Askin' questions all sly like, an' waitin' to see what I'll do. But I can't get out of seein' Mrs Laird. Iss like a law or somethin'. Even when I don't talk, she writes down loads of stuff. Today iss worse than usual, cos all she asks about is a man with sandy hair. I don't know where she got that from, cos I never told anyone the dream man has hair that colour. Iss funny. It feels like a trick. I say I don't know what she means. Then she gets cross an' brings out photos of my face all mushed up. Iss not the first time I've seen those. Rhona said the police took 'em.

31

'This is what you looked like when you came here,' Mrs Laird says. 'Don't you want to catch the person who did that?'

I look at the photos. They don't really look like me. Mrs Laird says some stuff about *progress,* an' *not being afraid.* Then she packs the pictures up an' lets me go.

I'm sad after the session, an' I want to go for a walk, but when I go to Rhona's office she's busy with a diff'rent girl. I scowl over her shoulder at the girl on the sofa. Iss the curly-haired one who had the party. Her eyes are all pink today. I scowl.

'Go by yourself, dear,' Rhona says. 'Some fresh air will be good for you.'

'No. You come with me.'

'I'm with Jess now. We can go for a walk tomorrow.'

'Not tomorrow. Now.'

Rhona sighs. 'No can do, hon.'

'Why can't *I* have a cake?'

Rhona looks surprised. 'What?'

'I want special cake. Like her. Cake an' candles.'

'You mean . . . for your birthday?'

'*My* cake an' candles.'

Rhona's face goes straight. She dumps her papers an' comes right to the door. Looks in my face, very close. Like she's cross.

'Kathy, what date is your birthday?'

'Let's go outside.'

'Listen, hon. This is important. Do you know what date your birthday is?'

'Will I get cake?'

'Yes, dear. You'll have all the birthday cake you want. Just tell me when the right day is.'

32

I look at Rhona. This is too annoyin'. I jus' wanted to go for a walk. But nothin's goin' to happen till I answer. I try to think. When is my birthday? The only birthday I remember is Jess's.

'Nine . . . teenth,' I say.

'The nineteenth?! Of what? Which month?'

I look past Rhona, to the calendar on her wall.

'April,' I say.

'So . . . it was your birthday two weeks ago?'

'No . . . uh . . .'

Rhona looks at her calendar too. She frowns. Looks back at me.

'We're into *May* now, Kathy. I just didn't turn the page yet.'

'I said May,' I say, an' look away from her eyes.

'Is your birthday in April or May?'

'May.'

'The nineteenth of May?'

'Yes.'

'Seriously? Are you sure?'

'Yes.'

My face is all hot now, but I don't think Rhona sees. She takes me in her office an' tells Jess to go. But that's as far as my luck holds. Instead of gettin' her anorak, Rhona picks up the telephone. She sits at her desk an' talks an' talks an' talks, an' writes on some paper, an' talks some more. Iss boring. Sometimes Rhona dials numbers into the telephone. Some- times it rings an' she picks it up. I jiggle my feet against the desk, an' that makes a glass ball thing fall off a stack of paper. I jump as it thuds to the floor.

'No!' shrieks Rhona. She drops to the ground an' comes back up with the ball in her arms. Iss purple, with pretty dark swirls inside it. 'Please don't play with this,' says Rhona. 'It's very dear to me.'

'What is it?'

'A gift from my mother. It's called a Caithness globe.'

'What's it for?'

'Nothing. Just ... Oh ... Kathy, why don't you go outside?'

'I want you to come too.'

'Go on. I'll catch you up.'

'Rho-na.' I scowl. But I don't want to make her cross, so I nod my head an' go.

The sea is super bright today, like silver. I stand on a rock by the back porch, lookin' at it. Iss funny bein' out here without Rhona. Somethin' shiny catches the sun an' winks back at me. I like that. Iss pretty. I walk slowly round the out-houses, an' while I'm doin' that some clouds come across. By the time I get back to my rock the sky is dark grey, but the silver light winks on an' on. Iss comin' from down the hill, jus' behind the perimeter fence. Jus' then, the porch door bangs open an' Rhona runs out.

'Get inside, Kathy!' she shouts. Her face is super mad, so I do like she says. She locks me in an' stomps downhill with her arms swingin'. I watch till her head drops out of sight.

#

Wednesday.

I'm not allowed outside today, an' I'm not allowed to sit in the conservat'ry. All the curtains are closed, an' that makes it feel like night-time. I sit in the dinin' room, pickin' at a slice of toast, as angry voices echo down the corridor. The telephone rings a lot.

I'm not hungry, so I creep to the hall an' stand at the end of the blue corridor. From here I can hear better. I think iss Joyce who's talkin'.

'—can't cottonwool the girl forever, Rhona. If you just do what they want, everything will be fine. They won't print the picture. The money keeps coming in. Everyone's happy!'

'This is not about *money*!'

'Ladies! Ladies! Please . . .'

'That poor girl's safety is in our hands, and all you can—'

'We could never afford to keep her here without those handouts. You of all people should—'

'I said no!'

'You'll be doing her a favour. Besides, she's not the only patient to consider. It's like Custer's Last Stand in here!'

'Animals!'

'What if they print pictures of the others? What if the families sue?'

'Exactly! They're animals, so why are you so keen to let them in?'

'Come on, Rhona, they're not that bad.'

Chingle-ingle-ing chingle-ingle-ing . . .

'Don't you dare pick that up!'

Chingle-ingle-ing . . .

'One interview, Rhona. One little interview.'

Chingle-ingle-ing . . .

'Over my dead body!'

Chingle-ingle . . .

'Oh, for God's sake!'

\#

Thursday.

I wake up early with a stabbin' pain behind my eyes, an' limp to the bathroom to be sick. For a long time iss hard to think straight. I lie on the floor in the dark, hopin' the pain will go away, but things jus' get worse instead. The ceilin' ripples when I move, an' there're patches missin', like I'm lookin' through a broken mirror. I close my eyes to the growin' daylight an' try not to think about goin' blind.

A face watches over me. Far off, hidden behind a bright light. I see my hands on that face. *His* face. A man. I feel my connection to him. Stubble scratchin' my fingertips. The tickle of his breath as he laughs.

Help me, I say. An' this time he hears. A smile surges out from the whiteness, an' as my heart flutters up to meet it an electric-blue eye stabs me to the ground. I jolt on the bathroom floor. Pinned underneath. A name punches into me with so much force that I start to cry. The air is painfully dry an' bright. Groaning, I rush back to my bedroom. Through the door. Across the carpet. *A pencil . . . Where's my pencil? There.* I grip it hard between my fingers, an' score six shaky letters on my pillowcase. I wilt forwards. Then pain crushes my eyes, an' I collapse into blackness.

#

Friday

Rhona sits in the conservat'ry with me, drinkin' hot chocolate. We sit far back, near the door to the dinin' room. I ask to go outside, but that's still not allowed. She gets cross when I ask, an' rubs her forehead a lot. I look through the window. From here I can jus' see rain.

36

'Why can't we? Is it dangerous?' I ask.

'Kind of.'

'But you said iss safe here.'

'It is. It's just that, well, there's newspaper people out there.'

'Is it the smelly men?' I ask.

Rhona laughs. 'No, sweets. It's not the *Western Courier*. The ones outside are from a bigger paper. They're the ones who made your fan club.'

'Why are they dangerous?'

'Well, they're not really *dangerous*. They just want to talk.'

I shiver.

'Don't worry, sweets. We told them no.'

'Are they outside *now*?'

Rhona nods. 'Rain and shine.'

'When will they go away?'

'Well, they *say* they'll go away after we let them talk to you. But that's something called blackmail, and it's not going to work.'

'So . . . they're never goin' to go away?'

'Don't worry, hon. We've got a lawyer on the case. He'll *make* them stop hassling us.'

I look out the window. The weather is bad. Iss hard to believe there's anyone standin' out there.

Rhona drums her fingers on her mug. After a while she says, 'You had nightmares again, didn't you?'

I whip round to face her. 'How do you know?'

'Well, I heard you screaming, for one. Then there's this . . .'

She unfolds a piece of white cloth. Doesn't take her eyes off me.

'Kathy, who is Magnus?'

I bang my cup down. The thing in her hands is my pillowcase. For a minute, I goggle. Then anger crashes through me, paintin' my cheeks bright red, an' iss all I can do not to slap her.

'Are you . . . *spyin'* on me?' I gasp, though iss *him*, not the spyin' bit, that's got me mad. That name holds power over me, like a terrible magic spell. If I say it out loud I will make the dream man real again.

'I'm trying to help you. You know that.'

'How'd you hear me scream from the staff wing?'

'Please, Kathy, I'm not the enemy here. You don't have to deal with these things by your—'

'Leave me alone!' I shoot to my feet an' start backin' for the door.

'You know who he is, don't you?'

'Get your hands off me!'

I drag myself free an' run out of the room. Rhona doesn't come after me, like I thought she might. I lie under my bed till the sun goes down, but no one knocks at my door.

#

Monday.

Rhona isn't at breakfast, an' neither is Mrs Laird. I sit alone in the corner of the dinin' room, scowlin' at the back of Joyce's head. Caroline comes over an' says Rhona had to sort out some stuff for her mother. Mrs Laird drove her to the bank in Invercraig an' they won't be back till late. I don't like it without Rhona here. It doesn't feel safe. For most of the day I stay in my room, cos no one but Rhona's allowed to come in here. For a while that's great. But there's not much to do, so I sneak downstairs for a book.

Like last time, there's no one in the library, an' that suits me fine. I take an atlas off a bottom shelf an' sit in the corner to look at it. On the fifth page there's a map of Scandinavia. I look at that one for a long time. Denmark is where they say I came from, so I look at that the most. If I really come from there, then a picture of it should make me feel somethin'. But it doesn't feel right. No matter how hard I look, all I see is a foreign country. The town names are ones I've never seen, an' I'm thrown by all the islands. If I'd lived there I'd've had to cross between those islands once in a while. But I don't remember that. Not at all.

Iss all very disappointin', an' jus' now I can't think where to go from here. Why can't I remember? The lullaby flutters round me, pointin' its glitt'ry little finger at Denmark. Denmark should be the answer. Ev'ryone wants it to be. An' I wanna tell 'em, 'Yes, that's right.' But I can't say that, cos deep down I'm startin' to think iss not true.

I sit starin' at the map on my knees. Iss funny. I can't close the book. Somethin' on the page is stoppin' me. Then I realise. The *top* bit of the map. Over the sea, an' up. It's *that* country my eyes keep driftin' to. I lean in closer, an' my skin starts to prickle. The shape of the land. That long, bitty coastline, stretchin' up into the Arctic Circle. The mountains an' the water an' the names . . . I *know* them . . .

Norway . . .

For a minute, the room swims.

I sway, an' touch my forehead, an' when I look up again I could swear the walls have moved. Slowly, I fold my arms to my chest, an' as I do this a horrible feeling spills through me, this horrible idea that I'm not really sittin' in this room any more. That those steady wooden surfaces aren't real at all, an' if I stretch out to check, my hands'd go right through. I *feel* the air changin'. Fleshin' out, like arteries, round my head. Growin' muscular an' dark an' dense with blood.

Pressin' down, all around, into ev'ry scrap of space, till a man-shaped thing stands above me in the darkness, an' I'm cowerin' underneath. Lungs punched empty. I clamp my eyes shut. Black hair tanglin' down ... He's right here. Breathin' in my face. Close enough to get me if I dare move ... a muscle ...

I breathe in. Whimper out.

The black-haired man ... I've seen him before ...

Please. No ...

The door yanks open. I scramble back an' kick an' kick an' ...

. . . . . .

Oh!

A woman.

My book spills onto the floor.

Joyce! Iss okay. Iss jus' Joyce ...

My God ...

I flop onto my back. Wheeze out air. An' jus' like that, the spell's broken. Joyce holds the door frame. Looks at me funny. Has she seen the atlas? I don't know. I stuff it behind some magazines.

'Come with me,' says Joyce, so I get up. She walks me through the house to her office, with her hand wedged in my back all the way. What does she want? Suddenly I'm not so sure I like this. But I daren't say no. We reach her office door, with the little engraved name plaque on it. No one else has one of those. Jus' Joyce.

'Go in, then,' she says, an' gives me a little push.

I turn the knob an' lean on it a bit. The door swings open. I jump. Crammed in the room are four people I've never seen before. One holds a black machine on his shoulder. There's a fuzzy thing on a stick. When I come in they jump forwards. Eight big eyes movin' all over me. A squeaky noise

40

comes up my throat, an' I try to turn round, but Joyce is like a wall.

'Well hello, Kathy! It's so lovely to meet you.'

'Come on,' grunts Joyce. She shunts me into the room.

'We've come for a little chat.'

'No . . .'

Heart's goin' crazy. Close my eyes. Somethin' hard comes up behind my legs. I tumble down.

'Five minutes, okay?' says Joyce.

'Of course. Doug, start rolling.'

Clickin' noises. Lights. Joyce's hand stays clamped round my arm. I go as small as possible. Joyce tuts. More hands creep onto me. Try to uncurl me.

'No no no . . .'

'Stop being silly.'

Voices prod me. Talkin' an' pausin', talkin' an' pausin', talkin' an' pausin'. Gettin' louder ev'ry time, an' the hands on my arms grab harder.

'Sit up straight.'

Beyond ev'rythin', a darkness creeps back. My throat closes up. I honk for air. Lights rush sideways. Then everythin' goes cold, an' all I can see is carpet.

#

Tuesday.

Rhona is so angry, her face is white. All day long it stays like that. At my bedside she whispers. Strokes my hand an' says *It'll never happen again.* When she's not in my room she shouts loud. Joyce shouts back. I hear them both. Backwards an' forwards. The telephone rings nonstop, an' no one answers it.

41

Later, Rhona tells me I'm famous. My fans have doubled since my face was on telly, an' apparently that's not a good thing. A blond man broke into the grounds this afternoon, but Caroline saw him an' called the police. He ran away long before they came, but some men stayed to guard the fence anyway. They said he prob'ly wasn't dangerous. That the fans jus' want to see me.

'Soon those people won't hound us any more,' says Rhona. 'The court order goes through any day now. Then it'll be *illegal*.'

'The lawyer man?' I ask.

'Yes, hon. The lawyer is sorting it out.'

'Will we open the curtains again then?'

Rhona's face stays pure white, an' the anger will not leave her eyes. But she nods yes. Makes her mouth into a smile.

4

>Katgrrl has logged on at 20.21.53GMT_17/12/2004

Katgrrl: Tim!

Katgrrl: Hey u ther?

Katgrrl: Tiiiiiiiiim! Come on! I gots da news :) :) :)

Katgrrl: Oi! Timbo!

>Katgrrl has sent a nudge

VinylVultures_666: Hey was jst eatin. Wait brb

Katgrrl: Heeeyyyy!!! Thank God. Yr alive!!

Katgrrl: Tim?

Katgrrl: Whats hapnin?

VinylVultures_666: Back. Sorry. Phone rang.

Katgrrl: Hi. Hey guess what

VinylVultures_666: You are secretly the antichrist :)

Katgrrl: I'm moving to Norway! Movin in w Magnus!

VinylVultures_666: Wow. Srsly? When?

Katgrrl: Aftr Xmas. Quit cafe today.

VinylVultures_666: U only met th guy like 5 minutes ago!

Katgrrl: Christ u sound lik my Dad

VinylVultures_666: Well . . . wow . . . When exactly? U booked it?

Katgrrl: Bookin ferry tomoro. All sortd out.

VinylVultures_666: Bloody hell. So I guess yr not movin down here aftr all then

Katgrrl: No. well, ykno. young love. hehe . . .

Katgrrl: Hello?

>Katgrrl has sent a nudge

VinylVultures_666: Sorry. Just can't really believe it. U sure about this?

Katgrrl: Yes!

VinylVultures_666: Whatd Mag say?

Katgrrl: He's happy. We gonna get married

VinylVultures_666: Bloody hell Kathy!!!

Katgrrl: I know! Crazy huh. Cant believe its hapnin . . .

Katgrrl: Tim?

VinylVultures_666: Sorry. Just thinking.

VinylVultures_666: Why ddnt u tel me before?

Katgrrl: Sorry hon. Just decided it all so quick . . . Youre 1st I told

VinylVultures_666: Well. Just . . . remember . . . if u need to come back I am always here

Katgrrl: Thanks hon. Yr my best friend u kno.

Katgrrl: U ther?

VinylVultures_666: So whatll happen with yr painting now?

Katgrrl: I'll still paint. Theyv got art stores ther too ykno ;)

VinylVultures_666: Hmm

Katgrrl: We can still do that group show together.

VinylVultures_666: Well actually we cant cos its oxfordshire artists only. That's whole point of u movin to Oxford.

Katgrrl: Oh hon . . . I'm sorry.

VinylVultures_666: Well. Not only reason. U need to get out. B with ppl like u. That towns killing u

Katgrrl: I am getting out

VinylVultures_666: Hmm

Katgrrl: R u not happy 4 me?

VinylVultures_666: Yes. Sorry. Just sad. I'll get over it.

Katgrrl: We can do another show. U could visit scandi. Get artist residency or somethin.

VinylVultures_666: I've got th record shop to run.

Katgrrl: Well mayb oneday.

VinylVultures_666: So what date u actually goin?

Katgrrl: 13jan.

VinylVultures_666: Bloody hell

Katgrrl: U shd come up visit before I go.

VinylVultures_666: I'll miss you, Katherine.

Katgrrl: Come up this weekend. We'll talk

VinylVultures_666: Cant leave th shop

Katgrrl: Well. We can write

VinylVultures_666: R u sure about this Kathy? Just all so sudden . . .

Katgrrl: I'm in love, Tim.

Katgrrl: U ther?

VinylVultures_666: Just b careful with this guy. Ok?

Katgrrl: Yessir!

VinylVultures_666: I'm serious. Any trouble, u call me. Ok?

Katgrrl: He's not a serial killer!

VinylVultures_666: Promise.

Katgrrl: Ok I promise. If u promise to stop freakin out so much.

VinylVultures_666: I just care.

Katgrrl: Promise

VinylVultures_666: Ok Cap'n

Katgrrl: Xx

VinylVultures_666: Xxx

>Katgrrl has logged off

5

On Friday we have a special teatime in the day room. There's a cake with my name iced on it, an' little square sandwiches an' jelly an' fizzy lemonade. Mrs Laird makes ev'ryone sing 'Happy Birthday'. Then she turns on the television an' we watch a film about a talkin' dog. That goes on for ages. When iss finished Joyce says iss time for bed, an ev'ryone goes out of the room. I'm goin' to go too, but Rhona comes out of nowhere an' says, 'Happy Birthday, hon.' At *birthday*, her hands make little rabbit ears in the air. Then she gives me a pot of nail varnish. We sit by the fire an' paint our fingernails gold. Rhona puts a candle on the last of my cake, I blow it out, an' we share the frosted slab onto our plates. My nails look strange, all painted up like that. I wonder if I used to wear nail varnish. Before. Together we look at our fingertips. Twinklin' like jewels as they dry.

'Are you ready to talk about Magnus?' asks Rhona. When she says that, she doesn't look at my face. Maybe that's somethin' Mrs Laird taught her. A brain trick. But it doesn't work. I jus' get mad. I stand up, throw my cake on the floor an' leave the room. She doesn't call out or try to stop me.

Back in my room, I scratch my nails clean with toilet paper. I can't bring myself to throw out the varnish, but tomorrow I'll tell Rhona I did. It'll hurt her feelin's, I'm sure, but right now I'm glad about that. I'll teach her not to say that name to me.

My face is hot. When I've calmed down a bit I find the hole in my mattress an' stick my hand inside. This is where I keep my bit of newspaper. They'd go mad if they knew I had this, but, like the nail varnish, I can't make myself get rid of it. I stole it from Mrs Laird's sittin' room on the day we opened the curtains.

Daily Post. Thursday, 11th May 2006

Snub 'n' Sly Girl

Lawyers dealt a **kick in the teeth** to our fundraising campaign yesterday, when they **forbade** further press access to their client — the Loch Oscaig 'Lullaby Girl'. The childlike amnesiac — now known as 'Katherine' — shot into the limelight last month after washing up on the banks of a remote loch in Scotland. Initially believed to be mute, she astonished carers one day with a rendition of a **Danish** lullaby, and continued to sing it compulsively.

Her story won the hearts of our readers and led to the formation of the Lullaby Girl Foundation, which has so far raised over £12,000 towards the brunette's psychiatric care. But now lawyers have **snubbed** our readers'

47

generosity by ordering the removal of Daily Post reporters from the vicinity of Gille Dubh Lodge in Cairndhu — where Lullaby Girl currently resides.

Reactions have been mixed since yesterday's ruling, with some doubting whether Katherine had a part in this decision at all. 'I saw her the day they pulled her out the water, and she **didn't know her arse from her elbow**,' comments photographer Malcolm Gray. 'We were inside Gille Dubh last week, and she'd barely progressed, mentally.' Our correspondent Zoe Rutherford, upon whose initiative the LGF was founded, had this to say: 'It's **just so selfish**, and so disappointing for everyone involved. After everything we've done for her, you'd think she'd give a little back.'

Lullaby Girl's mental capabilities have been widely debated in the media since her appearance on March 15th. But some locals, such as shopkeeper Gayle Paton, have been raising different questions.

'How can we protect ourselves if they won't keep us informed?' Ms Paton asked last night. 'As far as we know this was **attempted murder**, and until that loony remembers what happened,

we have to assume there's **a killer on
the loose.**'

Insiders say police are still to
receive any solid leads, either on
British or Danish soil, and this has
raised **further questions** as to why her
lawyers should try to remove Katherine
from the public eye. 'They can't very
well expect witnesses to come forward,
if there's no publicit

That's where the paper tears off. I fill my head with those
words, as I have a hundred times, an' try to gain strength
from my anger. *That loony.* That's all I am to the people over
the fence. How horrible to know they saw this newspaper two
weeks ago. That all this time they've prob'ly been talkin'
about me. A *killer on the loose* sounds bad. I don't like to think
about that bit.

I forgive Rhona, I think, but I still want her to say sorry.
Maybe she'll come up later . . .

The newsprint feels grubby in my fingers. I fold the clipping carefully, three times. Then I kneel an' put it back in the
mattress.

#

Saturday.

We have Internet at Gille Dubh, an' Caroline's the one in
charge of it. Most stuff is blocked, like email an' news, cos
Mrs Laird wants to limit *outside influences*, an' we're only
allowed Wikipedia if Caroline's sittin' with us. I suppose
that's to stop us gettin' upset. We're allowed fifteen minutes

49

per day, each, but not many of us really bother. Mary uses it more than me, but today she's not here. She's in the day room with the oldies, watchin' a film about tap dancin'. Outside, iss rainin'.

'I'm gonna pop the kettle on,' Caroline says as she heads into the next room. 'D'you want a cup?'

'Yes please,' I say as I scroll through a map of the moon's surface.

Caroline comes back with somethin' large an' square hidden under her jumper. She grins at me, then whips out the chocolate biscuit tin an' opens it under my nose. This is not chocolate biscuit day.

'Quick,' she says, lookin' over my shoulder at the doorway. I dive in an' grab a mint Viscount. Caroline an' the tin whirl away. Hot water bubbles, an' a teaspoon clinks on china. Then Caroline comes back with two steamin' cups, an' a Wagon Wheel hangin' from her teeth. I pick up my cup an' take a tiny, burning sip. The stripe round the edge is cornflower blue, but I don't have the heart to tell Caroline I prefer the green one.

'Thought you might be hungry,' she winks. 'Seeing as you missed lunch.'

'I slept late.'

'Figured,' says Caroline, an' takes a chomp out of her Wagon Wheel. Then she sits back an' starts her crossword. She does a lot of crosswords. She must be damn clever.

Five minutes into my session, Mrs Bell comes in an' asks for help to write a letter to her daughter in Hertfordshire. 'Sure,' says Caroline, an' they sit down at the word processor. I glance up from time to time. It seems such a waste of energy – lookin' up the right postcode an' checkin' the time of the last post collection an' the cost of stamps – when they could jus' send an email. It seems that so much of what we do here is about the *doing*. Not the end result. We faff around with things that don't matter so that we'll forget the bigger questions. About things that have hurt us, an' will hurt us again if we stop to remember.

#

We meet in the day room for music therapy. Mr Duff hands round the photocopied song sheets, an' we vote for the tunes we want to sing today. I put my hand up for 'Somewhere Over the Rainbow', 'Paperback Writer' an' 'Michelle', cos I like to sing the French bit. No one asks me to sing 'Solen er så rød, mor'. Thankfully, ev'ryone seems to have forgotten that. Or maybe they jus' don't care any more. I could never stand at the front an' sing like that now.

Rhona sits with her back to us in an easy chair by the window. I look over once or twice, but she doesn't turn round. It looks like she's readin', but there's no book in her lap. I'm startin' to feel bad about what happened. Maybe I should let her bring that hypnotist back, like she wants. Make up some stuff about Magnus. Would that make her happy?

At the end of choir time, Mr Duff puts his guitar away. He reads from his Bible in his boomy voice. Then he asks us to pray for old Mrs McRae, who runs the village post office. We seem to pray for Mrs McRae a lot. I've never seen her with my own eyes, but I often think about her an' her bad leg when I sit at the conservat'ry window. I have a picture of her face in my head. I think she smiles a lot an' has long white hair that she wears in a bun. Sometimes I wonder what'll happen when she finally dies. Who'll sort all the letters, an' dish out the stamps, an' cash Rhona's wage slips?

When Mr Duff has gone, Mrs Laird wheels in the gramophone. 'I've got a real treat for you today,' she says, 'from my personal collection.' Then she plays the same 78s she always plays, an' we get up to dance. As usual, Mary an' me are partners. We tango up an' down the room, bumpin' into the older ladies an' the furniture an' the walls, until Mrs Laird orders us to calm down. As we flop onto the old church pew I look round for Rhona, but she's not here any more. At dinner time she's not there either. When the sun goes down I sit in my room with the door open. Rain batters the window. Rhona doesn't show.

Why did Rhona have to find out about Magnus? That sleep lady told her, I jus' know it. See, I can't trust anyone here. An' that's no good, see, cos I can't have 'em all whisp'rin' about Magnus. Laughin' at me behind my back. Sayin' I'm weak. They'll whisper to the papers, an' the papers'll whisper to folk outside, an' then – jus' maybe – the whisper'll get all the way back to Magnus. I can't risk that. I couldn't handle it. I wouldn't do it even for Rhona.

Magnus. I want you to know that I know. I know about you an' I know about the pain you brought. I can't see your face prop'ly. Not yet. But you're here all the same. Hoverin' over me. For nine long weeks, my life hasn't had you in it. I ate my eggs from my green striped plate an' I sat at the conservat'ry window an' I slept under my mustard bedspread. When I could stand to be with people I joined in group therapy, an' when I could speak I spoke my first words to Rhona. I watched the sun rise an' I watched it fall. I watched the mountains change colour an' the winds shift direction. All of that time you weren't there. But that time is over now, an' iss time I admitted it. You first showed up in a dream, an' for some time I believed that that's all you were. Then the sleep lady saw you too, an' the cat was out of the bag. You *did* walk beside me once. You *did* hold my hand. You were part of my life – more than that, you were *ev'rythin'* – an' then, quite suddenly, you weren't. They don't know as much as me yet. Jus' your name. But now they know you're there, they won't give up. Rhona says you're the key. She's tryin' hard to bring you back out.

I'm scared of that, Magnus. I don't think I can ever let it happen. There's bad stuff tied to you, an' I can't risk settin' it free. I did that once before, I think, an' it turned me into a diff'rent person. I'm scared, Magnus. Damn you for coming back. If you'd stayed away, I wouldn't have had to deal with you.

#

The clouds are low this morning. I pick at a plate of toast, an' drink a cup of milky tea. As I sit in the conservat'ry, the wind sucks at the window. *Fwwwopp fwooopp* it goes, an' blasts the roof in little flurries. Today, like yesterday, I've eaten breakfast alone. Rhona has been missin' for three days, an' I'm too scared to ask anyone why. I think yesterday was my day to have Mrs Laird talk at me, but no one came to take me there. In the afternoon there's a keep-fit class in the dinin' room, an' I don't like all the commotion, so I go up to my room. I keep tellin' myself Rhona will appear soon. That the next face I see will be hers. But she doesn't come in. No one even comes upstairs. I stare out the window till the clouds come right down, an' after that I stare into the grey. Darkness grows, an' the house grows quiet. At dinner time I can't bring myself to go downstairs, so I lie on the bed an' try to forget how hungry I am. Voices come an' go. In the end, the room turns black.

#

Day number six an' Rhona is still missin'. Iss gettin' hard to think of ways to fill my days. I spend most of the day sittin' by my bedroom window. The pane is thicker in some parts than others, an' this makes the world outside look wonky. If I move my head around, it makes stuff move. A bird crossin' the sky might jump forwards by an inch, or a ripple might pass through the hillside. Before, it was fun to play with this super-power, but today is not one of those days. Sittin' perfectly still, I watch the long red gravel driveway. The path to the outside world. Rhona is out there somewhere.

Golds an' greens fleet across the moor. Clouds march from left to right, shiftin' in colour an' thickness an' shape. Faraway mountains step from the mist, then vanish again like ghosts. Once or twice I hear footsteps, but no one ever stops or knocks on my door. I haven't spoken to anyone all day, not even the cook, cos I've got too scared to leave my room. This is not good for me, an' I know it. How dare Rhona leave me for so long? I feel myself shrinkin'. All the skills I'd learnt are slidin' backwards, an' the ugly bits of me they'd covered are right back out in the open. It doesn't matter that I've spent three months amongst these people. Suddenly iss back to me an' them, an' the thought of havin' to talk to anyone makes my skin fizz cold.

The day passes slowly, like yesterday, an' the day before, an' the day before that. But this is a new kind of slowness, that I haven't felt before. Like I've fallen into a load of warm, sug'ry syrup an' been cut off from the world. Stuff is goin' on out there, I know that, but iss like those things don't matter any more. In here, they can't reach me an' I can't reach them. All I have left is myself.

Time gets stuck. I close my eyes.

#

Coldness wakes me, an' my eyes open into blackness. Neck hurts. Was I dreamin'? I push myself upright, an' the coldness sucks at my forehead.

Right. The window.

I'm on the window seat.

Pinpricks of light trickle down, an' I understand I am lookin' at the stars. My hand reaches out for the windowsill. Solid, an' cold, an' very real. My head doesn't feel good. Across the room, the clock's swallowed in shadow. Clutchin' my jumper to my throat, I get up.

Wait . . . Uh . . .

My knees buckle an' I fall onto the chair, almost missin' it in the darkness. Silence drills into my head. Gatherin' momentum, makin' me giddy. I shut my eyes against it. My heart squirms. Then, quite softly, things start to move.

What . . . What's . . . . . .

Uh . . .

Oh no . . .

No . . . .

Flakes lift an' drift. Up, up. Into my nose, makin' me sneeze. Zoomin' faster. Stronger. Sharper. They blaze an' froth an' multiply. A million lurid eyes, peeled inwards. Through my ears, through my nose, through my teeth an' my lungs an' my gulpin' tongue. Crowdin' like wolves upon a single dense atom. My heart swings out of control. They are in me. Behind my eyes. In my veins. Rushin'. Squealin'. Whippin'. So many pictures, so many feelin's. So fast. I can't stop it. I gasp. Gasp again. Jerk my mouth open. Then my

55

eyes. I am grippin' my collar. Shocked, I let go, an' the blood floods back into my hand.

Breathe . . . . . .

. . . .

. . . .

There. There . . .

. . . . . .

. . .

Breathe . . .

Iss over . . . . . .

Breathe . . . .

Fizziness crawlin' up my neck . . . my face . . . . .

Iss okay. Iss okay. Iss okay . . .

Curlin' sideways, I let my weight pull me off the chair. Here, I'm safe. I shrink as I stroke my neck, an' smell the flow'ry Shake n'Vac. Iss over. Iss okay. Iss okay.

. . . .

I drift back, an' realise I've been singin'.

That song. I recognise it. Of course. My song. *My* song . . .

. . . .

I retreat into cold, fresh light. And I know I am outside. For a moment I don't recognise myself, because my hair is white. Then I see my breath has turned it that way. Freezing clouds, coming from my mouth. My fringe a deathly skeleton. And beneath me, my clothes have frozen to the suitcase.

This place is like something off a postcard. Rickety wooden houses overhang the street. Lemon-yellow and brick-red and sage-green. Twisty gateways with hand-painted signs, and fat blue candles at every doorway, melting holes through the ice. A man-sized snowdrift hulks over me, banded with layers of grit. In the middle, a child's glove. Fingers sticking out, as if beckoning for help.

Come on.

Please . . .

My new lingerie feels tight beneath my clothes. I wish I hadn't put it on for him.

No. Don't think of that.

Close your eyes.

Stop.

Just another one.

Why did you come?

Why did you bother coming?

No.

Why did you even bother coming?

I punch Håkon's jeering lip. Blood spills over my hand. He looks up.

Why . . .

The spray hits my eyes.

Come at me, then!

One more of his sluts.

No!

Why did you come?

Come on, you bastard!

6

The room is pale. Risin' on one hip, I blink the sleep from my eyes. Is that an envelope, pushed under the door? Maybe iss from someone outside. I wonder about Mrs McRae.

No one woke me. Again. That means Rhona's not back.

I swing my legs round an' hop onto the cold floorboards. I'm wearin' my nightie with the strawberry on the front, an' that scares me cos I don't remember puttin' it on. When I pick up the letter I see iss tucked, not sealed. No postmark on the front, or an address. Jus' *Katherine* in nice curly handwriting.

> *Dear Kathy,*
>
> *As I'm sure you know by now, I have had to take a leave of absence. My mother's condition has worsened and the doctors doubt she'll make it to the end of the week. I'd only planned to be gone for the weekend, but I'm sorry to say circumstances have changed. Joyce will take over my duties for now, and I urge you to cooperate with her. As for your private psychiatric sessions . . . I know how you hate them, and how much support you need afterwards, so Vera has agreed to leave your next one until after my return. Having said that, please feel free to speak to someone if you need to. Vera, Joyce and Caroline are all there should you*

need them, and have been informed of the situation.
Your group sessions will continue as normal.
  Take care, dearest, and I'll see you very soon,
  Rhona
  X

I squash the letter to my chest an' try to get my breath. Suddenly I badly want a hug, but Rhona's the only one who can hug me, an' she's not here. I wipe my eyes on the back of my hand an' get back in bed.

Joyce can fuck right off. I'm not talkin' to Joyce.

Is this some sort of trick? Maybe Rhona made up the whole thing so she can go work somewhere else. The envelope wasn't sealed ... That means anyone could have read it. Maybe they're *all* in on it ...

What's the time? I peek over the bedcovers. Quarter to twelve says the clock. It'll be lunchtime soon.

If they give me a new case worker, will that person be allowed in my room? What if Joyce walks in at twelve on the dot an' forces me out of bed? Rhona never tried to push me past my limits. But Joyce doesn't know about my limits. What if she sends me downstairs before I'm prop'ly washed or dressed? Imagine! Chokin' down lunch in my nightie, with the others all pointin'. What if she asks me about private stuff? Magnus? Denmark? No! She doesn't get into my life that easily! She can't take Rhona's place! Not jus' like that! What is this? Musical chairs?

No ...

Suddenly my head is full of Joyce, an' I can't get her out again. I picture the door openin'. Joyce's bony face appearin', instead of Rhona's. Her voice rappin' on me like a fist. As the clock ticks the minutes off to lunchtime, I stare at the doorknob. Waitin' for it to twist. Waitin' for the loose floor-board on the landin'. Footsteps on the rug. A bossy voice callin' my name.

No!

Rhona wouldn't trick me like that. She jus' wouldn't. An' anyway, iss true about her mother bein' sick. She told me herself, ages ago.

The tears stay in my eyes, but a sort of hardness creeps in to join them. A coldness. Each time I swallow, it moves further in. Pressin' on my heart. Curlin' my hands into claws. I push myself into the dark, polished headboard. Beside me, the curtains are closed, but I can tell iss bad weather, from the light.

Damn Rhona's mother. Why did she have to get sick? An' damn Rhona, for lovin' her mother more than me.

By two o'clock I'm starvin', so I sneak downstairs. There's no one around, an' no food in the dinin' room. But the door to Mrs Laird's sittin' room is open, so I grab a banana from her fruit bowl an' slip out the back porch onto the moor. The air is super-still outside, like the sky's holdin' its breath. My shoes schlopp loudly through the mud, spittin' dirt up my legs, but I don't stop runnin' till I'm safely behind the out-houses. Here, I'm hidden from Gille Dubh. Across the hill-side, a dark, lumpy bank rises up, an' I remember Rhona sayin' that's where the farmers cut out bricks of peat. It looks funny from here, like a giant mouth has swooped down an' taken a chomp. There's a bitter, fresh smell, like somethin' alive.

I've never gone so far in this direction. Partly cos the ground gets dodgy to walk on. Wet in some places an' hard in others, an' never in the bits you expect. I try walkin' on the high bits, but iss hard to see the ground through the bracken, an' half the time I end up fallin' into holes. Flowerless thistles jab my knees. Clumps of black lichen sink me, bubblin', into mud.

I come to a sticky-out bit of land an' stop to eat my banana. Below me, there's a dip filled with heather, an' right in the middle of that there's a dark space, like a hole. What's that? I go closer an' find a perfectly circular pit, maybe ten metres wide, jam-packed with thorn bushes. Like the peat field, it looks like a bite mark. Only this one is long-healed. I lean over an' try to see the bottom. Birds dip an' flit through the bushes, too busy to bother themselves with me.

My legs are cold as I gaze downhill. Half a mile away, the perimeter fence cuts the hill in two. A long grey arm, holdin' me firmly inside. I stare at it with tears in my eyes. Then, socks squelchin', I climb back to the sticky-out bit. The roof of Gille Dubh creeps back over the horizon, an' I have a little chuckle to myself at how innocent the place looks from here. Who'd believe a bunch of nutters lived inside? Wind makes the bracken rush around my knees. I close my eyes an' it sounds like water. The sun pushes gently on my shoulders.

This will be my private place, I decide.

#

My back hurts. I sit at a wooden table in front of a window. Around me there is noise, like voices, but I cannot turn my head to see where this comes from. Outside, the sky is deep black. I sip from a hot cup, and blink my eyes, and feel the exhaustion. There are lights outside. Across the road. A factory . . . no . . . a wood mill . . . I watch the smoke rise. Calm. Vertical. I sip from the cup. I put down the cup. In the gloom between the window and the mill, a bus is parked. One sad street light looks down on it, and I see the name on its side. Then I know the bus is where I have come from. I am travelling on it, and will continue to.

The voices clatter on. More distinct now. *Bang bang bang. Bang bang bang.* And I try to turn around . . .

Was that my door . . . ?

Someone is . . .

Bang bang bang!

I gasp an' shoot backwards, bangin' my head on the head-board. My heart rattles hard as I stare into the dark. The bed-clothes are swamped with sweat.

'Who's there?' I hiss.

A *swoosh*. I wait. Then the ash tree groans. Out there, on the other side of the house. A gust like a human voice pushes the window, but I've already lowered my guard. There's no need to be scared. Iss jus' the wind. Iss jus' the tree.

I'm at Gille Dubh.

The bus fades away, leavin' a sense of great sadness in its wake. I sit up in bed, absorbin' this feelin'. The bus is nothin' new. Iss not the first time I have remembered the bus.

Rhona would have loved to hear about the bus . . .

It scares me when these bits of memory come out. Why can't they stay where they are? I don't like it, cos when they come out iss like they're real again. Crowdin' round me, blockin' me in. Rhona says that's the whole point of my ther-apy. To pull all those little bits from my head, stick em' together an' look at the full picture. After that, she says, I'll start gettin' better. But iss not as simple as that. I know there's some pretty nasty stuff still inside me. Stuff not even Rhona can protect me from. I never told Rhona this, but I don't think I *want* to let those things out. If I try really hard they might stay where they are. Then I won't have to be scared any more. This stopped-clock life is good enough for me.

The window beyond my curtains is a plain black square pasted onto a blacker, denser square. My eyes are used to the dark, but no matter how wide I open them I can't see more than the shape around the window. I wonder what the weather's like where Rhona is. Is she awake, like me, lis'nin' to the wind? Then I wonder, like I did all day yesterday, if she's forgotten me. Outside, the ash tree cracks an' swirls. It squeals an' prods the roof.

I wrap myself tightly in the sheets, but my sweat has turned 'em thin an' useless. Fear grows in me, slow an' dull. What if I freeze to death when I fall asleep? Without ever wakin' up? Is that possible?

I lie very still, wantin' to cry, but the ash tree never stops an' the cold never lifts from my bones. My shoulder is icy against the wooden headboard. I roll off the bed, draggin' the covers with me, an' thump slowly down onto the rug. There. I pull my knees to my chest. That's better, somehow. I doze, aware of shapes dustin' my eyelids. Fuzziness prickles through me, an' in little grey footsteps the bedroom retreats.

#

Wednesday.

My face looks slightly wrong in the bathroom mirror. Puffy. Cobbled together. As if my body was dismantled as I slept an' put back together in the morning. Today I was rebuilt in too much of a hurry, so I'm stuck with this patchwork face till bedtime. I don't like it. It doesn't feel right. I'm scared to look people in the eye, in case they see it too. They might force me to see someone other than Rhona, then. But I won't stand for it. Joyce can't have me. Nobody can. I'll turn my face to the floor.

63

I'm the first person to arrive for breakfast, an' the cook is not in sight. When I'm halfway through my porridge, Aggie walks in, an' we jump at the sight of each other. She hovers in the doorway, her face flushes, an' I see she's wond'rin' whether to come in or not. Obviously I'm not the only one who wants to be alone. My spoon is still clamped halfway to my mouth, but I manage to drop my eyes from Aggie's to the dog-shaped slippers on her feet. Their little pink tongues hangin' out, all happy. A second or two, then the dog slippers start to walk. I hear the spatula scrapin' the scrambled eggs tray, an' the whirrin' of the coffee machine. A couple of clinks, then the dogs walk back the way they came. I wait until the sounds have stopped, an' look up through my hair. There's Aggie, sittin' in the corner with her back to me. Suits me jus' fine. I neck my porridge an' leg it back to my room.

#

Mrs Laird calls me to her sittin' room after lunch. There's a telephone call for me, she says. For a second I'm scared. Then I realise what it means. There's only one person they'd make me use a telephone for.

Mrs Laird cradles the receiver to my ear an' I try to make my fingers grab hold.

'Hello?' I say, but as I breathe out the telephone makes a *hwooszzzhh* noise in my ear. I shrink away. I look at Mrs Laird. But she pushes the telephone back to my head. When I listen again, a voice is talkin'. Rhona's voice. To me.

'Hello?' I say. Rhona stops talkin'. Then starts again.

'Katherine? Can you hear me?'

'Yes. I can.'

'This is Rhona.'

'This is Katherine.'

Rhona laughs. It's strange to hear her laugh but not see her face.

'Are you coming home soon?' I ask. This time Rhona pauses.

'Not yet, dear. I'm still in Skye. How are you doing?'

'I want you to come back.'

Rhona sighs. I don't like that. I wonder if she's still angry about the nail varnish.

'Listen, dear. Vera and I have been talking, and . . . Well . . . We thought it might be best if you had a meeting with Joy—'

'No,' I say.

'I know how you feel, dear. But the thing is . . . It's not good for you to go so long by yourself.'

'Then come back!'

Rhona doesn't speak. I look at Mrs Laird, but she's over at her desk, cleanin' her glasses. I look at the doorway, an' a picture flashes through my head, of my hidin' place on the moor. But I don't want to run away. I jus' want Rhona to come back.

'What have I done?' I say, an' it sounds more like I'm cryin' than talkin'.

'It's nothing you've done, love . . .'

'I'm sorry about my birthday . . . I didn't mean . . . Can't you forgive me?'

'Look, you obviously need to talk to someone, and—'

'No! I won't!'

In the corner of my eye I see Mrs Laird gettin' up from her chair.

'You know that my . . . mother is . . . dying . . .'

Rhona's voice wobbles.

'Bring her here then. Bring her home with you . . .'

'Listen, Kathy. I've arranged it with Joyce that—'

'I won't talk to her. I want to talk to *you*!'

'Katherine. Listen to me. This is not forever. But right now, it's how things have to be. There's no other choice. My mother doesn't have—'

'I wish your mother would jus' *die*!' I yell.

At this point, Mrs Laird tackles me an' pulls the telephone from my hands. I make a break for the door but push Mrs Laird too hard. Backwards, mouth open, she tumbles over the coffee table, an' with a *plop*, the telephone unplugs from the wall. I look back an' see her clutchin' her side.

'Little rat!' she yowls.

I scuttle round the door frame on my hands an' knees. Mary's in the corridor, but I push her out of the way. We crash into the wall, like we do when we're dancin'. Then I untangle myself an' flee for the porch. I don't stop runnin' till I've reached the bite.

#

The crisis room is a twin bedroom on the ground floor, with permanently closed shutters. When they think someone's too sick to sleep alone, they stick 'em in here. There's one bed for the jailer an' one bed for the prisoner. Tonight the prisoner's me. Mrs Laird's still mad, so they picked Joyce to stand watch. It took 'em hours to find me. Joyce says they even called the police, cos they thought I'd gone over the fence. It was dark when they brought me in, an' they haven't been out of my face since. To be honest I could have held out longer, but I heard the search party comin' an' thought they'd find my secret place. There's no way I'd risk them takin' *that* away

66

from me. So I crawled uphill an' turned myself in by the out-houses.

Joyce is a horrible lady. I've never trusted her or enjoyed her company. She shows up for her shift with a cup of cocoa an' a *Christian Weekly* shoved under her armpit. She doesn't bother offerin' me a cocoa, an' in the back of my mind I know that that's on purpose. A sort of extra punishment. The room is very small, with no furniture besides Joyce's plastic night-stand, an' no pictures on the wall. Joyce controls the lamp an' decides when we go to sleep. I'm allowed to talk if I need to, but Joyce is not the sort of person I want to tell anything per-sonal. We barely speak all night, an' I get the feelin' Joyce is as happy as me about that. As she reads her magazine, I turn my face to the wall. I miss my soft mustard-coloured bedspread. This one's pink an' scratchy, an' far too heavy. The bed, too, is hard. I lie still so that the springs won't squeak, an' breathe through my mouth so I won't smell Joyce's cocoa. The wall-paper is a repeat pattern of flower posies, linked by a trailin', criss-crossin' ribbon design. If I look at it long enough I can see a dog's face in the petals. The dog has one pointed ear an' one curved, an' a dark spot above its nose. Both eyes are on one side of its head.

I think I had a dog once. Or . . . a cat. A small animal. It lived with me. I fed it an' played with it. An' I loved it. Yes . . . definitely a cat. Not a dog . . . I wish I could remember its name.

Iss hard to think straight when other people are there. I feel Joyce over my shoulder, like my very own bad angel. Ready to correct me if I do anythin' she doesn't like. I'm a grown-up. I shouldn't have to deal with this. But then, I *was* free once, an' look how well I dealt with that. I had a normal life, an' somewhere, somehow, I managed to mess it up.

67

I hate that they all *want* stuff from me. The huge, scary facts an' all the little reasons why. These are the things the newspaper men ask. That the people over the fence want to know. All of 'em want to solve me an' fix me. To dig that treasure chest out of me an' yank it wide open. An' I know that that's possible. I could please 'em all so easily, if I dared. I feel the chest inside me, as clearly as I feel my feet on the ground, an' I think if rooted deep enough I could find the key to open it. But the chest scares me so much. I feel the darkness in it. The evil. Sometimes, when I'm not lookin' for them, small bits float to the top, an' I get a tiny peek at that life. *Her* life. But I can't stand it. Not for long. Iss like lookin' right into the sun. If I stretch my eyes too wide, I'll do myself damage.

Joyce coughs into her cocoa, sendin' a sug'ry whiff my way. This sets off a chain reaction in my body, an' before I can stop it, my stomach makes a long, low groan. Suddenly I realise I've not eaten since lunchtime. But that rumble will please Joyce. If she feels I'm sufferin' in that way, she won't try to hurt me in others.

There is no clock in the crisis room, an' no daylight, so I must trust Joyce when she says iss night or day. Bein' in this room is about lettin' someone else take control. Goin' along with their view of the world. With any other staff member, that's okay. But not Joyce. I don't want to see the world her way for longer than I absolutely have to. Besides, iss not good for me to be away from the clouds. I think I'd miss the clouds more than the sun, if I were locked in here for a long time. I must be good. *Be normal.* If I'm normal, they'll let me out.

#

Pink fades into off-white. Yellowing round the edges, with a sun that makes me sneeze. I stand in a cornfield, talking to the local children. I have come to help them bring in the crop. They are glad of my help. I am useful. They hand me a hooked knife with an old, weathered handle. It is very sharp, but nobody tells me to be careful.

We bend our backs and work until our faces are red. My dungarees are covered with seeds and my wellies covered with mud. A dog runs around us, searching for attention. It is the youngest, the old farmer says. It has not yet learnt to be calm. We should not pet it, as it is not a pet. It is a worker. These dogs are different.

When we go back to the farmhouse we ride on a cart behind the tractor. The other girls have sandwiches wrapped in smooth paper, and they offer one to me. It is spread with red jam that has no seeds in it. Afterwards we play on the swing, and the mother brings an old woman out of a caravan to look at me. I walk round a darkened sitting room, between old people in brocade chairs. The clock on the wall has golden pine cones hanging from it. At bath time the water that comes from the taps is brown, but Mummy says it isn't dirty. We eat meatloaf, and soft peas which come from a tin. Tomorrow we will have the special meat pie from the butcher's. If I'm good I can have a stick of tablet, and they might let me ride the tractor again.

#

A hand shakes me awake. I flinch. But iss jus' Mary. I fling my arms round her, an' she hugs me back. I look round the room. We're alone. The walls are the same colour as when I fell asleep, but I see by the freshness in Mary's face that iss morning. Mary points at Joyce's perfectly made bed. Then she points to the door. Makes an *eating* sign.

69

'Am I locked in?' I ask. The smile fades from Mary's eyes, an' she nods. I return my head to my pillow. After a bit, Mary's hand touches my shoulder. She strokes my arm, then my hair. When I raise my eyes again I find her starin' at the floor. Not for the first time, I notice the lumps on her wrists.

'What time is it?'

Mary holds up one finger. I nod.

'Is it windy outside?' I ask. But I barely get the words out before burstin' into tears. Mary drags me to her shoulder. Her tight little fingers dig into my back. For ages we rock backwards an' forwards. Then I dig my face in her side, an' ev'rythin' goes still.

By the time I look up, Mary's eyes are back on the floor. As my breathin' gets more normal, her eyes drift back, an' we watch each other through the thickenin' film of tears.

'I'm scared,' I say.

Mary does not nod or smile. She jus' pushes the hair from my forehead. I droop back to the pillow, close my eyes, an' try to breathe. Mary's shadow casts a cool blindfold across my face, shieldin' me from the light bulb. Mary makes no sound, but I know she is still there.

7

January 13th, 2005.

The Tyneside skies are the colour of charcoal as the ferry coasts towards the open sea. On the land, Mum's face is so tiny I can barely tell it's her. But my instincts tell me it has to be. Poor old thing. In the car park there, on the easternmost tip of the land. One hand fluttering endlessly, the other raised to her head, probably holding Dad's binoculars. Can she see our smiles from there? I hope so, for her own peace of mind. Magnus's hand is warm around my own. He has stopped waving, but I keep going for my mother's sake. She hasn't changed position for a full five minutes. Around her, couples break off and amble to their cars, which are parked in a neat line behind them. Isn't that their Beetle? The rust-red one peeking out from behind the wall? It stings me to know Dad is sitting inside and did not come out to wave. Mum can't drive, so he must be there. His last, clumsy insult replays in my head and drives an involuntary scowl from me. But this time I refuse to let the pain take root. Today, my real life begins. I have Magnus, and Magnus is a better man than he'll ever be.

'I am frightened to speak, in case she reads my lips,' gottle-o-geers Magnus. I look at his face – uncharacteristically deadpan – and get a fit of the giggles. 'Let's start swearing,' he says, 'just in case,' and reels off an increasingly colourful list of English profanities. I stop waving and push him in the chest. The trademark boyish smile beams through then, and for a moment I am paralysed by his beauty. Magnus brushes the hair from my eyes, and it looks for all the world like he's about to kiss me. But a bloodthirsty cackle comes out instead, and he swoops to fake-bite my neck. I scream.

'You are not a vampire,' I scold, half-heartedly.

'Mwah hah hah!' he rumbles into my throat.

'Wait . . . my mum . . .'

'She's gone,' he murmurs, placing a kiss in the hollow above my collarbone. I look over his shoulder and find Mum still there. Alone now, and smaller, and still waving. Magnus puts his hands on my arse.

'It's champagne time!' he declares.

'Wait a minute.'

'Come on. I'm freezing.'

I bat Magnus away and raise an arm to continue waving. Seconds later I hear the clack of the door. I look through the porthole and see him striding through the Stardust Lounge, hands jammed in the pockets of his skinny jeans. Is he angry? It's difficult to tell from here. Well, let him have his tantrum. It's nothing I can't fix later.

At that moment an icy gust plasters my face, and I stagger as my hair does a full loop the loop. When I can see again, I find I'm the last one on deck. My mother is an inch tall now. Her red coat like a tea light on the asphalt. To her right, the industrial skyline could not be a more perfect symbol of my upbringing. Shipyard cranes rising from the wreckage like steampunk hand puppets – antique remnants of the Industrial Revolution. The North. A different north to the one I am going to, and in social terms a hundred worlds away. My new life stands before me like an unwritten page, intoxicatingly pure and simple, and I am drunk on the notion that anything

72

is possible. The most basic requirement – a roof over my head – is sorted, as I will be moving in with Magnus, but other than that I am going in blind. Aside from Magnus's tales, my knowledge of Norwegian society is limited to what I read in the *Learn Norwegian* manual. Shopping for groceries, ordering lutefisk, complaining about hotel room taps, that's all covered – but when it comes to the intricacies of the social security system, I'm stumped. It'll fall into place, as Magnus said, and with my university education I'm sure to find a job. Before, such disorganisation would have terrified me, but not any more. We could live in a barrel for all I care, because all that matters is that we have found each other. There is nothing left to wish for. Nothing else to achieve. I have found what all those millions of people have sought since the dawn of man. I have found him. We have found each other. I could cry with joy. I could sing. I could puke.

The ship is moving slowly. By the time Mum is out of sight, the sea winds will have frozen my arm off. Time to break away . . .

I put both arms up and try to indicate I really am going now. I blow a kiss, and make an *I'll call you* gesture, just in case she can see. Then I turn and enter the Stardust Lounge.

The bar is already filling with elderly couples, and at first I can't pick Magnus out of the crowd. The floor judders as the ship changes direction, and for a moment the world becomes unsteady. I stumble and grab a handrail. Christ, if it's like this the whole way I'll be in trouble. My seasickness pills had better work.

Surely he hasn't gone back to the cabin? I move to the middle of the room and hunt for his face. God, no. Not an argument. Not today. Then I see him by the cabaret stage, texting, and my worries melt away. As I approach his booth I glance round for girls my age, hoping to impress them with my uber-hot boyfriend, but to my dismay we are the youngest people in the room.

Magnus does not see me at first. In his striped sweater, he looks like a handsome spider. Mia Farrow cheekbones, and those heavy, twig-wristed hands. It strikes me for the hundredth time how ridiculously pale his skin is. I used to think *I* was pale before I met him, but my God . . . he's on a whole new colour chart. In the light from the window, he looks almost blue. When he sees me he claps his hands together.

'Right! Champagne!'

'Aye aye, cap'n!'

I melt into his arms and clasp his face like it's a priceless artefact. His skin stretches tightly around his jaw as I kiss him. Slightly weathered, as you'd expect from an up-north guy, or that might just be because he's several years older than me. A few wrinkles are definitely setting in. But they're good wrinkles. Laughter wrinkles. Part of me wishes I'd met him ten years ago – I've seen photographs of him aged twenty-five, and he looked like a fucking cherub – but in the end I'm just happy I met him at all.

On the pillar beside us there's a poster advertising short breaks in Newcastle to Norwegians, and I almost laugh at the sight of it. That concept had seemed unreal at first. That anyone in their right mind would want to take a holiday on *this* side of the North Sea. Yet that's exactly what Magnus was doing when we first met. A *boys' weekend* he'd called it, and when he failed to introduce me to the pals he was with I felt a secret thrill to have him to myself.

'Why Newcastle, though?' I'd shouted over the music. 'Why *here*?'

'Alcohol,' he'd replied, with relish, and I'd laughed, then

74

shrugged. Apparently the cost of spirits was extortionate back home. My memory of that night is peppered with drunken blanks, but the parts I do recall were nothing short of magical. We'd shared a jug of margarita at the back of the rock bar, and even before he leaned close to perch the cocktail umbrella in my hair, I knew he was the one. 'You have to let me paint you,' I'd pleaded, and so we had exchanged numbers.

How long ago was that, now? Four months? Five? Thank God I got stuck in Newcastle after my degree. These last two years I've been cursing myself for choosing to study Fine Art. I mean, it's not the easiest of disciplines to apply to the world of work and pretty much set me up for a life as a starving artist. But if I hadn't been working in that coffee shop, I wouldn't have been drinking in the bar across the street every weekend. I wouldn't have been there when Magnus first walked in, and I wouldn't be sitting in the Stardust Lounge with him now.

Magnus removes a ring from his large, delicate hand, pushes it onto mine, and gazes into my face. His eyes are richly, violently blue, and when he unleashes them on me it feels like a punch.

'Mrs Brudvik,' he murmurs, and though this will not become my name for several more months, I flush with delight. We've repeated this ritual over and over. More theatrical each time, as if trying to outdo the original proposal. Admittedly, that had not been the most fairytale of moments. There'd been no ring, for a start, and both of us were blazing drunk. On the end of Sunderland pier he'd chucked his fish and chips into the sea and blurted it out. 'Fuck off,' I'd said. 'Not until you do it right.' And we'd had a little fight about it. The next day, in his hotel room, he did it again and went down on both knees. Not one, but both! Maybe that's how

75

they do it in Norway, I don't know. That time I said yes, but Magnus got angry because I laughed. And so on, with little imperfections each time. He must have proposed about nine times now, and shows no signs of stopping. But we both agree that that first time was the most romantic.

I twiddle the ring on my finger and smile because it is far, far too big for me. It's made from tarnished silver, bent oval through repeated use, and to be fair it does look quite like a wedding band. I try it on my middle finger, then my thumb, but it fits neither.

'For now,' says Magnus. 'Next time there'll be a real one.'

Playfully, I push him. To our right, two elderly women are smiling.

'On your honeymoon?' asks the closest one in a broad Scottish accent.

Behind me, I hear Magnus stifle a snigger. British accents just tickle him that way. I'm amazed he can tell the difference when he can't understand all the vocabulary. Apparently he has an accent himself, being from a northern town, though my grip of his language is so scant that I'd never have noticed.

'Yes,' replies Magnus, at the exact same time as I say, 'No.' We look at each other, and his deadpan face snaps back on.

'No,' I repeat, smiling at the woman. 'Not yet.'

'Holiday, then?'

'No. Well, actually, I'm moving to Norway.'

'Ohhh,' say the two ladies, in unison, and the silent one makes a face. Mrs McBusybody grabs my hand and squeezes it, surprising me.

'So *brave*,' she says.

I laugh.

'So he's Nor*wegian*, then?' says the woman. Then, as if to a

child, she dips her head and asks Magnus, 'Do you understand any Eng-lish?'

'To be sure, to be sure,' quips Magnus, adopting the same
dippy-headed posture.

'That's *Irish*,' I whisper. He shrugs. The woman straightens
up. I can't tell if she is offended. The silent friend continues
to smile.

'So how did you two meet?' McBusybody asks me, ignor-
ing Magnus this time.

'In Newcastle.'

'You just met? In the street? And now you're moving to . . .'
Gales of laughter overcome the two ladies. The silent one
pipes up now – something about Viking plunderers – in a
broad Geordie accent most Brits would have struggled to
decipher, never mind Magnus. Hägar the Horrible is
mentioned.

'Yeah, that is what we Vikings do,' says Magnus. He rolls
his eyes. I giggle. Around us, people are starting to stare.

'So then, when exactly were you planning on raping me?' I
ask Magnus, in my best little-girl-lost voice. The women stop,
and for two full seconds you could have heard a pin drop.

'Graaaarrrrr!' roars Magnus, and sweeps me up in his
arms, knocking down the menu cards and missing
Geordiegran's sherry glass by millimetres. Screaming, I kick
my legs, and Magnus whirls me away across the bar.

'Let's get that champagne later,' he says in my ear.

'To be sure,' I laugh as he kicks his way through the double
doors. When I look back, McBusybody's mouth is wide open.

#

The car ride from Bergen takes an entire day, and Magnus is

77

in a bad mood from the off. This is something I've seen little of during our courtship, and I've yet to develop a strategy for dealing with it. First I try jokes, which barely raise a smile. Then I ask what's wrong, and he says, 'Nothing.' I ask if it's something I've done, and he shakes his head. 'I'm tired,' he says. 'It's a long drive.' So in silence we cover the next hundred miles.

The scenery outside is straight out of a travel brochure. Rugged and snowy, and curiously similar to the north-west of Scotland, only cranked up to eleven. I gaze through the window as mountains and fjords and frozen waterfalls rush past. Long, round tunnels feed us through mountainsides, and dense evergreens converge periodically to blot out the sky. The farms we pass are wooden and painted in contrasting toy-town colours. Red and white. Yellow and grey. Blue and cream. Raging rivers hug the road, then snake away to the bottom of impossibly deep ravines. Along the way we meet pockets of bad weather, and each time we plunge into one, the outside world switches off. Magnus swears quietly at such junctures, using words I do not understand, and tightens his grip on the steering wheel.

'Why the hurry?' I ask at one point, and he doesn't even bother to answer me.

An hour or so later he apologises. We park at a service station, he holds out his arms, and I climb across the cab into his embrace.

'I just want to get us home,' he says into the back of my neck, and to my relief there is kindness in his voice.

The service station is minuscule and has little on sale besides hot dogs and petrol. I look carefully at the shelf behind the counter. Apart from sweets and packets of crisps, there is absolutely nothing I can eat.

'You're in the wrong place to be vegetarian,' says Magnus as he stuffs a hot dog into his face, and it is hard to stop myself growling at him. I stare at the hot dogs, wishing desperately that they were tofu dogs, and suddenly this monstrous idea wells up in me, that I should eat one anyway. Like the Katherine standing in this cabin in the absolute back of beyond is not the same person as Geordie Katherine. British, northern Katherine, with a lifetime of personal ethics under her belt. A horrible chill goes through me, and for a moment I feel endlessly blank and lost. Like I've forgotten who I am.

A hand touches my face, and I jump.

'You okay?' asks Magnus. He looks concerned.

I smile weakly.

'Maybe you can eat some potato chips,' he says. 'It's a long way to the next station.'

'Okay.' I nod, and clear my throat in an effort to pull myself together. With cold-cramped fingers I open my handbag and extract the envelope containing my newly converted kroner. It looks like play money. So colourful.

'Jada, så ska vi ta oss en . . .' starts Magnus.

'No! I can do this.'

He holds his hands up. The clerk leans expectantly on the counter.

'Goddag. Jeg vill ha . . . en . . . salt-skruer . . . takk skal du . . . uh . . . please?'

The clerk replies with a torrent of unfamiliar words. I blush deeply. But I must have done something right, because he takes down the right packet from the shelf and holds out a hand for the money. I give him a hundred-kroner note. What's that? Ten pounds? Jesus. Beside me, Magnus is laughing.

'Fuck off!' I hiss. But he squeezes my arm and says, 'Actually that was not so bad.'

The clerk quips something to Magnus as he gives me my change, but I'm too embarrassed to ask what he said. Magnus buys me a chocolate bar called Plopp as a joke and a cup of strong black coffee for us to share. We guzzle this down in the front of the van, and Magnus kisses the tip of my nose. Then, in slightly better spirits, we continue our journey.

#

By the time Magnus shakes me awake, I feel like I have slept for a hundred years.

'Wake up, sleeping beauty.' He says this gently yet firmly.

'What time is it?' I slur.

'Half over nine.'

I peer through the windscreen at the black sky. Each time I exhale, it makes the air opaque.

'Come on,' he says. 'I have to take the van back.'

I allow Magnus to lift me down from the cab. Even though I have his arm to lean on, I slip and slam down hard onto both knees. Stunned, I notice the thickness of the ice beneath me. I've never seen anything like it. Magnus opens the back of the van, and with barely a pause for breath, we ferry my belongings onto the road. Magnus helps me transfer them into the communal stair of the building behind us. Then he gives me the house keys and gets back in the van.

'Go to settle in,' he tells me. 'When I get back, I will help move your things up.'

'What? We can't leave it there! Someone'll . . . It might get . . . It's . . .'

'Folks are good here. No one will steal it.'

'Are you *kidding*?'

'Don't worry,' says Magnus. 'I will be back soon.' He pecks me on the lips, closes the door and roars away. I watch until the van is a speck.

8

Friday.

Today I have a meetin' with Joyce. They said I had to, if I wanted to get out of the crisis room. The other thing I have to do is stay inside the house from now on. There wasn't much choice really.

The first thing Joyce brings up is the lullaby, an' actually that doesn't surprise me one bit, now I know for sure she's no better than the newspaper men. I tell Joyce – as I told all the others – that I don't want to talk about it. I don't tell her why not, but basically iss cos I'm ashamed. My failures are *mine*. Not entertainment for them. It embarrasses me now when they talk about the lullaby, cos it reminds me how loopy I was when they first brought me here. People are always draggin' that around. Pokin' me with it, tellin' me things I used to say an' do. Most of it, I don't remember for myself. But iss embarrassin' anyway. I hate it. I'm not playin'.

The conversation goes somethin' like this.

> **Joyce:** We have such a grand time in the ladies' choir, Katherine. You should join us sometime.
> **Me:** [No reply.]
> **Joyce:** You like singing, don't you? Do you remember the words to your nursery rhyme?
> **Me:** No. [Yes.]
> **Joyce:** That's a shame. I'd have liked to hear you

sing it for me. Do you think you might remember if you tried?

Me: No. I don't like singin'.

Joyce: All right. Maybe we could talk for a bit instead. Do you mind if we talk about holidays?

Me: Okay.

Joyce: Where do you think you would go, if you could go on holiday? Aaaanywhere in the world. Somewhere hot and sunny, or cold and snowy, or maybe a boating holiday? What do you think you'd like best?

Me: I dunno.

Joyce: Do you like boats? Would that be a nice holiday? Or maybe that'd be too boring?

Me: Dunno. Don't care.

Joyce: When I was wee, my daddy had a boat. We'd sail all around the islands, and spot birds, and catch fish. Sometimes we'd sail so far we weren't even in Scotland any more. Doesn't that sound exciting?

Me: I guess.

Joyce: Would you like to go for a boat trip, Katherine? That'd be a nice day out, wouldn't it? We could arrange that with the—

Me: No.

Joyce: We could phone the nice folks up at the fish—

Me: No.

Joyce: We could all go. The scenery round Loch Oscaig is lovely this time of—

Me: You go then. I'm not goin'.

[Joyce clamps her mouth into a line an' looks down. Her eyes grow small as she reads her notes.

For a minute, she doesn't speak. Then the smile
snaps back on, an' she looks up.]
Joyce: We could take a boat to *Skye*. Go visit
Rhona.
[I meet her eye, but just for a moment. A surge of
emotion flushes my face.]
Me: What about the bridge? There's a bridge, you
know.
Joyce: Yes, but it'd be so much *nicer* to—
Me: I'm thirsty. Can I have a drink of water?
Joyce: [Pauses. Then, irritated:] Yes. Yes. Of course
. . .

#

Joyce ends up all angry, but it doesn't matter. I've done what
they want, an' now they have to let me go. I climb the staircase in the dark, slippin' my hand easily up the polished rail.
On the landin' I walk slowly, hopin' to bump into Mary.
There's a blue glow from the skylight, which is good cos I can
see the way to my room without turnin' the light on. Mary's
door is across from mine, but tonight there's no strip of light
under it. I stand outside an' listen. Nothin'. Jus' some clinkin'
from the kitchen downstairs. I walk to my room, hit the light
switch an' sit on the bed. The clock says ten past eleven.
Eleven. Twelve. Thirteen. I watch the quick hand whizz. Each
second tappin' my heart like a hammer. Iss not till I peel back
the covers that I find the heather. Jus' a handful, tied up with
grass, but it smells amazin'. I clutch it to my chin an' crawl
under the covers. Bless Mary. She might be the only friend
I've got left.

Saturday.

Iss cold in the conservat'ry. For breakfast I have two slices of toast spread with blackcurrant jam. The moor is callin' me like crazy, an' iss harder to ignore than usual. In the afternoon I hang round the back porch, but whenever I get close to the door, a member of staff comes to whisk me away. Later on, I notice someone's taken the key out of the lock.

Mr Duff doesn't come today. Instead, we have an extra-long gramophone time. Mrs Laird hasn't brought enough records for that, so we have to play each one twice. I'm not in the mood to join in, so I go an' sit by the window. If Rhona was here now she'd say, 'What's up mopey chops? Come and dance!' An' for her, I would. But Rhona isn't here. Was I wrong to say no to the boat trip? It'd shut Joyce up for a while. But I don't believe they'd go to so much trouble without a reason. No, it feels like a trap. They think I came to the loch on a boat. That I fell off it, or escaped off it, or was thrown. I know they think that, an' I know they're dyin' to know for sure. Maybe they think I'll remember stuff if they stick me on another boat. Of course! That's it. What if the newspaper men are there, all watchin'? Waitin' for me to snap. No . . . No . . . Is a boat trip worth the risk? I mean, it might be true . . . I might get to see Rhona, but . . .

A hand touches my hand. I jump. But iss jus' Mrs Bell. She asks if I want to dance with her, cos I'm sittin' all alone. Joyce is watchin' from across the room, so I say okay an' Mrs Bell waltzes me round for a bit.

When gramophone time is over, we say a prayer for Rhona an' her mother. This time ev'ryone looks at me. Not jus' Joyce. I look at the floor an' pretend to be prayin' really hard.

When I look up again no one's watchin' any more. We don't pray for Mrs McRae today.

#

Sunday.

Today they let me telephone Rhona. Mrs Laird dials the number an' talks to Rhona behind her hand. Then she calls me over. I grab the receiver.

'We just came back from church,' Rhona says. Her voice sounds weird, like she's been runnin' really fast.

'What are the clouds like there? When are you comin' home?'

'Soon,' says Rhona.

I wait for her to say more, but she doesn't.

'The weather here is very fine today,' I tell her.

'Mm hmm? That's nice. Perhaps you should go for a walk.'

'I already asked,' I say, with my eyes on Mrs Laird. 'They won't let me.'

'Well, I'm sure they have your best interests at heart,' says Rhona. Then she goes quiet again. In the background there's a man talkin'. I think I hear a swear word.

'I have to go now, Katherine,' says Rhona.

My throat goes lumpy.

'Will you call me soon?'

'Yes. Yes, I will.'

I hear the man's voice. Louder this time.

'Goodbye, Katherine,' says Rhona, an' hangs up.

#

Monday.

Joyce brings boat-trip fliers back from the village. She hands them round an' says more than once that there's a

86

group discount. The other residents seem to like the idea of a trip to Skye. It scares me, cos it all hangs on me now. If I say no, the trip is off, an' ev'ryone will be angry.

After dinner the weather's really nice, an' ev'ryone except me is allowed outside. I watch them through my bedroom window, lyin' out there on the old striped deckchairs. Once or twice Joyce looks up, an' I jump behind the curtains, but not fast enough.

I count the heads below the window. Then I cross the landin' an' open Mary's door. Her room is on the other side of the house, an' from here I can see in the other direction. Downhill towards the village, with the long, flat tongue of sea an' jaggy mountains beyond. The ground inside the peri-meter fence is bumpy, like a wrinkled-up towel, an' I know that my secret place – the bite – is hidden in one of those wrinkles. But this is not what I've come to look at.

Skye. There it is, like a strip torn off the bottom of the sky. Dull grey an' featureless, above a brilliant white patch of sea. The bigger hills are to the left. Is Rhona to the left or right of them? I wish I could remember what Wikipedia said. On this side of Loch Ghlas, a cloud of seagulls twinkles to shore. The fishing boats must be coming in.

I squint my eyes at the place where the sea ends an' Skye begins. Rhona might be standin' on the beach there right now an' I'd never know. If only I had binoculars. I raise my hand an' wave a bit, jus' in case. Maybe *she's* got binoculars an' can see me standin' here.

A boat trip might not be so bad. If I manage to control myself, *if I try really hard*, there won't be a scene, an' I won't be the centre of attention. Anyway, it'd be worth it to see Rhona again. She'll hug me, an' smile, an' tell me how well I look. Iss been so long. She must be dyin' to see me. I might

87

even tell her about my dreams. Silly Joyce. I'll never tell *her* those things, no matter how hard she pushes.

Part of me is still scared of the sea, though I don't really remember bein' in it. In some ways, I think I might find my old self there. We switched places, me an' her, in Loch Oscaig, an' I'm the one who made it to shore. The newspaper men should pester her, not me. She knows exactly what she was runnin' from, or towards.

In the quiet moments I still feel her out there – sad an' cold an' all alone – an' this pain grows inside me, like I have to go back to her. But I know I'm not ready. They think they can force me to do that. Like jabbin' me in the back will get results faster. But things don't work that way. Until I'm as strong as the girl in the loch, her tales of foreign lands would only crush me.

The boat, I'm not sure about at all. I think she climbed out of the snow on her hands an' knees. An iceberg broke off from the land, with her on it, an' the Gulf Stream carried her away. On an' on, all the way here, till the ice melted under her an' her strength gave out. Then she handed me the song, an' I carried it to shore.

This heirloom isn't mine to keep. I can't make sense of it like she did, but I hold onto it till the day I can give it back. Maybe I will die then. I'll hand back the baton along with the song, an' she'll be the one they pull from the waves. Not me. On that day, I think both of us will find peace.

A scufflin' sound makes me wheel round. Mary stands in the doorway, wearin' a pink sun hat. Her forehead rests on the door frame, an' for a second I think the hat's caught on it. She hangs, an' stares, an' doesn't speak. My face goes hot.

'I'm sorry,' I say.

Mary holds out her hand, an' when I take it she leads me

away from the window. Into the hall we go, an' down the stairs. We step carefully, side by side, as Mary hangs onto the banister. She doesn't meet my eye, but that's okay cos I know she's concentratin'. I think iss a phobia she has. Somethin' to do with fallin'. At the door, we stop.

'I'm sorry,' I say again. But Mary jus' smiles. She opens the door, looks at me once an' leads me out into the garden. Joyce looks fit to explode, an' for a second I think she'll drag me back inside. But she doesn't. As long as Mary holds my hand, I'm safe. I know they think Mary is fragile. Iss why they bend over backwards not to upset her. I'm pretty sure Mary knows that too. We sit on the deckchairs till the sun goes down.

#

Wednesday.

I'm not hungry this morning, but no one tries to make me eat, cos Mrs Bell is havin' one of her bad days an' they're all busy with her. I sit in the conservat'ry, lis'nin' to the clatter of china an' the shoutin' of the staff an' Mrs Bell's shrill, short screams.

There are lots of ash keys on the roof. A magpie comes shufflin' round the path, peckin' between the stones. It keeps flyin' away then comin' back. I watch it for a long time.

I don't want to see the sun today. I wish the leaves would cover the roof completely. Swallow the house an' block out all the light. Then I wouldn't have to look at the outside. I wouldn't have to remember I'm trapped.

No one sees me sittin' in here. In the end I go back to bed.

#

89

Thursday.

Joyce comes upstairs to peck at me. Sittin' by the bed. On an' on, all pushy like. About the boat, mostly, an' hypnotist stuff. She wants me to do that again, the hypnotisin' thing. Says it'll help 'em answer questions. I say no, of course. But this is not good. Joyce has got powers now that she didn't have before. With her say-so, they could do all kinds of bad stuff. Like make me sing the lullaby, or let any of the staff come in my room, or stop me sittin' in the conservat'ry. Joyce can be a real bitch when she wants, an' I don't fancy bein' the one she explodes at. This is not good. I've got to be careful.

In the afternoon, iss Internet time. I want to read about Norway, but Caroline's sittin' real close, so I don't dare. Instead I look at pictures of dogs an' satellite maps of the Alps. When my time is up Caroline asks if I'd like to go outside today. I get all happy an' say yes, but all she says is, 'Well, you'd better talk to Joyce.' Then she goes next door an' makes herself a cup of tea. She doesn't ask if I want one, an' she doesn't give me a chocolate biscuit.

#

Friday.

The weather's really bad today, an' that puts me in a good mood. It rains all day, an' in the afternoon there's even a thunderstorm. Some people here are scared of storms, but not me. When the first boom goes off, I'm in the day room. Some of the ladies start wailin', an' in runs Caroline, goin', 'Shush, shush, it's all right.' Already people are gettin' up an' runnin' round, an' that's good cos none of the staff take any notice of me. What I really want is to go out in the rain, but I'm scared to push my luck that far, so I jus' run to my room

90

an' fling open the window. Straight away I feel a hundred times better. The rain smashes down, bouncin' off the sill, pricklin' my face with tiny cold drops. As I watch, a flurryin' movement pulls my eye to a herd of deer. I catch my breath. Under the lightnin' they look like holograms. Flickin' like pictures in a flip book. But they're real. I know they are, cos I hear their hooves. When the wind wafts this way, the drummin' comes with it. I feel their fear as they crash through the heather. Their confusion. They swarm towards the outhouses. Then left. Then right. For a second they run right for me. Then the whole sky flashes silver an' they shriek to a stop. Their leader swaggers sideways, an' they watch him. Trustin' him to show the way forwards. The wind blasts their coats. Then the buck bursts away, an' like ghosts the lot of 'em dive into the mist. My eyes stay glued to the place they disappeared, an' as I stand here breathless this funny feelin' hits me, that I should run out an' follow 'em. The moor is unrecognisable now. Gloomy one minute an' full of patterns the next, the air has become a giant Caithness globe. On an' off it flashes. On an' off an' on an' off an' on. I hang onto the window frame, hardly breathin' as this goes on, an' when the rain shunts to a stop I feel quite dizzy. Carefully, I lie down on the bed. Fat droplets dribble from the roof, an' as I look past 'em at the sky I wish I could see in the other direction. Downhill. What if I went to look through Mary's window? Nah, she's super-scared of thunder as it is. I shouldn't bother her.

If I was out in that rain, I'd probl'ly have run for the thorn bushes. I bet that's where the deer hide when it rains. Then again, maybe they don't bother. Do deer mind the rain? Iss prob'ly jus' the thunder they don't like. I wonder where they go to when they run away. What do they think is goin' on?

Another rumble fills the sky, an' my heart leaps. But straight away there's an absolutely gigantic crash. The room explodes with golden light. I jump off the bed.

'Holy *shit*!' I splutter.

Screams shake the house. I run to the window, but everythin's dark again. I can smell smoke. The screams grow wilder. Breathin' quickly, I run to my door an' fling it open. The hall lights have gone out, but I see shapes out there. Shona an' Mrs Bell are closest. Down on their knees, clingin' to the carpet. Mrs Bell is screechin' the Lord's Prayer.

'What's happened?!' I shout, but no one replies. Mrs Bell keeps screamin'. Then I hear feet runnin' upstairs an' Joyce's voice shouts, 'Ladies! Ladies! It's okay!'

Blue rectangles mark the open doorways, an' as I'm lookin' at 'em I notice one door's still closed. Mary! I barge in without knockin' an' stand pantin' in the dark. For a minute I don't see her there, under the window. She looks like she's cryin', an' the sight of that almost sets me off. I swing her round, an' her wet face flashes in the light. Then I see she's *laughin'*. Iss creepy to see her laughin' without really laughin'. Jus' a tiny, cute wheezin' noise.

'Are you hurt?!' I ask, but Mary looks through me. Grippin' her shoulders, I stick my head through the window. Outside, the garden is a mess of black an' white bits. Lightnin' flashes an' the bits glitter merrily. Then I see the gap. The ash tree on its side, on top of the conservat'ry. When I breathe in, the air is smoky. Mary laughs an' laughs an' laughs. I cradle her in my arms, an' wait, an' smile.

9

Saturday.

Today's music therapy is cancelled. Instead, some men come to check the storm damage. There's a hole in the dinin'-room wall, an' they spend most of the day tacking blue plastic sheets to it. The weather is wet an' blustery. Sometimes the wind blows the plastic away or fills the house with glass dust, an' when that happens the men shout a lot. No one was hurt last night, but we're all quite shaken up. They say we won't have the power back till tomorrow night, so we have to jus' make the best of things. Joyce walks up an' down, shoutin' orders at the men. Talkin' on her mobile telephone. The house is freezin', so we wear our anoraks all day. There's jam on bread for breakfast, an' cold beans on bread for lunch, an' cheese sandwiches for tea. I spend most of the day playin' snakes an' ladders with Mary, but now an' again I go down-stairs to look at the hole in the wall.

Iss hard to describe how lost I feel now the ash tree's gone. It almost feels like a person has died. The conservat'ry too. How will I manage now? That was the only room I could see Skye from, since they stopped me goin' outside. I'm ashamed to admit it, but the view from Mary's window is a big reason why I'm spendin' so much time with her.

#

Sunday.

Today the weather's calmer an' the clouds are low. When I come downstairs I find a lady with beautiful hair at the back door. She waves when she sees me, calls me by my first name an' explains through the letterbox that she *comes bearing gifts*. There's no key in the lock, so I have to wake up Mrs Laird to let her in.

The lady turns out to be from the church in the next village, an' she's driven up to bring us a thermos of tea. Iss round an' silver, like the boiler in the upstairs cupboard, an' iss got a little tap at the bottom. We gather in the library, which is the warmest room, an' share out the tea. There's sandwiches too, an' pink wafer biscuits, but the hot tea is the best thing of all. At first the church lady talks about Jesus. Then she starts askin' me about the thunderstorm. I tell her it wasn't really scary, an' she asks me what kind of stuff I *do* find scary. Then she asks about my mum an' dad. But iss nasty how she's starin' at me, all close, an' lis'nin', an' I don't want to talk about those things. My face goes red an' I shrink back towards the others. 'I think clowns are scary,' says Jess, but the lady jus' laughs an' keeps starin' at me.

Soon the food has all gone. The lady takes the Tupperware to her car an' comes back with a big blue parcel that she tries to give to me. Iss wrapped in fancy paper, with a big bow on top, an' a card. But Joyce dives between us, shoutin', an' grabs the present from my hands.

'You crafty swine!' shrieks Joyce. 'I just knew it!'

Shocked, I step back. Caroline comes runnin' an' the two of 'em march the lady to her car. The church lady says terrible words an' looks back over her shoulder, but by now Mrs Laird is leadin' me away. I see Caroline stuff the parcel through the car window. Then the front door closes an' Mrs

Laird takes me to a room on the other side of the house. When Joyce comes inside she stuffs a handful of black tape into the bin. Her face is tight with rage, but I'm too scared to ask why.

#

Monday.

I feel hemmed in today, like I can't breathe, an' though I'm scared of gettin' caught, I go to the back door. The key is in the lock, so I turn it quickly an' sneak out for some air. If I'm only a minute, Joyce will never know. But iss someone else I bump into. A fat red man, covered with sweat. There's a chainsaw in his hands an' bits of wood everywhere. The ash tree! My whole body shakes, an' I have to run inside.

Later they load the butchered remains onto a pickup truck an' drive her away. Prob'ly to the village, for firewood. This is the last time I'll see her. My good old friend. For weeks now, she's been the most stable part of my life. Never throwin' surprises at me, never makin' an unexpected move. I knew exactly what to expect from her, an' when. Like me, she thought she'd stand out there forever. Swayin' in the wind, never breakin'. But fate had diff'rent plans. With her gone, the world feels chaotic.

#

Tuesday.

The electricity is back an' the house is warm again. Ev'ryone sleeps in extra late, an' most of us miss breakfast. For lunch we have a big pot of potato stew, an' iss the best thing I remember eatin' in a long time. For the time bein', we'll be eatin' meals in the day room. We're allowed to use the dinin' room again, but no one wants to cos the blue plastic wall makes it so cold. There's glass dust over everythin', which keeps comin' back no matter how much iss cleaned off. I don't much fancy gettin' glass in my food. Mrs Laird says that that can kill you.

#

Wednesday.

I wake with a bad feelin' in my stomach an' can't get back to sleep. Have I been dreamin' again? I try to remember, but the details drain away as I try to catch them, leavin' nothin' behind but ripples.

A face flits in the corner of my eye. Somehow I know iss the face of a real person. Watchin' me, always, all this time. I turn over, draggin' my cold sheets with me, an' a terrible thought comes into my head: that I will never, ever be able to escape. That even when I can't see it, the face will keep seein' me.

My scalp is moist. I stroke it with tremblin' fingers, till the hair tangles. My eyelids flutter as my heartbeat rises. Bones soft an' cold, in a soup of sweat. The face looks on, an' analyses me, an' seems amused. It raises its fist an' I cower. Iss a man's face. Thick an' ugly, an' full of the threat of violence. Black hair strangles down. Darkness turns to red. Suddenly my mouth is singin'.

> Solen er så rød, mor
> og skoven bli'r så sort
> Nu er solen død, mor
> og dagen gået—

No!

A cold surge, an' I rush towards the light. Fast, the veil lifts. A sudden distortion. Then my nose is pricklin' hard an' I'm squashed against the floorboards. Tears leave my eyes. But iss okay. The song has stopped. I crawl to the corner an' stuff myself into it. Cold waves rush through me. I am full of sharp edges. The face has gone away, but the fear will not.

#

When I wake I find Joyce at the end of my bed. She snores on the floor, inside a royal-blue sleepin' bag. There are three empty mugs beside her, an' a copy of *Christian Weekly*. Her hair is frizzy.

I look at the square of light behind the window. Iss hard to tell, but it looks like it might be a nice day. I look back at Joyce. She hasn't moved. I feel heavy.

It feels like the window is open, though the curtains are too still for this to be true. I think about gettin' up but find I can't move. Instead, I move my eyes to the ceilin' an' count the half-moons in the cornice. I keep losin' count somewhere around sixteen. Joyce turns over at one point, but doesn't wake up. I want to look at the clock, but iss extremely hard to turn my head. By the time I start countin' again, the room is brighter. Birdsong echoes down the chimney – starlings, I think – an' iss so loud it sounds like the room is full of 'em. I crane forwards an' see Joyce has gone.

#

Today. Slow. wanted, wanted so badly.get out. of bed. My face. tight an' bloated. Like cryin' a. lots. a cryin' a. ah. ugh.

97

Spend time. Lookin'. at hands. back. of *my* hands. an' think. they look. wrong. Remember hand. Diff'rent hand. Face raisin'. a hand. spoon of hot. Spoon. to mouth. My mouth. an' the sleeve. Lace. an' tiny cup. Sweeties. in they go an'. an' an' after I. *can't* move my. mouth. Wasn't *my* hand. see? Not *stupid*. know that now. How could it be? How could it . . . That's why that's why that's. I *know* it. the cornice. an' an' the seam. in wallpaper. Up. above headboard, I see it. seam. crack. seam an'. sound. voices. somewhere. quiet. think they were. think came tryin'. feed me. sweeties, but then. When I see. Foil. the foil. *Pop.* blisters. *Pop! Popple.* An' I. know. pills . . . I glide through. long. dull expanse. brown. gentle stream. The voices. the whispers. An' the room. goes away.

#

Iss warm, an' soft. Wind throwin' gravel at my window. I know that. Like the nights. *Smash trickle, smash trickle.* A hand snared in gold an' opal. Rings. Bangle. Magazine. Smell coffee. That magazine moves, fraction. Does not reveal face. But she's on other side. I try to say *Joyce*, but. my mouth . . . body feels. wrong.

try again. arch my neck. suck in. Then,

'Joyce . . .'

Magazine moves. Joyce's face.

I was right.

'Go to sleep, lassie,' says bitch Joyce. But her voice. like mine. Unnatural.

Want to reply. But. all breath used. Hands chatter. Feel my . . . I . . . Watch her face the . . . The mole . . . jowl . . . The twist of . . . *mouth*. coffee smell strong. Saliva. My bottom lip i.waterfall. Stop . . . Can't move arm. Can't nt'n'tt wipe.

blooms. Warm into into pillow. Quick cold. Then . . . cold cheek. Joyce. Fades.

Hand comes back. scratchy tissue. wipes my lip hard. Close my eyes. wish she had not done that. Things swing back. I'm *here*. I can hear *ev'rythin'*.

'Shush now,' says her voice.

Upupupblistering lights! swarms, see it. coming, no, from somewhere. out. around. sinuses. hurts. can't. Stop! Can't . . . stop! Catch . . . it . . . stopGasp, an'

whooshesdowndown down downdowndowndowndown-downdownaround. inhale. I am . . . movin' backwards . . . faster than. I . . . oh. jelly.lights.an'. an'.ican't . . . keep. up . . .

#

I realise my voice is talkin', an' I jerk my eyes open. Joyce sits beside me, wearin' diff'rent clothes. Her eyes stretch when she sees me lookin' back, but she finishes her sentence.

'—did it make you feel when he did this?'

I look round, then back at Joyce. I think she's askin' a question. I look round again.

'What?'

The room is much cooler than before. I'm not in my bed, or even my bedroom. This is a room I haven't seen before. I jump. The woman is not Joyce.

'Aaaaaah . . .' I say, startin' to panic. Somethin' below me rips, an' then I see a wide blue sheet on the bed. Like toilet paper, but too big. Hands appear on me, an' a sharp pain stabs my arm. Faces appear, smoosh to one side an' droop into shapes. A smile tingles on my face as all the world turns soft. Voices overlappin' from somewhere in the sky. The air is not real. I breathe chiffon. Blue paper cracks as my weight drags down. Slow earthquake, comin' apart in bits. Soon the gap will swallow me. Ears rumble. Voice has stopped talkin'.

#

Joyce drives me back from the clinic in Inverness. *An emergency* she says. *Only for your own good* she says. But I know the truth. They've been dyin' to hypnotise me again an' this was the perfect excuse. Joyce seems pleased. She says we've made progress. I barely speak back to her.

Mist hugs the road, forcin' us to drive slowly. Every so often, headlights blunder out of the greyness, an' we reverse to the closest passing place. Joyce keeps her eyes on the road. Rust-coloured trees flash past. Yawnin' ravines an' sullen, stationary sheep. They appear an' they leave. A cloudy slideshow. The world starts to feel as unreal as one of my dreams. This is a place that never sees the sun.

#

We pass a sign that reads *Milk Bar*. Joyce stops beside a tall hedge an' reverses back to the sign. She drags the map from the glovebox an' studies it, peekin' once in the rear-view mirror. Then she pushes back into first gear. We creep through a hole in the hedge an' up a narrow track. Gravel purrs under the wheels. Wet rhododendrons stroke the windows.

'Are we stoppin'?' I ask. I picture a tall, cold glass of milk.

'Mm,' says Joyce, hunchin' over the steerin' wheel. Then the car bucks, an' we swing to the left. Joyce swears under her breath. Then it happens.

Through the undergrowth I spy a wooden house. Painted white. Log pillars. Pointed roof. A plungin' sensation drags

100

my chest down, an' all at once I am fallin'. Somewhere down there my knees are movin'. My lungs heave an' catch hold of nothin'. Door handle in my fingers. Ev'rythin' turns cold. I flounder head first into branches. Shriekin'. I lurch. Run. Fall. Roll into a dark, swampy place. The house is still there, behind my shoulder, an' I can't get far enough away. The weight in my chest is too strong. There's mud under my nails. In my mouth. In my collar. Damp creeps through my clothes, I swoon into blackness, an' when the stingin' in my palms hauls me back I find myself clingin' to the ground. I vomit, an' water comes up. Behind me, Joyce is shoutin'. The car squeals, whirrs an' crunches. A mechanical grunt, then the gravel patters in a diff'rent way.

'Kathy!' bellows Joyce. 'Kathy! For God's sake!'

I hear the plants swing behind her. Then she stops, an' everythin' goes quiet. Her hands touch my shoulders, an' angrily I shake her off.

'Sorry, lassie,' she says.

I spit acid into the dark. My knees are hot an' soaked, an' it takes some time to clean myself up. By the time I'm ready, my heart has stopped hammerin'. I go back to the car an' find Joyce leanin' on the bonnet. Her hands are in her pockets. Her coat covered in seeds. For a moment I feel sorry for her. She looks like she actually does care.

'You ready?' she asks. I nod.

We get back in the car an' drive to the top of the track. There, the car park is empty, but the sign says *Open*, so we go inside. The front porch is full of glass animals. I pause, thinkin' we've strayed into someone's home, but when Joyce opens the next door, we see the tables an' chairs. An old woman in a housecoat brings two handwritten menus. We're the only customers. Joyce shoots me a look as we sit down, but I don't know what this means so I pretend not to have noticed. A plastic inflatable parrot in the window takes my fancy, an' when the woman comes back I ask if I can have it. Again Joyce glares at me, so I shut up an' look at the floor. The woman says no.

Joyce has a cheese sandwich an' a cup of coffee, while I have tomato soup. We eat in silence. To my disappointment, there's no milk on the menu. We have scones with pear jam that the woman says she made herself. Then Joyce pays an' we head back to the car. I close my eyes as we drive down the path, to make sure I don't see the house in the wing mirror. Iss nightfall by the time we reach Gille Dubh.

#

I dream of a dark, dense room with a paintin' of a ship on the wall. When I wake up, Joyce is sittin' by my bed. She's brought me some tea an' a plate of oatcakes with cheese. I'm impressed that Joyce brought the green-striped cup, even if it was by accident.

'Thank you,' I say, an' she nods.

I take a sip, tryin' to avoid her gaze. Iss strange to have her here in my room.

'So,' says Joyce. 'Do you think you could tell me some more about your mother?'

I freeze. Suddenly I see the machine in her lap.

'My . . . mother?' I gasp.

'Yes,' says Joyce. 'We were really getting to the bottom of that, I think.'

I look at the tape machine. Iss switched on. The little tape goin' round an' round.

'I want to go for a walk,' I say, an' slam my cup down on

102

the nightstand. Joyce's eyes follow my cup. One large splosh heads her way, an' she dodges to avoid gettin' it on her dress. By the time her eyes return to me, I'm out of bed. Joyce shoots upwards as I reach the doorway an' the tape recorder clatters to the floor.

'Well you can't!' she commands, but by now I'm runnin' down the corridor. My nightgown glues my legs together, slowin' me down. At first I think I'm goin' to get away. But Joyce comes crashin' after me an' wrestles me to the carpet at the top of the stairs. She pins my arms above my head, like a marathon winner.

'Caroline!' she yells. 'Caroline! It's Kathy!'

I raise my head an' see faces.

'I want to go *outside*!' I scream, an' wriggle free.

Joyce lunges an' misses me. But jus' then Caroline appears. Hands grab me, an' the weight on my back becomes more than I can fight. My knees hit the ground, an' all of us go down. Someone holds my head still, an' a hand with a needle swings close. As I sink into the floor, I recognise the pattern of my bedroom carpet. The tape recorder – still runnin' – on the floor. Then the sounds blur an' stretch, draggin' away from my ears, pullin' me away, an' around, an' down.

When I wake it is dark, an' I'm alone. I try my door, but find that – for the first time I can remember – it is locked.

#

I sit in the far corner of the dinin' room, eating my toast an' jam. I drink my tea from the mug with flowers on it, now that my green one's broken. When no one's lookin', I put my arms round myself. My wrists are bruised, yellowish-tan. They don't hurt any more, but the sight of them still upsets me.

They're the crownin' glory of my awful, lost weekend in Inverness, an' a reminder that sooner or later I'll be dragged back up there for more. What will happen then? Will they make me talk about Magnus? Or my mother? Maybe they know where my mother is, an' that's what Joyce meant when she said we'd made progress. My memories of my mother are faint. I jus' know she was thin, with short, black hair. No matter how hard I try, I can't picture her face, but I do remember her dressin' gown, which was flimsy an' dark with a brightly coloured print of fruit on it. I remember her wearin' it while cookin', with her back to me. It breaks my heart to think of her sittin' by her television now. Seein' my story on the news. Not carin' enough to pick up the telephone.

The workmen have built a plain brick wall across the hole where the conservat'ry door used to be, but iss not insulated yet, so the house is still freezin'. Who decided to build a wall instead of a new conservat'ry? It feels like somethin' Joyce would do to punish me. I mean, it was no secret how much I loved the conservat'ry. I spent every single morning out there. Evil witch. I bet iss her idea to keep me inside, too. Caroline took people out for a walk earlier, but I wasn't allowed to go.

The workmen's voices echo through the house. They talk about football an' pop stars whose names I don't recognise, an' sometimes without warnin' they bark with laughter. When their voices get loud I throw my arms up to protect myself. I know they talk behind my back. I've seen them lookin' an' dread what they might be plottin'. I wish they'd jus' finish an' go away.

When I've eaten I take my dishes upstairs an' push them under my bed. If I wash them later on, I won't have to bump into the men.

I sit draped in my mustard bedspread an' watch Caroline's

walkin' party from the window. Every so often I lose sight of them behind dips in the slope. Mary walks two steps behind the others, clutchin' handfuls of wild flowers. Each time she passes, the bunch of flowers is bigger. She sees me one time, an' waves. I wave back. By the time I hear the front door, iss dark.

10

January 19th, 2005.

Everything around me is still so exotic. Six days since my arrival, I remain thrilled by the unfamiliar brands. The champagne-flavour pop. The tins of 'Bog' and 'Sodd'. The lighter fluid I mistook for mouthwash. The ridiculously long tri-language ingredient listings. Those three, cheeky extra vowels. The strangely named chocolate bars. The weird, dense little cakes, the open sandwiches and the elk jerky. The fruit soup and the sour cream porridge. It's all so bloody exotic. The supermarket has become my church, and I bow to its novelties with ceaseless delight. In the daytime, when I am alone, I cross the main square to Rema 1000, just to gawp at the products. On the first day, I learnt to gawp rather than buy. The prices, by British standards, are seriously high, and if I bought everything that took my fancy, my savings would be gone in a week. For now, Magnus buys our food. It's not something I'm comfortable with, and I certainly don't intend to become a kept woman, but I content myself with the knowledge that it's a temporary arrangement. The petrol, van hire and ferry tickets depleted my meagre life savings, and now I'm down to my last three hundred pounds. It's the poorest I've been in my whole adult life, but with Magnus by my side I'm not afraid. When I get a job I'll treat him in return. Teamwork! Isn't that what marriage is all about?

For the first week we play house. In the morning Magnus

puts on clothes and goes to work. In the daytime I scour the Internet for a job. In the evening Magnus returns and we climb back into our tiny loft bed. Occasionally we remember to eat. Night after night we meld and contort, hot skin glued together in the freezing air. Sometimes in the light, and sometimes in the dark, hours fly past like seconds. I doze in between, his heart thudding strongly beneath my hand, and feel happier than I ever thought it possible to be. Sometimes a lock of hair tickles my neck, and when I go to brush it aside I realise it is his, not my own. At night, I truly feel we have become one.

Magnus works at a teen community centre where they have bands and a café and all this other cool stuff. Loop the Loop, the place is called. He's like the Godfather to those kids. On Saturday nights he works late, and originally we'd planned for me to hang out there during his shift. I'd looked forward to seeing the place at night-time, after months of hearing how great it is. But on Saturday he comes home at six with a bottle of aquavit. 'I pulled a sickie,' he grins, and pours me out a massive shot. By midnight we can barely walk, never mind scale the loft ladder. Magnus drags some coats from the wardrobe instead and we build a makeshift bed on the hall floor.

My job hunt is not going well, and this is largely to do with my language skills. I learnt it all from a book, you see. The Queen's Norwegian. It looked so easy on paper. Paul and Eirin and their delightful conversations about verbs. Their jaunts to Aker Brygge to order coffee in perfect Bokmål. The reality is more daunting. The book never warned me about the dialects people speak up north. It never warned me how *fast* people speak, and the fact that though most of them speak English, they don't particularly want to. I was naïve to think I could just continue speaking English. I see that now. But it never once struck me that the Norwegian I'd learnt would also largely be useless. Maybe if I pretended to be deaf, things would be easier. If I could have my conversations slowly, on paper, I might get by. But my God . . . even then I wouldn't understand the colloquialisms.

'You're the Geordies of Norway!' I tell Magnus, but instead of laughing with me he rasps, 'Well, get used to it.' At first I'm enraged by that comment, but as the days go on I realise he is right. Sure, I'm more of an outsider in this place than I'd anticipated, but I can't hide under Magnus's wing forever. I'm not a child. Why should he go out of his way to help me settle in?

So much for my glittering art career. Things were supposed to have been different out here. I'd imagined landing an art director job at a magazine or museum or whatnot, and doing my own paintings on the side. Becoming a famous expat artist, with Magnus by my side. But suddenly it's not that simple. There are plenty of arts sector jobs, but all of them require experience, or some form of vocational training. As a native university-leaver, I might have found a company easily, but as it stands I require a dictionary to carry out the simplest of transactions. It says so in the adverts – *all* of the adverts actually – 'Fluent Norwegian essential'. I'm beginning to know that phrase by heart. Right now, even the kebab shops wouldn't hire me.

'Have you considered . . . um . . . moving to Oslo?' I ask Magnus one night.

Without looking at me, he shakes his head.

'You could ask for a transfer or something,' I press. 'They must have community centres down there. Or some other council job . . .'

'I'm staying here.'

'It's just . . . it might be easier for me to get a job down there.'

'Mn,' says Magnus, and I can tell he is not really listening.

'You see, my Norwegian's not good enough for—'

'Speak English then. Everyone speaks English. They *love* to speak English.'

'But all the ads say—'

'So speak Norwegian. Do a course. *I* had to, when we moved up from Aarhus.'

'You were a kid then! You've had plenty of time to—'

'Just do the course! It's not *that* hard!'

'I can only do the free course if I've already got a job . . .'

'Uff. So get a *dictionary*!'

The shortness of Magnus's tone stings me. I fall silent against my pillow, and watch him trying to pluck a hair from the smooth desert of his chest. With every failed attempt, his skin grows pinker. I consider slapping him in the face, or at least telling him I already have a dictionary. That if people here spoke normally, like Paul and Eirin, I might be able to understand them.

'The way they speak on TV,' I say. 'Do they speak like that in Oslo?'

'Hmn.'

'Magnus, I'm serious. If I don't get a job soon, I'm fucked. I can't tell NAV I'm here until I've got a job. I can't get a doctor until NAV know I'm here. I can't renew my prescriptions until I've—'

'I can't leave town,' smiles Magnus. 'What would the kids do without me?'

He has turned around now, but instead of looking at my face his eyes are fixed on my body. Under the covers, his hands move across me. I flap a hand at him. But it's hard to stay mad when he turns on the charm.

'I'm sure the kids will be fine,' I whisper as he kisses my hands. 'Rock 'n' roll will find a way to survive without you . . .'

'Hysj,' he murmurs, and touches his mouth to mine.

'I'm serious,' I repeat. Then his kiss flows into me, and the real world swoons into pieces.

#

In the blink of an eye, another week passes. By now, my job hunt has taken on a different slant. Having been refused by the local newspaper, art gallery and tourist magazine, I've adopted the hope that a hotel – with its yearly influx of foreign tourists – might welcome a native English speaker onto their staff. I present myself to each major hotel, wearing the cheap skirt suit I begged Magnus to buy me. One after the other, I lay my heart on the line, and one after the other they turn me down. After this I try the English pub and the Irish pub. I try the tourist office, the museum, the cinema and the library. I even try to sell some paintings in the cafés. Everywhere, the answer is no, and with every rejection a little more spring goes out of my step. 'I'm scared,' I tell Magnus, several times. I need him to understand my predicament. To realise this is not working and open himself to the possibility of a Plan B. But every time he kisses my tears away, we somehow just end up having sex.

#

Saturday comes round again, and Magnus is due to work the

110

evening shift. It's now five days since my meds ran out, and the side effects are kicking in. I sit below the dark skylight, crying into Magnus's pillow, and for one whole hour it feels like I am going mad. This morning Magnus left without waking me and took the single set of house keys with him. This basically means I can't go out, because once the door has closed I have no way of getting back in.

I hate this feeling. This weakness that descends when I stop taking my meds. It usually happens by accident, when I forget two doses in a row or go on a trip without them. But now I have no choice. I must learn to live without such luxuries. Be strong, where Dad never managed to be. I can do this.

Loop the Loop is a twenty-minute walk away, down by the marina. I've been past it once, on my way to a job interview, but until now I haven't been inside. Annexed to the main building there's a windowless wooden outhouse covered in graffiti. If Magnus's descriptions are anything to go by, then that is the rehearsal block. That's where he spends his day-times – allotting session times to bands, fixing faulty amps and kick pedals, hiring out microphones. All that guff. But it's after six now, and that means the rehearsal block is closed. By now, Magnus will be in the main building.

A shiver passes through me, and with disgust I wriggle it away. Why am I so afraid of going there? I wasn't afraid before. They're only kids. Not *aliens*. They may speak a different language, but that doesn't make them *dangerous*.

God, I'd do anything for a valium right now. But aquavit is all I've got. Aquavit will have to be my new drug.

Taking another swig, I look at the clock. Seven thirty. That's not so bad. Magnus is only working till nine. I should go down and surprise him, with a nice dress and a smile. I don't think he's seen me crack a smile all week.

Right. Pull yourself together.

I slide one foot over the edge and find the first rung of the ladder. Cautiously, I descend to the bedroom floor and make myself ready to leave. By the time I reach Loop the Loop it is after eight.

As I approach the door, my feet slow. The place looks bigger than I remembered, and darker, and louder. This is the first time I've been out alone at night-time, and I'm shocked by how scared I feel without Magnus. Tears form in my eyes as I scan the teenagers outside the entrance. Leaning on walls, sitting on the kerbs, drinking from plastic bottles. Now and again they squeal with laughter, and my eyes dart towards them. But they're so self-absorbed they've barely noticed me. Pulling my hood low, I go through the front door.

'Magnus?' I ask the girl at the café, and she points across the crowded dance floor. 'Takk skal du ha,' I say, like they do in my *Learn Norwegian* book, and wander self-consciously into the dark. As I walk, I realise how many of the kids are drunk.

He was right, though. This place is cool. God, I'd have been a much more well-rounded kid if I'd had a place like this to go to. It'll be fun to hang out here.

There, I think I see him. Smiling with relief, I smooth my dress down and push my way towards the back wall. Past the really tall Hanoi Rocks kid, round the punk girls doing the tango. People move to one side, eyeing me suspiciously. Then I make it through and Magnus is right before me. It's his face I see first. Sitting laughing by the stage. Drink on one knee, and a blonde girl on the other. Her arms are wrapped around his neck, and until his gaze jerks onto me, his arm is around her too. A cold pain stabs my stomach, and for a moment the floor whirls beneath me. Someone shoves my back and I pitch forwards.

'Magnus?' I ask, in barely more than a whisper. Lights flare. Then my hearing slams back, and Magnus is on his feet. His eyes are rounder than I've ever seen. Intently, he speaks into my face, and the voice that comes out is panicked.

'Katty. What you doing here?'

'I—'

'You shouldn't be in here, it's members only.'

'What the *hell* do you think you're—'

'Hysj! Not here! I'm at work.'

'Who the fuck is she?'

'Not *here*!' Magnus jerks my arm, hard, and my neck jolts. People are staring as he pulls me to one side. He takes a deep, angry breath. Again, those eyes. Then his arm flies forwards and rapidly yet covertly pushes the house keys into my hand.

'Go home,' he whispers. 'We'll talk later.'

I look behind him and see the girl staring at me. She's even younger than I first thought. Silky, golden shoulder-length hair, fresh skin, ripped black clothes. Her piercing blue eyes are fixed on me, scowling, and as she steps up to take Magnus's arm, she says some words I don't understand.

'Piece of shit!' I spit, and throw the keys at his feet. Then I turn on my heel and storm through the crowd.

11

Friday.

The dinin' room wall is finally fixed, an' Mrs Laird summons us to say a special thank you to the workmen. I don't speak or look anyone in the eye. Mrs Laird does most of the talkin'. One of the men is a trained blacksmith an' makes a big show of presentin' Mrs Laird with a real horseshoe. Ev'ryone coos an' wants to touch it, so they end up handin' it round so we can feel how heavy it is.

'I bet the horses dinnae feel so lucky, luggin' four ae them around aw the time!' says the head workman. Ev'ryone laughs except me.

Later, I see someone's hung the horseshoe on a nail above the kitchen doorway. The nail doesn't look strong enough to hold it there, an' this makes me anxious beyond words. Over an' over I picture the horseshoe fallin' on someone's head. The blood an' the fuss an' the screamin'. The roar of ambulance sirens, an' the scar such an injury would leave. I want to ask them to take down the horseshoe, but I don't know how to say it in a way they'd understand. Soon the thought of askin' them grows as terrible as the horseshoe itself. Each time I see it, it reminds me of the workmen. As if they never left, an' never will. I no longer dare to walk through the kitchen door, an' sooner or later someone's goin' to notice that.

#

I fall asleep in the afternoon, an' by the time I go downstairs dinner is over. Usually this wouldn't bother me, but tonight I am starvin'. I sniff the air in the back porch, kickin' myself for this mistake. I should, of course, go to the kitchen an' ask for leftovers, but that'd mean walkin' under the horseshoe, an' I can't do that. Somewhere nearby, I can hear Joyce singin' scales.

On my way past Mrs Laird's sittin' room I notice her door is open. I peer inside to see her hunched at her desk. Her head is in her hands. I'm about to ask if she's okay when she speaks, an' I realise she's usin' the telephone. I shrink back into the corridor, glad that the rug hides my footsteps.

'Mm hmm ,' nods Mrs Laird. 'I know, I know, but . . . no . . . Listen . . . sweetheart . . .'

She falls silent, one finger raised in the air. But the person on the telephone doesn't stop talkin' for a long time. Bit by bit, Mrs Laird's finger lowers an' returns, unused, to the tabletop. Several times, she sighs.

'It's not . . . it isn't . . . Darling, it's *not* your obligation! You have to put your own health first . . .' says Mrs Laird. She listens some more, till another gap comes an' she jabs, 'Well, *no*, I haven't told her yet, but—'

I gasp, an' Mrs Laird's face swings towards me. Her eyes look tired. I wonder if I should run. But iss too late. She's seen me.

'She's here,' Mrs Laird mutters, between her teeth. She raises her hand an' flaps it at me as she rises. I back away, along the wall. When she reaches me I think she will say somethin' else, or shout at me for eavesdroppin', but all she does is pull the door closed.

I wander away uneasily an' climb the stairs. Jess is cryin' on the floor of the landin', but I can barely handle my own

115

problems, let alone hers, so I slip past without a word. I sit at my bedroom window for what feels like hours, watchin' the sun sink away. Outside, Jess's sobs rise an' fall. Dispersin' into abstract sounds, till I almost forget what they are. As I braid an' unbraid my hair, my reflection in the glass grows brighter than the outside world. Bit by bit, till I've eclipsed it all, an' the only light left comes from the bulb behind me.

Tonight, my faith is at a low. Ev'rythin' feels uncertain, an' laughably, bottomlessly pointless. But I know it wasn't always this way. I have this misty memory of pickin' bilberries on a vast green hill. Droppin' 'em into a sand-castle bucket. I can see my stained fingers on the ride home, an' the sense of pride when the bilberry pie came out of the oven. There was a beginnin', a middle an' an end, an' all of it was worth doin'. My days have none of that now. Is that because there's no one left to *tell* me these things are worth doin'? To threaten or hurry me along? Rhona was the last one who bothered to do that, an' now it seems she's abandoned me too.

#

This mornin' I take care to get to breakfast on time. I've never made it down so early, but I must be sure to get some food before iss cleared away. I also take some for later. Oatcakes an' two little tubs of jam. This goes well. Nobody notices.

'Golly, you've got an appetite today, Kathy!' says Mrs Laird as I refill my plate. I stare at her. Is she on to me? On my way back to my seat I pass Jess. She's talkin' all serious with Aggie an' Liz, but when I walk past all three of 'em go quiet. Jess's eyes are swollen. She looks at me once, then at the floor. I don't like the way they're lookin' at me, so I switch to the seat facin' away from them. As I sit down a tub of jam slips from my pocket. I fluster to pick it up. Did they notice?

'Ladies!' says a voice, an' I look up to see Mrs Laird. She's on her feet now, at the end of the dinin' room, an' she looks like she's goin' to say somethin' important. My eyes move to the horseshoe hangin' inches above her head. Suddenly the horseshoe's all I can see. Balancin' on its nail. Temptin' gravity . . .

My foot starts jigglin'. I have to lean on it to keep it still.

'I have an announcement to make,' says Mrs Laird. 'A piece of good news, which may brighten your day. Some of you more than others . . .'

I feel Mrs Laird's smile on me, full of teeth, an' daren't raise my eyes. I picture the horseshoe smashin' into those teeth. Scatt'rin' them in a bloody arc across the floor. Into the cauldron of porridge, roots an' all. The blood seepin' in, like jam. People's teeth crunchin' into Mrs Laird's teeth as they feed on the red porridge . . . Swallowin' sharp edges . . . Chokin' . . .

Baboom goes my heart. A yelp comes out of me. I clutch my mouth.

'As you all know,' Mrs Laird says, 'our dear friend and colleague Rhona has been away. I know this has been hard on some of you, and I want to thank you for your patience while we've been *one man down*. But! I'm happy to say Rhona will soon be back with us!'

My heart leaps. Several people gasp happily, an' some of the oldies start clappin'.

'When is she coming?' asks Aggie.

'Thursday afternoon. She'll be back to work on Friday.'

Joyce noisily clears her throat.

'Oh, I clean forgot,' says Mrs Laird. 'Joyce has some news, too. Don't you, Joyce?'

'Thank you, Vera. Yes. No doubt most of you already know about the local production of *My Fair Lady*. Well, I'm thrilled to tell you my audition went well, and I've been chosen for the part of Eliza Doolittle!'

'Ooooo,' say the older ladies.

'Thank you. Thank you. Yes, it's quite an honour. For the next month I'll be attending rehearsals at the village hall. Now, this will mean rearranging my Thursday sessions. But I'm sure all my girls understand. And of course, when the time comes, you'll get free tickets for the show. A little *culture* for you!'

A dribble of applause rounds off the announcement. Joyce milks the attention for as long as possible, while Mrs Laird returns to her toast an' jam. I gulp some tea from my flowered cup an' gaze at the wall where the conservat'ry used to be. Suddenly I feel really happy. Not cos of Joyce's announcement. I don't give a shit about that. But the rest of it . . . Rhona . . . She's really comin' back! Soon my life will be back to normal.

#

I spend the followin' days wrapped in a delicious haze. My weekly session with Mrs Laird goes ahead, but iss more straightforward than usual, cos she doesn't try to talk about heavy stuff. She basically asks how I'm feelin', an' I tell her fine, which is pretty much the truth since Saturday. She asks a couple of simple questions. Then she nods an' says, 'All right, run along then.'

'That's it?' I ask, an' she nods again.

118

'Why don't you go for a nice walk?'

'But Joyce said I'm not allow—'

'Never mind what Joyce said.'

I take a long walk around the perimeter fence. Dark blotches dribble like ink across the hillside, sendin' the gorse in an' out of shadow. That night I sleep like a log.

#

Thursday.

I wake at dawn an' can't back to sleep. I lean out of bed an' drag my skirt off the chair. The pockets are still full of oatcakes. I eat them slowly, tryin' not to get crumbs in the bed. There's one tub of apricot jam, which I eat last of all, as dessert. The room is quite cold, so I roll back under the covers an' close my eyes. For a while I try to sleep sittin' up, but this doesn't work so well.

I feel like I should feel happier than this. It puzzles me. I should have been out on the moor by now, turnin' cartwheels. But I can't even bring myself to get up.

The cold pushes down, rootin' me to my bed. But iss not jus' the cold that keeps me here. Deep inside, my body knows somethin' is wrong. I feel it there, alongside that damn lullaby, but no matter how hard I try I can't make sense of it.

As I stare at the brightenin' window, shapes creep from the dark. A chair, a curtain, a table, a lamp. Sharpenin' in detail till the whole room is filled. In the mirror on the dresser, a sliver of sky pokes through the curtains. Pure white. Then dappled grey. A whorl of cloud looks down, like a huge, forgetful eye.

Somethin' is wrong . . .

119

Mr Duff comes to visit in the afternoon. He's two days early, an' all of us are in the day room when the car pulls up. I hear its slow wheels on the gravel, followed by whispers. I crane my neck but see nothin' through the window. They must have come in the back way, on the other side of the house. Mr Duff sings really loudly today, an' even Caroline joins in, which she's never done before. Music therapy goes on for much longer than usual, an' when iss over Caroline unpacks what she calls a *special picnic tea*, right here in the day room. Afterwards most people head to their rooms. I set off to search for Rhona, but Caroline stops me an' makes me go upstairs. At Mary's room I stop an' tap on the door, but though I know she's inside, there's no reply.

Later, I look through my bedroom window an' see Rhona. Jus' beyond the outhouses, walkin' away from the house. I bang on the glass, but she doesn't turn around.

Friday.

I'm woken by the sound of a car an' look out in time to see it roarin' away. Iss a white car. Small. When it reaches the perimeter fence I wait to see who'll open the gate, but the person who gets out turns out to be Joyce. I creep back to bed.

When I come down for breakfast, nothin' seems to have changed. Mrs Laird says Rhona has gone shoppin' an' will come back this afternoon. I suppose that could be true. I didn't think to check if there were two people in the car. I fill my plate with toast, takin' care to avoid the kitchen doorway, an' sit beside Mary to eat. She looks surprised when I sit down, but doesn't scowl or move away. Instead she turns her face down, towards the tabletop. Suddenly I realise iss been days since she smiled at me. Have I done somethin' wrong? I watch her anxiously, but Mary fails to meet my eyes. She stares instead at her plate, where she's crushed a single dry oatcake into pieces. I stare at it too. I look round to check no one's lis'nin'. Then I whisper, 'Are you okay?'

Mary's eyes wake up. She jerks her head up an' down, an' pulls her mouth into a smile, but this jus' highlights the sadness in her face. Her eyes seem glassy an' far too fragile, an' don't match her mouth. I glance over my shoulder at Mrs Laird. Should I tell someone?

'Aren't you hungry?' I ask, pointin' at her destroyed oatcake.

Mary shakes her head. She takes a deep breath an' looks away, then returns to studyin' the backs of her hands. I notice that her legs are shakin'.

'What can I do?' I whisper, but Mary keeps her face turned away. Silence spreads between us. For an awfully long time Mary does not move. Then she lifts a hand an' nudges me away. I'm not used to being pushed.

'*Mary*,' I say, an' she raises her head. Her eyes fill up, an' for a moment I almost believe she'll speak. But the fake smile returns instead, harder at the edges, an' with much more force she pushes at me.

'No,' I say. 'Tell me what's wrong.'

Mary rolls her eyes. For a minute nothin' happens, an' I wonder if I should apologise. Then Mary grabs my hand an' drags me out of the dinin' room. We climb the stairs in her usual, painstakin' fashion, an' all the way there the tears don't stop slidin' down her face. In her room she goes to the

121

nightstand an' takes something out of the drawer. Then she kneels on the rug below the window. In her hands there's a Jiffy bag. A rip across the top showin' iss already been opened. Not knowin' what to do, I sit down beside her.

Mary's face is rigid now. Shallow, huffy breaths spill out of her as she snatches somethin' white from the bag an' throws it into my lap. I stare. Iss a greetings card. But no salutation graces the front, jus' a small silver cross with a halo an' some doves. I open it up.

> *Mary. Today you are one year older, and one year closer to death. Each day we pray for the salvation of your soul. That God may cleanse you and restore, by His grace, your place by His side in Heaven. Murder is the most heinous of sins, but with God's help we may one day find a way to forgive what you did. Only through prayer will you find the path to redemption.*
> *Father and Mother.*

I stare at Mary, open-mouthed.
'What the . . . !'
Mary's eyes have gone dull.
'Iss your birthday?'
A nod.
'"Murder"?'
A scowl. She goes back to the nightstand, comes back with a biro an' scrawls something on the back of the Jiffy bag, so hard that the pen punctures through.
Abortion = 'Murder'
'You had an abortion?'
A nod.
'But . . .'

122

Mary writes somethin' else an' shoves the Jiffy bag back at me.

Got raped. Got pregnant. Got abortion. Now going to hell.

'What?' I splutter. 'You believe that?'

Mary grimaces. She shakes her head. Then she points at the card an' nods. I stare at her, aghast.

'Is that why you . . . why you tried to . . . kill yoursel—'

A nod.

So now you know, she writes. *Happy?*

I try to hug Mary, but she pushes me away. Her eyes are even duller than before. She scribbles *Please leave me alone.*

'I jus' want to help y—'

She pushes me roughly an' I tumble off balance.

'Mary!'

She pushes me again. Then I know I must go.

There's no one in sight as I burst through the back porch onto the moor. I run till my lungs are on fire an' my legs are black with mud. Finally my knees give way an' spill me into the bracken. Only then do I let myself cry. I hunch where I've fallen, squashed low to the ground. Thorns stick in my back. The air is eerily still, an' there are no birds in the sky.

#

Lunchtime comes around, an' I sit at my usual table. As I pick at my stew I try to find the right words to say to Mary, but this ends up being a waste of time, cos she doesn't show. I stay here till long after the dishes have been cleared away. *She's fine,* I tell myself. *Iss not my job to keep tabs on her.* After all, I don't come down for every meal myself. These thoughts give me a headache. No, she told me to leave her alone, an' in

123

here that's somethin' you must respect. When Mary wants help, she'll ask for it.

After lunch I feel drained, so I go back to bed. I dream about my mother. At least, I think that's who it is, only her face is blotted out. In the dream I have a red an' yellow satchel with a picture of a bear on it. The window on its front pocket holds my name, but when I try to see it the words bend an' dance. We walk through the rain hand in hand, wearin' long hooded coats which I think look silly. I love the satchel but don't want to wear the coat.

'No one's looking at you anyway,' says the woman. 'Why would they look at *you*?'

The rain makes my hand slippery. Iss cold, an' I don't understand why there are so many people here. They move fast, an' they're all too high up, an' every face is hidden. We're movin' an' weavin' between the bodies, an' I'm strainin' to keep up. Our coats are indistinguishable from the others. Our faces featureless. The woman does not look at me. I know that soon she will let go, an' that when this happens I will not find her again. The rain flashes down. Her grip hurts my hand. I want to cry.

12

Saturday.

When I walk into the dinin' room my heart almost explodes. There, in the corner, sippin' from a blue cup, is Rhona. Ev'ryone watches as I float towards her, but for once I don't care about that. Already I can feel the smile spreadin' across my face. Rhona lifts the napkin from her lap, drops it on the tabletop an' stands up.

'C'mere, you,' she says, an' opens her arms. I rush into them. When I look again, most people have gone back to their food. Beside us, Joyce clears her throat.

'Did you miss me, sweetie?' asks Rhona.

'Yes.'

'Well I missed you too. Listen, honey, I'm sure you have lots to tell me, but right now I need to talk to Joyce. Why don't you get some breakfast and we'll see each other later.'

There's a new edge to Rhona's voice that I do not like. A commandin' edge. It was never there before.

'But you're only jus' back,' I say. 'I want to tell you . . . things.'

Rhona sighs, an' for a second it looks like she'll change her mind, but Joyce clears her throat again an' the steeliness springs back into Rhona's eyes.

'I know, love,' she says. 'But we'll talk about it later. I promise. Why don't you get some eggs, and make a list in your head of everything you want to tell me?'

125

'But—'

'Run along now, Kathy,' says Joyce. I bristle. Rhona sits down an' replaces the napkin on her lap.

'I'll . . . get some toast,' I say to the side of Rhona's head.

She nods but doesn't look at me. 'Okay then,' she says, casually. 'See you later.'

#

For the first time in ages we meet in Rhona's office, an' this makes the meetin' feel uncomfortably formal. On her desk there's a pile of folders, an' with a sinkin' heart I realise what they are.

'So,' breezes Rhona. 'I see you've been to the big city.'

'I . . . don't . . . I . . .'

Rhona grabs the topmost folder an' leafs through it. There's so much paper inside – typed an' stamped an' signed. I wish I could see what they've written.

'Looks like you made some real progress. The parts about your family are fascinating.'

'I don't know. They wouldn't let me read it.'

'Do you want to read it now?' asks Rhona.

This throws me off guard. I stare at the beige folder an' feel light-headed. There is so much paper inside.

'Can't we talk about somethin' else?' I whisper.

'What do you want to talk about?' asks Rhona, tentin' her hands below her chin.

I look at her, an' struggle to hold back tears. 'I . . .'

Rhona looks at her stack of folders. She swipes a hand across her nose.

'Look. Kathy. We have to talk about these things sooner or later.'

'But . . . Can't we jus'—'

'It's in your best interests to read these transcripts, love. You've obviously got a lot bottled up. If you don't let it out you might get sick again. You don't want another trip to Inverness, do you?'

I stare at my lap, strugglin' to find the right answer. A puff of air lifts my fringe as Rhona chucks a folder over the desk. It slides to a stop in front of my face. The only word on it is *Katherine*. The rest is all numbers. I look at Rhona.

'This is the transcript of your first Inverness session,' she says. I think you should read it.'

'But—'

Rhona leans across an' takes my chin in her hand.

'I'm trying to help you, Kathy. Seriously, the Inverness stuff has opened some exciting doors. Don't you want to find your mother?'

I withdraw as far as my chair will allow. I look at the file. I scratch my chin in the place where Rhona put her hand.

'I want to go for a walk,' I say.

A small silence. Rhona exhales.

'Read the file, Katherine.'

'No.'

A rustle of paper.

'I'll read it to you, then.'

I shoot to my feet an' my chair clatters over. I cringe.

'Oh *come on*, Katherine!' cries Rhona. Her face is all hard an' pink. I've never seen her face look like that. I back away.

'You won't find the answers out there!' she calls, an' her tone of voice shocks me into lookin' back. Almost immediately I crash into something hard. But iss not the wall. Iss Joyce.

Christ, the woman really is made of steel . . .

I dodge sideways an' flee along the corridor. Jus' before the corner I look back. Joyce has her hand on Rhona's arm.

#

Sunday.

It feels wrong to see Mr Duff so soon after our last session. Nobody is very enthusiastic about singin' or dancin'. Instead, we watch Mr Duff sing songs at us. I'd hoped Rhona would come to apologise, but she's nowhere to be seen. Mary's not here either, an' I miss her. Specially when it comes to dancin' time an' I have to pair up with Jess. There's no gramophone today cos Mrs Laird is away an' doesn't like us touchin' her 78s. Instead we have to dance to Mr Duff's guitar, which feels extremely strange. I know Mary would have found this as funny as I do.

For lunch we eat meatloaf, which I don't really like. I sit in my corner near the new brick wall, pushin' bits round my plate. Is Rhona eatin' in her office, jus' to avoid me? The thought of this enrages me. Joyce fillin' secret plates for her. Passin' them under the door.

When I've finished eatin' I get up to leave, but Aggie loudly points out I haven't cleared my dishes away, an' this attracts Caroline's attention.

'Go on, lazybones,' says Caroline. 'Take your stuff to the kitchen.'

I look at the horseshoe-door.

'I . . . can't . . .'

'*Katherine*, I'm warning you.'

Ev'ryone's eyes are on me. I press myself against the wall, wantin' to leave. But this would cause problems. They'd tell Rhona, an' she'd get angry again.

My legs feel disconnected from the rest of me. I command them to move, without luck. *Move. Move. Move!* This burns a huge amount of energy. I stand glued to the carpet while my heartbeat quickens A dark, fizzy patch slurs across my vision an' settles there, right in the middle.

'What are you waiting for?' demands Caroline.

I swing my head towards her voice, but her face is hidden behind the fizzy patch. I open my mouth. The darkness slips to the left. Something swishes towards me. I gasp. Hands appear. Fasten onto me. Yank me forwards. Voices babble. Too late, I flail. The ceilin' light slams down into my eyes. Then away. Out, back, to somewhere behind my head. I trip backwards, followin' it. The fizzy patch rushes up my nose, an' then . . .

#

Floor. Hands. Light. Faces. Dark.

#

Wild faces watch me, inhuman and grand. Legs swishing through the grass. They're coming to see what I am. I can't stand that sound. Those strangled vocals, like a giant, hurt man. Getting closer. Closer . . .

Unless, of course . . . Unless it's . . . What if it's . . .

I lie flatter, hands sinking deep in the soil. Is this mud thick enough to hide me? Above, there are stars. Framed on all sides by a dark, swinging fringe. Lukewarm dots swarm behind my eyes. I feel them there. Pale tangerine. They are what I see inside me. Waiting for their time. Waiting to explode when a weak moment comes. When my instinct outgrows my fear and my legs raise me up to run.

Heavy.

Pink.

Dim light.

Of course. The crisis room.

'Hey,' says a voice.

I turn over.

Rhona is tucked up in the other bed. In her hands, a dog-eared copy of *Flight to Terror Mountain*. She puts down the book an' tilts a smile at me.

'You all right, ya weirdo?' she asks, kindly.

I look at her carefully. I nod.

'You don't have to talk. I've got my cheesy book.' She winks.

I smile.

'I tried readin' that one,' I say. 'I didn't get very far.'

We lie quietly. Rhona drifts in an' out of focus. Sometimes I hear her readin' the words under her breath, an' this sound reminds me of the wind in the ash tree.

'I'm sorry for the other day,' I mumble.

'That's all right.'

'I went onto the moor.'

I hear Rhona put down her book. 'You like it out there, don't you?' she says. 'We should take a walk sometime.'

I turn, an' smile hopefully.

'Like old times,' I say. But this time she doesn't answer. Instead she slots a knitted bookmark into her book an' places it face down on her lap. For a while she fiddles with the tassel on the bookmark. Then she flicks through the pages with her thumb.

'Do you still pray?' she asks, without lookin' up. I watch

the pages flutterin'. Beneath my head, my folded arm grows tingly.

'Mm hmm,' I answer, finally.

'What do you pray for?' asks Rhona.

I twist my mouth to one side. Is it allowed, to tell another person such things? Aren't there rules? Like on my birthday, when I blew out the candles? Rhona sees me pause an' thumps me gently on the arm.

'Hey,' she says. 'Don't worry. I'm just making conversation.'

I smile.

'Sometimes,' I tell her, 'I pray for Mrs McRae.'

'Oh,' says Rhona. 'Didn't she pass awa—'

I stop. Rhona stops too, an' turns her face away. Suddenly I understand she's made a mistake.

'I mean . . . I meant . . .'

'Mrs McRae is dead?'

Rhona sighs. 'I think so, yes.' She doesn't look at me, but I see the frown wrinkles on the side of her face.

'Who will . . . run the post office now?'

'I don't know, love.'

A great gust of wind rattles the shutters then, breakin' apart the silence that has fallen. We wriggle at the sudden chill, an' Rhona shifts further under her bedcovers. I look at her mess of backcombed bed-hair, an' cackle.

'What?' she laughs.

'You look like a ginger lion.'

Rhona cackles too an' flaps at me with her book. I duck.

'Cheeky sod!' she says, but I know she's not really mad.

#

People stare when I enter the breakfast room. I fill a plate with toast an' carry it to my usual table. Caroline is not here. I like to imagine she got into trouble for last night. My appetite is pretty good today, an' the shakiness has disappeared. I worry that when Mrs Laird returns she'll make me talk about yesterday. They never learn that fuss makes things worse. Iss not like I *chose* to faint, is it? Maybe I should tell someone about the horseshoe. They might go easy on me then, an' take the bloody thing away. My God, I'd love that. I'd throw it over the *mountains* if I could. I'd throw it into the sea.

We're meant to talk to Joyce this week instead of Mrs Laird, but there's no way I'm tellin' Joyce my super-private stuff. I don't believe she's clever enough to do the deep brain stuff anyway. Yesterday I heard Liz talkin' about Joyce. That Joyce once did a night class in the stuff Mrs Laird does an' now she thinks she knows it all. Could that be true? God, imagine if Joyce took over Mrs Laird's job for good! I couldn't bear it.

As I pick at my food I think of the Inverness transcripts an' know that sooner or later I'll be made to read them. But God knows what horrors I'll find at the end of that path. Why is ev'ryone so anxious to send me back where I came from? How can I explain this fear to them? That I don't *want* to leave this place. That I can't. That if I lost Rhona, I think I might die . . .

After breakfast I go upstairs an' ponder by my bedroom window. Outside, a spider is buildin' a web. For hours, I watch its progress. Gettin' battered by the wind. Hangin' on by one leg.

By nightfall I've made my decision. I get up from my chair an' go downstairs. The lights are turned off except for one dim wall lamp, an' this makes the hall look smaller than usual. It feels strange to be down here so late, an' I'll probl'ly get in trouble for it, but this can't wait till mornin'. I have to tell Rhona right now. I'm not goin' to read the files. If I show her how scared I am, she can't get mad. Can she? I'll jus' tell her straight.

A light flickers through the sittin'-room door, throwin' a jerky pattern into the hallway. I stand for a moment, watchin' the shapes. Then I peek inside an' see Caroline lookin' at the television. On it, a man with long hair is kissin' a woman with short hair. I clutch my throat as I inch past, but Caroline doesn't turn round. She looks younger from the back than the front. I wonder where ev'ryone else is. They can't all be in bed already.

Then I hear Rhona's voice. Unmistakable. I approach her office, expectin' to find her on the telephone. But jus' as I reach the doorway, I hear a second voice. Joyce! I leap back.

'—blame yourself. You've got to have the courage of your convictions.'

'If I'd only done it a different way . . .'

'Listen to me. It was *not* your fault! She was old! No one could have saved her . . .'

'If I'd remortgaged the house sooner . . . we could have paid for private treatment sooner, and—'

'No, you can't think that way!'

'Now she's gone . . . and the money's gone . . . And this debt . . . I can't keep it up . . . I . . . I just . . .'

For a long time there are no real words. It is Joyce who breaks the silence.

'Be honest with yourself, Rhona. You're just not ready to be back. You're not . . . bloody *superwoman*. Take some time off.'

'I have to make money, Joyce. The repayments are astronomical . . .'

'Look. I'm sure if you just—'

'I'm going to lose the house . . . *Generations*, we've lived there. *Generations* . . .'

'I'll cover your patients. If I can cover Vera's sessions for a week, I can handle a bit of paperwork.'

'No . . . There's Kathy . . . I can't just . . . I just . . . I've got to . . .'

Rhona cries diff'rently now. Faster, an' snottier, an' without pause for breath.

'Let me deal with Kathy,' says Joyce.

My skin turns cold.

'Bu . . . bu . . . but . . .'

'Shush, lassie, I know how you feel. But you've got to put yourself first for once.'

This time Rhona doesn't stop cryin' at all. I listen for as long as I can bear. Then I creep away an' climb the stairs.

13

February 5th-6th, 2005.

In my heart of hearts, I should have known Magnus would not chase me. I wait outside our building until midnight. Stamping my feet. Watching the street from end to end. When I'm certain he is not coming home I return to Loop the Loop and find it shut. The wind slices through my 15-denier tights, and I'm worried about my toes, which I haven't been able to feel for an hour. So far anger has kept me going, but there's only so much longer I can hold out in this weather. Magnus is not answering his phone. I decide, against all common sense, to find a hotel.

Stupid girl, I think, over and over. *Why didn't you just take the keys?*

There are no single rooms left at the NordLys St Olav, and the doubles cost sixteen hundred kroner. Stunned, I ask after cheaper alternatives. The man says this is the cheapest I'll find, this time of night. I tell him I need to make a phone call first and collapse on the lobby sofa.

What can I do? It's the last money I have – more than that, it'll put me in the red – but if I don't stay here I'll fucking freeze to death. Three deep breaths. I dial Magnus's number. Like before, it goes straight to voicemail. I hang up, grit my teeth and go back to the reception desk.

'Okay,' I tell the man, and give him my credit card.

The room is spartan. I sleep like the dead.

I wake to the sound of a phone and groggily pick it up. A man's voice starts talking, and I jump at the memory of Magnus.

'Mrs Fenwick?' says the voice, and then my heart droops. It's just the receptionist. 'Check-out time is ten,' he snips.

'Oh . . . Thank you.'

'It is now half past ten. Will you be staying for one more night, Mrs Fenwick?'

Shit. I sit up straight.

'No, no . . . I'm sorry, I'll be down in a minute.'

When I step back onto the street, last night's indignation has all but disappeared. I feel small and foolish as I walk the half mile back to the old town. My clothes, which I slept in, feel grubby and wet against my skin, and I can't wait to crawl into a hot bath. Perversely, the foremost image in my mind is of Magnus, waiting up for me behind the front door. It was probably a case of bad timing and we missed each other by minutes. Was he worried? Will he hug me and cry and apologise when I finally show up? Some self-righteous part of me hopes so. But I'm tired of being angry now. All I want is for this to be over.

The downstairs door is propped open. That's a good sign. I go inside and start climbing the stairs. When I reach the third floor I try our front door, but it's locked. I knock once and wait. Nothing. Again. Again. Nothing. I try the bell. Nothing.

Where the fuck is he?

Suddenly my ears prick up. Just for a second, I could've sworn I heard a creak. So quiet it could almost have been the wind. Neighbours. Traffic on the street. But my gut instinct tells me it was none of these things. That the creak came from the other side of this door.

I put my finger on the bell and hold it. The creak comes again, louder this time. A pause. A little crash. Then footsteps approach the door, and it whooshes open to reveal Magnus. His face is like thunder.

'What?' he barks, engulfing me in whisky fumes.

'What do you mean, *what*?!'

Muttering, he walks back down the hall. I dump my bag and follow. My anger has returned fully fledged, but there's something about this that puts me on edge. We've fought before, dozens of times, but this is different. This is something much, much more . . .

'Would you like to explain?' I demand, when we reach the living room.

'Explain what?'

'The *girl*! Who the fuck was she?'

'She's no one.'

'Where have you been all night? With her?'

'Where have *you* been?'

'I stayed in a hotel! I had to!'

Magnus makes a face. I realise now that he's still drunk.

'Are you seeing that girl?' I demand.

'No.'

'Who is she?'

'One of the kids. She's in love with me, I guess.'

'But you're with *me*!' I cry, exasperated.

Magnus makes the face again. He mutters something.

'What?'

'*You* don't love me,' he repeats.

I reel. 'How can you say that?'

He mutters again.

137

Suddenly I feel light-headed. I float away to the sofa and sink to the floor beside it.

'I spent my last money on the hotel room,' I whisper.

'I gave you the keys. Should have taken them, shouldn't you?'

'I have nothing now.'

Magnus snorts. 'So how are you going to eat?'

I glare at him, and he glares back.

'That girl,' I start, but Magnus slams his hand down on the door frame, shocking me into silence.

'She's innocent,' he says.

'Have you told her you have a girlfriend?'

'It's not as simple as that.'

'It's extremely simple!'

'She's fifteen. She's just flirting.'

'So you haven't told her you're with me?'

'Nobody knows. Not yet.'

'What? You haven't told *anyone*?'

'It's too soon.'

'It's been *five months*!'

Magnus shrugs. His eyes are like steel. Something in me snaps, then, and my shoulders start to shake. I curl into the floor and weep, while Magnus's feet remain planted to the floor before me.

Time drags. My head aches. By the time Magnus pulls me into his arms, hours could have passed. I cry myself out against his chest, smelling the salt of his skin through the whisky-stained shirt. His heat against my cheek.

'You're mine,' he whispers, from somewhere above my head. 'No one else. But for now we must be secret. We must let people down easy.'

I don't reply. I can't.

'They're just kids,' he says. 'They're vulnerable. I could never live with myself if they did something stupid.'

I want to say *They?* But I don't have the energy for that argument. Instead I squeak, 'Okay.'

'I love this job. I don't want to lose it. So no more dramatic shit, okay?'

'Okay.'

'I've got debts to pay, besides food for you and me. So you need to get a job, right? Try harder. *Smile.*'

He brings up a hand and pats my head with it. It feels like a lead weight. And as I submit to this comfort, I feel some important part of myself draining away.

#

Friday, 11th February 2005.

In the aftershock of Saturday's events, Magnus is extra patient with my fluctuating moods. Maybe that's because he feels guilty. Or it could simply be that my reasons for feeling bad are more tangible to him now. It's hard to believe a Scandinavian could fail so completely to understand depression. As if I enjoyed feeling like shit, or did it on cue. Anyway, a shaky truce is formed, and I agree – against every bone in my body – to keep our relationship a secret.

There's a party tonight at a rock club in the old town, and most of Magnus's friends will be there. Before going, Magnus sets several ground rules: no hand holding, no clinging and no crying. I bristle inwardly as he recites this list. But until I can afford to feed myself, I have little choice in such matters. To hold on to Magnus, I must start making compromises.

'Just for now,' he says.

'I know. Just for now.'

'Come on. Cheer up.'

I do my best to smile. Magnus kisses me.

We have our own little pre-party in the flat – knocking back the bottle of rum we bought on the ferry – and this goes a long way towards softening the atmosphere. We play some music while picking out clothes to wear, and Magnus dances me round to a couple of our favourite tunes. He looks so handsome tonight. Ghostly pale in his dark shirt. At midnight, we head downtown.

Along the back streets, Magnus walks in step with me. The air is frosty, making me shiver, and as we walk through the gloom I take his gloved hand in my own. I catch his eye and he smiles. Relief floods through my chest, and just for that moment I wonder what I've been so upset about. Then a throng of drunks bursts, singing, round the corner, and Magnus yanks his hand from mine. In the space of two seconds, he's put several paces between us. Reeling, I fold my arms round myself. Has the *just friends* act begun already? Magnus parades ahead, as if I was not there, and, feeling like a fool, I trot after him.

Råkk is a squat timber building adorned with a lightning-bolt-shaped sign. Through the darkened windows I see heads bobbing. As we approach, someone comes out of the door and the sound of AC/DC fills the street. Without a backwards glance, Magnus flounces down the steps and makes his entrance. It seems like he knows every person in the place, and under different circumstances I might have found that adorable. But not tonight. I stand awkwardly by the door, waiting for the hellos to stop and the girls to stop pawing him. A long-haired guy in a Motörhead cut-off nods at me and, grateful for some recognition, I smile back. He hurls a string of words at me, which I can only assume is a greeting.

He looks at me for a reply. But at that moment, Magnus dives between us and throws an arm round the guy's neck. They exchange words.

'Don't mind him,' Magnus tells me, in English. 'He's drunk.'

Then a fresh barrage of friends greets him, and he's gone again. I stand near the door, scanning the room, and suddenly it hits me that I have absolutely no friends here. Not a single one. I look round for Magnus and see him laughing with two stunningly beautiful women. One of them, a redhead with pixie-like cheekbones, is playing with his tie. At his side, a really young girl is vying for his attention, and with rising anger I recognise her as the girl from Loop the Loop.

'It was n-ai-ss too meet yoo,' sing-songs a voice, and I whip round to find the Motörhead guy in my face. His accent tickles me into laughter. Until this moment I have never heard anyone sound so Norwegian. With a big smile, I shake the huge, pale hand he has thrust out.

'I am Håkon,' says the guy. 'Yoo are Magnus sin friend?'

'Yes.'

'Yoo are Scot . . . uh . . . Scots . . . *Scot-tish*?'

He looks so pleased with himself for remembering the right word that I don't have the heart to correct him. Anyway, he's not the first to misplace my accent. Sometimes even British people think I'm from Scotland. Smiling broadly, I nod.

'*Train-spot-ting*!' exclaims the guy, and to my astonishment he reels off a heartfelt, perfectly remembered Sick Boy soliloquy. I gape at him, impressed.

'Whisky! Yoo like whisky? Single malt . . .' He gestures enthusiastically, sloshing me with the contents of his pint glass, and in an instant the front of my top is soaked.

Swearing, I shoot backwards. But Håkon hasn't even

noticed. I look round for Magnus, hoping to extricate myself, and see him by the bar, handing a drink to the Loop the Loop girl.

'Excuse me,' I tell Håkon, and drift over to Magnus's side. The girl's hand is on his chest now. She sways slightly, and Magnus pulls her upright.

'Hall-lo,' I say, as brightly as I can. They turn to look at me. I'd hoped Magnus would notice the warning in my tone, but as far as I can tell, he has not. Suddenly I feel nastily sober. The girl tugs at Magnus and says something that makes him laugh. Then she takes a pack of cigarettes from her pocket and puts one in Magnus's mouth. I stare at the packet and a surge of longing passes through me. I can no longer afford my own cigarettes.

'Hold this,' says Magnus, and puts his glass in my hand, before following the girl outside. Dumbstruck, I watch them go.

'Sin-gull malt!' blares a voice into my ear, and I turn to find Håkon beside me. I shove Magnus's glass into his hand. Then I storm to the ladies to dry my top.

#

For forty minutes I try to talk to Magnus's friends. Occasionally I recognise English words and jump on the chance to join in. But it never lasts more than a few seconds. People get bored of me, or don't understand my humour, or return to speaking in dialect. I try in vain to identify words, to get some gist of the conversation, but it's useless. My bottle goes and I get sick of grinning into empty air. I retreat into the corner and sit on a stool. By the time Magnus comes back to my side, I am sober.

'Whatssz wrong with yurr face?' he glowers. There's a beer in his hand. I glare at him, wanting to slap him, but he's so drunk by now he wouldn't even realise why I'd done it.

'Nothing.'

'Why won't you speak to people? I'm sick of you . . . be-ing so . . .'

'So what?'

'Cheer *up*, Kathy! For *helvete*!'

I push Magnus and he teeters off balance, taking a bar stool with him. The clatter makes people look. Magnus looks at me with undisguised contempt and drags himself upright. Suddenly I realise I've never seen him as drunk as this. In fact, I've never seen this level of drunkenness in *anyone*. People usually pass out when they reach this stage, or puke, or start drinking water. But here he is, still on his feet. For a moment, the pain is so great I can barely breathe. I close my eyes, do my breathing exercise and try to hold the tears in. When I open my eyes again, Magnus is glaring at the floor.

'Can we go home?' I ask.

Magnus tuts. I look at his hands, wrapped tightly round the stool, and try to lay mine on top. He jerks away, swears and returns to his friends.

For some time I sit with my head on the bar. No one tries to talk to me or move me on, so maybe this is a normal sight in here. My head starts to throb, and with growing bitterness I realise the hangover's already kicking in. Until 3 a.m., the clock on the wall keeps me company.

From here I can see the top of Magnus's head. He's been sitting with two well-dressed men for a while. They've moved to a table at the back, so I can't see them well. The big guy with the black hair has his back to me, and over the bulk of his frame I only catch narrow glimpses of the thin one's face.

Magnus is slumped between them, barely moving other than to sip from his glass. I watch his face for a while, trying to work out if he's falling asleep. If he does pass out I might need a hand getting him home. Maybe those guys could help. The big secret would be out then, wouldn't it? I laugh to myself, bitterly.

Suddenly, a commotion draws my attention. I look up. The black-haired guy is on his feet, in the corner by the door to the toilets. Some girls are pushing him, without much effect. He tilts to one side, and I see then that he has a girl pinned against the wall. Blonde, pretty, falling out of a low-cut dress. The Loop the Loop girl. She stands there, visibly trembling, as he speaks into her ear. Now and again she tries to respond, but her jaw is hindered by the huge hand he has clasped round her face. Slowly, carefully, he turns her face from left to right, and inspects her as a vet would an animal. Then he slides his thumb down her cheek, croons some more and uses it to part her lips. For a moment she lets it rest there. Then, quite suddenly, she bites.

The man yells, draws his hand far back, and wallops the girl in the face. She falls to her knees. The girls around them go bananas. I get to my feet. But in the bedlam that follows, Loop the Loop girl makes a break for it. I follow her through the exit and run up the stairs to the street.

At first I don't see her. Then a wail cuts out of the shadows, and I see her on the ground behind the bus stop. Rivulets of mascara stain her face, and she is spitting something red – either blood or lipstick – into the gutter. I run to her side, just as her band of friends bursts out of Råkk.

'Sølvi!' they yell. '*Sølvi!*' Then they see her, and run towards us.

'Is she okay?' I gasp, but no one replies.

144

The girl cries and cries. Someone is dabbing her face with a napkin. Another strokes her knee. Just then, Magnus blunders through the door and Sølvi pushes all of us aside. As she runs into his arms he makes a meaningful face at her friends, and like a troupe of butlers they shrink away.

Magnus leads the girl into the alley behind Råkk. They sit down on a doorstep, and for a long time he just rocks her backwards and forwards. I stand by his side, waiting. When she's stopped crying I whisper, 'Is she okay?'

'Fuck off,' slurs Magnus, and goes back to stroking her hair.

'Why did your friend do that?'

'This is not your business.'

I retreat to a doorway on the street corner and hug myself against the wind. Magnus and the girl talk in hushed tones. Eventually I sit down on the ground.

14

Tuesday.

'I want you to bring that lady back,' I tell Rhona.

She lowers her notepad an' stares at me. '*What?*' she says.

'That hypnotist lady. I want to talk to her.'

Rhona's mouth drops open. For a moment she jus' stares. Then a lovely smile spreads across her face an' she pushes her hair behind one ear, like she does when she's thinkin' hard.

'Are you sure?' she asks.

'Yes.'

'Well . . .' says Rhona. 'Well . . .'

'I'm sure.'

'I'll have to give her some notice . . . maybe a few days . . . You *do* mean Susan, don't you? Dr Harrison?'

'Yes, Dr Harrison.'

'Right! Well . . . I'll give her a call,' says Rhona. Her eyes are sparkier than they were all day yesterday, an' I'm proud to be the one who made this happen. Huh. Maybe this *isn't* such a bad idea . . .

I play with the hem of my sleeve while Rhona writes some notes. When she's finished she pulls her feet up onto the chair edge an' hugs her knees. She smiles at me, an' again I feel good.

'I'm glad you came to this decision,' she says. 'You know,

I've been dying to talk to you about Inverness. You may not remember this, but you made some real progress in those sessions.' She pauses, as if amazed I haven't stopped her yet, an' asks, 'Is it okay for us to talk about this?'

This is hard to answer, cos Rhona usually knows when I'm lyin'. But my *yes* seems to satisfy her.

'I still have the transcripts, if you're ready to read them,' she says. Then she adds, 'Or one . . . We could start with one, if you like.'

'Yes please,' I blurt, before she can withdraw the offer. One at a time is as much as I can handle anyway.

Rhona looks at me more closely, an' I wonder if she's seen through my fake bravery. But she jus' says, 'Righto,' an' goes to root though the filin' cabinet.

I watch her back as she stands on her tiptoes, there. Her hair is knotted tightly at the base of her neck, an' I can't help wond'rin' if iss as painful as it looks. She never used to wear it that way. After a minute she comes back holding a cardboard folder.

'This is the main one,' she says. 'It's a summary of the most important parts. We have the full-length version, of course, but I think it'd be hard for you to make sense of.'

I stare at the file, tryin' to keep my eyes dry. Rhona kneels at my side.

'I know you're afraid,' she says. 'You're not as good an actress as you think. But trust me. The sooner you face these things, the sooner we can get you home.'

I nod. My throat feels like iss full of tissue paper.

'I'm here for you,' says Rhona.

I nod.

Rhona hands me the file. I hold it in my hands, breathin' hard. I square my shoulders. Then I open it.

MmhorGDRegP89/10
Name: Katherine (Fennick?)
Gender: F
DOB: Unknown (Est. age 30)
Date of session: 16/06/2006
Duration: 55min
T: Therapist, P: Patient

Excerpt 1:
T: So the farmer lives in the other half of the house?
P: Yes.
T: Was this the house where you were born?
P: No. I come in the summer. With Mummy and Daddy.
T: Is it the first time you have been here?
P: We come every year.
T: Does your daddy work here, on the farm?
P: No. He looks at the birds with his telescopes. But I work sometimes. I help push the sheep in the big bath. I get the eggs, with Coral.
T: Who is Coral?
P: My friend.
T: Did Coral come here with you, in the red car?
P: No, silly. She lives in the caravan with her mummy.
T: Which caravan do they live in?
P: The brown caravan. With the swing.
T: Are there other caravans there?

P: No. It's got nettles under the steps. I play with Coral on the swing.

Excerpt 2:
T: Why are you afraid of Daddy?
P: He shouts. Loud.
T: Has your daddy ever done more than shout at you?
P: He's not like the other daddies. Sometimes he acts funny.
T: What does your daddy do when he acts funny?
P: He cries. He hits me when I haven't been naughty.
T: Why do you think your daddy cries? Is it because he is sad?
P: He hits Mummy too. She says she'll pack her bags. She'll leave us at the bus stop.
T: Which bus stop is that?
P: Mummy doesn't say. But she says it a lot.

Excerpt 3:
T: How far is the farm from the sea? Is it a long way?
P: No. Usually we drive there. I get tired when we walk. We drive to the post office too.
T: What does the post office look like?
P: White. It's long. With postcards.
T: Can you see the words on the postcards? Can you see the name of the town?
P: No town. The towns are far away. We buy the shortbread in Edinburgh.

T: You drive to Edinburgh to buy shortbread?
P: No. We drive there on the way. We walk round the fountain. The other kids are at school.
T: The other kids? Who are they?
P: The Scottish kids. They aren't on holiday. But I am. So there's no one to play with.
T: But you play with Coral?
P: We play on the swing. And I help Mr McLennan.
T: Is Mr McLennan the farmer?
P: Yes.

Excerpt 4:
T: Why don't you like taking a bath?
P: The water's dirty. The hot tap makes brown water.
T: The water is brown when it comes out of the tap?
P: Yes.

Excerpt 5:
T: Maybe you make sandcastles at the beach?
P: [Laughs.] No, silly.
T: What do you do at the beach, then?
P: Climb the rocks. I saw little jellyfish . . . they were all round my feet . . . they might sting me, and Daddy's walking away . . . I'm calling and calling and he won't come back. He won't lift me up. [Patient becomes agitated.]

Excerpt 6:

T: But you felt safe when your mother was around?

P: Yes.

T: Do you think she was a good mother to you?

P: She tried her best.

T: Do you remember the last time you spoke to your mother?

P: [Patient makes sounds. Facial tic. Seems confused.]

T: When you parted with your mother, were you on good terms?

P: She was happy for me.

T: What had happened, to make her happy for you?

P: I was happy. I was getting on the boat.

T: Was your father there too?

P: No.

T: Where was the boat going?

P: [Facial tic intensifies. Further prompts are unsuccessful. Patient wakes.]

Session ends

In the corner of my eye, Rhona's face looks on. I lower the beige folder to my knees an' look into the floor. Water falls an' falls from my eyes. Down my cheeks, down my nose, into my collar, onto my knees. Rhona does not speak, an' neither do I. The folder turns moist in my fists.

'I need to be alone,' I whisper.

'I understand.'

I feel myself floatin' down the hallway. My shoulder bangs into a door frame, hard.

'Do you need help?' asks Rhona's voice.

'No.'

I go into the darkness. I go past Mrs Laird's sittin' room. I go upstairs, close my door an' crawl into bed. I pull the covers round my head an' bury myself far beneath.

Wind brays at the window, an' for once this does not sound beautiful to me. I push my head deep, an' swallow, an' try to think of nothin'.

#

Wednesday.

This mornin', Rhona brings a cup of tea. She doesn't hang around. Jus' sets it on the nightstand, looks at me a little too long an' heads back to the door.

'Come to me when you're ready,' she says.

I lie on my side, lookin' at the wall. The tea is cold by the time I reach for it, but I drink it anyway. Rhona has brought the mug with the blue stripe, an' if I half close my eyes I can trick myself that iss the green one.

As I sip, I try to get my head in order. The shock I felt last night has died down, but I'm still pretty shaken, an' need to make sense of things before talkin' to Rhona.

Part of the Inverness transcript really struck the bullseye. The rest jus' puzzled me an' sounded exactly like what it was. A story told by someone else. I know I should remember ev'rythin', cos those words came out of my mouth. But I can't connect the dots. In the end those things happened to that little girl, not me.

My memories of Coral are the clearest of all, an' I think that's because they are good ones. The swing by her caravan was blue, with rustin' chains that squeaked. I remember sittin' on it with one foot up an' one down. Playin' acrobats. Takin' turns to hold the frame steady. In a barn we made bird's nests out of hay, an' tried to make the chickens sit in them. We ran in green wellies, rubbed dock leaves on nettle stings, an' raced twigs in a beck. I remember callin' by too early one morning, an' her mother's mouth shoutin' at me through a frosted-glass window. I remember lyin' on my back, with a black an' white dog runnin' round me an' a woman with veined cheeks peggin' sheets to a clothes line.

But that's the end of the good memories. Cos on the other side of the spectrum, there's my father. The parts about him chilled me to the core. I remember him. Or I remember the *fear* of him. The anger an' shame an' frustration that were never to be spoken of out loud. I remember knowin' his behaviour wasn't normal. That when he lashed out, it was not really allowed.

The more I think of my father, the jumpier I become, an' though his image is hazier than Coral's, it has glued itself onto me. I'm scared, cos I know this is jus' the beginning. Why did I ever read the transcript? I should have known I wasn't strong enough yet.

#

'Well. What do you think?'

We are sittin' against the old sheep fold, huggin' our knees to keep warm. A bank of thorn bushes shields us from the house. I trail my fingers down the scratchy grey stones, trying to distil my feelin's into words. Bits of lichen crumble off, stickin' to the sleeve of my jumper.

'It made me sad,' I say.

'Your father?' asks Rhona.

153

I shoot her a glance. I nod.

'Can we talk about the farm?' asks Rhona. 'I really think the farm is the key.'

'I don't remember much. The bits I remember are sort of useless.'

'None of it is *useless*,' she says brightly. 'Just talking about it is a step in the right direction. Let's get it all out in the open.'

'All?' I say, an' regret it straight away. Then the wind blows my hood down, an' my hair billows out. It whips round my mouth like iss trying to gag me, an' for several seconds I find myself engulfed. When I've battled it back into place, my hair smells like gorse.

'You do realise,' says Rhona, 'that that farm you described was probably in this area?'

'Why do you think that?'

'Well . . . the peaty water, for a start.'

The thought of my old life being so close by makes me uncomfortable. I drop my eyes from Rhona's an' look past her instead, to the sun-spotted hillside. It looks dark an' bright at the same time. Golden an' peach an' black. The gorse bushes startlingly yellow against the horizon.

'I don't want to leave this place.' I say. 'Please don't make me leave.'

Rhona doesn't answer for a long time. I watch the side of her face, but iss her turn to be evasive now, an' she keeps her eyes well away from mine. Wind toots through the gaps in the wall.

'If we find your mother,' says Rhona, 'you could go back home.'

'*Have* you found her?' I ask, a bit too sharply.

'No,' says Rhona as she plays with a piece of grass. 'But I think we might be able to.'

I imagine sittin' at a table with a strange woman, watched on all sides by newspaper men. All of them holdin' tape machines. Lis'nin'. Waitin'. In this vision I feel nothin' for the woman, an' I know she feels nothin' for me.

'I don't know,' I say. 'I don't think she'd want to talk to me.'

'Why ever not? You're her daughter!'

'She hasn't come here. I jus' . . . I jus' don't think she cares . . .'

Rhona sighs. We look at the sky. A black cloud is advancin' from the sea. I think it'll rain soon.

'If we find her, you can *ask* her where she's been. It couldn't do any harm, could it? Just to talk?'

'I don't want to see her if she doesn't care.'

'She's your mother!'

'I don't want her! I want to stay with you.'

Rhona doesn't look up for a long time. I wait desperately for her to answer. But the black cloud beats her to it an' empties the first spats of rain.

'Quick!' says Rhona. She jumps up an' grabs her raincoat, which we've been sittin' on. I tumble sideways as she shakes off the grass stalks an' hurls it over her head. Within seconds, the sky is alive. We make a break for it over the boggy ground. Both of us fall at least once.

#

Thursday.

After breakfast, Rhona tells me ev'rythin' has been arranged. Dr Harrison will get here on Saturday morning.

'Great,' I tell Rhona, when in truth I'm scared witless. I'm supposed to read the rest of the transcripts to prepare for my first session. Or, well, that's what I agreed. All mornin', my belly's in knots.

Is it too late to change my mind? I want to make things easy on Rhona. She's been unhappy, an' doin' this stuff will make her feel better. But I also have to protect myself.

When lunchtime comes round I'm too scared to go the dinin' room. What if Rhona's there, with the transcripts? My belly's growlin', but I can't take the risk, so I sneak outside an' hurry across the moor. When I reach the bite I feel calmer. Here, I am hidden from Gille Dubh. I stop an' let the wind push me onto my back. The bracken crunches under me as I land, an' gladly I raise my arms to the sky. Clouds cavort like a magical, untouchable landscape, an' suddenly nothin' feels quite real. I'm a girl in a paintin' hung on a sittin'-room wall. Part of a lush, overgrown dream. I lie on my back with my legs danglin' over the edge, an' for a moment it feels like I am floatin'.

Am I able to swim? I've tried so many times to remember. If I really travelled here on the Gulf Stream, I suppose I must be able to. Sometimes when I'm lyin' in bed I move my arms an' legs like the people we saw on television. But it never feels familiar, an' iss hard to believe such small motions could prevent me from sinkin'. I have come to regard swimmin' in the same fanciful way I regard flyin'. Maybe I did fly here. The thought somehow seems less ludicrous. If the water could have delivered me here, then why not the air?

I push my palms together an' practise my swimmin' movements. As always, it doesn't feel right, so I lower my arms an' look at the clouds. If only I could fly away. Imagine that! I'd watch from far above as Dr Harrison's car wound its way to Gille Dubh. Search parties would be sent out when she realised I'd gone, an' I'd smile downwards as they fumbled round the grounds. How long would they bother for? One day? Two? I'd wait as long as it took, till Dr Harrison got mad an' drove back to Inverness. Then I'd ride back down on a gust of rain, an' come inside for supper. Hah! That'd teach them!

Wait . . .

Tremblin', I lower my hands. Something above me is shiftin'. A dark cloud barging down, pinnin' me here on my back. My beautiful vision shrivels away, an' as my heart rears up in shock, a tremendous rip cuts the clouds in half.

Bam, goes my heart.

!!!

A wet screech clogs my throat. I grab sideways.

Spilling through. Dripping towards me. A soft black tendril, searching to take root. I gasp. The tide turns. Then it's in me, lodged hard and growing. I think I make a noise. I turn and fill my hands with bracken. I can't get away. The sky crashes down, taking the landscape with it, and suddenly I'm alone in an empty frame. Stuff bleeding from my fingertips. Reassembling itself. Turning back into something real . . . What is the picture? I know it . . . A black ship, half swallowed. I see it there, scratched in the clouds. All around me. The sad masts. The waves. The rushing sky. I trace them with my fingers. I've seen them before. But it's slanted . . . Falling . . . Falling towards me . . . I want to make the picture straight . . . To push one corner up . . . But it's too high . . . Too far . . . No . . . My fingers scream . . . I cannot grab it . . . I cannot make it right . . .

The motion makes me sick . . .

No!

Darkness punches my chest. Rain hits my face. A long, slow fall. Then I know no more.

#

I wake into twilight an' a cold, solid drizzle. Water pools in my eyes, makin' me blink, but I'm too weak to roll over. Cold crawls from the ground like a livin' creature. Climbin' through me, stealin' heat from my flesh. It's tryin' to freeze me, as it freezes the thorn bushes. It doesn't know I'm a person. That such treatment would kill me.

I'm still on the lip of the bite. Summoning all my strength, I rise to my knees an' the house swings across the horizon. Just an orange glow from here, an' I know the sight of it should comfort me, but no. No . . .

Unseen grasses whip my hands. Rain dribbles through my hair.

What . . .

My ears start to pound.

No . . . Please . . . Not again . . .

The shakin's uncontrollable now. My feet rooted fast. The taste of metal on my tongue. Is that ice below my knees? A figure framed in blood. Suckin' me into its arms. I screech. A rush of acid. Then I'm breathin' hard, an' runnin'. Wet foliage smacks my knees. The house swings back into view, an' as it does a voice appears in my head. My *own* voice. Disembodied.

Everything has gone wrong.

I stumble. Bite my tongue. Get up. Keep runnin'.

He can see me . . .

I skid across the gravel. Flounder round the outhouses. Claw at the back door. For one dreadful second I think it's locked. Then it flies open, an' I spill onto the carpet.

15

Friday.

I wake late – still dressed an' still wearing my shoes. My bed is full of dead grass. I know something scared me last night, but I still can't make sense of what happened. Sooner or later Rhona will turn up, demanding answers, and I haven't the slightest idea what to tell her. At one o'clock there's a knock on my door. I lie very still. But nobody speaks or comes in.

#

Rhona is sitting in the chair. My eyes dart to the clock. Five minutes past four. Is there time to close my eyes? No, she's seen me. Painfully slowly, she clears her throat. It feels like she's frying my brain with her eyes, superhero-style. I picture Rhona wearing a red cape, flying through the clouds, an' just for a second this almost makes me laugh.

'So what's going on?' she demands, in that weird, controlled voice. The one she uses when she's really, really furious. I stare at her. Rhona waits. Delicately, slowly, she blinks. 'I *said* . . . what's . . . going . . . on?'

'What?'

'Bloody *hell*, Katherine! Talk to me! Tell me what's filling that . . . head of yours!'

I draw my knees up to my chin an' retreat as far as I can go without fallin' off the bed. I can't bear it when Rhona's angry. My head starts to hurt. I close my eyes.

'Kathy . . .' says Rhona. 'Please. Just tell me . . .'

I turn my face away. The bevelled edge of the headboard presses into my forehead, an' as I roll my head from side to side I feel it brand a pattern into my skin. My thoughts get muddled. Rhona doesn't speak again. There's soil all around me, pooling in the folds of the sheets, gathering under my legs, mixing with my sweat. My body feels filthy. Camouflaged, like a soldier. If only it could help hide me from Rhona.

A small weight settles on my feet. Then a cold hand takes hold of mine. We stay this way for a long time, an' all the while I daren't look Rhona in the eye. I resent myself for accepting her affection, cos all I really want now is to be alone. Rhona pats my arm, an' though this is a huge comfort, I wish she wouldn't do it. Time drags. The room grows dark. I feel sick.

#

When I come around, someone's sitting there. Two bony hands curl round a magazine. The face is hidden, but I know who it is.

My throat feels raw. I cough and the magazine lowers, revealing Joyce's face. I watch her watch me. Neither of us speaks. I cough again.

'Aspirin?' asks Joyce tartly.

'Yes please.'

It hurts my throat to speak. Joyce moves out of sight, then returns with a blister pack of pills. She pops out two and puts them in my hand. Then she sits down and crosses her legs.

160

I look at her and say, 'I need water.'

Joyce pauses. Then gets up again. As she walks to the sink I take a quick scan of the room. The open curtains are bathed in sunshine, and the clock says twelve minutes past one. My clothes and bed are still a mess. Someone has, however, taken off my shoes and placed them by the door. Joyce returns with a small glass of water, and I see she's used the glass I keep my toothbrush in. There's a creamy white film round the bottom.

'Where's Rhona?' I croak.

'Downstairs.'

I choke down the pills, wincing at the minty taste. Though I'm extremely thirsty, I don't want to drink more from this glass. I lay against the headboard and look at the wall, wishing Joyce would go away.

'Dr Harrison is here,' says Joyce.

I don't answer.

'Your session's at two o'clock. You'll have to go in cold, I'm afraid. We've informed her of the situation.'

'I feel sick,' I whisper.

But Joyce just snaps, 'Dr Harrison has come a long way.'

I close my eyes.

'She came a long way because you asked for her to come. And now that she's here, we have no intention of wasting her time. She has other patients, you know. Patients who've waited a long time for appointments. Dr Harrison could have stayed in Inverness and helped those people today, but she *didn't*. She was kind enough to drive here. For *you*.'

I feel my body wantin' to cry yet not having the energy or moisture to accomplish it. I open my eyes and watch the backs of my hands – muddy an' dead on my lap.

'I don't want—'

'I haven't got time for your games, Kathy.'

'But I'm not—'

'Take your bath now. We don't want to keep Dr Harrison waiting.'

'Can I talk to—'

'Rhona is tired,' snaps Joyce. 'She watched you all night. Now it's your turn to give a little back. You can't just take, Kathy. It doesn't work like that.

I stare at my hands.

'Chop chop,' says Joyce.

#

The water is clear as it pours into the bath, but by the time I pull the plug it is light brown. It reminds me of a dream I had, about a bath where the water came out of the taps that way. Dirty, but not dirty really. But today things are different. Today, the dirt has come from me.

When I get back to my room I find a clean dress laid out. My mustard bedspread has been replaced by a scarlet one with yellow stitching. They should have laid out a final meal while they were at it an' called Mr Duff to read the last rites. Each time I look at the bedspread I feel my heart rate rising. It's like a panic attack made out of wool.

I drag on the clean dress an' tights, an' sit on the chair instead of the new bed. I wonder if they'll come to get me or not. The clock on the wall says six an' a half minutes to two. I watch the quick hand going round. My belly grumbles. Should I go downstairs by myself? Will Dr Harrison will be kind? I wonder if Rhona will be there. Or Joyce. Probably Joyce.

A knock at the door makes me jump.

'Yes?'

My voice sounds like the wind on the moor. Airy, invisible.

A pause. Another knock.

'*Yes?*' I say, forcing myself to say it louder.

'You're to come down now,' Caroline's voice says.

My heart crumples.

'Oh.' This time I barely hear my voice at all.

On the way downstairs, my legs don't feel steady. I grip the handrail tightly, like Mary, an' find this helps calm my nerves. Is that why Mary does it? If it was up to me I'd stop walking altogether and cement my hand to the rail. Nothing could hurt me then. Nothing could ever move or change or happen to me, as long as I stay in this spot. How simple that would be! Centuries trickling around me. Ice ages covering and uncovering me from the sun. I breathe, and for once the air reaches the depths of my lungs it ought to. But this feeling doesn't last long. Caroline nudges my back, an' my feet are forced onwards. This time we descend at a swifter pace, an' Caroline's hand doesn't leave my back till we reach the bottom. In the hallway I glance back at her, an' she nods along the blue corridor, where the second-last door stands open.

'Can I have a glass of water?' I whisper.

'You can have some when we get there.'

I shuffle along the hall, an' Caroline walks behind me. The floor sends a chill through my feet.

'Come on,' says Caroline, with a touch of impatience.

Breathin' carefully, I push myself through the door. I haven't been in here for a long time, an' the first thing I notice is a pot-pourri sort of smell. Maybe it's Joyce's perfume or somethin'. God knows. Rhona's office smells nothin' like this.

Why couldn't we do this in Rhona's office?

I stand by the door, not wantin' to go further than necessary. Dr Harrison sits at the desk, behind a stack of paper. I look across the room at the poky little sofa. That's where Joyce's patients sit when they tell her things. I'll probably have to sit there too.

'Kathy!'

My eyes dart back to Dr Harrison. She's standing up, beaming. Behind me I feel Caroline shift position, like she thinks I'll make a run for it. And I must confess it had crossed my mind. But Dr Harrison flaps her hand at Caroline and clucks, 'Shoo! Patients only!'

With a nod, Caroline disappears. Dr Harrison comes right over then and shuts the door. I watch her from the corner of my eye. If I squint, I can almost pretend she's Rhona.

'Well, here we are again!' declares Dr Harrison as she returns to her papers.

I stand where I am, fiddling with the hem of my dress. It's strange to think that the last time we spoke was in Inverness. That she remembers it and I don't.

'Come and sit down,' says Dr Harrison. I obey.

Dr Harrison sits in Joyce's swivel chair and shuffles closer to the sofa. There's a beige folder on her knees, which she taps with her biro. I'm scared she'll make me read something from it.

'So,' she begins. 'I'm told there was a little drama yesterday. And I wanted to clear—'

'It wasn't my fault!'

'Now, this is my point exactly. If you're feeling defensive or tense in any way, this session won't be successful. So I want you to forget what happened yesterday. It's not important right now, and it's certainly not important to me. This is a safe place, and all we're going to do is talk.'

164

Dr Harrison waits for a reply. When she doesn't get one, she says, 'Is there anything I can do to make you more at ease?'

I frown.

'Maybe if I dim the lights? Would you like to leave the door open?

'Can I have a glass of water?'

'Ah, of course.'

Dr Harrison takes a plastic cup to the sink, runs the cold tap for a while an' fills it.

'Are you going to make me talk about my mother?' I ask.

'I'm not going to *make* you do anything you don't want to. Okay?'

I'm not sure if I believe her.

'Okay.'

'I'm here to *help* you. That's all we're going to do today.'

'Okay.'

Dr Harrison asks me to lie down on the sofa. It's not as big as Rhona's so I have to have my feet hanging off the end. I put my head on the armrest an' try not to think of bad things. Instead I fixate on the noticeboard, where Joyce has pinned sheet after sheet of song lyrics. I suppose they're from her play. Soon we'll all be dragged to see it and for God knows how many hours I'll have to endure the horror of Joyce singing.

'Now,' says Dr Harrison, 'just forget any negative feelings you may have had this morning. This is a safe place. A place where—'

'Okay.'

'Shh. Try not to speak. Just *relax*.'

I close my mouth firmly. Dr Harrison pulls her chair closer. I look at her an' try to relax. The armrest is hurting my neck.

'Now,' says Dr Harrison, 'just close your eyes, and listen to the sound of my voice.'

There is a light pat on the sofa next to my arm. Knowing I'm not allowed, I don't look to see what it is. I wonder if she'll give me an injection, like before. Will it hurt, like it does when they hold me down? Maybe she'll get Caroline to do it for her. Her dirty work. That's why she wants me to close my eyes! Maybe Caroline's already in the room!

'I want you to put your hand on my hand,' says Dr Harrison, 'and press down as hard as you can.'

I breathe out, heavily.

'Put your hand on my hand.'

'Where's your hand?'

'Here.'

I feel Dr Harrison take my right hand an' place it on top of her other hand.

'Press down,' says Dr Harrison, so I do, but not as hard as I can, because I don't want to hurt her.

'Harder,' she says.

'Okay,' I say, but still don't press harder. She breathes out then, an' I worry I've made her angry, so I lean forwards an' push on her with all my strength. I hear her chair squeak against the floor.

'One,' says Dr Harrison.

'What?'

'Shh!'

I stop pushin'.

'No,' says Dr Harrison. 'Push my hand.'

'Like this?'

'*Relax*,' she says. 'Don't speak.'

I wonder if I'm pushin' hard enough.

'Two. Your eyelids are drowsy and sleepy.'

Her chair squeaks again. The sound hurts my head. I pull away.

Dr Harrison sighs. Her hand disappears.

'Okay,' she says, 'let's try something else.'

'Did I do it wrong?'

'It's okay. Just *breathe deeply*.'

I hear the chair move again.

'In your mind,' she says, 'I want you to imagine a staircase. There are a hundred steps curving down and down and around, and though you cannot see the bottom, you know there's a wonderful place down there. A beautiful, perfect place, waiting just for you.'

I imagine running over the moor on a clear day. The clouds are soft and from there I can see all the way to Skye. Rhona is standing there, waving a red handkerchief. I look closer. But her face is not happy. She is scowling.

'You are standing on the top step, with your hand resting lightly on the rail. The rail is smooth and polished and feels good under your hand. I want you to start walking down the staircase, Katherine. Niiice and slowly. And with each step you take, you will find yourself getting more and more relaxed . . . One . . . Two . . . Three . . .'

Rhona's mouth is moving. 'Bloody *hell*, Katherine!' Rhona is saying. My throat quivers.

'Four . . . Five . . .'

Let me deal with Katherine, says Joyce.

'Six . . .'

Dr Harrison's chair scrapes back, an' she stops counting. I think she sighs. I hope that wasn't a sigh. Have I done something wrong? I listen to her feet walking away. Paper rustles. Her feet walk back. She clears her throat.

'Seven . . . eight . . .' says Dr Harrison.

167

Will she jab me in the arm? Is the syringe in her hand right now? I wait for the grab, and the sting, and the slow, cold surge.

'Nine . . . ten . . . eleven . . .'

I'm still thirsty. Can we still stop? I think of my toothbrush glass. Joyce smiling as she hands me a glass of dirty water. Drink! Drink! And again my tears well up. Falling hotly down the back of my throat.

'Twelve . . . thirteen . . . Keep counting . . . Keep counting . . . Down and down you go, towards your lovely, special place . . . Fourteen . . . fifteen . . . You can't wait to arrive, because you feel so safe and happy there . . . Sixteen . . . Keep counting . . . I want you to keep counting in your own mind . . . always moving closer to the bottom of the staircase . . .'

Phlegm creeps further back in my throat. Rhona stands at the bottom of the staircase, holding my mustard bedspread in her arms. It is covered with mud. She is crying. Joyce is there too, scowlin' up at me. I will be in trouble when I reach them.

'Down and down and down . . . Keep counting . . . Keep counting . . .'

I'll deal with Katherine, Joyce is sayin'.

Rhona!

It doesn't work like that, Kathy . . .

'Down . . . Down . . . Closer to the bottom of the staircase . . . You can almost see it now . . . It's just around the bend . . . Down . . . Keep counting down . . .'

I reach out for Rhona, but she's no longer there. It's Joyce who stands waitin' for me, and the bedspread is red with blood. She moves slightly, an' I see the butcher's knife in her hand.

You have to give some back, Kathy . . .

'Down and down and down . . . Closer . . . You feel relaxed . . . Extremely relaxed . . .'

No!

'Shhhh . . . very . . . very . . . relaxed . . .'

Joyce starts hacking my bedspread to pieces. Rhona has disappeared, but I hear her crying.

'Veryyy . . . relaxed . . .'

Rhona is crying.

'You are now very deeply relaxed, and everything I say will go deeply into your mind.'

Too busy for you . . .

'Katherine? Can you hear me?'

'Rhona!'

'Can you hear me, Katherine?'

'Yes.'

They want me to think it's Rhona, but . . .

'Good. I want you to visualise your safe place now. You are feeling very relaxed and at ease, and you notice that there is a door in front of you. I want you to walk through that door, Katherine. Nice and slowly . . . In your own time . . . Just step through the door . . . Can you do that?'

It's him . . . he can see me . . . he can see me . . . he can . . .

'Yes.'

'Have you stepped through the door now?'

'Yes.'

'Good. Very good. Now, in your own time, look around and tell me what you see.'

The bite . . . but it's not . . . it's . . .

'Grass . . . dark . . . I'm . . . I can see . . . stars . . .'

'Move your head to the side and look at what's there. Can you see?'

'Yes.'

'What can you see?'

'Grass . . . no . . . plants . . . wheat . . . I'm lying down . . . There's light . . . on the other side . . .'

'I want you to focus on the light. Look past the wheat and focus on the light. Can you see anything else there?'

'It's . . . far away . . .'

'What can you see?'

'A house.'

'Good. Very good. What kind of house is it?'

'It's . . . wooden. Like a . . . log cabin . . . It's blue . . .'

'Do you know who lives in the blue house?'

'I do . . .'

'Does anyone else live in the blue house?'

'I wasn't supposed to be here . . .'

'Does anyone else live in the blue house?'

'He'll see me . . . He's coming . . .'

'Relax. Just breathe. Breathe deeply and relax. You're safe. No one can hurt you. I want you to come back now, to your place with the wheat and the stars. I want you to rise up, far above the ground, and look at the place where you were lying down . . . Can you see it?'

'Yes.'

'Tell me what you see.'

'It's a big field. There are trees . . . all around . . . my house is there, on the edge . . . I'm . . . scared . . .'

'Why are you scared?'

'Noises . . . animals . . .'

'Can you see any other houses, around your house?'

'They're further away . . . They're near a . . . a railway track . . .'

'I want you to go closer to the railway track, and see where

170

the tracks are going. I want you to follow the tracks. Can you see the tracks?'

'Yes.'

'Where do the tracks go to?'

'A city . . .'

'Do you know the name of the city?'

'There's water . . .'

'Go closer now. Imagine you are on the train, and it is pulling into the station . . . You are arriving at the station in the big city. Now turn your head and look out of the window as the train stops . . . You are standing up, and you are ready to get off, onto the platform. Can you see the sign on the platform?'

'Yes.'

'What does the sign say?'

'Oslo S.'

'*Very* good. Now, come all the way back. Back into the sky, and back along the tracks. Back to your safe place . . . Back to your place in the field . . . Go down . . . closer . . . closer . . . Are you there?'

'Yes.'

'Good. See yourself lying there. From the outside, as if you were someone else. You feel everything that that girl feels, and you know everything she knows. You are looking through her thoughts. Browsing through them. Can you see her thoughts?'

'Yes.'

'Good. Now, tell me if you see Magnus.'

'I . . .'

'Is Magnus there?'

'I can see him . . .'

'Tell me, where is Magnus?'

171

'Oh God . . . He's coming . . . I hear him . . .'

'Where is Magnus?'

'He said he . . . he said . . . he . . .'

'Concentrate. Where is Magnus?'

'Bastard . . . drittsekk . . . drittsekk . . . jævla . . .'

'Relax, relax, you're safe. You—'

'He's coming! He'll kill me! He's going to kill me!'

'You are feeling relaxed—'

'Bastard! No! I—'

'Okay, Katherine. It's okay. I'll count to five, and as I do so, you will start to wake up. One . . .'

'No . . .'

'Two. You are becoming aware of my voice and the room around you . . .'

'I . . .'

'Three. You are starting to wake up from the trance state. You are aware of your body, your arms, your legs . . . Four. Stretch your arms out, all the way to your fingertips. You start to open your eyes and wake up. You feel refreshed and positive . . . Five. Wide awake and you are feeling fantastic. There! Well done!'

Dr Harrison sits above me. My neck hurts. Her smile looks wrong. I know she can't protect me. No one can.

'I'm scared,' I say.

'Shhh. You did really well.'

'I want to go back to my room.'

Everything is wrong . . .

16

February 17th, 2005.

On Thursday night, Magnus throws a party. It's fun at first, and Magnus is on his best behaviour – introducing me around as his British pen pal. I get drunk quickly as the evening progresses, mostly on the bright-yellow home-brewed beer that Håkon brought, and end up passing out in the kitchen. When I wake, the party's still going. Six a.m. passes. Then seven. Then eight. By nine a.m. I accept that people won't be leaving, and resume drinking. But that's just the beginning. Four whole days, the party lasts. Night and day, with fluctuating attendance and levels of intensity. At the time I don't know it's four days. The alcohol makes it hard to keep track. But the weekend takes its toll on me nevertheless. In the night-time I waver between laughter and tears, loneliness and claustrophobia, delight and frustration. In the daytime I fall asleep wherever I'm sitting, only to wake with a fresh set of people around me. It comes to a point where my hangover runs simultaneously with my drunkenness, and so many girls follow Magnus in and out of our bedroom that I can no longer find a place to recuperate. Several times I go to Magnus and beg him to end the party. But he never really listens. His friends seem bemused to find me still here. They ask when I'm going home, in a tone that suggests I've outstayed my welcome. Girls eye me suspiciously, particularly when I go to the bedroom.

'What about your job?' I ask Magnus, because he's not been to work all week, and the people around us greet this with gales of laughter. Magnus quips a reply, and they crease up again. I leave the room in humiliation, but Magnus doesn't follow.

#

The next time I wake, I am crushed beneath a killer headache. Around me, daylight. I push myself upright, upsetting a cup of water someone had placed on the floor. It pools coldly into my clothes.

My knuckles are skinned. How did that happen? I shift sideways, trying to steady myself against the wall, and as I do so a vague memory drifts back. Of me sitting on Håkon's chest. Hands pushing me back. My fist swinging. And his face, laughing at me. I remember my fury. He'd called me something . . . A slut. *One of Magnus's sluts.*

Wait. That's the shoe rack beside me. Of course. I'm in the hallway, behind the front door. And there are only two pairs of shoes: Magnus's and my own.

'Hello?' I call. My voice echoes.

Is the party over? God, I hope so. I stumble to my feet, but my balance betrays me and sends me crashing back onto the shoe rack. For several moments, I am winded.

Stupid girl. Get up . . .

I hobble into the living room. Empty. The spare room too. And the bedroom. I stand looking at the loft bed, delaying the climb to the top. But there's no snoring. No breathing. *He's not up there*, I reflect, with a pinch of bitterness. Of course not. He'd rather be with his friends than with me.

#

Magnus returns after seven, laden with waffle mix, and barely looks at me before whirling into action. He upends the coffee table, sending a pile of debris onto the floor. Then he dumps his shopping on the newly cleared tabletop and starts bagging up the rubbish. His eyes are unreadable behind his sunglasses. His mouth tense. Is he still drunk? It's hard to tell. I stay on the sofa, cowed by this sudden activity. A rank smell fills the air. Cigarette butts marinated in beer. Magnus dumps them in the sink and carries on.

'What's the rush?' I ask.

'Visitors,' he replies, without looking at me.

'Who?'

'Will you get dressed?'

'I am dressed.'

'You know what I mean. Get changed.'

'Why?'

'Because you smell bad!'

'Fuck you!'

'*Come on!* They'll be here soon.'

'Who will?'

Magnus stops, with his back to me. His shoulders rise up, then down, and despite my unease, I find myself hypnotised by the nape of his neck. I will love that neck till the day I die. Skin the colour of milk. Spine rising beneath like a lost mountain range.

'Look, I know this is the wrong time to tell you. But . . . uh . . .'

Magnus turns round and takes off his sunglasses. With careful eyes, he probes my face. Then he comes over and crouches on the floor. My heart rushes as he takes my hands

175

in his, and for a second I believe he will apologise. Proclaim his love for me, like he did in the beginning, and say everything's going to be all right.

Mrs Brudvik . . .

With one thumb, Magnus strokes my hand. Briefly, his mouth softens. Then, in a quiet, confident voice he says, 'Katherine . . . I am a father.'

Blankness.

Horror.

I gape at my beautiful true love. The enormity of his statement polluting the air between us. Expanding. Multiplying. Pressing on my skin, my lungs, my eardrums. Magnus holds my gaze. His mouth forms, then unforms, a tiny, hopeful smile. I try to take my hands back, but cannot make them move.

'You're a . . . You're . . . You've got . . .'

'Kids.'

The room feels like it is moving. I am vaguely aware that I'm on my feet. Shuddering backwards, as far as I can go.

'How old?' I hear my voice say.

'Seven. And nine.'

'Who's the . . . mother?'

'Mathilde. You don't know her.'

I scowl in an effort to hold my face together. Several teardrops spill onto the carpet.

'Are you married?' I manage.

'Yes,' says Magnus, after a pause. 'But it's over.'

The shaking in my arms is unstoppable now. Magnus stands somewhere between me and the light. His hand touches mine, but this time I manage to withdraw.

'Does *she* know it's over?' I ask stiffly.

'She is still in love with me, but . . .'

176

A sob gushes out of me. I can't hold it in any more.

'I'm with *you* now,' Magnus insists.

I shake my head from side to side, blinded by tears. 'If you're with me, why won't you tell anyone? Why do you let your friends think I'm some . . . *stalker*?'

'Fy faen . . . Are you *still* complaining about Håkon?'

'It's like you're embarrassed to be with me!'

'It's not that easy! Mathilde's crazy! She'll take the kids away if she thinks—'

'So you'll just have me *and* her? Is that it? Oh God . . .' – I swing my eyes up to his – '*That's* where you went, isn't it? That first night, when you were gone for hours?'

Magnus doesn't answer. But the look in his eyes is all the proof I need. He holds my gaze for a moment, then clears his throat and grabs the rubbish bag.

'There's no time for this,' he snaps. 'The kids are coming.'

My stomach lurches. I back away, and the sudden movement makes me light-headed.

'Here?' I gasp.

'Yes. For the night.'

'When?'

'Now.'

'But . . . Do they know about me? What . . . What am I supposed to—'

'Look, I would have liked more time to tell you. I didn't want it to be this way. But you've been drunk. I didn't have a chance.'

'What?'

Magnus grabs the bag of empties, feverishly ties it and starts filling a second one. When that's done he fills another, and another. He dumps them in the hallway and flounces into the bedroom. Banging ensues. I go to the door and find him on the loft bed, chucking cans onto the floor. On the back of a chair, there's a sky-blue bra that doesn't belong to me.

'What's that?' I ask, pointing at the bra.

Magnus freezes, then scoffs and carries on. On his way back down the ladder he jabs, 'If you won't help me, get out of the way.'

For a moment I am so filled with rage I think I might throw up. Then his words unravel in my brain, and I realise Mathilde will be coming here as well as the kids. In an instant, my anger turns to fear. I look to the window and want to run. But where could I go? It's minus twenty out there, and the only public building in town closes at five. The other indoor places will only shelter paying customers. Money is something I no longer have.

Swallowing hard, I pick up a can. It's wet and disgustingly sticky.

'Don't crush that!' orders Magnus. 'We can't . . . uh . . . pant it if you crush it.'

I squint at him, momentarily distracted.

'Pant?'

'Pant. Money. You know.'

'Recycling?'

Magnus drags the rubbish bags to the door, taking care not to get dirt on his clothing. Suddenly I realise I've never seen that outfit before. A perfect crease runs down each sleeve, and this proves that the shirt at least must be brand new, because Magnus never irons anything. Did he dress up nicely for Mathilde?

Bristling, I clear my throat. Magnus turns around.

'You mean, don't do . . . this?' I say, and pulverise the can in my fist.

Magnus stands up straight, and a shadow falls across his face. I draw a breath. The change in him happens so quickly and so completely that it's hard to make sense of at once. It happens in the eyes. A complete transformation from the inside out, as if a malevolent spirit has commandeered his body. I look into those eyes and meet a part of Magnus I've never noticed before. A brutal, inhumane part, more than capable of striking me. I wait for the fist to come up. An elbow, or at least the palm of his hand. Deep inside, I almost believe I deserve this.

Magnus tilts his head back and regards me from beyond his nostrils. For a second, neither of us seems to breathe. His eyes have never looked so beautiful, and this makes the moment even harder to bear.

But already the blackness is leaving him. Wisp after wisp, like ink diffusing into an ocean, and as it does so, the tension of the moment drains away. Magnus makes a dismissive sound – something similar to *Pah*. Then he pushes past me and returns to his work.

I stay where I am, closing my eyes to keep the tears in. Is this actually happening? The whole thing feels like a practical joke. Banging sounds filter through from the hall. Brusque footsteps, swishing bin bags and the clatter of beer cans. Backwards and forwards he goes, no longer bothering to acknowledge my presence, and during this time I remain rooted to my spot below the bed. The metal ladder grows painful in my fists. It takes Magnus ten minutes to clean the flat, and another ten to do his hair.

#

Mathilde doesn't enter the house, but the kids' arrival is no

179

less dreadful for this. I perch on the end of the sofa and try to make my mouth smile. The youngest one, Isak, will not come near me. The older, Tor Olav, just scowls. Magnus bustles around. Making dinner. Being a dad. Beneath the lemon-scented bleach I can still smell remnants of the party, and I wonder if the kids can smell it too. Maybe *that's* why they're acting strangely. I wrack my brains for conversational phrases, but none seem suited to the occasion. Anyway, I've never been good with kids. It's hard enough to talk to them in my own language.

When waffles have been eaten and cartoons watched and teeth brushed, Magnus makes a bed for the boys on the sofa. They talk in quiet voices. Then Magnus kisses them good-night and turns off the living-room light. Gravely, we go to the bedroom.

'We need to talk,' Magnus says, as he shuts the door behind him.

'Yeah, I know,' I say.

'Come on.'

Magnus climbs the ladder in two big steps and settles himself on the bed. Methodically, I follow. The sheets up here are freshly changed, which confuses me, as I didn't notice Magnus doing that. Then I realise he must have done it while I was hiding from Mathilde in the bathroom.

Magnus positions himself at the opposite end of the bed to me and, cross-legged, we face each other. The smile he used for the kids has disappeared. Silence rings out as I wait for him to apologise.

'This is not working,' I whisper. 'I'm not . . . happy.'

'Pfffff!' exclaims Magnus, and laughs. His eyes dart to me, and desperately I search them for compassion, but find none. Magnus says something in Norwegian.

'What?' I ask, and he says it again.

'That's not fair! Talk in English!'

'You're *never* happy!' he blares.

The force of his scorn takes me aback. For a moment I can think of nothing to say. Magnus puts both hands to his head, and says, 'It's true, though. Things have to change.'

'What?'

'I need a wife, Kathy. Not a . . . third child. You don't try to get a job. You don't like my friends. You don't like my kids. I don't think you even like me.'

'How can you say that?' I gasp.

Magnus looks away.

'Look. I sorted it out. There's a place you can live, near Oslo. I'll buy your train ticket.'

A jolt goes through me.

'Please! Don't!'

I move forwards, but Magnus pushes me back.

'You changed, these last weeks. I don't know who you are any more,' he says in a quieter voice.

'I'm me! I'm the same!'

'This guy, near Oslo. You can live with him for a while.'

Tears bleed down my cheeks.

'Please,' I say. Then the pain kicks in for real, and I can no longer keep my body from reacting. When the first howl comes out of me, Magnus jumps. His hands fly out. But instead of offering comfort, they shake me. For some time, the real world leaves my side. Then a hand slams across my mouth and I resurface to find Magnus's face inches from mine.

'Stop it,' he hisses. 'The boys!'

I gulp and shake. Magnus watches awhile. Then he says, 'It's for the best. Living with Hans. Making money of your own—'

'Doing what?'

'Working!'

Gravity overwhelms me and I wilt head first into the pillow. Fizziness. Darkness. When I speak again, my voice does not sound like my own.

'I don't even know him! Why should he give me a job?'

'He's a friend of Kolbeinn's.'

'Who's Kolbeinn?'

'A guy I know. Look, you can still visit me . . . On weekends . . .'

I pull down the pillow and look at Magnus. At first he doesn't see, and I catch him with a bored expression on his face.

'We need a break from each other,' he says. 'Lots of couples do.'

'I came here to be with you! Not hundreds of miles away!'

'Grow up, Kathy. You'll wake the boys.'

Darkness and death bleed into my heart, obliterating his face.

'How can you treat me like this?' I blubber.

'Pfff. Pain is a part of love. Haven't you learnt that by now?'

I feel my eyes grow dull, though the tears keep coming and coming. They course down my face and throat. Down the front of my body. Into the sheets. Into the floor. I am melting. The world glazes over.

Game over. Game over. Game over.

'Where's that girl I met?' Magnus asks. 'That happy girl . . . What happened to her?'

'I love you,' I whisper, and the ghostliness of my voice horrifies me. I am not really here any more. I gaze beyond the pillows. Seeing nothing. Feeling nothing.

'Fy faen,' Magnus mutters.

His hand moves towards me and I prepare myself to be shaken, but instead I feel a warm palm on my head. I had not expected this. My body starts to wobble, and the tears bleed out until I almost forget where I am. When he starts to sing it takes me by surprise.

The tune falls from him quietly, and though I do not understand the words, I can tell it is some sort of lullaby.

'My mother used to sing this,' he says. The look in his eyes suggests he thinks he is being kind.

17

Sunday.

I watch the rising sun from my window. Blood red as it slides out of the mist. For one full minute the moor turns a dull, brooding pink.

After last night's session I went straight to bed, so I haven't yet seen Rhona or Joyce. I wonder what I said to Dr Harrison. She seemed pleased, but I don't know what that means. Will they force me to do another session before she goes? Will they still expect me to read the Inverness stuff? I'm scared that the people around me might now know my thoughts better than I do. To take that advantage from them I might *have* to read the transcripts. The clock on the wall says five minutes to five. Sooner or later, someone will come up here and tell me what to do.

I remember small pieces from last night. Or rather, small *feelings*. They rush at me like waves onto a shore, but each time I grab for them they drain back through my fingers. The whole process makes me dizzy. *Oslo* keeps coming back to me. Just the word, by itself. An' that scares me cos I know it means I was there. The atlas in the library was right. There's something else too. A man. I can't figure out who he is, but I do know he's not Magnus. That bit is what scares me most.

The room is turning tangerine. Outside the window, a calm line of gulls crosses the sky and watching them I flood with the urge to feel the wind on my skin. I have to get out.

Even just for a moment. I wrap my robe around myself and shuffle into my slippers. I go to the door and turn the handle.

I don't believe it . . .

The door is locked.

My face grows hot. I look through the keyhole, but there's no key on the other side. I can see right through, into the hallway. Again I try the handle. But it's no good. I'm a prisoner.

Shit . . .

I stagger backwards onto the bed.

Joyce. I'll bet anything it was Joyce. Why did she lock me in? Did I say something bad in my session?

I stare at the door for a long time. My head throbs.

What the hell could I have said?

#

Heavy limbs. I am lying on my belly. Around me, the dark, sweet-smelling dirt, and that glow on the horizon. The orange-lit house, my tomb, so close. Between it and me, two legs are planted. Magnus's legs. I follow them to his face, and find it dead set. That alien side of him that was always underneath. How could I have been so blind? He tenses a fist, and gleaming metal draws my eye.

Bastard . . . you bastard . . . you bastard . . .

I am on my knees. When I shout his name it sounds different to how the others say it and this marks me as the outsider I truly am. The butcher's knife glints, and I scream again. His name smacks off the trees, shatters, and comes back to me. I sob amongst the fragments. My fear laced irrevocably with love. Then darkness swallows me completely, and I am alone.

#

I wake drenched in sweat. Heart pulsing.

Curtains are bright.

I need to be with someone. Anyone.

I stumble out of bed. Up. Onto the landing. Breakfast sounds drift up from upstairs. I clatter towards them. But already my panic is ebbing. Magnus is not here. I'm at Gille Dubh. I'm safe.

Rhona and Caroline are nowhere to be found, but I check the sitting room instead, and to my relief Mrs Laird is back from her trip. I ask for aspirin, but she's got none left. She tells me to ask Joyce, but there's no way I'm doing that. Instead I go to the dining room and make a fresh cup of tea. There are people here an' that is good. Dr Harrison is in the corner with Joyce, but neither of them sees me. I take my cup an' retreat into my spot. I won't stay here long. Just till this feeling passes. I press myself back in my chair, an' this helps stop me shaking.

It's okay. Nothing's going to happen. I'm safe. I'm safe . . .

I know this is important. That the stuff in my dream really happened. But my God . . . Would Magnus really hurt me that way? I'm scared to let the staff in on this. Visions slide through me as I sit here, of being on my knees behind a door. Trapped and confused, and afraid. Then I remember the door to my bedroom and how I thought it was locked last night. Did I dream that too? Am I going mad?

A presence grabs my attention. Mary. She peers at me through oily strands of hair. When I grab her she barely moves.

'*Mary*,' I hiss, 'I've got to tell you something!'

Mary's eyes remain slits. She floats there, kite-like, on the end of my hand, a blue vein bulging in her forehead. Dark lava, flowing dangerously close to the surface.

'I've got to tell you something,' I repeat. And as I say the words, I realise it's the perfect solution. Mary is the perfect confidante. She won't judge me, or betray me, or try to send me away from here. But her face shows no sign of understanding. I want to shake her. Make her listen. Has she gone deaf as well as dumb?

Mary's eyes finally connect with mine. She teeters backwards, taking my hand with her. When I'm on my feet she drags again, and with several stumbling steps we find ourselves in the porch. Out here, the hollows round her eyes are darker.

'What—' I blurt, but Mary shakes her head. She glances over my shoulder, as if checking for something, and I look too but find nothing. We are leaning against the back door now. Mary's mouth trembles into a smile. Falteringly, she blinks. She takes my hand, pushes something into it, and hugs me for a very long time. Her breath is shallow across my shoulder. Her spine like Lego. I blaze with the need to tell her about the knife. But this is clearly not the time.

Mary pulls away, opens the door and retreats. I watch from the doorway as she drifts towards the outhouses. She turns back once, waves, and is gone. When I open my hand I find a small, heart-shaped counter from the snakes and ladders set.

#

After lunch, Rhona comes to my room. She sits on the end of my bed while I sit on the fireside rug. Cold air sucks at my back, but I like this cos it makes me feel linked to the outside.

'I'm surprised you're still indoors,' says Rhona. 'Lovely day like this.'

187

'I had a headache.'

'Well, I'm glad I found you. I wanted to talk about your session.'

'Am I in trouble?'

'No! God, no. Quite the opposite. Dr Harrison had some interesting things to say.'

'I'm sorry for the other night. For running away.'

Rhona comes to sit beside me.

'Why did you do that?' she asks. 'Were you frightened?'

I nod.

Rhona pushes a bit of dirt with her foot. The fireplace whooshes at our backs.

'Well . . . that's understandable,' she says.

'Did Joyce burn my bedspread?'

'No! Of course not! Why should she do that?'

'I thought she might still be mad. Lockin' me in an' ev'rythin'.'

Rhona looks puzzled. 'Locking you in where?'

'In here. Last night.'

A pause.

'Honey, no one locked you in.'

'They did. I couldn't open the door!'

'You didn't just dream it?'

I frown at the floor. Suddenly I'm not sure.

'So,' Rhona says, 'Dr Harrison leaves tonight, and we'd like you to see her one last time.'

I sigh.

'Do I have to read the transcripts?'

'I'm afraid so.'

'But . . . It's all written down already. Isn't that all you need? Why do *I* have to read it?'

Rhona pulls my fringe out of my eyes. Usually I'd find that

comforting. But today I know her motives are different. I scowl an' she pulls her hand away.

'Sweetie . . . you're the one who has to understand this. Not us. We're only here to help you. If you never sort through all that information in your head, you'll never get better.'

I don't answer.

Rhona clasps her hands between her knees. When she speaks again, her voice is quieter.

'I just want to help you move on.'

'Then don't make me go back. Don't make me talk about . . . him.'

Rhona's eyes sharpen.

'You remember Magnus. Don't you?'

Her eyes dig into my face. The fireplace sucks at us once more, and weakly I turn my head towards the window.

'Bits.'

'If he's the one who hurt you,' says Rhona. 'I mean . . . There are people who can help us—'

'No.'

'People who can make him pay for wha—'

'No.'

'Anything, Kathy, it could be anything at all . . . If not his surname, then his nickname, or the colour of his hair, or—'

'I don't remember!'

'Then tell me what you *do* remember!' she rasps.

I swing round. We stare at each other.

'Why are you protecting him? I know you know something!'

'I'm not!'

'Do you want me to show you the pictures again?! Because I'll go and get the file right now! I'll show you the state you were in when they dragged you—'

'He loved me!'

'Did he throw you out of a boat? Were you trying to escape? What happened? Kathy, you've got to *tell* me!'

'Stop it!' I scream, and drop to the floor.

Silence holds for what feels like minutes. I keep expecting the floorboards to creak under Rhona's feet. But no. Nothing. When my heart has slowed, I look up and see her standing in the same place.

'Rhona?' I tremble.

She looks up, weary-eyed, and studies my face. Finally she says, 'I just want to help you. You know that, right?'

I break eye contact. Rhona sighs.

'Don't you want to know what happened?'

'It's in the past. We can't change it . . .'

'Hmm,' she says, and flops into a chair. She looks like she has more to say, but I'm glad she doesn't.

#

I lie on my bed, watching the sun go down. As my session with Dr Harrison draws closer, it gets harder to hold myself together. At one point the sound of singing puzzles me. Then I remember this is music therapy day and that the voices I hear belong to the other patients.

Now that I'm alone, strange things are settling back into my mind. Maybe they're part of the fear. I don't know. They feel like memories, or the kind of memories you have inside dreams. A whole life story, condensed and ready to go. Lights, cameras, action! It takes all my concentration not to get dragged into them. I'm scared of what I'll see if I let my guard down. They brush past my skin. Making me wriggle.

Magnus, is that you?

190

Is this real?

Did these things really happen?

The field is the clearest memory of all. Hiding in the dark from something dreadful. Magnus was not there that time. He fits in somehow, but not there.

At one point someone knocks. My stomach twinges. They've come to take me down. I wait. But nothing happens.

Fucking Joyce.

I hold my breath. Seconds later, a shadow moves under the door. The floorboard on the landing creaks. Then nothing.

Time drags. As the room gets darker, bad feelings lurk back. I close my eyes in a bid to shut them out, but it's no good. In this silence, they are all around. Nodding. Conspiring.

Snow closes in, streaking lines across me as wide and as white as the sun. I watch through the gaps. Overlapping in my wake, marking the places I have been. Outside, gusts carry the flakes to places I can no longer reach, and with every howl and gasp I feel my dreams scatter further away. All the hopeless wishes. Wishing he had stayed the man he pretended to be. Wishing he had meant the words he said.

We huddle in our seats as the wind rocks the van. Around us, the stink of hotdog meat. Filter coffee. Sweat. The chill against my back and the hard, tall sleeve of his arm. Magnus glares forwards as he drives. Hands clamped round the wheel. This is not how the first day should have been. Why isn't this romantic? It should have been romantic. I try to make him smile, and cannot. The cold becomes unbearable. I ask him to turn the heating up, but he mutters something about the thickness of my blood.

'Penny for your thoughts?'

191

Magnus stays silent.

We pass another service station, and I persuade him to stop for fresh coffee. We troop inside and refill the travel mug. They have white-chocolate syrup here, which costs extra, but we tell the clerk we didn't put any in and he believes us. We stand inside the doors to drink it, relishing the warmth of the floor against our feet. When we set off again, Magnus takes my hand, and my heart floods with relief.

'I love you,' I say loudly, and now his smile blooms back to greet me. Weak with relief, I allow Magnus to pull me close. He lowers his scarf, leans down to my height and kisses me. The gale gasps and tears at us. His lips are as cold as ice.

#

I swing into the headboard. *Clang!* goes my head. My hands fly out.

Wait . . . it's the headboard . . . just the headboard . . .

I fumble around to make sure. Yes. It's the bed. *Idiot.*

Rubbing my head, I lean forwards. The room is invisible. Every molecule of light gone. Someone has veiled the house like a birdcage, and now it is time to sleep. I can't hear a single sound. For a moment I feel quite peaceful. Then I remember my session, and sit bolt upright.

What time is it?

I feel for the edge of the bed. Swing myself out. Three cold steps and I'm at the wall. Then, hand over hand over hand, I fumble for the light switch. The room flashes on, and I sneeze in the brightness.

Quarter past one.

What?

What about Dr Harrison?

I try the door knob.

Shit!

It's locked again.

What the *hell* is going on?

I double check. Triple check.

Did Joyce do this to punish me? Would she really be such a bitch? But I didn't *mean* to miss my session. I just fell asleep!

This is madness.

Why did no one wake me up?

18

Monday.

The dining room is packed when I go down for breakfast. Rhona and Joyce share a table by the kitchen. They look up as I walk in, and I'm pretty sure they see me, but they don't come over to explain my missed session. Confused, I fill my plate. The bread seems tasteless today. At one point I notice Dr Harrison sitting amongst the staff. Am I going mad? Did I miss a day, somehow?

I sneak a second glance at Dr Harrison. She looks quite normal. Like nothing strange has happened at all. Maybe I *did* get the wrong day. I eat my toast quickly and leave the dining room before she has a chance to grab me. I really would have liked a cup of tea, but I daren't hang around.

Outside, the weather is bad. I stay by my bedroom window, wrapped in a blanket, and worry about the upcoming session. What do I do? I haven't the nerve to hide again. Water pours down the window, blurring my view of the moor.

At eleven o'clock I go to the Internet room, but Caroline's not there so I sit on the shoe rack in the back porch and wait. After a while I hear a car. Caroline bursts through the door, laden with plastic bags, and jumps when she sees me. A pool of water forms around her as she takes off her wellington boots. She says she's been buying wool in the village, for a weaving class this afternoon.

To my surprise, no one mentions Dr Harrison. Hours go

by, but no one comes to take me to her, and no one comes to explain about yesterday. I don't like this. It's too weird. At six I pop my head in at the library, but Rhona's nowhere to be seen. Caroline tries to talk me into weaving.

'I'm supposed to see Dr Harrison,' I tell her.

'Not that I heard.'

'But . . . when's she going home?'

'I dunno. Come on now and join us. Here's a nice blue one!' She pushes a ball of wool into my hand.

Half-heartedly, I sit down. Caroline hands round cardboard squares cut from cereal packets, and everyone takes one. Mine is Shreddies. As we start cutting slits in our cereal packets, I think I hear Rhona's voice outside. Then a door slams and the voice cuts off. Caroline is glaring at me, as if warning me not to get up, and I know by now it's a bad idea to pick a fight with her. When the class is over everyone filters into the day room. I slip off in search of Rhona, but her office is deserted. The rest of the house is empty too, without a staff member in sight. The only sound comes from the television in the day room. It looks like we'll be allowed a film today, and though this is a rare treat I can't muster any enthusiasm. Instead of joining the others I sit in the darkened dining room and strain my ears for signs of life. Bit by bit, the electric voices of the television replace real ones, and I'm almost asleep when people filter through for dinner. Unusually, there is no hot food. Just a big plate of cling-wrapped sandwiches and a bowl of custard creams. I go to Caroline and ask, 'Where is everyone?'

'What do you mean? We're all here.'

'Where's Mrs Laird? And Rhona, and everyone else?'

'Oh right,' says Caroline as she puts a sandwich into her mouth. 'They went to the pub.'

'But they've never—'

'It's Susan's birthday,' says Caroline as she takes another bite.

'Dr Harrison?'

'Yes.'

'Is that why we didn't do my session?'

'Must be.'

I nod. I suppose it makes sense.

Caroline takes her cling wrap and rolls it into a ball. I watch for a moment. Then I pull out a chair and sit beside her.

Caroline sighs. 'What's up? Not hungry?'

'No.'

'You should eat something. There won't be any supper, you know.'

'Will there be cake?'

'What?'

'Birthday cake.'

'Oh . . . No, Susan is a little old for cake.'

I study Caroline as she eats a custard cream. She has such an unreadable face. Maybe that's why they always leave her in charge.

'Katherine,' she snaps. '*Please*. Have a sandwich.'

'I'm not hungry.'

'Look. There won't be any food later. So if you come down whining that you're hungry . . .'

'But—'

'*Kathy*,' warns Caroline, an' this time there is anger in her voice. Sighing, I get up. I go to the food, take the smallest sandwich and nibble at it, standing up. This seems to satisfy her. I walk past her table in silence. Then I go to my room.

It's late when the cars return from the village. I hear them crunching up the track, followed by footsteps and slamming doors. No matter how hard I strain, I can't hear voices. Even after they have come into the house.

#

Tuesday.

At breakfast, Rhona and Joyce are sitting together again. Rhona sees me and waves, so I get up and approach their table.

'Hey you,' she says. Joyce keeps eating, not looking at me.

'Hi. I just wanted to ask . . . I mean . . . Dr Harrison—'

'Oh yes,' says Rhona. 'There was a wee get-together last night, so we shifted round the schedule. Sorry I didn't tell you sooner.'

'But . . . wasn't it supposed to be on . . . Sunday?' I ask.

Joyce puts down her butter knife.

'No . . . It was supposed to be yesterday,' says Rhona. 'Did you get it wrong, silly?'

'Yeah . . .'

'Silly billy,' she says, and continues to smile.

'Is there . . . I mean . . . Do I still have to . . . Is Dr Harrison—'

'She's still here,' says Joyce. 'Your session's at seven o' clock.'

I glare at her, irritated by her presence.

'Run along, Kathy,' says Joyce. 'Get yourself some breakfast.'

I look at Rhona. She nods.

'Why don't you have some eggs?' she says. 'Put some flesh on those bones!'

'All right,' I say.

'Run along then.'

Rhona and Joyce return to their breakfast. I put some eggs on my plate because Rhona asked me to, pour a glass of orange juice and carry these things to my table. Once or twice I look over and see them deep in conversation. I don't like them being close like that. They never were before.

#

I'd wanted to take a walk with Rhona, but for the rest of the day she's nowhere to be found. Her office door stays closed, and when I knock no one answers. The third time this happens I try to let myself in, but Caroline catches me an' sends me packing. The fourth time I pass, I hear someone crying inside. I wait on the bottom of the stairs, looking down the blue corridor, but nothing happens for a very long time. In the end I get sick of waiting, so I go out alone and have a long walk down by the fence. It's good to get out in the fresh air. For some reason the loch makes me think of Bonnie Prince Charlie. I imagine myself running towards it through the heather, dressed in tartan. The redcoats would be following with their guns, but I'd give them the slip through sheer cunning. My God, even the bracken looks like an oil painting today. It all looks like an oil painting. Maybe there's something different with the light. Yes, that makes sense. I gaze at the loch and sigh. I wish I had someone to discuss this with. Once or twice I stand on my tiptoes an' look at the house. But Rhona never appears.

Poor Dr Harrison, having to spend her birthday away from her family. Even at her age, that must be tough. If she'd gone home without seein' me, I wouldn't exactly have complained.

By the time I come inside, Rhona's office is deserted. The clock says ten minutes to seven. Not long till Dr Harrison turns up. I flop down in the big swivel chair and scratch my nose.

I like this chair. Sometimes during our sessions Rhona lets me sit in it. We swap places and joke that she's the patient. The back of the chair is very springy. I push myself round in it till I grow dizzy. Then I wheel it back to her desk and sit looking up at her noticeboard. At the top of it, like a trophy, is the keyring my fan dropped when he came over the fence. It gave me the creeps before, that thing. But later it just made me feel sorry for the guy. God knows how he got home without it. There's a couple of door keys on the ring, an' a car key an' a black, circular fob.

On the desk is Rhona's in-tray. We call it the mountain. Today it's particularly tall. I don't know how Rhona deals with all that paperwork. Sometimes she says she'd like to just burn it. A section near the top catches my eye. It's a different sort of paper. Rougher, and not as white as the rest. I look at the door, but there's no one there, so I slip to my feet and approach the mountain. The interesting section is folded, pressed flat beneath the globe paperweight. But already I have recognised it for what it is. I gasp and glance over my shoulder. A newspaper! I haven't seen one since I found that old *Daily Post*. It makes me nervous to see another one. It's forbidden to go through Rhona's papers, and way more forbidden to read a *news*paper. But . . .

I snatch it from the pile and dash behind the sofa.

She'll never know . . .

At first I daren't even open it. I sit on the floor below the window, staring at the front page. On it, there are words. Lots of words, written by people I don't know. The *Western*

Courier is the name of the paper. That's the local one, with the cigarette men. As I thought, the headlines are nothing special. They've stretched them out to fill the whole page. Something about a fisherman winning some lottery money. I look at the name of the man who wrote the story. Donald McTavish. I wonder if he's the man who eats all the chocolate biscuits.

The novelty is wearing off already. There's a full-page advert for a knitting supply shop, a piece about a lost dog, something about the council, an advert for *My Fair Lady* and a local weather report. I read the lost dog bit for the longest, but even that is boring. The dog's name is Pepper and it belongs to a family from the village. They think it might have fallen into the sea, cos they lost it during a walk along the cliffs. There's no reward for its return, just a photograph of the little girl who owns the dog. I look at the photograph closely. It is strange to see a new face. She looks very sad.

Sighing, I flip through the back pages. Cars for sale. Border collie puppies. Second-hand farm equipment.

Okay. Nothing special.

Standing up, I fold the paper. But wait . . . I stop. I look again. A small piece is missing. A perfect, random square cut out of the football results. How strange. Why would someone bother to cut *that* out? Then I realise. I turn the back page and look at the other side. There. In the middle of the obituaries page. Someone has cut out an obituary.

As far as I know, no staff member has family in the village. Rhona's talked about this several times. They're all specially qualified and came from other parts of Scotland. Rhona is the most local of the lot and she's from Skye. So why should she be bothered with a local obituary?

Mrs McRae. Of course. It must be for her. I close the paper and check the date. But this is today's paper.

Huh . . .

The sound of footsteps makes me jump. I stuff the paper behind my back.

'Are you in there, Sue?' calls Rhona.

I freeze. Why didn't I close the door properly? I crouch lower behind the sofa an' kick over the little tissue-box table. *Clatter.*

Shit!

'Susan? Can I come in?'

The door creaks. I stuff the paper under the sofa an' stand up straight. Rhona stands in the doorway.

'Oh!' she exclaims.

'I . . . was looking for . . . you,' I blurt.

Rhona's eyes dart around the room once, then back at me. Her face looks weird without make-up on. Swollen.

'Kathy, this is my *office*. You're not meant to be in here by yourself.'

'I just . . . wanted to see you before . . . my session . . .'

Rhona sighs as she crosses the room.

'You know you have to wait outside.'

I blush.

'Nervous?' she asks. I nod. She gives me a hug.

'I had nightmares,' I say.

'What? When?'

'The last time.'

'Shhh. I know it's hard,' she says. Her throat makes a funny sound, and for a moment I think she'll say something more. Then a rap at the door startles us, and we turn round to see Dr Harrison.

'Speak of the devil!' announces Rhona, and marches to the

201

doorway. She keeps her back turned to me, and this upsets me because I'd wanted to say goodbye. Dr Harrison nudges the door closed and shrugs her handbag onto the desk.

'Happy birthday,' I say.

'What?' Her face hovers between surprise and confusion.

'I have a present for you,' I say. 'A pot stand. I made it.'

Dr Harrison blushes. 'Oh no no, dear . . . That won't be necessary!'

'It's okay. You can have it. I don't have any pots.'

'Right. Well. All right. Thank you.'

I smile.

'Should we get started?' asks Dr Harrison.

'Okay.'

I hover next to Rhona's sofa, knowing this is the point of no return. Once I sit down, that's it. I scan the shadows beneath it, but the newspaper is not sticking out. My stomach twinges with guilt. I'll have to find a way of sneaking it back.

'Sit down then,' says Dr Harrison. 'Make yourself comfortable.'

My chest feels tight as I obey. Dr Harrison is fiddling with the height control on Rhona's chair. I look around the room while I wait for her. This is quite a low sofa. From here I can see all the dust under the furniture. It looks like no one's vacuumed in years.

'God*damn* . . .' says Dr Harrison. She rattles the chair and her clipboard *whoomphs* to the floor. The papers on the mountain flutter.

Just then, something catches my eye. A bit of paper. A tiny, square bit of paper, sailing to the ground. My heart jumps, and I leap off the sofa to catch it.

'What are you . . .' says Dr Harrison.

Uncupping my hands, I look at the square. Dr Harrison moves towards me. I turn the square over, and read.

Wishart, Mary Annabel
Aged 28 years.
Taken from us suddenly, on Sunday
16th Jul,
at Gille Dubh care home, Cairndhu.
Beloved daughter of Mike and Helen.
Big sister
of John and Rory.
'Earth has no sorrow that heaven
cannot heal.'
Funeral Sunday 23rd Jul, at St Mary's
Catholic Church, Thurso, Caithness.
Friends please gather at church at
1pm.

19

March 18th, 2005.

Rimi is the last store I pass on my way to the night bus, and as such it's become my last port of call. Me on a bus! I would never have believed, before, that I'd be able to handle these eight-hour bus rides. Back in the UK I only ever travelled by train. But it costs money to cushion yourself from claustrophobia, and I don't have a lot of that now. So the night bus it is. I just have to distract myself. I'm getting quite good at it.

In Rimi, I splash out on snacks for the trip. Rosinboller, mini carrots, an apple, fizzy water. I'm not used to saying the full-length phrase for *thank you*. Sometimes I force myself to say it, but it sounds unnaturally long-winded coming out of my mouth, and I never know which syllables to stress. So mostly I just bark *Takk* and wince in the knowledge of how rude I sound.

Suitcase in tow, I cross the walkway to the bus station and plunge through the revolving doors. Inside, some men are sheltering from the snow. One of them grabs at me as I pass, but I pull my arm away and keep walking. After that I make sure not to meet anyone's gaze. Down the escalator I go, under the departure boards and past the kiosk to the long-distance stands. Here, I slip outside and chain-smoke Marlboro Golds. As the departure time approaches, more people sidle out to join me, braving the cold in exchange for a good seat. I shuffle and jiggle and stand my ground. Then the bus swings into the bay, and like groupies we lurch at the door. The other people have pyjama bottoms and travel pillows, something I always try – and fail – to remember for next time. The queue moves slowly. I puff on a dog-end to keep warm, waiting till the last possible second to throw it away. Then it's my turn, and I dive inside to claim a seat. I stuff my water, book and snacks into both seat pockets, then stretch out under my coat and pretend to sleep. I learnt this trick on my second trip north, and if I'm lucky it wins me a double seat for the whole journey.

As we leave the city lights behind, the bus quietens down, and it's safe to raise my head. Trees close in, obscuring the fjord from view. My eyes are heavy, but the armrest gouging into my hip makes it hard to sleep. On occasion I look up and catch moonlit glimpses of churning rivers, or herds of elk. Unfamiliar road signs swing past my face like fists.

This is my fourth visit to Magnus since moving south. I'd come every weekend if I could, but on my current wage there's no way I can afford that. Fifty kroner a day is more like pocket money, really, but it's better than nothing, and at least it's *mine*. Plus, the roof over my head is free, cos it's Hans's roof too. I live in the guest apartment on the bottom floor of his house, while he lives at the top. It's really not bad. My first week here, Hans gave me jobs around the house. Washing, ironing and the like. After that he shifted me to his barber shop in town, because one of his stylists had quit and Lina needed help to run the place. Hans doesn't cut hair – he leaves all that hands-on stuff to other people – but he certainly hoovers up the money.

I'm not sure I like Lina. She's been cold since day one, and I secretly suspect she's one of those girls who doesn't like other girls. One day when we were alone she got all snotty with me and suggested I should find myself another job. But after four weeks, I think I've figured it out. You see, Hans has a thing for Lina. She pretends not to notice, but it's as clear as day and I'm pretty sure she loves the attention. One day he even brought her flowers, and though she acted cool when he presented her with them, she kept them next to her barber's chair till the petals went crispy. Maybe she's worried he'll stop lavishing attention on her now that I'm around. Anyway, I'm trying my best to make friends with her.

#

In the middle of a deep valley, the night bus parks outside a diner, and those who are still awake tumble indoors. Animal heads furnish the rough pine walls, while antique skis and weapons hang from the beams. I buy a hot chocolate from the round-faced clerk and sit by the window to drink it. Each place mat tells the story of the battle that took place here, between the natives and the Scottish invaders. From what I can make out, the natives won.

On this journey, the driver is king. Everyone eyeballs him while they eat, to make sure they don't get left behind, and when he finishes his meatballs we pretty much sprint after him. Outside, he lights a cigarette before unlocking the bus, and like funeral guests we bow our heads and wait. I peer across the road, where the chimney of the wood mill releases a tall finger of smoke. Finally the driver discards his dog-end, and we slide carefully across the ice to the bus. Before setting off he makes some announcements – the same phrases each time – and I try to extract words from the tumult. In the beginning I believed the first of his announcements was about travel sickness, and it wasn't till I checked a map that I

206

realised he was talking about the town in the valley. Its name sounds just like the word for nausea and for weeks I thought this route must be a particularly bumpy one.

The second stretch of the journey is as long as the first, but I pretty much sleep it away. Just before seven, the driver announces our arrival and the yawning passengers sit up. The thick virgin snow makes the outside world seem unreal. Wild and unexplored, and full of adventure. Despite my hatred of long-distance travel, I've come to love the night bus.

#

Three hours I sit outside the house. Three motherfucking hours. By the time my patience breaks, I can barely feel my fingers.

I back away from the house and glare at Magnus's window. Someone has closed it in too much of a hurry and trapped part of a curtain in the frame. I recognise the pattern on the curtain, and it reminds me of that perfect first week we had together. Under lamplight, I would gaze through the window and watch the moon rise. How I wish I was on that side of the curtains now. The trapped corner flaps sadly in the breeze. Taunting me.

What the fuck is so hard about opening a door? He knew I was coming. He's known all week. I stamp to the middle of the street, where a trail of grit has been recently distributed. Some of it has frozen into the road, but some has not. With my foot, I scrape some into a pile, take a handful and chuck it at the house. But it sprays over a wider area than I'd anticipated and collides loudly with several other windows besides Magnus's. I jump, fearing I've cracked the glass. If a neighbour calls the police, I'll have to run.

An elderly couple strides out of the mist, hand in hand, and I blush as their eyes flick towards me. I know what I look like by now. The snow has built up steadily on my fake fur coat and I've long since given up brushing it off. Walking snowmen must be quite a novelty for the locals. I fish my phone from my pocket and look at it, but there are still no messages. I hold the phone to my ear anyway and bash out one half of a conversation. *Hi love. Yeah, it's me. Yeah, I'd love some help with my bag.*

Bit by bit, whiteness swallows the couple from sight. I wonder where they are going and if it is warm there. If I ran after them and begged, would they give me shelter? Or something to eat? The air smells of newly baked bread and it's driving me crazy. I am so hungry. But I only have two hundred kroner, and that has to last me all weekend. I'll get some noodles later. Bunnpris noodles and a bottle of plonk.

Answer your fucking phone! Why don't you answer?

Just then, the window next to Magnus's fills with a face. I cringe as the window opens and a man's head sticks out of it.

'Sorry!' I call. The guy is young and skinny, with long, messy hair and a Burzum T-shirt. Suddenly I recognise him.

'Håkon! Let me in!'

Håkon wobbles slightly and squints. Behind him, I can hear music. Jayne County, if I'm not mistaken. Party music. Fuck, I should have known. That's why Magnus didn't answer.

Håkon disappears from the window, and in the two minutes of inactivity that follows, I fear he has forgotten me. Then I hear footsteps from inside the hall and a girl with blonde hair swings the door open. Wordlessly, she ushers me upstairs.

The hallway is full of shoes. I stand there for a moment, stunned by the noise. The door to the spare room is closed, and I don't feel like braving the living room, so I head for the bedroom and sidle through the door. Inside, it is blissfully calm. On the bed I hear Magnus half-breathing, half-snoring, the way he does when he's really, really drunk. But my anger is dissolving already. All I want to do is go to sleep. Kicking off my shoes, I climb the ladder.

There, I see his shoulder in the shadows. He can't have been that drunk if he managed to undress himself. I lie by his side and am about to put my arm round him when I notice the girl. I jolt upright. Sølvi! She's stark naked, pressed snugly against his side, and sleeping just as soundly. For a moment I cannot move. Tears well up in my eyes. But no . . . Wait . . . Magnus is only naked from the waist upwards . . .

I put both hands on my forehead and take a breath. I'm well within my rights to raise hell. I know that, and I know that I probably should. But I'm also dead on my feet . . .

Stiffly, I lie down on my back. Magnus's arm is warm against my frozen skin and already I feel him thawing me out. Sensation prickles back into my fingers, and then my feet. For a while I close my eyes, trying to pretend Sølvi is not there. But the pain soon usurps my fatigue, and I find myself wobbling back down the ladder.

#

The living room looks like a lorry has driven through it. Seven people lie draped across the two sofas, but clearly it took more than seven to make all this mess. Håkon is nowhere in sight, and the only person I recognise is the girl who opened the door. I perch in an empty spot by the window and take the plastic off my packet of cigarettes. Within forty minutes I have chain-smoked the lot.

One by one, people fall asleep or disappear. I boil the kettle, add some more coffee to my karsk and look out of the window while I wait for something to happen. For the hundredth time, I feel like I'm going mad. Why the fuck do I keep coming here? It's like letting him punch me repeatedly in the face. But I know that if he says *I love you* between each punch, I will allow it to continue . . .

Eventually Magnus and Sølvi come through. Magnus jumps when he sees me. Sølvi goes to the fridge and leans over, looking inside. Her bare legs are supermodel slim and she's wearing the hoodie Magnus wore on our first date. Magnus remains frozen in the doorway and smiles at me with that simpering expression I hate so much. That look that shows he's waiting for me to explode. Maybe all his ex-girlfriends used to do that. But I'm not an exploder. I see him see the weakness in me, like always, and choose his course of action. His expression exaggerates into sourness, and his bottom lip juts out. He rolls his eyes dramatically.

'Oh come *on*,' he says.

'What?'

'That look. You know.'

'I didn't—'

'Well, fuck you if you're going to be like that,' he says, not looking at me as he lights a cigarette. With a *whoomph*, he sits down on the other sofa. 'Why did you bother coming?'

Sølvi comes over and sits beside Magnus. She smiles a private smile, which he returns. Then she takes the cigarette from his fingers and takes a long, slow drag. During this transaction they do not lift their eyes from each other. I look away, wishing I had not already smoked my cigarettes.

What am I doing here?

I cup one hand over my face and try to blink the moisture

from my eyes. Sølvi stares at me. There are so many things I cannot say in front of her. I know I should trust him. That the kid probably just pawed him all night. But that still doesn't make it all right.

'Sleep well?' I ask Magnus, tartly.

At this moment Håkon swaggers into the room and all of us look up. He flops down next to Magnus, and the three of them start joking in local dialect.

I look through the window at the river. In the middle the water has cut a path through the ice, and small clusters of snow bob along this surface. From edge to crumbling edge they pinball along, and for some time I find myself dazzled by this display. On the opposite bank, candles cast pastel reflections in the snow. Behind my head, the stream of words I do not understand. A magical, poetic language, like ambient music. I sink away till the only thing rooting me here is the pain in my heart. It's the only link I've had left for a while, and it's time I admitted it. The real world is drifting away from me.

Oh Magnus, how I'm coming to hate your beautiful face . . .

I realise the voices have stopped, and look up to find the room deserted. Only Håkon is left, snoring in a mound of spilled cigarette ash. His thin, freckled arms are crossed over his chest, and I see now that someone has covered him with marker-pen tattoos. Under normal circumstances this would make me laugh. But right now I can't even smile. I feel like I've been beaten with a baseball bat, and despite Sølvi's presence my first instinct is to go to Magnus. He's the one I came to see. He's the one who's supposed to love me. I go to the bedroom and try the handle but find the door locked. Some people come into the living room then and resume drinking. I join in, pretending to be drunk so they'll leave me alone. I recognise one of the new arrivals. She's a friend of Sølvi's, from that crazy night at Råkk. I try to ask what happened, but she is very drunk and doesn't understand.

'That man was wrong to hit your friend,' I tell her, and she just squints her eyes.

'You mean Hans?' asks another girl, in perfect English.

'What?'

'The man at Råkk, who hit Sølvi. Were you there?'

Suddenly, I feel horribly sober. I think of the man with the black hair. Those big shoulders. I only saw him from behind, but . . .

'Hans?' I repeat.

'Yeah. From Oslo.'

'How does she know Hans?' My voice is faint now.

'She doesn't. He's her dealer's boss. But she owed some money, and . . . well, he wanted it back . . .'

For a second, I cannot breathe.

'It's just business to those guys,' says the friend. She shrugs. 'It could have been worse.'

20

I make it upstairs in less than twenty seconds an' hurl myself at Mary's bedroom door. The hinges are bright. Brand new. I pump the door handle as hard as I can. Again an' again an' again. I drop to my knees an' stare through the keyhole. Inside, iss dark. No Mary. Nothing. I can't see anything.

'Mary!' I screech. 'Mary! *Mary!*'

Dr Harrison appears, followed by Rhona and Joyce. Joyce holds a blanket. Rhona is shouting. They run at me.

I hammer my fists on the door. Behind me, people are comin' out of their bedrooms.

'Mary!'

They rush at me, an' as I roll along the floor I feel the blanket snare my limbs. Strong hands appear an' stop mine from movin'. Joyce and Rhona are shoutin' at the same time. My heart surges and curls. I cry so powerfully that it chokes me.

Hands roll me over an' a sky full of faces rolls in. Other people are screaming now. Dr Harrison holds Liz by the wrists. Rhona is arguing with Joyce. Joyce leans on me with her full weight.

'Where's Mary?' I howl. 'Where's Mary? Where's Mary?'

I free my left hand an' swipe at Joyce. But something gets in the way. My wrist snaps under a great weight an' I'm pushed even further under the blanket. More runnin' feet. Along the corridor, Caroline appears with a syringe. Her feet

213

pound closer. Joyce leans on my throat. 'Wait!' shouts Rhona. 'Wait!'

I scream. Caroline crashes down. The syringe hits my arm an' my veins rush cold. I feel her push it in. Roughly, like a shove in the back. My heart swells and trips, an' I fall back. My eyes shut. Clunk. They open. The corridor is melting. Down. Down. A syrupy collage. My leaking eyes bounce the lights into crystals. Icicle daggers, dashing in all directions. My hand swoops to catch one. Then the world slides away and there is only darkness.

#

I spend two nights in the crisis room. On the second day, Rhona tells me the others spent the night on the library floor. Everyone is upset, she says. Last night was the biggest crisis they've ever had at this place and we need to stick together. Is this is an attempt to make me guilty? I don't know. But I have no room for any more guilt. I'm already so full that no more will fit.

Rhona cries with me during that second day. When she cries, I catch glimpses of a huge weakness in her. Eternally deep an' black, like a mountain chasm. Since Rhona came back from Skye I've often sensed its presence but never seen it with my own eyes. It makes me feel closer to her, cos it proves that she's not perfect. But it also scares me, cos isn't Rhona supposed to be the strong one? If we've both fallen into the chasm, what hope do we have of escaping? Who'll lower the rope to me if there's no one on the outside?

I want to go to Mary's funeral, but Rhona says the family doesn't want it. None of us are invited. Not even Joyce, who was Mary's case worker. We decide to have our own ceremony

214

on the day of Mary's funeral, and in the end this thought is what holds me together. Rhona says the police have already combed Mary's room, but there's little doubt over what happened. Mary was found hanging from the curtain rail in her bedroom, two days ago. She'd taken Mrs Laird's keys and locked herself in. There was no note, but as the keys had gone missing four days before, the police said the act was *premeditated*. They'll come back to tie up loose ends, but the case is pretty much closed. Till then, Mary's room is out of bounds.

I ask why Joyce didn't notice Mary's state of mind, but Rhona just says, 'She can't be held accountable.' This answer puzzles me, but when I press her about it she keeps changing the subject. On the third day, she admits Mary's last psych session had been cancelled by mistake. Mrs Laird was away that week, and Joyce was supposed to take her appointments. But Mary's session clashed with a *My Fair Lady* rehearsal, and when Joyce changed appointments round she forgot to pencil Mary back in.

Rhona keeps saying Joyce wasn't to blame, but the more she says it the less believable it sounds. The final insult comes when she asks me to keep quiet, cos if word gets out Joyce could lose her job.

On Thursday I am released from the crisis room. The atmosphere is subdued by now, and it seems like everyone's in mourning. Activities are cancelled for the rest of the week, though Mr Duff drives up every day to give extra support. No one really laughs or smiles or raises their voices. My meds have been increased these last few days, and the others are so dopey-acting I think theirs probably has too. Quietly, together, we mourn.

#

Sunday.

Mr Duff comes earlier than usual, and without his guitar. In an eerie break from tradition, he leads us onto the moor and asks us to put our hands together. Then he clears his throat, and without readin' out from anythin', recites a prayer for Mary. Jess cries loudly, which annoys me cos she and Mary were never close.

When it's over we file back inside for breakfast. I stand at the door, watchin' people fill their plates. They take their food. They bustle. They sit down. I walk to the hotplate an' stare at the sausages. I stare at the disposable egg cups. I stare at the congealed beans. Then I leave the room an' go back outside. I try to remember which way Mary was walking the last time I saw her, an' head off in that direction. When I reach the sheep fold I lie down on my back. The sky is clean and empty. I feel in my pocket for the heart-shaped counter an' squeeze it until my hand hurts.

This isn't over yet. Our official memorial thing will take place at sea, due to Mary's love of the outdoors. They've printed programmes an' everything. Whose decision was that? It seems tacky. And, I mean, they've been tryin' to make me go on a boat for weeks. Are they using Mary's death as a tool to get into my head? Would they stoop that low? I jus' don't know any more.

Dr Harrison is staying longer than planned, to lend a helping hand. Rhona says I should talk to her, cos it'll help me deal with my grief. We'll have a special talk tomorrow that'll just be about Mary. *A light session*, they said. I said okay.

#

Rhona stays up with me, long after the others have gone to

bed. We share a carton of milk and play draughts in the darkened dining room. It feels good to have something different to do. The evenings have been hard on me this week. I keep wondering if what happened to Mary was my fault. I shouldn't have let her walk away that day. I should have told someone she was actin' weird. But I didn't. I forgot her. Little Mary.

'You're quiet,' says Rhona as she packs up the board.

'I guess.'

'Thinking about her?'

I nod.

'Want to talk about it?'

I look up. Rhona's eyelids are puffy, like old balloons. I reply with a shake of the head.

'Okay,' says Rhona, and gets up from the table. She collects our empty glasses and heads for the kitchen. My stomach churns.

'Rhona!' I shout.

She jumps.

'What?!'

'Don't go in there . . . I mean . . . don't walk under there.'

'What?'

'It's not safe.'

Rhona frowns, then turns and looks behind her.

'This?' she says, pointing at the horseshoe.

I nod.

'Hmm,' she says. She plonks the milk glasses on the nearest table, pulls a chair to the doorway and stands on it. Then she grabs the horseshoe, takes it to the window and flings it outside.

'Thank you, Rhona,' I say.

'No problem, ya freak.' She picks up the glasses again, one

217

in each hand. 'C'mon now. Get to bed, or they'll have my hide.'

On my way past Mrs Laird's sitting room, I notice the television is on. But the person sitting on the sofa is Joyce. She sings along to the film on the screen, and with a heavy heart I recognise the song. It's one she's been practising for weeks, for that bloody musical. The one she's still going ahead with, despite all the damage she's done. Her back is turned to me, but I can tell by the sounds she makes that she is eating. All at once, my shoulders tense up. I listen to the slack-mouthed crunching. The high-pitched trills.

My eyes are full of tears. But I'm not strong enough to have that fight tonight. I force myself to go upstairs.

#

Monday.

I wake to find Rhona asleep in the bedside chair. What is she doing here? Frightened, I nudge her arm.

'Rhona?' I whisper, and she looks up.

'Mornin', squirt,' she says.

'What are you doing here?'

'Don't you remember?'

'No.'

'You were screaming.'

I feel my face grow red.

'For your mother,' she adds, carefully.

My heart booms.

'Oh . . .'

'Do you remember what you said?' asks Rhona. She is fully awake now. For the second time I notice the pouches under her eyes. They make her look old.

'I think I was dreaming . . .' I say. 'I think you were there. You were my mother . . .'

'That's right,' says Rhona. 'You thought I was her. But do you remember what you said?'

'No . . .'

'You said you were sorry. For killing me.'

My mouth drops open. The smile has gone from Rhona's face. I swallow, an' my throat feels hard.

'It was . . . a dream . . .'

Rhona leans forward and takes my hand.

'Kathy. I really don't think things can go on like this. I know you remember things. Why won't you tell me? Don't you trust me?'

'There's nothing to—'

'Is it because you're ashamed? Do you think I'll be shocked by the things you tell me?'

'I . . . I don't remember—'

'I *know* you remember! We have to make some progress sooner or later!'

'Why do we? Who says we have to?'

Rhona frowns into her lap. She clears her throat, an' her brow wrinkles so much that I think she might burst into tears. But all she says is, 'Things change, Kathy. None of us can help that.'

All the heat drains from my body.

'What things?'

'I won't be here forever, Kathy. And I really want to help you, before—'

'Before what? Where are you going?'

My voice comes out far away. Tight and small, as if I was speakin' through a cardboard tube. The back of my neck is burning.

Rhona's eyes flick across my face, then away. She sighs, heavily.

'Nowhere, love.'

'Promise you won't leave me.'

'Kathy . . .'

'Promise!'

Rhona sighs. 'All right. All right.'

'Say it!'

'I promise.'

I search Rhona's face for some back-up. But her eyes fail to meet me. I hear myself wheezing, an' it sounds like an old hoover.

'Kathy, love. I'm not your mother . . . But I *am* your friend. You have to help me with this. We need to find your *real* mother.'

I yank my hand away.

'I didn't kill her! It was a dream! I told you, it was a dream!'

'No one's saying you *killed* her, Kathy. We just . . . *oh* . . . You need to give a little back.'

'I didn't ask you to come in here! Who said you could sleep in here, anyway?'

'Kathy, calm down!'

'Get out!'

I leap out of bed an' stand on the other side. I hold the pillow out between us.

'Kathy—'

'Get out! Get out get out get *out*!'

Rhona tries to walk round the bed. I throw the pillow at her.

'You're not my friend! You're not *anything*!' I yell.

Rhona's face hardens. Out she goes, an' the door clicks

shut. My hands are still shaking. I stare at the doorknob for a long time.

#

MmhorGDRegP89/10
Name: Katherine (Fennick?)
Gender: F
DOB: Unknown. (Est. age 30)
Date of session: 17/07/2006
Duration: 35min
T: Therapist, P: Patient

[Session notes: Patient too agitated to achieve somnambulist state. Light relaxation only possible after extended pre-talk.]

Excerpt 1:
T: I'd like to talk about your mother, today.
P: No. I said I wouldn't.
T: Take a deep breath. If you relax, you'll find this much easier.
P: We were meant to talk about Mary.
T: Well, we're coming to that. We can talk about Mary as much as you like. But first I need to go over a few things. Do you think you can help me?
P: [Long pause.] All right.
T: So, in one of our previous sessions we talked about your holidays on the farm. When you were small. Do you remember these things?
P: A bit. I read the transcript.

T: But you also remember that farm? You can picture it, if you think hard enough?

P: Yes. A bit.

T: Good. I'd like you to imagine you are at that farm right now. You have just arrived with your parents. It's a beautiful day and you are feeling very happy. Very glad to be there. Can you see yourself there?

P: Sort of.

T: Good. Very good. Now, I'd like you to imagine you are getting out of the car. You look at your mother and—

P: I said I wouldn't talk about her.

T: Okay. Okay. Well, maybe we can talk about the farm instead.

P: This is stupid.

T: Whatever you tell me will be utterly confidential.

P: No. I've changed my mind. They'll read it.

T: Who will read it?

P: Rhona. Joyce.

T: Don't you trust Rhona? I thought you and her were close?

P: No.

T: All we want is to help you.

P: No you don't. You want to get rid of me. You'll disappear.

T: Why would we disappear?

P: You will. You always do.

T: People you've loved have disappeared before?

222

P: You're going to leave. I can't do it again.

T: Who has left you?

P: Mary. Magnus. Mum.

T: How do you know your mother left you?

P: She didn't come to get me.

T: When was this?

P: After the newspapers . . . She didn't come.

T: Did she leave you before this, too?

P: Yes.

T: You remember this?

P: No.

T: How do you know, if you don't remember?

P: She's not here, is she?

T: Is your mother dead, Katherine?

P: Stop it!

[Patient becomes agitated and gets up from chair. Takes several minutes to return her to relaxed state.]

Excerpt 5:

T: Earlier, you said that Magnus left you. I'd like to talk about that, if you—

P: No.

T: You don't want to talk about Magnus, or you didn't mean what you said?

P: [No answer.]

T: Why don't you want to discuss Magnus? Is it because he hurt you?

P: [No answer.]

T: Concentrate, Katherine. Is Magnus the one

who hurt you? Is he the one who put you in
the loch?

P: No.

T: I know there's someone you're afraid of.
You just have to tell me who it is.

P: [Patient cries. Speaks incoherently.]

T: Do you remember how you got to the loch,
Katherine?

P: I don't know.

T: Did Magnus take you to the loch?

P: He loved me.

Excerpt 8.

T: You were close to Mary?

P: Yes.

T: Were you best friends?

P: It was different. She didn't talk. But she
understood me.

T: You felt that you could trust her?

P: Yes.

T: Was this the first time you've been able to
trust someone in this way?

P: [Pauses.] No.

T: How did it make you feel when Mary died?

P: Guilty.

T: What made you feel guilty?

P: I wasn't there. She needed me and I wasn't
there.

T: You didn't fail her. You were her friend.

P: No. I was worse than Joyce. She trusted
me. I should have seen.

T: What did Joyce do?

P: She left her. Like Rhona's going to leave
me.
T: You're afraid that everyone will leave
you?
P: Yes.
T: What do you think will happen then? After
they've left you?
P: I deserve it.
T: What do you think you deserve?
P: Punishment.
T: But why should you be punished? You're a
lovely girl.
P: I'm Miss La-di-da.
[Patient wakes abruptly. Gets up and tries to
leave room. Extremely agitated. Attempts to
calm patient/resume session unsuccessful.]
Session ends
[Note: Try 'La-di-da' as bridge in
somnambulist state.]

#

Tuesday.

I spend most of the day in my room. Rhona hasn't shown
her face, and I can't bring myself to go to her.

At five o'clock I hear voices, so I go to my window an' peer
through the curtains. The first thing I see is Joyce's head. I
know it's her from that cast-iron hairdo. No one else in the
world has hair like that. She's leaning over a green car, talkin'
to the person inside. I strain to hear their conversation, but
all that reaches me are the high tones in Joyce's voice. I hate
that bloody voice. The pure noise of it. Joyce steps back an'

225

the car swings round. Through the windscreen, it's Dr Harrison. Her hand flutters once. Then the car creeps round an' makes for the gates. I watch till she's out of sight. So does Joyce. I don't think Dr Harrison is coming back.

Last night, Dr Harrison tried to trick me. She asked all the things she said she wouldn't. She thinks Magnus dumped me in Loch Oscaig, like nuclear waste. I found myself wonderin' if this was true, an' suddenly, clear as day, I saw a face. A handsome face. Sandy-haired, with stubble and super-bright blue eyes. I knew straight away it was Magnus. My chest reeled from the impact. I felt that wild devotion, as if for the first time, and it made me want to laugh and run and sing. For a second, I was almost there with him. But his face bled away, then, an' a diff'rent one rose its place. Pinpoint eyes, hairy arms an' a mane of black hair. A calloused fist swung down. Veins in his neck, an' the dark thrum of violence. I felt my hysterical hatred of this man. The shame an' desperation, an' the fear. That man's been in my nightmares for weeks, an' now for the first time I saw his face. A name flashed through my head. *Hans*. An' in an instant I knew who he was.

21

Wednesday.

Rain clouds loiter, like they're waiting for an opportunity to soak me.

I haven't eaten for thirty-six hours, an' I'd planned on holding out longer, but I snap this morning when breakfast smells float up the stairs. I think I smell waffles, which are my favourite. Waffles and golden syrup. Oh, that'd be fab right now. Crispy brown edges. Fluffy inside. I imagine prising the lid off the syrup. Licking my sticky fingers. Loading my fork with sugary goodness. They said I'm not allowed sugar right now. But maybe I can sneak some anyway. They'd never know.

I slip out of bed and follow my nose downstairs. Rhona is in the dining room. I jump as we clock each other, an' for a second my hunger turns to nausea. This is the moment I'd dreaded. But Rhona is talking with Joyce and only glances up for a moment.

I hover by the doorway, recalculating. Did I overreact the other day? Should I apologise? Storm out? But my belly has taken control now an' won't let me do anythin' that results in me not eatin'. Lookin' straight ahead, I approach the hot-plates. There are no waffles, and before I can take anything else the cook swoops in to stop me. She microwaves my 'special meal' porridge – made without seasoning – and I shuffle off angrily to eat it. If I swallow it fast I can almost trick

227

myself it's sweet. It's just a question of replacing the thoughts I don't like with ones I do.

Joyce seems to be dominating the conversation with Rhona. Sometimes Rhona holds her head in her hands, an' sometimes she nods. It makes me sad to watch them, so I go back upstairs an' play snakes and ladders on the floor. The clouds grow closer each time I look up, as if they'll end up comin' right through the window. At four o'clock I crawl into bed, pull the pillow over my head an' close my eyes.

#

Men's voices. Right outside. I stiffen and grip the pillow to my face. The crack beneath my door moves with shadows.

'—much longer, madam.'

'Well please, for the other girls' sakes, do try to be quiet.'

Was that Mrs Laird?

'Of course.'

Heavy feet pound the floorboards. Mrs Laird must be cross they didn't take their shoes off in the hall. They sound like big shoes. Boots. Full of mud and mess.

'Come on, people, you heard the lady. Let's get this done.'

'Yes sir.'

A soft thud, like a woolly animal falling over. Coughing. 'Sorry,' says a voice. Footsteps walk around, further away. Muffled sometimes, like they're walkin' on a rug. Then I know for sure. The men are in Mary's room. My first instinct is to run out and hit them. I leap out of bed and stand behind the door, hands clenched. But the feeling passes quickly. Bit by bit, my fists go slack. I go to the window and wipe a looking-hole in the condensation. A big white van is parked below. Police.

A ghoulish desire gathers pace in me, to look at Mary's room one last time. If they lock the door from now on I might never see it again. Creeping forward, I touch the door handle. But I can't make myself go further. Why not? It doesn't make sense to be so frightened. They're policemen. No more likely to hurt me than Mr Duff. But I can't open the door. Not with all those fists on the other side. All that weight and hair and sweat, crushing their big shoes into the carpet. Smiling teeth and black eyes.

The back of my neck is on fire. I try to move my arm, but my body has turned into a suit of armour. Behind my eyes, bright shapes boogie. I lower myself to the carpet an' wipe my sweaty hands on it.

The voices outside seem to have stopped, and a great rustling noise has taken over, like a forest of paper bags. Swishing this way, then that. Close then far. A creak from the loose floorboard in the corridor. The swishing diminishes. Then, quite suddenly, the corridor falls silent. I sit up straight. Outside, a motor starts. I raise myself up and inch the door open. There is no one in sight, but my bravery has come too late. Mary's door is padlocked shut.

#

Thursday.

Gentle rain lulls me awake. The room is darker than usual, but when I get up to look I find it is indeed morning. Thick fog has come down low outside the window, so all I see is a hellish spotlight of red gravel. I slog back to bed and lie very still. But my thoughts are too morose to let me drop off again. Shadows rise and fall beyond the curtains, and the glass sucks and creaks. Sometimes the wind changes direction and

229

smacks rain into my window. When this happens I get a lump in my throat. I think of the conservatory, and then the ash tree. She's probably burned up by now. The thought of it repulses me. I wonder if the logs went to one person's house, or if they shared her out like slices of cake. Then I think about birthday cake, and how everyone lied to me about Dr Harrison. This makes me cry. It seems an unforgivable crime, to conceal death with something so joyful. I push my hand under my pillow and close my fingers around the heart-shaped counter. It came from a cereal packet originally. I remember the day the cook gave it to us.

'I'm sorry,' I whisper. Then the tears flow harder and will not stop. I think of Mary's smile as she waved goodbye. That last, clinging hug.

Everything is changing. I thought I could stay here forever, like the ash tree. But now it seems that won't be possible after all. What will I do if Rhona abandons me? I know what a mess I am. That I couldn't survive on the outside. Maybe they're right. Maybe it is time to tell them I've remembered Magnus. I lost my chance to confide in Mary, an' if Rhona leaves too there'll be no one left to listen. I don't think it's good for me to keep it all in. Unravelling inside me, making a mess. Things are startin' to get squashed, an' the nastier stuff gets, the less I want it to stay inside me. Someone has to help. I must break my silence.

\#

At lunchtime I go looking for Rhona. I check her office an' the library an' the day room an' the dining room, but she's nowhere to be found. *Maybe she's in her bedroom*, I think, so I go through to the staff wing an' knock on Rhona's door.

230

There's a pause. Footsteps. The door swings open. I leap back.

Joyce!

A yellow blanket hangs over her arm, semi-folded.

'Kathy. You know you're not allowed here. What do you want?'

'I'm . . . looking for Rhona.'

'Rhona isn't here.'

A chill wriggles through me.

'Where is she?' I croak.

Joyce sighs as she finishes folding Rhona's blanket. I can hardly stand to watch her.

'You won't see her for a while. She needed a wee break.'

'But . . . she would have told me . . .'

'Get used to it, Kathy.'

'What about . . . our sessions?'

'I'm taking over,' snips Joyce.

I feel my jaw fall.

'For how long?'

'As long as it takes.'

I stare at her. Or, rather, I stare at the dark place where her face should be. As Joyce refolds her arms round the blanket, a sunbeam sends a blizzard of lighted squares through her rings. Stupefied, I watch them dust the walls. Joyce clears her throat.

'Look. I know you don't like me very much. But it's still my job to help you. We'll be having a long talk tomorrow.'

I grab the wall to steady myself.

'But . . . Rhona . . .'

'Go on,' sighs Joyce, flapping a hand. The swirl of bright squares envelops me like sparkles from a wand, and inwardly I bristle at the idea Joyce could ever put me under her spell.

231

'What about Sunday? Isn't she coming?'

'Sunday?'

Joyce has no idea what I'm talking about. Rage crashes through me, nudging the shock to one side. I want to scream an' shout an' hurt her.

'Mary's ceremony,' I splutter.

'Is that Sunday?'

'Yes!'

'Well then no. No she's not.'

'But doesn't she . . . How can she . . .'

I convulse. My vision blacks out for a second. Then the world rushes back an' delivers me onto the floor. Joyce towers over me, barking, 'Stop it this minute!'

I try to sit up, an' can't. Joyce's eyes are like glass-topped pins. She swoops, seizes my wrists an' hauls me up. But my legs still don't work, so her efforts just sort of stretch me.

'You stop this charade right now!'

'I think I'm goin' to—'

'Don't defy me, Katherine!'

My belly bubbles. I stumble. For a second I almost free myself. But Joyce is quick. She grabs my wrists an' shoves me back down. I start to cry.

'Ohhh ho ho! No, missy . . . That might work on Rhona, but it won't work on me!'

'I want Rhona!' I shout.

'Well Rhona isn't here!'

I propel forwards. Upwards. Joyce's face centres in my vision. Circled in black, like a noose. I feel the blood pumping through me, my hands reaching forward. In my ears, Joyce's voice. *Put yourself first . . . I'll take care of Kathy . . . I'll take care of Kathy . . .* I think of Joyce's singing. Of the horseshoe. Of Mary. Blackness explodes across my vision, taking

232

every ounce of my strength with it. Then the noose slides back an' returns me to the room. Before me, Joyce's face drips with water. Spit. *My* spit.

For a second neither of us moves. A low breath grumbles out of Joyce. Then her palm swipes, hard, across my face. I stagger but don't fall. Trying to hide my pain, I lick the inside of my cheek. I look at her. Then I run.

At first my flight takes Joyce by surprise. But two steps short of the door she grabs my legs. We clatter forwards. My forehead strikes the desk. Joyce sits on my back, twisting my hands.

'Little madam!' she shrieks.

'Go on then! Kill me like you killed Mary!'

'You little—'

Her hand bats my head. I gasp as my teeth hit the floor.

'I'll tell them!' I screech. 'I'll get you sacked!

Joyce leans hard against my back. Her heart hammers into my spine. My wrists are twisted to breaking point. I yell, an' the taste of blood fills my tongue.

Holy shit. Is this how things will be from now on?

The door springs open, spillin' running feet.

'What are you doing?' shouts Caroline's voice.

'Help me! Hold her down!'

'Joyce, what the hell? Take it easy!'

'Don't touch me!'

'Hey . . . *Hey!*'

My spine jolts. Several knees jut into my kidneys. I slide sideways. Behind my head, Joyce yowls. Hands grab me, then release me, then grab me again. A cry of pain. A snarl. A foot slides across an' cracks into my spine. Hands claw my back, like a cat. Then, incredibly, the weight lifts from my body. Hands release me. The sliding noise continues, like a lazy tap dancer. I cradle my wrists to my chest. Suckin' in air. My whole body hurts.

'Shhh,' says Mrs Laird's voice. I shrink further, an' the hand follows me.

'Don't play her game!' Joyce shrieks.

'Get her out of here,' says a voice.

The footsteps scuff away, carryin' Joyce's shoutin' with them. Mrs Laird puts her hand on my shoulder. By the time my pulse has slowed, the room is dark.

#

Saturday.

I think they tried to wake me yesterday, but my memory of that is muddy. Today Mrs Laird summons me to her office. What happened was very wrong, she says. Joyce has been suspended an' so Mrs Laird will take over her duties. She stresses that this is a temporary solution. I ask to see Rhona, but Mrs Laird says I can't. She asks if I want to press charges against Joyce. 'It's your right,' she says. But she seems scared I'll agree, so I shrug an' say no. Besides, I'm scared loads of policemen might come here. Joyce would get revenge for that sooner or later, an' I can't live with that over my head. No. The best I can ask for is that Joyce isn't here for Mary's ceremony. Talk about perfect timing. I'm proud I could do Mary this small service.

At dinner, I eat fast. Both of my eyes are bruised, an' a hard grey lump crowns my forehead. I'm not a pretty sight, an' I know it. Each time I look up, someone's eyes dart away. I wonder if people know what happened by now.

My wrists still hurt, though the doctor assured me they are not broken, only torn. He gave me painkillers that make me mega sleepy an' told me not to move too much. In the evening I play snakes and ladders with myself, cos I'm too tired to do anythin' else. I play with two counters. One for me and one for Mary. Whenever it's Mary's turn I throw the dice for her an' move her counter. We win roughly the same amount of games each.

22

April 2nd, 2005.

Magnus has moved back in with Mathilde, for the good of the kids. I should have fucking known. On the first day of my visit, he breaks the news. He kisses my face and says this is not the end. That he still loves me deeply. Or, rather, he loves the old me. If that version comes back, he says he'll be powerless to resist. I say I will try.

The five of us take a walk through the playground. Isak and Tor Olav run ahead, throwing sticks at each other. Mathilde does not speak to me, and I do not speak to her. The way Magnus gazes at her makes me nauseous with pain, but somehow I hold myself together. He has told her I'm a friend of Håkon's, and though I could easily blow that lie apart, I daren't risk driving him away.

They sit on the climbing frame and nudge each other and whisper, but each time I approach they move to a different spot, so I stand in a snowdrift and wait for them to finish. The spring thaw is still some way off at this latitude, and as the sugary top crust of snow skitters round my legs, my hands shake inside my gloves. I play counting games with my heartbeat. *I want to die . . . I want to die . . . I want to die . . .*

Magnus pays for me to stay in a hostel, and I barely see him for the rest of the weekend. On Monday he's too hungover to walk me to the night bus, but he comes out to meet me in the street outside Mathilde's house. He tells me not to cry. That Mathilde likes me. That he'll bring her to visit. Then he reaches out and shakes my hand goodbye.

'I need to talk to you,' I tell him, as I have all weekend. But Magnus shakes his head and says, 'Not now.'

In this weather, the half-mile walk to the bus station takes forty minutes. The pavements are compacted with snow, so I have to drag my bag down the middle of the road. By the time I get on the bus, my face is raw with tears. I crawl onto my seat, curl up under my coat and try to sleep. On the way across the mountains, I catch my first ever glimpse of the northern lights.

#

The next three days are hellish, but I restrain myself from telephoning Magnus. *Absence makes the heart grow fonder,* my mother always said. I must make him miss me. In a box under my bed there's a box of UK stuff, with my old mobile phone in it. It's the first time I've looked at it in months, because I never got round to buying a local SIM card. On my knees beside the bed, I switch it on. The little screen turns blue; the welcome tune hums. I scroll through the phonebook to Tim's number and sit looking at it for a long time. His name on the screen comforts me. There's probably a few pence left in the phone. I might hear a few seconds of his voice, and he'd probably call me right back. But I can't call. I'm too ashamed. Several times I almost press the green button and stop myself. I'll never hear the end of it if I tell him what's going on. Tim hates Magnus with a passion, even if he never admitted it to me. It comes from the heart, though. I know he's just looking out for me, and that makes it worse in a way, because so far he's been 100 per cent right. No. I'll show him. Maintain radio silence. When things with Magnus are fixed, I'll be glad I didn't jump ship.

#

On Wednesday, Hans is not at the shop. After I have made the coffee and swept the floor and cleaned the windows, I go to the sofa, where Lina sits in between customers. She does not look up as I sit beside her. For a while I pretend to be looking out of the window. Then I glance at her copy of *Se og Hør*, but the photographs are all of Norwegian celebrities and I don't recognise anyone except the princess, Mette-Marit.

'What?' sighs Lina.

My eyes shoot to her face. But she doesn't look pissed off.

'Um, can I ask something? About Hans?'

The muscles around Lina's mouth harden. But she says, 'Okay.'

'It's just . . . he seems so rich. With that big house, and the car, and the clothes . . . And this shop is . . . well . . . not exactly *busy*. So I was wondering where he gets all that money from?'

Silence follows my question. Thick, substantial silence. For a split second, Lina's eyes film with moisture. Then she puts her magazine on the floor and makes a big show of picking a tangle out of her hair. With her back to me, she mumbles something about a new shampoo. I watch until it becomes clear she won't turn back. Then I touch her arm.

'Lina. Please. This is important.'

'What is?'

'I . . . heard something. About Hans. And I just need to know . . .'

Lina's face is red now. She smoothes her fringe back with one hand and blinks her eyes at the ceiling.

'I tried to warn you,' she whispers.

'About what?'

'Him.'

Silence descends again. I stare at Lina, bursting with questions but afraid to ask the wrong ones.

'The girl before you . . .' starts Lina. She stops and looks around. The shop is empty. 'We shouldn't be talking about this,' she whispers, and vigorously rubs her eyes.

'Is he *dangerous*?' I ask, feeling ridiculous to say the words out loud. But Lina is on her feet now and heading for the door. I watch through the window as she lights a cigarette. By the time I join her, her face is back to normal. I accept a cigarette, and we sit down on the kerb. It feels good to smoke something decent instead of the cheap shit I've been relegated to.

'"Hans" is not a normal man,' says Lina. She does not speak his name, only mouths it, and even then she takes a good look round for eavesdroppers. 'But you're okay, for now. He is always shy with new ones.'

Before this afternoon, that statement would have made me laugh. Hans is so brash, it's hard to imagine he could ever be shy. But I don't feel like laughing now. In my mind, I picture Hans smashing Sølvi in the face. Then I picture the flimsy lock on my apartment door. I shiver.

'I *live* with him . . .' I say.

Lina turns to face me. Her eyes are dry now, and very serious. It's the same look she's been wearing for months. The one I had mistaken for snottiness.

'Listen,' she says. 'Bring your passport to the shop. I will hide it for you.'

I stare at her.

'Why? Do you think he'd take it?'

She brushes her hands through her hair again.

'Has he done it before?'

Lina folds her hands and looks at the floor.

'You'll be okay,' she says. 'You have your man to protect you.'

This time it is my turn to be silent. For a while, I look at the floor too. Then, faintly, I reply, 'Yeah.'

#

Summertime wraps around me like a bubble, and as the days flick past I allow my routines to numb me further. My sleep pattern grows ever more erratic, and some nights I don't sleep at all. On those occasions I go outside and walk down the track to the farm. By now the wheat is almost head-height. I pick my way to the middle of the field, lie on my back and sing my lullaby to the stars. Animals come close sometimes, when I'm lying there. I hear their legs swishing through the crop, their voices calling to each other. It scared me a lot, in the beginning.

My telephone calls with Magnus grow shorter as my depression grows. It's hard to think of nice things to talk about, because the only bright point of my life here is the growing friendship with Lina, and at my most paranoid moments even that is thrown into doubt. Day after day, I pray Magnus will tire of Mathilde. That he'll forget the parts of me he does not love and come down here to save me.

'It's in my genes,' I tell Magnus when he tells me to cheer the fuck up.

240

'Faen i helvete! Stop blaming other people! You're the one in control.'

'But I'm not in control,' I wobble.

'How can I love you when you can't love yourself?'

'It's not like I can choose! I need a doctor!'

'Then get one!'

'I've told you why I can't—'

Magnus sighs loudly. 'Call when you're feeling better,' he says, and hangs up.

#

As the days become hotter, it gets hard to concentrate on anything. At work, I perform the tasks required of me, at lunchtime I eat the sandwiches Lina puts into my hand, and in the evenings I walk home. The weather is gorgeous, without a cloud in the sky, and in different circumstances I might have enjoyed this. But I've lost the ability to enjoy anything. Day after day, a little more hope dribbles out of me, and my participation in the world feels increasingly ethereal. I stop bothering with make-up, or my hair, or washing my clothes. At home, I stare at the wall while waiting for sleep to liberate me. Sleep is all I care about now. It's the only thing that makes the pain stop.

This is the longest that I've ever gone cold turkey, and it's shocked me to learn how much I need my pills. Medication has veiled me from my true self for so long, I barely recognise the monster that's festered beneath. I'm embarrassed to exist, in this unrecognisable skin. Everything is changing – my reflection in the mirror, the way I hold a spoon, my perceptions of space and sound and other people. In the night-time my mind drifts to Dad, and I shiver to realise I am turning into him. The weaknesses I had hated in him as a child. The irrational mood swings and flashes of violence. I recognise all of them in myself now. Or, at least, the potential for them. Does this mean I was wrong to hate him? That despite everything, his behaviour was justified? Maybe I'm being punished now, for the conclusions I jumped to back then. After all of it, my father has had the last laugh.

#

July 21st, 2005.

I am crying on the sofa bed when Hans lets himself into my apartment.

'What is wrong?' he blares.

I sit up, incensed by his sudden presence. Instinctively, I bring my arms up to conceal my chest. Under my vest top, I am not wearing a bra.

Hans is either high or drunk. He sends a hand towards me and hits my teacup. Off the table it goes. Over the floor. Into three perfect pieces. Hans follows it with his eyes, one beat behind. By the time he looks back at me I have retreated. His hand moves back, and I realise there is an envelope in it. On the front, my name. Recognising Mum's handwriting, I grab it.

'What is wrong?' he repeats.

'Nothing, I'm okay.'

'Do you want a line?'

'No. Thank you.'

'When your husband coming, Katty?'

'He's not coming any more.'

'Oh. That is why you crying?'

'I'm not crying. I'm okay.'

Hans drops his plank of an arm round my shoulder.

'Have a line. You can have a line. Do you want some?'

Wiping his nose, he reaches in his pocket. But I've already escaped his grip. Rushing to the kettle, I try to busy myself. What do I do? I can't ask him to leave. If I offer him coffee, he'll stay longer . . .

Hans snorts in my ear, and I realise he's followed me across the room.

'Have a bit,' he says. 'Get a bit.'

I look at the wrap of white powder in his hand. He jabs my arm with it.

'No thanks. I'm really tired. It'll keep me awake.'

'Come up to drink with me,' he says. 'I have beers.'

'No. Really. Thanks. But I'm going to go to sleep now.'

Hans sways, and for a moment his brow darkens. But all he says is, 'Well I party alone.'

I hold my breath as he walks to the door.

'You make him come live here,' he shouts over his shoulder. 'You have rent to pay. Thirty thousand kroner.'

The smile freezes on my face.

'Rent? I thought—'

'Five months. Thirty thousand. No time to visit your husband. You will not leave. Not to your mother. Not to nowhere.'

Panic streams through my veins, but somehow I manage a nod. Hans swings round and starts to climb the stairs. I daren't close my door until I hear his TV come on. Only then do I look down and see Mum's letter has already been opened.

Fuck!

I rip the letter out of the envelope and scan it for sensitive information. But aside from the return address, it's clean.

Thank God my mum leads such a mundane life, and thank God she doesn't know the truth about Magnus. If Hans knew I was alone, I dread to imagine what he'd do.

23

Sunday.

The weather is dreadful, which immediately puts me in a bad mood. I'd had such strong visions of how today would look. The clouds should have been high and fluffy. The bay should have been calm as glass and airbrushed in a hundred tones of sepia. Clad in black, we would gather on the sun-warmed deck and hang our heads for Mary. I'd throw a single white flower an' then we'd head for home. It would be warm-hearted and dignified and serene.

But no. It's not going to go that way at all. The sun has been eaten by a dense fog. The sea not even visible. And a lusty rain jibbers round the house, spittin' mouthfuls at the glass. Enraged, I clutch the windowsill.

Half past nine, the clock says. Another blast punches the window, and angrily I punch back. But I'd forgotten my injured wrist. Shrieking, I recoil. The fight goes out of me and I crumple to the floor.

At twelve o'clock people gather in the hallway. When I peer over the banister I see they're wearing raincoats. I look down at my dress, which was loaned from Mrs Laird's niece. The colour is perfect – a dark, bluish sort of grey – and I don't want to hide it under my yellow cagoule. What kind of funeral party is this? Dumb, rainbow-coloured freaks. But I'll never get away with being the odd one out, so I take my cagoule from the wardrobe and join the others downstairs. Mrs Laird appears and starts to count heads.

'One . . . two . . . three . . .' she says.

It feels horrible to know there'll be thirteen of us, an' not fifteen. Fifteen, there should have been fifteen . . .

'. . . eight . . .'

Mrs Laird taps my head. Counted, I sit down next to Mrs Bell. Unlike the others, Mrs Bell's coat is black. That makes me feel a bit better. Old ladies know how to do funerals properly.

'. . . eleven . . . twelve . . . thirteen . . . fourteen. Okay, ladies, hoods up. It's blowing a gale out there!'

Everyone starts shufflin' forwards. But I stay glued to the spot. Faces mill past me an' I search them excitedly. *Fourteen?* Is Rhona here after all? Did she have a change of—

Then I see her.

Joyce.

All of my body heat rushes out through my face. Away, away, leavin' me shaking and sick on my step. I look for Mrs Laird. What the hell's going on?

She's not supposed to be here . . . She's . . . She's not . . .

'Come on,' says Mrs Laird.

'What's . . . *she* doing here?' I manage. Halfway through the door, Joyce turns to glare at me. But it's Mrs Laird who meets her eyes. For a moment Joyce looks like she'll say something nasty, but Mrs Laird raises a hand in the air an' Joyce's mouth snaps shut. I can't stop shaking as I watch her go out the door.

'Now now, dear,' says Mrs Laird. 'It's only right that she should come.'

'Keep her *away* from me,' I splutter.

Mrs Laird rubs my back.

246

'It's okay, dearie. No one's going to hurt you.'

'It's not right . . . It's—'

'No one's going to hurt—'

'She killed Mary!'

Mrs Laird's eyes turn sharp. But all she says is, 'Shush now.'

I search my pocket for the heart-shaped counter.

I'm sorry, Mary . . . I'm so sorry . . .

Mrs Laird walks me outside, where a red minibus is waiting. The wind smacks us around as Mrs Laird struggles to open the door. Gaily-coloured figures huddle within, like people trapped in a washing machine. Suddenly another thought strikes me.

'Where's the vicar?' I ask.

'A vicar?'

'There was meant to be a vicar!'

'Oh. No, dearie. Who told you that?'

'Who'll say the prayers?'

'We will, silly.'

I stare at Mrs Laird.

'Get in,' she says.

As we pass through the perimeter gate I hold my breath. I know I've been out here before, but . . . Well, that was *before* . . . Suddenly I'm grateful for the limited visibility. The world is too big to swallow in one go.

Wind chases us down the track, pushing the bus from side to side. Caroline hunches over the wheel, an' I'm amazed she can see anything at all. The windscreen wipers slosh from side to side, shoving sheets of water to the left and right. Rusty leaves splat down and get stuck. It takes a good ten minutes to reach the sea, and during that time no one speaks to each other.

The boat is smaller than I'd expected, an' much shabbier. The name on its side is *Elspeth*, and we board her across a rough plank bridge. The skipper has to drag us across the last bit cos there's no handrail, but judging by the horror everyone greets this with, I think they'd rather just have fallen in. On board, I hear Mrs Bell asking about life jackets.

'It's okay,' Mrs Laird tells her, 'we booked in advance.'

'No, the life preservers.'

'Well, it's a cruise boat, so it's fully equipped,' says Mrs Laird. She tries to walk away, but Mrs Bell makes a fuss an' demands to have a life jacket before we leave the harbour. When it's brought out, Mrs Shaw decides she wants one too. Then Aggie, an' Muriel, an' Mrs Smith. The skipper decides to give everyone one, then, so we all end up clad in neon.

Though the wind has lessened since we left the house, it looks pretty biblical out there. We chug out of the harbour, clutching our seats like terrified puffins. Suddenly this whole idea seems like madness. Freezing sea spray blends with the rain, stinging my face as the boat enters the bigger waves. I dig my hands in my armpits and try not to be scared. This is Mary's day. Not mine.

The *Elspeth* climbs a particularly large wave, and everyone's attention shoots towards the prow. Up we go. Up. Up. Then the horizon shifts an' we crash down into a glossy black pit. I try to see the harbour over my shoulder, but the mist has closed in, an' we're alone out here.

Mrs Laird totters round with a demented smile. 'Isn't this *fun*!' she shrieks to Jess and Aggie. They agree that it is. I look away in disgust.

We travel for what seems like hours, pitching further and

further into the grey. At one point the water is full of slippery, bobbing heads, which the skipper says are seals. Then we chug past the mouth of a huge cave, and everyone reaches out to touch the rock. By the time we stop, the winds have calmed considerably. The skipper cuts the engine and the background sounds drift back. The gentler, simpler sounds, which the shrieking of the motor had hidden. I fill my lungs deeply with sea air. Water gurgles and laps. A beam of sunshine stabs the clouds.

'Gather round, ladies,' says Mrs Laird, and starts handing out the programmes. Obediently, people follow her to the front of the boat. Nobody chatters. Surprised by this orderliness, I take my copy and join them. Photocopied onto the paper is a picture of Mary's face. *M. Wishart. Rest in peace*, it says. Inside there are two prayers and the lyrics to 'All Things Bright and Beautiful'.

'Put your hands together and close your eyes,' says Mrs Laird. We do this. She clears her throat and reads out the first prayer on the programme. At one point someone sobs, and I glare across, expecting it to be Jess. But it's Mrs Bell. Good old Mrs Bell, in her black coat. She blows her nose loudly into a cloth handkerchief. Someone pats her on the shoulder, and then Mrs Laird continues. It's a very long prayer, and when it's over everyone says Amen.

Next, Joyce steps up. She tells a long, cryptic story about a child losing her way in a forest, and how the shadows she had mistaken for bears were actually cast by herself. Nobody sobs during her story, and nobody says Amen.

We sing 'All Things Bright and Beautiful' and the second prayer follows. Then Mrs Laird asks if anyone else would like to say something. She's looking at me, but I daren't raise my eyes to her gaze, so the moment passes. On the journey back to the mainland, I dwell deeply on this. Did I let Mary down?

To the portside, the clouds seem to be lifting. I rest my chin on my hands and watch. A shimmering slab of droplets hangs across the waves, neither falling nor rising. It looks like time has stopped over that small portion of the world. My heart flutters, and as it does so it seems like a vast white lid has opened above the sky. The shadow in my heart lifts with it, tugging me upwards. I turn my eyes down and circles rush out of the waves. Illuminating me like a Blackpool ballroom dancer. I breathe in deeply and taste the salt. Something in me sways. Then the bad feeling begins.

No. Please. Don't.

Everything starts going too fast. Dancing. Diving. Reflecting. I lean back. But it's too late to stop. My heartbeat rises high from my chest in a solid, rushing column, and as it spews out I must tip my head back to make way for it. My heart gasps open and the whole world plunders in. Concentrated. Reversed. All the dots, and the dark, and the ice. I see Mary's face. I see Magnus. I see my mother. I claw at my burning neck, and with a clack the weight catapults from my back. I am coming to the bright place, where I was before they pinched me back. It was the pure thing to do. Beautiful. Logical. I recognise it. Can't believe I forgot. I strain to the patterns. Stroke at my fingertips. Then the wind swoops to catch me, and I dive into the ice.

Darkness. Salt water in my mouth. I sink down. Down. Bubbles pummelling my face. I look up and see the side of the boat. So far. A cluster of heads, plastic clad. Red. Yellow. Blue. Their mouths chorus my name. Then a wave curls between us, and I go down.

#

There you are my love come run with me it's all right it's all all right and it does not hurt. Your arms are reaching, dark like pins, through the long deep hole . . . reach and reach and never touch . . . ah but closing . . . over it goes and the light slams out . . . I know you are there . . . you still listen . . . you know it and you feel my pain but you will not take credit . . . you say you love but not me enough . . . never you never did . . . know that now i know . . . i do . . . and it's all right . . .

Hi Dad . . . Oh la-di-da . . . get yourself on a plane why not? she's on life support . . . Well bring Magnus . . . well come alone . . . this is serious . . . but no why what's wrong with you . . . what kind of daughter . . . but how can i . . . how can . . . no i can't ever leave he will find . . . will find me . . . Stai-tunn Street. Eleffen Stai-tunn Street . . . see? but . . . but lots of couples . . . but . . . no Dad I can't make it . . . this is it . . . bastards just drove off . . . doctors say this is it . . . what kind of daughter are . . . he will kill me will kill me too will always find . . . lots of couples . . . can't hide . . . not anywhere in the world . . . can't . . .

She's been asking for you . . . one last time . . . pity's sake . . . come say goodbye . . .

#

I don't know which day it is, but I think I've been in bed my whole life. I watch the pink covers an' taste the tang of sedatives. Sometimes I wake full of tears an' can't remember where they came from. I watch myself from the inside, fillin' an' emptyin'. My throat stuffed with wind, then sandpaper. But I'm far below the surface now. I've stopped tryin' to join in. Instead, I focus on simple things. The patterns an' the flowers

251

an' the waning light. Sometimes arms hold me. Sometimes there are syringes. Sometimes tablets. Sometimes I shiver an' sometimes I slur.

A hobbling block fills my chest. Heavy as an anvil. I feel it – always there – draggin' my face into the pillows. I think it's the only thing holdin' me in place. Without the block I wouldn't have made it this far.

Sometimes, a woman's face. Her old eyes crinkle shut. When she comes close I smell the sea. I think the arms that embrace me are hers.

You're safe now. You had an accident. But you're all right.

There's no longer anythin' I want. I breathe, an' I look at the pink, and I feel the block. I think I used to want things. I recognise the memory. But now there are no victories or failures. In here they're not needed. The bed has become my world.

#

My first week passes painfully slowly. I spend most of it in my room, sittin' in a chair by the window. They check on me once an hour an' leave a baby monitor in here the rest of the time. The newspapers were here last week, but to Mrs Laird's credit she wouldn't let them through the gates. Fucking vultures smelled the drama an' came running. I bet the guy with the boat told 'em. Or maybe it was the coastguard.

I think it's Saturday today, cos earlier I heard singing. It's the only thing to set this day apart, since this routine took over my life. At three o'clock someone comes to change my dressings. They ask how I feel. I say fine. At five o'clock my food tray comes. I won't eat it. At nine o'clock my pills come. I swallow them. Then my evening will dissolve into a patchwork landscape, and Magnus will return to my side.

In the mornings they send someone in to 'chat', and thankfully that's mostly been Mrs Laird. I don't know why they make me talk at that time of day, when I'm still so high on the drugs. Half the time I don't even realise what I'm saying. I'll wake up in the middle of a sentence to find Mrs Laird scribblin' my words down. Maybe that's the point. Fuck it. Of *course* it's the point . . . But I don't care any more. Not in the mornings. The drugs make it hard to care . . .

#

Stop it, *you're saying*. Stop it.

Shaking me. I'm shaking anyway, all by myself. But . . . Stop it! *And you shake me again. Black shapes fall across me. Forming patterns, pathways, windows. So dark I can barely see out. My body howls, and I know I must stop. Across the room, your boys are asleep. Only metres between us. But my body is in charge now. I have never been more injured in my life, and the pain must escape from somewhere. Like a burning photograph, I curl smaller. Harder, frailer. Please, let the bed swallow me up. Eat me alive and get it over with.*

Shut up!

This time you shake me so hard my teeth clack. I gulp and fall down. Down, down, down. Past your stretching hands and the pine-clad living room. Through the black window like a bullet, and as the glass shatters around me, the whole scene switches off.

#

When I open my eyes, I can still hear Magnus singing. The

253

sound darts around me for many minutes, mocking my pain, and with growing anger I realise just how long that song has been mocking me. That nugget of suffering, veiled in the promise of love. Saint Magnus bequeathed it to me as his mother did to him, and God, how I clung to it. Night after night, drowning myself in that poisonous little coping mechanism.

But there's more to this than heartbreak. I know it, deep in my gut, and I'm dreading the day when the full truth returns. It tickles the corners of my memory, like a hair in the eye. Magnus. *Hans*. They're like performers in a play who only know their lines for the first act. I remember the beginning. My love for Magnus. My banishment to the south. I remember hating Hans. But that's as far as it goes. The worst is yet to come, and it terrifies me that I don't know what to expect. Suddenly, I feel unsafe. My stopped-clock life ready to burn down around my ears. New monsters lurk, and I must equip myself to deal with them.

Wake up, Kathy.
It's time to talk.

24

September 17th, 2005.

Lina and I are mopping the floor when the Porsche pulls up outside. 'Oh God,' says Lina as Hans stumbles out of it and bangs, shoulder first, into the glass door of the shop.

'What?'

'Drunk again,' she says, rolling her eyes. I look back at Hans. Lina disappears with the bucket of dirty water.

'Ladies!' trumpets Hans as he swaggers through the door. Arms outstretched, he makes a beeline for me. In the back room I hear Lina stifle a giggle.

'Ladies! What are your plans tonight?'

'Uh . . .'

'Well it don't matter. You both coming out to dinner. Both of you. Okay? I am paying.'

Lina sticks her head round the corner, catches my eye and makes a *shoot me* gesture. She wipes her hands on her apron and walks out, smiling, to join us. But at that exact moment, the shop door swings open and a second man walks in. Lina makes a strangled noise in the back of her throat. I turn to find her frozen, mid step. She opens her mouth, once, but no words come out.

'Kathy,' announces Hans, 'I want you to meet Kolbeinn, my business associate. Lina already knows him, don't you, Lina?'

'Actually. Katherine and me. We had, we were, already had . . . We are going to eat with. My boyfriend. In Oslo.'

My heart jumps. I shoot Lina a glance before turning back to the newcomer, who has barely moved from the doorway. Though he is not tall, he has a foreboding presence, and it's clear that – unlike Hans – he has not been drinking. His face is thin, wizened by age or harsh weather, with icy-grey, inquisitive eyes and perfectly combed white hair. His clothing is sombre, made of expensive-looking cloth, and on one hand he wears a sand-coloured driving glove.

'I'm sure Stian can wait a few hours,' he says, without lifting his eyes from Lina. I look at her too. Her throat is trembling.

'Let's go,' instructs Hans, and this time there are no protests. Like children, Lina and I are ushered into the car, and Kolbeinn roars smoothly out onto the main road.

We drive for what feels like hours. First along highways. Then down small country roads. We pass a few houses, make a right onto another highway, and follow it towards a big illuminated sign that says KRO. Kolbeinn pulls into a car park beside a cosy-looking wooden building, and we all get out.

'Eat anything you like,' blares Hans, as we sit down in a booth. Straight away he orders a double whisky on the rocks and a bottle of white wine for *jentene*. Kolbeinn orders water.

'I'm not actually very hungry,' I start, but Lina shoots me a warning glance, so I order pasta arrabbiata and hand the menu back. Everyone else gets steak. Hans fills my wine glass to the brim, then Lina's. 'All in one!' says Hans, and we clink glasses. Lina and I only manage to sink half, but Hans doesn't berate us for this. He just fills our glasses up again, and we repeat the process. I must admit, my nerves soften considerably after the first few. When they bring our food the mood is quite relaxed, and I start to wonder what all the fuss was about. My pasta is not half bad. Hans makes a joke about the antique moose head above our booth, and we all laugh. Feeling braver, I ask Kolbeinn how he knows Hans, and he replies that they ply similar trades. That he sometimes puts business Hans's way, and vice versa. 'So you have a salon too?' I ask, but this time he is busy with his steak knife and the question slips by unanswered. I take a sip of wine and tell him about the kitten Lina got me last weekend. She said it'd be good company for me, and so far I must admit it's raised my spirits. I don't tell him that bit, of course. 'It's called Bobble,' I announce, but no one raises a smile, so I go back to my pasta. This meal must be costing them a fortune. I saw the prices on the menu and the drink tab alone must be approaching a thousand kroner.

'So I hear you are not happy at your job, Lina,' says Kolbeinn, casually. Lina chokes. Her eyes flick up at him. I catch my breath.

'No. I'm happy,' she squeaks through a mouthful of food.

'Oh. What I hear is that you're planning to leave us. You and Stian and your bastard child. I heard you're going to run away, through Sweden, with a fake passport, and that Stian will send the police to pay your employers a visit. Teaching them a lesson. That is what I have heard.'

'It's not true!'

Silence rings out. Even Hans has stopped eating now. I uncross my legs, painfully slowly, and square my feet against the floor. But there's no point even trying to run. We're hemmed in. That's the whole point. It's been the point all night. I look around the room and see we're the only customers. There are no staff in sight, and no CCTV cameras.

There are tears in Lina's eyes.

'Please,' she whispers. 'I have a daughter.'

'Yes. And how old would she be now?'

'Three.'

Kolbeinn leans forward, tenting his fingers beneath his chin.

'Such precious years.'

'Please, Kolbeinn—'

'She must be missing her mother. Why don't we drive you home to her?'

Lina starts to cry. I feel the blood drain from my face.

For many moments, nobody speaks at all. I stare at the tablecloth beneath my face. Looking at the sauce stain on the edge, beside the plate. Suddenly I'm aware that Lina is on her feet. She stands up straight beside Hans, sobbing into her chest. Like me, she's wedged into the end seat, and can't get out unless Hans moves.

'I need to. Go to. The bathroom,' she stutters.

Hans's face is stony now. He is sloshed and looks uncomfortable at the escalating situation but refuses to meet Lina's eye. Instead, he looks straight across at Kolbeinn and does not budge.

'No,' announces Kolbeinn, standing up and throwing his napkin on the table. 'Let's just take you home now.'

The drive into Oslo seems to last hours, and for the whole way Lina grips my hand like a vice. At one set of traffic lights I see her looking to the side and realise she's thinking about jumping out. But there are no back doors to jump out of. Just a tiny, sturdy window. Hans makes several phone calls, in Norwegian. By the time we reach Lina's home, the sky is dim. We pull into the driveway and four men I've never seen before approach the car. Kolbeinn gets out to join them, just as the front door of the house opens, and two more men drag

258

a thinner, younger man outside. His head is covered in blood. Lina shoots up.

'Stian!' she shrieks.

The men drag Stian along the porch and lay him on his back. Lina is already out of the car and running towards the house. Through the open door, I hear a child wailing.

'No!' screams Lina, but a man pulls her back. They struggle to their knees on the lawn. One man pulls Stian's arm straight and positions it carefully against the top step. Bodies converge, blocking them from view. Then something shiny flashes through the air and a sickening crack rings out. A bellow. More commotion, a crunching sound, and after there is more noise than I can deal with.

Hans drives me home, drunk. The car swerves all over the road. On the way he makes jokes. Talks about the food at the diner, and his favourite burger chain, Tom's, which the bigger, international chains are trying to drive out of business. There is blood on his shirt and on his face. I try not to look. When I get home I grab Bobble and crawl into the bathroom. At first she lets me hug her, but when I start crying she scratches herself free. I lie down in the shower stall and hide my face. Through layers of numbness, I can hear her hissing. Tiny and useless, in the corner behind the toilet.

#

September 20th, 2005.

Hans and his 'associates' have gone on holiday. Lina and I had looked forward to the lift in atmosphere this absence would bring. But things have not turned out the way we thought. Each day, a man comes to the shop. He doesn't say anything. We don't know him. But he's clearly one of Hans's spies. All day he sits watching us, and we are too scared to make him leave. Before Stian's arms were broken, we might not have cared so much. But now we know what's at stake. Since that night, Lina and I have our conversations on paper.

It's the end of the day. Lina and I watch the man in the corner. He is short, with receding blond hair, thick-framed glasses and a Gore-Tex jacket. We call him the Duck, because of the way he purses his lips.

'Better count the money up,' says Lina, in English. Her eyes burn into me.

'All right,' I say.

The Duck gets up and approaches the desk. Lina counts out the money. The Duck watches. He looks at the final figure. Then he watches her put it in the safe. When she has finished, he leaves.

Lina and I look at each other. We look at the door. She grabs an envelope from the waste-paper basket and scrawls, *I cannot take much more of this.*

She smiles at me, with tears in her eyes. I take the pen off her and write, *The Duck is better than Hans . . .*

She takes the pen back and writes, *You are lucky. You have no children.*

I've got family.

Far away. They would never find them.

Maybe that's why they went to England!

Ha! ha! :-S

But your family's Lithuanian. You could go back there.

No. He has my passport.

I flip the envelope and write, *Would Hans really hurt your daughter?*

I don't know. Maybe.

'What the f—' I say out loud. But she widens her eyes to

260

shut me up. Then she glances over her shoulder, and writes, *It is okay. She is safe so long as I stay.*

Has he said that?

Yes.

I stare at Lina.

Tell the police! I write.

No. It is higher than that.

For a second I feel dizzy, and have to sit down.

Lina turns the envelope inside out and writes, *You will be all right. They do not know you so well. Aušra, the girl before you, Hans gave her to Kolbeinn. Business deal. But you are not same as her.*

What do you mean, gave? What does Kolbeinn do?

Sex work stuff. Illegal girls, no passports. He has business in Oslo.

I stare at Lina. She makes a face and scribbles, *You have hidden passport. You can still run.*

I'm too scared.

Can Magnus help?

I called but he was in bad mood. Said had own stuff to sort out.

You still more lucky than me. Hans not in love with you.

Lina raises her eyebrows wearily. Suddenly I feel ashamed for ever believing her situation was easier than mine.

Maybe that's why they haven't hurt you.

Hurting Stian is same thing. Same to me.

'How *is* Stian?' I ask, before remembering not to speak out loud.

It could have been worse.

My eyes glaze over. Several seconds later Lina nudges me, and shows me her reply.

I saw him last night. He will be okay.

This is insane!

261

Welcome to hell.

Let's just win the lottery. Then we can hire bodyguards!

We laugh out loud. Then Lina takes the pen back and writes, *Only way we will get out.*

I look at her. She raises her eyebrows. But our smiles have gone. I can't think of anything else to write.

'Let's get this floor clean!' announces Lina, loudly. Then she takes the envelope, carries it through the back room and flushes it down the toilet.

#

January 20th, 2006.

I'm on the track that curves round the edge of the big field. Above me, stars gleam like bullets. It is dark, this last stretch, because the street lights stop at the main road. They don't clear the snow off the track, either. Maybe they think it's not worth it. This is the end of the line. The unworthy bit. Or maybe it's because I'm the only one who ever walks it on foot. Hans, like everyone else in this area, has an SUV. A big, sleek American fucker that would be perfect for picking up his own shopping. But no. Why do that when he can send me?

My hands are burned raw from the overloaded Rimi bags. Progress is slow, because the snow in the middle is thigh-deep and the thinner parts are slicked with a perfectly smooth slab of ice. During the last hour, I've fallen more times than I can count. Suddenly I understand why old ladies are scared of walking on ice. Each step I take I'm braced for another fall, and the tension has turned into a permanent backache.

In the summer this walk was all right. I could gaze across the field and pretend I was on my holidays. The little wooden farmhouse looked enchanting. The contrasting gables and the vintage stabbur. Now the darkness is so complete I can't see any of it. I still describe it nicely to my mother, though. She loves to hear about that.

'Tell Magnus I say hello!' she said during our Christmas phone call, and I told her that I would. She still thinks I'm living the dream, up north. The truth would break her heart. I'm not even sure what the truth *is*, to be honest, or how I'd explain it to another person. Humiliation has been a big factor in keeping this clusterfuck under wraps. God knows my mother's had enough worry to last a lifetime, and I don't want to add to that. To keep her happy, I reeled off a description of Lina's Christmas dinner, despite the stumbling block that Lithuanian Christmas food is different to Norwegian. Not that my mum noticed. Her voice was so smiley I could almost see her face over the phone. She didn't mention my dad and I didn't ask about him. She sounded content, though, which surprised me, as always. It had always stunned me that she never left him. *I* certainly got out as soon as I could.

My feet start sliding around, so I pick my way to the verge and grab the fence. Here, I remove a mitten and try to rub some life back into my hand. But the shopping bag I'd laid down makes a squeaky sound and slides away. I reach out for it and lose my balance. The ice rushes from my feet and I slam down, hard, onto my left hip. For a second the pain takes my breath away. Through the dark, I hear the Rimi bag still slithering downhill. It's too dark to see if anything has rolled out of the bag. Fuck. Hans will be furious if anything's missing. I clamber downhill on my hands and knees, fling myself forwards and intercept it. My mittens are full of snow. I slide to a stop.

This is insane. This is officially insane. Where did my

self-respect go? The old me would have been horrified by this subservience. But at least I'm not the only one in this situation. I've seen how Lina shrinks from Hans when he enters a room. Maybe that's why the fight has gone out of me. I'm coming to wonder if it's normal for men to treat women this way and if *I'm* the strange one for expecting anything different. Is Magnus's treatment of me normal too? He's reduced me to the level of a performing dog. *Yes sir, no sir, I'll smile nicely and wiggle my arse for you, sir. Yes, go fuck those other girls till I come up to your standards.* Christ, even his lullaby has attached itself to me. That nasty little symbol of everything he's reduced me to. How I hate it. Yet in moments of fear, I still find myself singing it. It will probably follow me to the grave.

Close by, something shuffles through the undergrowth. I freeze. Was that on *this* side of the fence? It sounded big. Big enough to attack me. I try to remember if any dangerous animals live in this country and for some reason my mind settles on badgers. Aren't they meant to be aggressive? Fuck ... Håkon said there are *wolverines* in Norway ... Do they attack people? I don't know what wolverines looks like, but I'm sure they've got lots of teeth.

Stop it. Stop pissing about.

My knees feel like they've been slashed open. Clutching the shopping bag, I use the fence to drag myself uphill. In less than a minute, I reach the second, escaped bag. Okay. I drag myself upright and negotiate two slippery footholds.

When I reach my building I cringe to find the motion-triggered porch light on. Has Hans been out here, looking for me? Is he angry I took so long? As I place my foot on the first step, a clatter makes my heart jump. Then four deer scramble round the veranda and hurdle the balcony, into the trees.

Thank God. Only deer. The trees crack and crash as the deer go, marking their escape route. Downhill to the field, near the place where I buried my passport. My eyes fill with tears as the sounds grow fainter, and suddenly I realise I want nothing more than to run away with them. My legs shiver. The porch light blinks off.

As I enter the vestibule, my door is unusually quiet. It's so warm in here. My face aches as the heat wakes it up, but it's a good ache. The ache means I am safe again. It means I made it.

I don't want to see Hans. Just the thought of him gives me the creeps. Couldn't I just leave his shopping *here*? He's bound to come downstairs eventually, and find it outside his door. If I leave a note, and put the frozen stuff outside . . .

Fuck it. I don't care any more. That's what I'm going to do. I'll tell him I tried knocking.

I leave the shopping bags where they are and unlock the door to my apartment. There's a pen by my bed. The sooner this is done with the better.

'Bob?' I whisper.

She's usually running round my ankles by now.

'Bobble?'

Closing the door behind me, I flick on the light. The room looks normal. Just the same as when I left. Confused, I walk around the apartment. As usual, the bathroom door is closed. I look under the bed. Bobble is not there. I look *in* the bed. She is not there. I look in the wardrobe. I look in the bathroom. Not there.

'Bob?'

Where the fuck . . .

I check the windows, but they're closed. I check everywhere for a second time. And a third time. And a fourth. I

265

start to run faster. I even look in the microwave. Nothing. Maybe she's sick. Don't cats crawl away and hide when they know they're going to die? I hover round Bob's feeding bowl and scan it for clues. She might have swallowed a pebble or a bit of plastic. Or maybe she finally had a reaction to the chamomile. Since Hans had that rant about the noise she makes, I've been putting it in her food. But there's no sign of anything unusual.

Heart thudding, I rush outside. The porch light clicks on as I tumble down the steps. I look left. I look right. I look at the trees. I look back at the hallway. Nothing. Around me, the undergrowth is black. I wade from the path and stand waist-deep in snow, looking up at the house. But the first-floor lights are off. On the steps, the only footprints are my own. Hans hasn't been here since the last snowfall.

'Bob?!' I shriek. 'Bobble!'

I climb back up and check the veranda for paw prints, but the deer left such disarray in their wake that it's hard to tell. In the end, all I can do is go inside. I take the kitchen knife from under my pillow and sit on the floor for a long time. When Hans's car roars onto the driveway, I lock myself in the bathroom.

25

I wake to find Mrs Laird there. Confused, I look at the wall clock. It says ten past four. The room is dim.

'What do you . . . want?' I ask. It irritates me that I can't get this out in one breath.

'How are you, dearie?'

'What do you . . . want?'

'You have a visitor.'

I stiffen. Maybe Rhona's back. But wouldn't she just come right in?

'Who?'

'Normally we wouldn't allow this sort of thing. But in this case we thought it might be good for you.'

Mrs Laird smiles. Her wrinkles deepen, lit up by the weakening daylight.

'Good for me, how?'

'It's someone you've met before, love. It's . . . Well, it's Coral . . .'

'What? Caroline?'

'No. Coral. Remember your wee friend Coral? With the swing?'

My mouth drops open.

'So,' says Mrs Laird, 'shall I send her in?'

'How do you know . . . it's her?' I gasp.

'Why don't you talk to her for yourself?' says Mrs Laird.

My stomach does a little jump, as I realise how terrified I

am of speaking to an outsider. A real adult from the real world. I feel my cheeks flush. How much have they told Coral? What must she think of me?

'I don't—'

'Come on. She's a very nice lady. I'll be right down the hall if you need me.'

'Do I have to?'

Mrs Laird sighs. 'She's been travelling all day. We can't very well send her away now, can we?'

I look down at my hands.

'Okay,' I mumble.

'Good girl,' says Mrs Laird.

#

The woman pauses in the doorway, but I sense this is merely through politeness. She is freckled and pretty, with tidy brown hair and a tweed overcoat. A bobbly wooden necklace flatters her perfectly sculpted collarbones, and her manicured hands clutch a tan leather satchel. She looks fit and confident and much older than me, though I know that if it's really her, this isn't true. Coral was one year my junior.

'Coral?'

'*My God*, Kathy. Is that really you?'

I nod.

A lovely smile breaks across the woman's face, and then I know for sure. She runs across the room and squeezes me so hard that my spine cracks.

'They told me you were here,' she gasps. 'I had to come.'

'Who . . . told . . .'

She pushes her fringe out of her eyes and beams at me.

'Your hair,' I say. 'It used to be red.'

'Aye, well. You know. I dye it.'

'It really *is* you,' I wheeze. Then my emotions gain control and I have to take a moment.

Coral sits on the edge of the bed.

'Do you . . . still live on . . . the farm?' I ask, as I struggle to get my breath back.

'No. Oh dear me, no . . . We moved to Edinburgh when I was nine. And I've been in France since my PhD.'

'So what are you doing . . . up here?'

'Oh, just a wee holiday. I've been showing my fiancé where I grew up. He's from Paris, you know. This place is like the moon to him.'

'But . . . how did you know . . . it was me . . .'

'The people at Jack's old croft! They said some woman phoned up, saying the Lullaby Girl might've used the holiday annex once. Then they said *Katherine* and I just—'

'Oh . . . Yeah . . . They call me Lullaby—'

'I know! They showed me your picture in the paper! I recognised you right off!'

'The paper?'

'You were in the newspaper. Didn't you know?'

'What did it say?' I gulp.

'That you'd been dragged out of the loch . . . for a second time. You're really a celebrity round here, huh?'

'Different loch,' I mumble, but Coral doesn't seem to take this in. Her smile fades away as she watches me.

'What *happened* to you, Kathy?' she asks. 'How did you end up here?'

I laugh bitterly, and this makes me cough.

'Well. That's the big question . . . isn't it?'

Coral presses her hands between her knees and looks at the floor.

'What about your parents?' she asks. 'Don't they know you're here?'

'I don't know . . . They haven't been able . . . to find them . . .'

'Why don't you just call them?'

'I don't know . . . the number.'

An awkward silence. Coral scratches her nose.

'Coral?' I ask.

'Yes?'

'What was my . . . mother like?'

She shoots me a glance before returning her eyes to her lap. 'Ach, Kathy. I was just a bairn . . . She had dark hair, that's all I remember.'

'My father . . .'

At this, Coral's jaw clenches. She swallows hard. Then, in a quieter voice, she replies, 'He was dark-haired too.'

'Do you know my . . . second name?'

'Wow, you really are the *mystery girl*, aren't you?'

'Do you?'

Coral shakes her head. 'I guess the McLennans would've had it in the visitors' book. But hell, they were really old . . . I doubt they'd still be alive . . .'

I suck air into my lungs. Then I say, 'Coral . . . About that last summer . . .'

Her head darts upwards, and with a little tremor, her eyes fill up. It takes several seconds for her to answer.

'You mean . . . your dad?'

'You remember?'

'Heavens! The game? How could I ever—'

I catch hold of her arm. 'We were kids,' I wheeze. 'It wasn't . . . our fault.'

Coral brings her hand up to her mouth and shoots me a

glance from behind her thumb. For a moment, she looks eight years old again. I find myself checking her face for scars.

'How come you remember that,' she says, 'if you don't remember the rest?'

'I don't know . . . I think I always remembered . . . But . . . hearing your voice now . . . I just . . . It just came . . . out.'

'I never told my mum, you know,' says Coral. 'I said I hit my head in the barn.'

'Why didn't you . . . tell her?'

'I don't know. Maybe the same reason you didn't stop him. I figured we'd deserved it. Like, two girls playing doctor and nurse isn't exactly normal . . .'

I put my head in my hands. 'I wanted to stop him . . . But he was so big . . . He was my dad . . .'

'Well,' she mumbles. 'It's in the past now.'

I look at her, and in my mind I see it all over again.

'In the . . . corner . . . He shook you . . . so hard . . . There was so . . . much blood . . .'

Coral wipes her eyes. 'I'm sure he didn't mean for me to fall,' she says.

'Did it scar?'

'Yeah. But it's faded a lot.' Coral lays a hand on her temple but does not lift the thick fringe of hair that covers it.

'I should have . . . stopped him . . .'

'It's in the past.'

'Did you . . . hate me?'

Coral snorts. 'Do you really think I'd have come here if I hated you?'

Suddenly I feel extremely tired. Hugging my knees to my chest, I pull the bedcovers round my shoulders. I think I am going to cry and hate to think Coral might see this. For a moment the room wafts away from me.

271

'You must really . . . think I'm . . . a freak,' I whisper.

'You've had a bad time of things. That's all . . .'

Outside, the wind screams.

'How . . . old . . . are you?' I ask.

Coral doesn't answer straight away. I feel her turn around but can't see her face from here.

'Are you serious?'

I try to nod my head.

'Twenty-six.'

'Oh . . .'

'Why?'

'I'm older . . . than you . . . aren't I?'

'I don't know. I think so. Maybe . . .'

I sigh. The first tear rolls down my face now, and I'm glad Coral cannot see it.

'Funny how . . . things go,' I gasp. 'Huh?'

'Aye,' sighs Coral. 'Aye. It sure is . . .'

\#

Mrs Laird is overjoyed by Coral's visit and says it's the first stepping stone to recovering my past. On Monday she'll drive north to the McLennans' croft, and after that it's only a matter of time before they track down my family. No one has asked my permission to do this. They're all so excited. Gambolling from clue to clue like children on an Easter egg hunt. And the grand prize is that they get to get rid of me.

Several hours after Coral's departure, I hear another car. I go to the window and see Mrs Laird ushering Dr Harrison to the house. Their arms are stacked with paper files. Dr Harrison glances at my window. Then they pass behind the clematis and out of sight.

At nine o'clock Caroline brings my pills.

'Is Dr Harrison here?' I ask, but she just says, 'Get some sleep.'

'I thought I saw . . . Dr Harrison . . .'

'Oh?'

I can tell I won't get any straight answers tonight, but this does not put me in a bad mood. Dr Harrison is here, and unlike the others she might actually listen to me.

'Did you brush your teeth?' asks Caroline when I have swallowed all the pills.

I shake my head.

'Come on then, best do it quick!'

She hovers behind me as I stand at the sink. These pills act quickly. Suddenly it gets hard to push my toothbrush around my mouth. By the time I'm done, the room has turned psychedelic. I think I hear my voice talking, or crying. I'm not quite sure how I get back to bed.

#

When I stir, I am still clutching my toothbrush. Shocked by this alien presence, I jerk backwards and the brush tumbles away. With fuzzy dismay, I hear it skid into the dust. My right palm stings. I touch it with my other hand and find a wavy pattern etched there.

My face hurts, like I've spent hours hanging upside down. For a long time I lie here, opening and closing my eyes. My brain is full of blood, and too heavy to lift from the pillow.

I recognise this. It's a drug hangover. But I'm puzzled, because I don't think I took more than my usual dose. Wait. No. I didn't eat much yesterday. That explains it . . .

The clouds move peacefully. Steadily. It's no wonder

273

people imagine heaven as being in the clouds. I wouldn't mind hanging around up there all day.

There's a picture in my head today of a tiny, messy room bathed in sunlight. I'm there, sitting on a wooden floor, and somehow I know I've been there lots of times before. There's a blond man next to me, and he is not Magnus. Dried paint stuck in patches up his forearm, blended on his hand, spattered in his hair. He turns to me, clutching a brush and looks like he's telling a joke. His eyes are wild, but I feel safe. Narrow, twisting stairs, with crates of records on each step. Laughing like drains, we carry a pizza up to the light. Turpentine. Rags. Canvas. That face . . . I know it. A name tickles my brain, too vague to touch . . . Ka . . . ? Sa . . . ? Ti . . . ?

Somebody knocks. I stiffen.

'Kathy! My hands are full. Can you open the door?'

Whose voice is that? If I pretend I'm asleep, will they go away?

'Kathy!' repeats the voice.

Is that Mrs Laird? Caroline?

A bump, followed by a clatter. Someone swears under their breath. Then the handle squeaks and the door flies open. If I'd been more alert I'd have pretended to be asleep, but in my present condition I am too slow. Dr Harrison stands in the doorway, beaming.

'Well, good *morning*!' she clucks. She stumbles towards the bed, carrying a massive two-handled tray. The crockery rattles boisterously. My eyes widen.

'Morning. Afternoon. What's the difference?' winks Dr Harrison as she sets the tray on the nightstand. 'There! A nice breakfast. Get the day off to a good start. I made you a smoothie with my own fair hands. Chock-full of vitamins! And there's toast, and jam, and honey from my local—'

'I don't . . . usually . . . eat . . .'

'Everyone needs a good breakfast,' she says as she shakes out a napkin. 'Come on, sit up! Your egg's getting cold.'

What is this obsession they have with eggs? I think as I push myself upright. Dr Harrison tucks a napkin into my collar.

'I heard you took a tumble into the loch. Are you all right?'

'Yes.'

'Shall we have a nice chat later?'

'I don't know.'

'Good. Well, tuck in and we'll get started in an hour.'

Dr Harrison glides to the door. I look at the tray, which is packed with enough food to feed an elephant.

#

Caroline arrives to dress me. This is the first time I have worn day clothes since the accident, so it is also the first time I have had to endure this.

'I *can* do this myself,' I say.

'Of course you can,' mutters Caroline, without looking at me, and this makes me flinch, because her tone of voice turns the phrase into *Of course you can't*.

'Why do I still have to take . . . all these bloody . . . *pills*?' I ask, with effort. My bottom lip feels absolutely massive. I can feel the blood pumping through it.

'You know why,' says Caroline as she pulls my socks on.

'No, I don't . . . Why don't . . . you . . . tell me?'

'Don't be difficult, Kathy. Not today.'

I glare at Caroline. She starts putting my arms into my cardigan. I detest being this weak. It wasn't so noticeable when I

275

spent all my days in bed. But my God, this is awful . . . Caroline fastens my top button and starts fiddling with my hair. I scowl and swoon under the force of her hands. When she's finished she thumbs something off my cheek and stands back.

'Pretty as a picture. Ready to go?'

I glare at her. Without waiting for an answer, Caroline puts my arm round her neck. She heaves, and we topple to the right. My feet feel like they're cut from paper. Caroline grunts to a stop. Tries again. Staggers to the left.

Jesus!

Caroline seems as amazed as me. She hauls me further over her shoulder, and I dangle there like a Santa sack. I want to ask what the fuck they've drugged me with, but my mouth won't even form the words. Cold flushes trickle down my neck, and my eyes flutter shut against the light. Caroline takes another step, swears and lays me back onto the bed. I stare at her, aghast. The light moves fast around her head, making her look like a huge, pouncing animal.

'Okay,' she pants. 'Okay . . . Let me think . . .'

'Don't . . . hurt . . . me.'

'I'm not gonna *hurt* you!'

The light bulb cuts the air into patterns. My vision shivers.

'I don't . . . feel . . .'

Caroline lays the back of her hand on my forehead.

'Huh. You're very cold.'

I swallow and close my eyes against the light. My heart is fluttering in my throat. I can't control it.

'Kathy? Kathy!'

What did you give her?

I didn't give her anything!

What did you do?

276

Nothing! She just . . .
She's already had forty milligrams!
I didn't . . .
Hey . . . hey . . . look . . . look!
Kathy!
Katherine!

I fall into a cluster of white. Faces. Talking. Mouths. I gasp, cough, and my eyes go wide. Then the mouths hit full volume and I am plastered back onto my pillow. I am in my best clothes. Skin saturated. Stinking of sweat. Someone fighting with my buttons.

'What?'

'Katherine! Thank God!'

Mrs Laird.

'What's . . . going on?'

Mrs Laird drags my arms out of my cardigan. I flop from the sleeves, hot and patchy. Ice-cold, hot, cold . . . I lie here and try to breathe. Someone is fanning my face. But it's no good now. It just makes me cold. I start to tremble. I don't understand. Voices are jabbing.

It's okay . . . I think it's okay . . . I think it's just shock . . .
Shock from what?
I don't know. Delayed shock . . . from the loch . . .
Don't be absurd! It's been a week!
You didn't give her more than the usual dose?
What did she eat? Has she eaten anything different?
I gave her breakfast.
What? You're not supposed . . .
I thought . . .
She's on a strict hypoglycaemic diet!
What? She wasn't on that last time I was here!
It started right before you left. We were trying to keep her stable.

Oh . . . Oh no . . . I'm sorry!

What were you thinking?

I didn't know!

What kind of breakfast?

I don't know . . . toast . . . honey . . . eggs.

Did she eat the honey?

I . . . I think so . . .

(sighing)

Oh blazes, I made her a smoothie too . . . With the last of the bananas . . .

(sighs)

(more sighs)

(muttering)

Well, the worst is over. The sugar spike set her off . . . but . . .

I'll stay and keep an eye on her.

I'm so sorry . . .

Just ask next time, will you? You have to ask . . .

(sighing)

I'm sorry . . .

#

Everyone is angry with Dr Harrison except me. We are the bad guys. It feels good not to be the only one. She sneaks up to apologise for yesterday. 'It's okay,' I tell her, 'it wasn't your fault.'

We talk quietly. Dr Harrison asks if I was trying to commit suicide when I jumped into the loch last week. I actually hadn't considered this, and need a moment to decide.

'No,' I tell her.

Dr Harrison seems pleased.

'Have you told them that?'

278

I shake my head. She urges me to tell them, because it's the main reason they've got me so drugged up. I'm on suicide watch, she says. It's the reason she came down here so fast.

'Mm hmm,' I reply. I have no intention of doing this, though.

'I'll try to get us a session tomorrow,' says Dr Harrison. 'I think I can convince them. As long as I don't try to feed you again.'

We smile. She gets up.

'Okay,' I say.

Dr Harrison pauses at the door and presses her forehead to the door frame. When she speaks, her face is deadly serious.

'Do you trust me, Katherine?'

Cautiously, I nod. It seems like the best option.

'You see, there's something that's been puzzling me,' she continues. 'Something that's written in your file.'

I sit up straight.

'It's about Magnus. I'm sorry. I know you don't like to talk about that. But I need to know. What kind of accent did he have?'

I stare at Dr Harrison.

'He's from . . . Norway,' I reply.

'So he had a Norwegian accent?'

'Well . . . yeah.'

'You're positive of this?'

'Yes.'

Dr Harrison looks at her feet. She looks through the open door. Then she steps back inside, closes the door behind her and comes to sit on the bed.

'A man called the police hotline,' she says, quietly. 'The same day you were found.'

I swallow. Dr Harrison's eyes are harder now. More careful.

'What did he say?' I whisper.

Dr Harrison looks me in the eye for a second. Then looks away, as if regretting opening this can of worms.

'He said . . . Well, he asked if you were still alive, and he called you Katherine. The police asked how he knew your name, because that information hadn't been released yet, and he wouldn't answer. He asked where you were being held, and when they wouldn't tell him he got angry. He said to tell you he'll be waiting. And he said these weird words. They tried to keep him on the line, of course, but he hung up. He was the only lead, back then. The only lead they ever had . . .'

I stiffen against the headboard. Suddenly my whole body feels like stone.

Hans . . .

'What were the weird words?' I ask.

Dr Harrison shakes her head. 'It wasn't any language I'm familiar with.'

A little sob escapes me. Dr Harrison shoots a hand out and puts it on my arm.

'Look, I'm not saying this to scare you,' she says. 'You're safe here, no matter what. But it would help us a great deal if you could tell us who that man was. You've been remembering things in therapy, and—'

'It wouldn't do any good,' I whisper. Suddenly my plan to come clean about my past seems laughably naïve. Talking about my ex is one thing. But *Hans* is another completely.

'You're *safe* here,' repeats Dr Harrison.

But this time I cannot find the words to answer. All I can do is shake my head.

26

March 10th, 2006.

A rustle in the dark stirs me out of sleep, and I open my eyes. For a moment, all is still. A faint glow comes from behind the curtains, indicating that the porch light is on. Then a shape moves across it – a shape that is in the room with me – and approaches the bed. I rocket backwards. Forgetting the knife. The shape comes closer.

'Katty?'

I scream. Then the shape moves faster and a familiar voice says, 'Kathy! It's me! It's me!'

'Jesus fucking Christ . . .'

I flump back down and click the lamp on.

'Magnus, what are you doing here? How did you get in?'

'Door was unlocked. Can I get in the bed? It's freezing.'

I wipe the sleep from my eyes. 'What time is it?'

'Six thirty.'

'What the fuck!'

He flops into bed, reeking of alcohol.

'Me and Mathilde had a fight,' he says in a broken voice. There are tears in his eyes. He tries to put his arms around me, and before shaking him off I realise he is trembling.

'So?'

'I came to see you.' Then, in a bitter, fake-happy tone: 'I brought party snacks!'

He jerks an arm sideways, to indicate a bottle of aquavit in the middle of the floor. Or rather, two-thirds of a bottle. I can only assume the rest of it is inside him. For a moment I am speechless. Magnus sways closer, almost headbutting me in the process, and folds me in his arms.

'Warm me up,' he blurts, and sinks coldly into me. Time drifts, and despite my shock at this situation I am thrilled to be close to him again. Almost as if the last year never happened.

'I'm sorry,' he whispers into my neck. 'I'm sorry. I'm sorry.'

I lie here awhile – Magnus sprawled on me like an octopus – my eyes flicking round the ceiling. Then he whispers 'I love you' and an angry lump rises in my throat. Unlike me, he has not spent the last three hundred nights alone. There's a different woman for him to curl up with, and he probably tells her those words every night. I think of him lying in bed with Mathilde. Stroking her face. Kissing her. Fucking her. Suddenly, this is all I can think of. I look into his scrunched-up face and feel that curious blend of rage and love. Then my eyes wander sideways and fix on his jacket, which lies draped on the kitchen counter. It's the only item he seems to have brought, besides the alcohol. I imagine shredding that jacket with the knife beneath my pillow. So close to my hand. How long would it take for me to snatch it and get across the room? I think I could make it before he stopped me. Then I'd throw him out. Fucking parasite. Out of my bed. Out of my life. Back to Mathilde.

No.

Fucking lunatic. How can you think such things? Stop it.

I look at Magnus. The long black eyelashes. The cheekbones. That perfect, photogenic symmetry.

Look at him. Look at *me*! It's a wonder he came to visit at all.

Mathilde is the mother of his children. His first true love. Her eyes are clear turquoise and untarnished by failure. The world is hers. Magnus is hers. It's all fucking hers.

But I'm still here. I'm still here . . .

I drift sadly, wondering what to do, and cannot come up with an answer. Magnus snores snottily. Eventually I close my eyes.

#

I wake with a bitterness on my lips. The clock says 4 p.m., but that can't possibly be right. My limbs are like lead, and my head even heavier. What happened? Strange visions crowd me, of Magnus showing up at my bedside. Of crying in the dark, and gritty-tasting water. Hauling myself outside, I find Magnus smoking on the veranda. In the snow, he has made a pile of cigarette butts. Dirty, grey, smoked down to the filters. When he sees me he takes a last, long drag and crushes the butt with his unlaced boot. His eyes are red. Part of me wants to hug him. Another part still wants to hit him. He hunches there, dead-faced, and stares at me as if he has no idea who I am.

'Hangover?' I ask, neutrally.

'I shouldn't have come here,' he says, almost as if to himself, and his Adam's apple bobs.

'Why did you come?'

'I had to,' he says. A pause, then, 'I had to see you.'

'You're a bit late,' I jab.

But he doesn't rise to this. Instead he takes out a fresh cigarette, lights it with a cooking match and takes a slow, squinting drag.

'I still love you, you know,' he says, without looking at me. 'I always will.'

'You're going back to her. Aren't you?'

He looks at me silently, blows out a cloud of smoke, and nods.

'The kids,' he says, and with these words a fat tear wobbles down his face. Behind him, dusk is already well underway. As we stand here the porch light blinks off and the snowy garden's glow takes over, like a smooth, elegant ghost. Since last night, a fresh topcoat has fallen. We stand side by side and look at it.

'Things are not good here, Magnus. I won't stick around much longer.'

He turns sharply.

'What do you mean?'

'I tried to tell you on the phone.' I look behind me and lower my voice. 'It's not *safe* here . . .'

Magnus looks hard into my face, and for a second I think I detect concern. Then he tips his head back and says, scornfully, 'Are you still talking about *that*?'

'I can't take it any more. I'm going back.'

'Back?'

'To the UK.'

'When?'

'I don't know. In a few days. Maybe a week.'

'You can't!'

'Why not? You're already back with Mathilde. There's nothing left for me here. Even Bobble's gone.'

'Bobble?'

'Fucksake, Magnus. I told you a hundred times. My cat.' I look over my shoulder and hiss, 'I think *he* did something to her.'

'Don't be stupid!'

'Shhhh!' I stuff my hand to Magnus's mouth. But he takes

this opportunity to throw both arms around my waist and pulls me to him.

'Don't go,' he croons.

'Are you crazy?'

'I love you,' he sobs into my neck. 'You've got to believe me . . .'

I hang in his arms, confused by these mixed signals. I want to hit him and get angry. To tell him there's not a chance in hell. That he blew his chance with me a long time ago. But it's no good. I can't extinguish that flame.

'You're killing me,' I gasp.

He buries his face deep in my hair, and together we sway in the darkening twilight. Tears leak down my face. By the time Magnus says, 'Let's get drunk,' the world around us feels unreal. Wearily, I nod, and he leads me inside.

#

By six o'clock we've emptied a good chunk of the bottle. Magnus plays music at full volume and sits on the floor, singing along. Though the aquavit has loosened my nerves, I'm still not as smashed as Magnus, and the commotion from the radio makes me uneasy. I turn down the volume several times, but Magnus turns it back when I go to the toilet. Bit by bit he stops singing and just sits, staring at the blaring radio. On one occasion, I come back to find tears on his face.

'Not much left,' he says, holding up the bottle.

I reach to take a swig, but Magnus grabs it back.

'Wait,' he says. 'Let's drink this like my mother used to.'

'What?'

'The Danish way.'

'What's the Danish way?'

'Colder!'

'I don't have a fridge.'

'Uff,' says Magnus. 'Then we'll put it in the snow.'

Just for a moment his smile reminds me of our first, crazy night in Newcastle, and it softens me.

'All right,' I smile.

Magnus holds the bottle out and measures with his fingers how much is left.

'Little more shots first,' he says, and hands the bottle to me. Wincing, I take a swig. It burns my mouth.

'I fucking hate aquavit,' I say.

'I know,' he says, and we laugh.

There's not much left in the bottle by the time we go out-side. Magnus gives me a piggyback round the veranda, his feet leaving thick holes in the snow.

'Shhh,' I hiss. 'Hans will hear us!' And I giggle some more.

We stop at the top of the steps, and I touch the veranda ceiling to steady myself.

'Down there!' I say, pointing at the garden, and wordlessly Magnus starts downwards. The steps are encased in ice, and at first I'm impressed by his sure-footedness. But this lasts all of three seconds. Magnus jolts forwards, grabs for the hand-rail, and I fall right over his shoulders. I reach my arms out, catch a shoulder on the bottom step and wallop head first into the undergrowth. Blackness punches into me, and for a second I don't know where I am. Then I look sideways and see Magnus halfway down the steps.

'Sorry,' he winces. In front of him, a trail of broken glass. The last remains of the aquavit.

A dull pain gnaws my ribs. I rock myself forwards, and as I

turn to look at the hollow my body has made in the snow, I notice a twisted brown object, half hidden from sight. That must be what I landed on. But what is it? It doesn't look like a rock . . .

'Looks like the party's over,' says Magnus as he reaches for my hand. His serious face is back.

'Wait.'

'What?'

'There's something down here.'

I lean forwards and tug the lump out of the snow. It's spongy and greasy, with hard bits inside. I poke at it, and a smell like rotten eggs fills the air. Then I see the eyeball.

'Oh!' I cry, and drop it.

'What?'

I kneel where I have fallen, looking at the body, and a horrible feeling suddenly grips me. That this is not a wild animal. That it's . . . It's . . .

I crawl back to the body. Lean really close and squint through the darkness. There. It's unmistakable. She looks tiny with her fur plastered flat. Her face squashed sideways, as if yawning.

'Oh God . . . Magnus . . . It's my cat . . .'

Magnus pokes Bobble with his foot and shrugs.

'Looks like it froze to death.'

'How did she get out?' I wail. 'I always kept the door closed . . .'

I push Magnus's foot away and dust more snow from Bobble's head. Black liquid oozes through my fingers, but I can't give up yet. I have to know how she . . .

There.

Oh God.

That hard thing round her neck is a belt. I see the buckle

now, fastened at the throat. The woven leather wound tightly. Round and round, leaving no more than an inch in the middle . . .

I place Bobble back in the snow. Magnus is in front of me, somewhere, but I barely hear his words as I stumble into the house. Dumbly, I start packing a bag.

'—anything stupid.'

I get on my knees beside the washing machine and extract the plastic bag I'd taped behind it. In the bag is six hundred kroner, give or take. My life savings. I put it in my bag, next to the rest of my stuff.

'—you doing?'

In go my phone, my wallet, my miniature torch. An apple from the kitchen. The book my mum sent for Christmas. I zip the bag closed. I carry it to the door and start putting on my boots.

'Kathy!'

I look up. Magnus looks furious. My hands have still not stopped shaking. I force them to tie my laces.

'You have to believe me now,' I tremble. 'He's not right in the head . . .'

'What are you talking about?!'

'*Him.* You saw what he did. He killed my cat.'

'Your cat froze to death!'

'She had a belt round her neck!'

'What are you doing?' He stands over me and bats my hands. '*Stop* it!'

I finish tying my laces and look up.

'I'm going. I told you. It's not safe.'

Magnus hovers over me. There's something akin to panic in his eyes, something unnatural, and I can't figure out why. He's been acting weird ever since he arrived. But I don't have time to deal with that. For the first time in months, I must put myself first.

'No!' says Magnus as I stand up, and this time there is more force in his tone.

'What do you mean, *no*?

'Just. Please. Sit down.'

'Don't you care that I'm in danger?'

'I need you to stay!'

'Magnus, I'm not your fucking pet!'

He moves in front of me and starts removing the coat I'm trying to put on.

'You don't understand! You can't . . . You . . . *Take off the jacket!*' He starts to cry now in a crazy, childish way. Snotty, uncontrolled, with his mouth curled wide open. I've never seen a grown man cry like that, and it scares me. I stop struggling, and with a great sweep of his arm Magnus flings the coat away.

'What's going on?' I can barely squeeze the words out.

'I had to do it,' he groans. 'I had to. For my family . . .'

A chill moves through me. I start backing towards the bed.

'Do what?'

'You don't understand . . . They made me choose . . . Between you and the kids . . .'

'Who?'

'They won't hurt you. If you don't fight them . . . He promised me that—'

'Who promised you?'

'Hans.'

I reach the bed now and snatch my knife from under the pillow. Magnus's eyes go wide.

My mind is racing, trying to make connections. One

answer is more prominent than the rest, but I can't convince myself Magnus is capable of it.

'You said Kolbeinn was your friend,' I gasp. 'You lied, didn't you?'

'There's no other way.'

'Who is he? Did he lend you money? Is that what it is? Money?'

Magnus squares his jaw. The gap between us closes.

'I can get you money,' I cry.

'I can't let you leave,' says Magnus hoarsely. Then he lunges.

On the first try, I almost get away. I'm halfway across the veranda when he catches me, and for the second time in one night we clatter head first down the steps. The butcher's knife flies out of my hand, disappearing with a *plop* into the snow of the garden, and I scramble forwards in an effort to regain my footing. Behind me, I feel movement. Orange light blinding me. Pinning me to the ground. I see my hands, bright red against the ice, and my blue woollen sleeves. The squeak and clink of shoes on ice. Then I get my balance and dive onwards, into a surface as hard as steel. Everything jars. Magnus's feet in front of me. I raise my eyes higher, trying to find his face. In his hand, my butcher's knife. His breath spumes out in clouds. My blood smudged on his sleeve.

'Please, Magnus!' I scream. 'Magnus!'

His knee comes up fast. My nose explodes.

Sobbing.

Down.

Down.

So sorry . . .

Static.

27

MmhorGDRegP89/10
Name: Katherine (Fennick?)
Gender: F
DOB: Unknown. (Est. age 30)
Date of session: 12/08/2006
Duration: 45min
T: Therapist, P: Patient

[Note: Patient is in a hypnotic trance and has just visualised stepping into a room.]

T: What can you see?

P: It's dark. Quiet. I'm in the house.

T: Which house is that?

P: Hans's house. On the hill.

T: Is Hans here with you?

P: No. He's upstairs.

T: Are you alone?

P: There's a kitten. It's scared of me.

T: Where did you get the kitten?

P: Lina got it for me.

T: Who is Lina?

P: I work with her.

T: Where do you work?

P: Not real work. He pays pocket money.

T: Who does?

P: Hans.

T: What work do you do for Hans?

P: I clean. Wash. Mop. Sweep. Make coffee.

T: Do you like working for Hans?

P: No. But now I have Bobble.

T: What is Bobble?

P: The kitten.

T: Why do you stay, if you hate him?

P: I can't leave.

T: Why not?

P: He'll hurt me.

T: Who will hurt you?

P: [No answer.]

T: Is Hans the one who hurt you?

P: I have to go back now.

T: Is there someone who can help you? A best friend?

P: Tim. From art school. But I don't . . . I can't . . .

T: Tell me about Tim.

P: He wants me to go back.

T: Back where? Where does Tim live?

P: Above the shop.

T: What about your parents?

P: No . . . Don't hurt my mother . . .

T: Who will hurt her? Magnus? Hans?

P: He's with Mathilde now. But I love him . . .

T: Earlier you said you need pills . . .

P: I can't get them now. But I promised I'll be happy . . .

T: What kind of pills do you need?

P: Blue and white.

[Patient becomes twitchy.]

T: What's happening now, Katherine?

P: He's back.

T: Who's back?

P: I locked the door. But I think he has a key.

T: Katherine, can you tell me what Hans looks like?

P: I locked the door.

T: Does Magnus ever get angry with you?

P: He's coming!

[Patient falls out of bed. Brought out of trance.]

Session ends

#

At eight o'clock Caroline comes with my pills. I stare at her, confused by this break in routine.

'Come on,' she says as she holds out the beaker of water.

'It's . . . not nine o'clock.'

'I know. Just take them.'

'But . . . why are . . . why isn't . . . why . . .'

'Take your pills, Kathy. You need rest.'

'I want to talk to Rhona.'

Caroline counts the pills out of the Tupperware. First up, as always, are the big red ones. She puts them in my hand and, grudgingly, I take them.

'It's *important*,' I say.

'You need rest.'

Caroline hands me the white pills. These are smaller, and

smoother, and easier to swallow. I put all three on my tongue at once.

'Why hasn't she come back yet?' I ask.

'Dunno,' says Caroline. She hands me the yellow pill, and I swallow it. Last of all come the two plastic capsules. I swallow these too. 'Good girl,' she says. 'Did you clean your teeth yet?'

'Yes,' I lie. The pills will hit soon, and I don't fancy being manhandled into bed. Caroline takes my empty beaker.

'Okay. Well, good night.'

I try to stay awake, but it soon becomes clear this won't be possible. Darkness sinks me below the surface, gluing me into a monstrous limbo. Joyce loves the pills because they carry me out of their way. I'm swept under the rug, dirt and all, and everyone assumes I am safe. But the pressure down here is immense. It'd be more humane to slug me with a hammer.

Memories become clearer now. I tremble as they crowd around my head. Nudging me. Snickering. I see Hans, fist raised high in the air. Waving treetops. A halo of screams. He recites my parent's address to me. Mispronouncing everything. I think I am weeping. My mother appears next, standing at the kitchen door. Whistling with both fingers in her mouth. *Teatime*. And I run to the house. Soil pounds down, cold and hard around my head. My arms cannot move. Then the edges contract, and I slide into blackness.

#

It's not your responsibility. She's not your daughter!

She might as well be!

Look. There's nothing you can do for her when you're like this. You have to let go. Let us take care of her.

294

But that's just it! You're not! Drugging her to the eyeballs is not taking care of her!

It's for her own protection.

Look at her. No, look at her! Does that look like protection to you? She's higher than the fucking moon!

It's standard procedure, post trauma, for—

Would you listen to yourself! Good God . . . You make it so that I can't leave! You're failing her . . . You . . . Oh . . .

Shhh. You're upset—

Damn right I'm upset! If you did your job properly, I wouldn't have t—

So go back to your sick leave. Let us deal with her.

You're not listening . . .

#

When I wake, there is no one in the room. I look at the clock. Twenty minutes past one. Someone has closed my curtains. I look at the chair and try to assemble my thoughts.

Was that Rhona's voice I heard? Is she here?

I barely have the energy to breathe. But this is serious now. I miss Rhona, of course I do, and I'm hurt that she's been gone, but right now I have bigger motives for needing to see her. That phone message Dr Harrison mentioned – I can't get it out of my head. I'm a sitting duck in here, just waiting for Hans to come and follow up his threat. I must tell Rhona about him. Get her to protect me. She's the only one who might take me seriously.

Embracing the nightstand, I haul myself sideways. The wood is like ice.

Can I do this?

I have to.

I take a deep breath, tense my stomach and haul myself out of bed. I had meant to land on my feet, but my ankle flops sideways beneath my weight and splays me head first onto the carpet.

My God, I think as I dab my chin. *When did my legs stop working?*

I gather my breath and try again. This time I make it to the door before my legs give up. I claw at the wall, hoping to rest against it, but gravity has other ideas and hauls me back to the floor. I loll onto my back. The ceiling looks so far away.

It's okay . . . it's okay . . . it's okay . . .

Fuck it. All right. I'll crawl.

Painstakingly, I drag myself to my knees. Four deep breaths. Then I fall at the door handle. It jolts beneath my weight, and opens. Two seconds to get my breath back. Then I nudge my way outside. The corridor is empty as I drag myself to the landing. This takes a long time. Cheerful voices drift upstairs. When I reach the banisters I collapse, panting, on my belly. My heart pummels the floor like the movements of some hideous internal parasite. Pushing that metallic fizz through my gums. I close my eyes, trying to regain control. The air presses down like a centrifuge.

Keep still. Keep still. Breathe . . .

nonono . . .

oh . . .

no . . .

I don't think I'm out for more than a few seconds, but the experience drains me all the same. I lie on my side, pushing my head to the gap in the banisters.

As long as no one comes, I'll be all right. If I can just lie here . . . get my breath back . . .

A door opens below, and my eyes widen.

'Rhona!' I gurgle.

She stops and looks up.

'Jesus!' she shrieks, and clatters up the stairs.

I try to grab her arms.

'Shhh,' she says. 'Don't try to talk.'

'Please . . . You have to . . . listen . . .'

Rhona pushes her hair back, revealing a shockingly run-down face. I jolt. Her eyes are dull. Her skin puffy. She is smaller. Harder. Frailer. And somehow much, much older.

'Come on,' she sighs. 'Let's get you back before Joyce sees you.'

She tries to walk me along and I do my best to cooperate. Somehow we make it back to my room. Rhona dumps me on the bed, closes the door and falls into the chair beside me. I loll against the pillow, overjoyed that my mission succeeded. When I get my breath back, I'll explain to her. Rhona holds a hand to her forehead and kneads the skin there. I watch her left eyebrow rising and falling. Her skin is so stretchy. Old.

'I'm not feeling good, Kathy,' mumbles Rhona, without meeting my eyes. Her hand moves faster as she talks. 'I wasn't going to tell you yet, with you being so ill. But . . . I'm really not doing well.'

Her statement hangs, and I am unsure how to deal with it. The concept of Rhona being sick is unthinkable. Like a hilarious joke.

'I lost the family home this week. The bank repossessed it. Do you know what that means?'

My neck begins to tremble beneath the weight of my head and, fearing the onset of a panic attack, I lie down flat. Breathing raggedly, I try my best to nod. Rhona continues.

'I had to remortgage it, to pay for some things. But I didn't get a good deal . . .'

For one terrible moment I think she might cry. But that moment passes.

'I missed you,' I mumble.

Rhona's mouth curves upwards, and for a second I snatch a glimpse of the old her. My heart leaps. Then her mask snaps back, and she's gone.

'I missed you too,' she says. 'But . . . See . . . I'm not well enough to be here.'

A lump appears in my throat.

'But you're back now.'

'Hmm.'

'Please. It's dangerous . . . Make them stop the pills . . .'

Rhona's mouth remains shut. She rubs her forehead as she looks at the floor. When she replies it sounds even less like her.

'That's not my decision.'

'What?' I croak.

'Look, hon. I don't know if you knew this, but Joyce is back. More than that. As of today, she's taking over your case.'

'What?'

'She has to, for now. Do you understand, love?'

My mouth forms the word *No*. But no sound comes out. Rhona sighs heavily, and sits forward in her chair.

'Look. We're very short-staffed. I'm not strong enough to help you right now. We need all hands on deck, and Joyce is the only one here who can do my job.'

'What about Mrs Laird?' I whisper.

'She's sixty-one years old, Kathy. There's a limit to how much extra work she can take on.'

My collar is getting tighter. I claw at it. Trembling, I meet Rhona's eye.

298

'I'll be good. I promise . . .'

Rhona shoots me a weary look.

'Please,' I croak. But the room is rushing away now, and it's hard to make myself stay with her. Whiteness wraps around my head, swallowing all but the sound of my breathing. I think my eyes are crying, on the outside. But as I slip further, it gets hard to tell. Sounds falter, like distant radio waves. Handful by handful, the static gains precedence. Then I float right down, and all of it goes away.

#

My sores have almost healed. Caroline turns my hands over and over before deciding I don't need any pink ointment today. She clicks a biro open and writes something in her notebook. I wish I could see what else is written in there. Would she show me if I asked? I'm sure that'd be a thrilling read. *This Is Your Life*, in Caroline's handwriting. Hey presto!

'Has Rhona gone away again?' I ask. Caroline looks sideways at me.

'No,' she replies. 'No . . . She's still with us.'

'Why doesn't she come up here any more?'

Caroline clears her throat. 'Rhona's . . . *sick* right now.'

'I know. She told me. But—'

'Oh, she did?'

'But still . . . I thought . . . Well, I hoped she might have come to see me . . .'

Caroline doesn't reply.

'Will you tell her I need to talk to her?' I say.

'Yeah,' says Caroline, though her body language tells a different answer.

299

'Please?'

'Kathy, I said I would!'

I sink into the pillows while Caroline bustles around. She goes to the curtains and unveils me to the world. The light hurts my head, but I don't look away from it. I mustn't. It's my last link to a future outside of this room.

'When can I go outside?'

'When you're better.'

'I *am* better. My hands are better—'

'You know what I mean,' snaps Caroline.

'What about my legs?'

'What about them?'

'I'll forget how to walk.'

Caroline puts her hands on her hips.

'See . . . This is exactly why Rhona doesn't come.'

'What do you mean?'

'Just . . . oh . . . Forget it, Kathy. When Joyce gives the word, we'll reduce your meds. Then you can go downstairs again. All right?'

'How will *Joyce* know I'm better? She never even sees me! Why can't Rhona—'

'Rhona's *sick*!' blusters Caroline. 'She's *resting*. My God, Kathy, don't you listen to a word I say?'

'It's just . . . I'm scared . . . I—'

'Exactly. You're sick too. And until you are well, young lady, you're staying in bed!'

'My legs—'

'That's the *end* of it!'

'Caroline!'

'What?'

'Are you going already?'

'Yup.'

'Can't you stay?'

'Shush now. Get some sleep.'

'I'm sick of sleeping!'

'Shush,' says the dark gap behind the door. 'I'll be back at five. You know that.'

'Please!'

The door seals shut, and I am alone.

#

'What day is it?'

'Sunday.'

'Sunday the what?'

'I dunno . . . the 10th, I think.'

'Of what?'

'September.'

'I thought it was August?'

'Come on now,' says Caroline as she lifts the plate of stew. 'Sit up.'

'Why don't I have breakfast any more? Dr Harrison brought me breakfast . . .'

'My, aren't you feisty today? Come on, sit up.'

'Is Dr Harrison still here?'

'Nope.'

A lead hammer strikes my chest, taking my breath away. There goes another of my allies.

'But . . . why didn't she say goodbye?'

'You were sleeping.'

'Mrs Laird, then. Will you ask her to—'

'Nope.'

My stomach twists.

'But—'

'*Kathy*,' warns Caroline. I realise she is waiting. I look at the stew. It's dark green.

'I'm not eating that.'

'Of course you are. It's superfood!'

'Why can't I have proper food?'

'This was made just for you. Chock-full of potassium!'

'It looks horrible.'

Caroline glares. 'Do you want me to send Joyce up?'

The name sends a shiver through me.

'Send Rhona,' I say.

Caroline's jaw stiffens. 'That's enough. Eat your dinner.'

'No.'

'Don't make me get Joyce,' she growls, and stabs the fork full of stew. I dodge as she aims it at my mouth, and the fork hits the cut on my lip. I scream and flap my arms up, hitting Caroline in the face.

'RIGHT!' roars Caroline. She scrambles to her feet and out of the door.

I drag myself off the bed. Maybe I can make a run for it. But my legs are like twigs. I crash straight to the ground.

'Help!' I shout. '*Help!*'

Nearby, footsteps approach. A pause. Then Mrs Bell's face appears in the doorway. She looks terrified.

'Help me!' I gasp. 'I'm begging you, get Rhona!'

Mrs Bell opens her mouth. Then Caroline reappears with a syringe and pushes her to one side. I yell. Caroline swoops and pins me with her full weight. I grab her arm. It's then that I turn and see Rhona standing over her shoulder. Relief cascades through me. Now everything will be all right.

'Rhona!' I cry. 'Get her off me!'

'I'm warning you, Kathy,' pants Caroline.

I look up once more, but Rhona has not moved. Her sad

eyes are fixed right upon mine. With a sudden rush of emotion I realise she does not mean to help me, and in that split second my relief turns to rage. I feel it gush through me. Throttling me, turning my face red hot.

'God*damn* you!' I roar. 'You old bitch!'

Suddenly Caroline is behind me, and my fists are full of Rhona's hair. With a tremendous yank I roll forwards, and Rhona rolls with me. Her mouth opens, and a wobbling, womanly cry comes out. We tumble into the door frame. Someone is battling to loosen my grip, but it's no good. I work my fingers well in and tug with all my strength.

'Kathy!' screams Rhona, but this just makes me angrier. Somewhere underneath us, the needle scrapes my arm but does not hit. My sleeve turns wet.

'You're just like them! *You're worse!*' I scream.

'Rhona! For God's sake. Get the syringe!' shouts Caroline.

The tears are taking me over now. Weakening me. Blurring my vision. I wilt onto the ground and look into Rhona's face. She leans forwards, and just for a second I think she's reaching out to comfort me. Then I'm on my back and Caroline is holding my wrists down.

'Got it,' says Rhona, and jams the syringe in my arm.

28

March 10th–11th, 2006.

When my eyes open I am on a wooden floor. The room is dark, save for the glow behind the curtains. Not the porch light. I know that because the colour's dark blue, not orange. I'm in the flat. The kitchen floor, I think. But things are not right. Something's not right.

Oh Christ. My nose.

I touch a hand to the wound, crispy now, and pain radiates through my forehead. I yelp, buck backwards and suck in a breath. My nose whistles.

Magnus!

Fuck. Fuck!

Flailing, I turn around. I look behind me. Then the other side. Clear. I make my hands into fists.

Okay. I'm alone, I think. *Okay. Okay . . .*

I rise to my knees. Crawl to the window. Push my face to the curtains. I feel sick. Weak. Like I might pass out again. Alarm spreads through me, rising higher than the pain, to take control. I open the curtains fully and drag myself up on them. I mustn't think of Magnus. I mustn't cry. Concentrate. Sounds pulse through the darkness. Guttural. Moving in time with my heart. Outside, the stars are bright, like the stars you get in fairytales, and another layer of snow has fallen. What time is it? How long is it since Magnus . . . since he . . .

Wait! On the veranda, there are fresh footsteps. Who's here? Hans? Kolbeinn? Are they already inside?

Calm down. You're awake. You can still get out.

As softly as possible, I go to the door. I try the handle. Jammed. Try again. No key in the lock.

No . . .

It's hard to keep from crying now. Wait! No light in the keyhole. I get down and look. There, the key *is* there. It's on the outside of the door.

Magnus locked me in . . .

I return to the window and study the footprints. There are several sets, and all of them lead into the house. What kind of shoes? They overlap so much. Hard to tell. I close my eyes and try to remember. Was Magnus wearing his baseball boots? I think he was. There are no prints like that on the veranda. That means . . .

I wilt away from the window. With wet eyes I go straight to the bed. But my knife is not there. Of course not. Magnus took it.

Fuck . . .

I go to the drawer below the kettle and fish through it for a weapon. The sharpest thing is a fork, so I grab it and retreat to my place below the window.

How can I get out? The bathroom's internal, with no window to the outside. In the laundry room there's just an air vent. The windows at the front are barred by metal grilles, and there's no door to my apartment besides this one.

Concentrate.

Could I tunnel through the walls? They're made from wood. I know that. But what would I tunnel with? A fork? And maybe there's something else in them, like concrete or insulation. Is insulation hard to tunnel through? Fuck knows.

I don't know how the fuck they build houses in this fucking country. Fuck. *Fuck!*

Breathe.

I close my eyes.

Music is playing upstairs. Bass-heavy music, with female vocals and a heavy, rattling beat, like ragga. Masked beyond that, other noises. Bumping, like feet. Stamping. Dancing? The blood drains from me as I remember the last time Hans had a party. His guests were all men and they pounded my door so many times that I turned the lights off and hid under the bed.

Bangs. Banging. It's rhythmical. Short. Underlaid by a softer sound. A voice, partly muffled. A woman's voice. Is it saying my name?

Idiot. Don't cry. Concentrate. Listen.

Kathy . . .

A crash. Then a second voice, and a third. Two men, laughing.

Bumping.

Banging.

Drumming.

No . . . A bed.

I stiffen against the wall.

Bam bam bam bam. Getting faster. Then the female voice comes back.

Bang bang bang bang bangbangbangbangbangbangbangbang.

Quiet.

The male voices have stopped now, but the female voice has not. Her cries keep going. Then, quite suddenly, the banging stops, and I hear her clearly.

'Kathy!'

I reel into the wall.

Lina. That's Lina's voice.

The floorboards groan as footsteps cross the ceiling. Lina's voice rises several octaves. A man's voice rumbles through the floor. Lina screams, then coughs, then howls. And the banging starts again.

My heart hammers.

'Ne! Ne! Ne!'

I have to open this door. I've no idea how, but it's my only chance.

With shaking hands, I put my weapon on the floor. Then I kneel and try to fit my finger in the lock. Every few seconds Lina shrieks, and I must stop myself from shrieking with her. My finger won't reach the key, so I try with the fork. A prong snaps off and tinkles to the floor. Cheap shit. I look through the keyhole. No key. I must have pushed it out! I look under the door. There it is, on the floor.

Then!

Footsteps. On the stairs.

I skid backwards across the room. The steps on the staircase keep coming. The banging bangs on. I hold the fork out in front of me.

Quite suddenly, I hear a snigger. Right there, on the other side of my door.

'Kaaaatt-eeee,' coos a man's voice.

A whimper falls out of me.

'Hysj,' says a voice. Giggling.

A jingle of metal. Through the keyhole, I see movement. A flash of cloth and skin. Then the door handle jolts. This time I can't hold myself together. A scream belts out of me as I run at the far wall. I no longer know what is or isn't in my hands. The curtains are all around me. I try to bury myself in them. But when I look again, the door has not opened.

Didn't they see the key on the floor?

I drop to my knees and try to see through the keyhole. But I'm too far away. The men are still there. I can hear them arguing. A scuffle, and the door jolts. I jam my hands across my mouth. But the lock holds strong.

'Katt-eee,' sings a voice. 'We come to party with you.'

A small pause. Then laughter explodes. I cry out.

Silence.

The door handle jiggles.

Silence.

Muttering.

Every muscle in my body is poised to run. I watch the shadows.

More muttering. Creaking. A click, and the curtains flash orange. Once, twice, small sounds scrape the windows. Floorboards creak. Then all the noises shrink away.

Lina's gone quiet. Is that good or bad?

The porch light extinguishes, sending me back into darkness. I steady myself against the wall and strain my ears for clues. There's a faint sound, like a car, but it might just be my ears playing tricks.

Who was that? Have they gone?

On my belly, I creep back to the door. The crack beneath it is half an inch high. I put my eye to it and look.

No feet. But also no key.

Just then, an almighty crash shakes the upstairs floor. I jolt, bang my head and jump up. Without stopping to think, I kick at the door.

Banging again. That's the music back on.

I ram the door with my shoulder. I kick it again. I kick at the handle. No good. My heartbeat is frantic now. Fluttering in my throat, in my chest, in my ears. I slam on the light switch and look round the room. There. The microwave. I yank it away from the wall, hug it to my chest and fly at the door.

theeee

A smash. A flash. My neck cracks. I fall forwards and sharp bits stab my arm.

eeee

When I lift my head, the light is dim. A smell like burnt metal taints my tongue.

I'm in the vestibule. I did it.

. . . ee! Kathy!

Lina. Her voice is louder now. Shriller. I hear her above the scream of the music.

I look at the front door and know this is my chance. Through the glass, the porch light is off. I could run now. Right now. I could be out of here. Down the track, towards the main road. But . . .

'*Kathy!*'

Hans's door is partly open. I can see inside, to a pine-clad entrance hall. Several coats hang on hooks. A pair of motor-cycle boots. A bunch of keys. On the wall, a framed picture of Elvis. Ice slush dots the stairs.

I suddenly think of Coral, screaming behind my father, and tears rush down my face.

Fresh blood where her head smacked into the wood stove. That same terror-stricken plea. My own name.

I clamber upwards. From here, I see the ceiling of the room above. The stark, white bulb of an unshaded table lamp. Lina's pale-blue parka hanging over the banisters.

In the living room, three sofas surround a black glass coffee table. The floor is strewn with beer bottles, and on one edge of the table someone has snorted powder through a thousand-kroner note. By the CD player I pass a Louis Vuitton handbag, with the price tag still attached.

I can't do this, I think. But still I press onwards. The door at the end of the room is closed. Lina's voice has stopped, but I know she's in there. I know they both are. A sob shakes my chest, soundless amongst the thrashing of the music.

I can't do this . . .

The door glides open and I slip inside. The smell of urine hits me first. Then the dull crimson of the bedside lamp. My eyes skim across her bloated face and rest upon the painting above the bed. Hans's voice is in my head, dark and loud, and the sweat and skin and blood is overpowering, but all I can see is the painting of the ship. A red line smears the wall below it, as if Lina had tried to crawl right into the picture. Hans is moving forwards, half naked, and the noise and tension advance with him. He is getting closer, and Lina is trying to get off the bed, and my feet are cemented to the floor. His mouth moving fast, spitting words. A swish. My nose explodes with pain. I bellow. Then he's on me, and my hand swipes up into his face . . .

Staggering backwards. No sound now. Only thrashing. My vision tunnelled in onto that single dense spot. *The picture is not straight.* The fork stuck thickly in his temple, like some harpooned, slapstick monster. His hair straggles into my mouth. That awful, slow grunt as the light goes out of his eyes. The veins in his hands slacken and release me. Then his full weight comes down, and I am pinned to the floor.

#

For some time, all I hear is Lina. Her voice is so broken that the screams are no longer screams. Guttural, continuous, the noise fills the air. I try to look at her, but Hans is so heavy I can barely move my head. His skin is sweaty against my own. Again I struggle, and manage to free an arm. Levering myself sideways, I crawl away. Hans rolls the opposite way, along the back of my legs, and I kick at him desperately. But he doesn't leap after me. He doesn't move at all.

'Lina!'

I can see her now, bundled small in the corner. From here I can't tell if the marks on her body are real. I crawl to her, and she explodes. One kick lands square in my chest, sending me back against the bed. Lina scrambles to Hans's side, and from our new positions we watch each other.

'Come on,' I hear my voice say. 'We have to go.'

'What have you done . . .'

I barely hear her say it. I move towards Lina, and again she freaks out.

'I can't leave y—'

'Ne!'

She's on her feet now. Breasts swinging. Hands clawing. A massive bruise on her hip.

'Please, Lina,' I sob. 'They'll come ba—'

'Get *away*!' she howls, and swings both fists at me.

At the door I look back and see Lina bent double beside Hans. Her cries are so muddled I can no longer tell what language she's speaking. With both arms, she embraces him. Then the adrenaline takes hold, and all I can do is run.

29

A tapping sound alerts me.

What? Why is . . .

'Katherine?' calls a voice, and I slur, 'Yes?'

A click. Feet. Shuffling. I open my eyes.

'Hallo, dearie, how are you?' asks Mrs Laird.

I'm so shocked to see her, I don't know how to react. My mouth trembles into a smile. Overjoyed, I start to shake. Then my eyes flood with tears.

'Oh! No!' she exclaims, and breaks open the box of man-size tissues she has brought with her. 'I must confess, this isn't the reaction I'd anticipated,' she chuckles as she dabs my face. I titter. It takes all my strength not to grab her hand. I want to chain myself to her, to make sure she can't leave.

'Have you come to . . . get me out?'

'Out? What do you mean?'

'Can you . . . stop . . . them . . . ?'

'Ah . . .' Mrs Laird lowers herself into the chair, and her face becomes serious. 'You're on quite a lot of medication, aren't you?' she says.

'Joyce . . .'

Mrs Laird sighs. 'It's for the best, dear.'

'But—'

'You've had a lot on your plate lately. And what with Rhona . . .'

312

She trails off and turns her head away. I wait for her to elaborate, but she does not. Her face sinks behind her hand like a setting sun, and as it does so all the warmth seems to go out of the room.

'I have to . . . get out . . . of here . . .'

'Katherine. I've come to talk to you for a reason.'

I blink and stare. 'What?' I try to say. But I don't have enough air to push it out.

Mrs Laird's mouth tightens. She picks my freezing hands from my lap.

'I have to talk to you about your mother,' she says.

I look at the box of tissues, and suddenly things make sense.

'Oh . . .'

'I don't quite know how to tell you this. I thought you should be the first to know . . .'

My hands go slack. I raise my eyes to Mrs Laird's and see the answer emblazoned there.

'She's dead. Isn't she?'

Mrs Laird blinks. Then says, 'Yes.'

I stare at my hands.

'A traffic accident,' she continues. 'Eighteen months ago. The police confirmed it.'

And that's it. I look at Mrs Laird. She looks at me.

'I'm so sorry, Kathy,' she says.

'What about . . . my . . . father?'

'I'm afraid we couldn't trace him.'

This is strange. I ought to be crying by now. Mrs Laird knows it as well as I do. I see the anticipation in her face. But . . .

'Shhh,' she says, though there is nothing to shush, and leans in to hug me. I hang in her arms. Feeling her grief for

313

me. Her confusion. The tension as she waits for me to fall apart.

But there's nothing left to fall out of me. My mother is dead. I knew that . . . didn't I? I always knew. How could I have forgotten?

'Shush,' repeats Mrs Laird, sounding ridiculous now.

'S'okay . . .' I whisper, to make her happy. Whether this is true, I don't know, but it feels good to say it.

'You're in shock,' says Mrs Laird. 'The tears will come.'

I look at her face, so far away. Eventually she takes her tissues and leaves.

#

I wake and instantly know I have been dreaming. Magnus was there, and me. Just the two of us, struggling in the snow. As I lie here the memory sticks to me. Sucking at me. Sapping my power.

The clock says ten past seven. I stare at it. Trying to latch myself on to something real. Finally I convince myself I am really here with the clock.

Softly, I begin to shudder.

Magnus. My love. Would he really do that to me? Sell me, like a cow, to save himself? He's just like Rhona. Saying he loves me, then plunging the knife through my back. My God, I've been such a fool. The only one I can count on is myself.

A sudden crash startles me.

'Knock knock,' says a voice. I look up.

Rhona.

She barely gets two steps into the room before I yell, 'How could you?'

In her hands there's a tray, with soup on top. She halts and the bowl slides sideways. It's orange. Probably carrot.

'Don't be silly,' she says. But her tone is far from confident. We look at each other. Then she moves forwards and the gap between us closes. She sets the tray down on the nightstand and perches herself on the bed. I shove at her.

'Look,' she says. 'I need to ask you something.'

'How can I ever trust you—'

'Would you just listen?'

'You said you'd help me!'

'I'm *trying* to!'

Silence rings out. We glare at each other. The urge to cry is stronger than the urge to lash out, but somehow I manage to do neither.

'You're your own worst enemy,' snaps Rhona, and reaches for the tray. I look at the floor, and when I turn back I see it's not a tray at all but a folder. With a sigh, Rhona opens it.

'I noticed something,' she says. 'When I read through your last session. This Hans guy. It's him you're scared of, isn't it? Not Magnus?'

I close my eyes.

'Look, Kathy. Things can't go on this way.'

I look at Rhona's face – so weak beneath the well-meaning eyes. Wishing I could trust her.

'I can't bring him back,' I say limply. 'I won't.'

Rhona's face hardens. She looks away, and for a second it seems she is wiping her eyes. The rhythm of her breathing is odd.

'You've been asking for me for weeks. Day in, day out. Pleading. Saying how desperately you need to talk. Well, here I am! I'm listening!'

'Changed my mind,' I mumble defiantly.

'Is this a game to you? Cat and mouse?'

I glare.

'No one else will be this patient with you,' whispers Rhona. 'This really is your last chance to—'

A jolt passes through me.

'What do you mean, last chance?'

Rhona pauses. Studies me with those sad eyes.

'I'm leaving Gille Dubh,' she says. 'For good. And if you won't let me help you before then, your future will be pret—'

My body drains of blood. I feel it all go, from top to bottom. Plunging through my limbs. Leaving nothing behind but my eyeballs. Rhona's mouth is moving, but I no longer hear the words. Suddenly I realise my hands are moving. I watch them striking her. Ripping at the folder. Picking up the soup and throwing it. Rhona's eyes widen as she falls off the bed. Anger rushing through her face. The soup in her hair like alien blood. She touches her cheek. Then the pain rises, godlike, to choke out everything else, and I step off into purest blackness.

#

It feels like I've been asleep for centuries. I see the darks, the greys and the closed curtains. They look like the old curtains. The curtains I closed to stop Hans seeing me. I lived in the dark then too. I hate the dark. I want to be outside. I want to run. I will never get out. I must trick them . . . but how . . . I want it to stop it hurts and . . . oh . . . I feel sick . . .

a cat outside . . . Bobble . . . no it can't be . . . The curtains turn white, then black, then white again. My ribs grow.

Caroline puts spoons in my mouth. She holds up a cup,

316

and I swallow. How long has this been going on? I try to focus on her face. What day is it? The air is dark now, thick like syrup. Memories prowl like slow monsters.

#

Joyce sits by my bed. Impulsively, I make a face, and though it was not my intention for her to see this, it is nevertheless obvious that she has.

I look around us. There is no one else in the room. Joyce is wearing her best dress.

'Good evening, Katherine,' she announces. 'I've come to talk to you.'

I remain silent. Something is badly wrong. With barely a pause, Joyce launches into her speech.

'Do you have any idea how much it costs to keep you here, Katherine? I mean, per year. For your therapy. Your bed and board. Your medication. Social activities. Heating. Light. For running water and sewage removal and council tax. Your clothing. Your personal toiletries. Dr Harrison's visits? Do you know?'

I stare at her.

'Do you know?'

'No.'

Joyce looks triumphant. She sits back in her chair.

'Twenty-three thousand, four hundred and forty-six pounds. Did you know that? Did you?'

'No.'

'And who do you think pays for that?'

I look at Joyce.

'The Lullaby Girl Foundation!' she exclaims. 'Or they did, before Rhona saw fit to set the lawyers on them. Almost half

317

of the funds they raised were used to pay for legal action against them! All to keep you out of the news! All for you, Kathy! And now that the charity money's gone, someone *else* will have to foot the bill for your upkeep. Do you know who *that* would be?'

I blanch. But Joyce seems to be enjoying herself tremend-ously and blusters on.

'The taxpayers! The hard-working citizens of the United Kingdom. With some National Lottery handouts, of course. But mostly . . . the blood, sweat and tears of good, honest people. Now, at any one time, we have funding to support ten residential patients. Until Mary popped off you may have noticed we were, in fact, eleven, and that's because your stay was financed by *Daily Post* readers. But that's changed, Katherine, and so we find ourselves at a crossroads.'

I remain silent. Joyce folds her hands in a complicated way and tilts her face to one side. She pauses dramatically. Then continues.

'This is not a long-term residential home. A place where people live indefinitely. It's merely a resting place. A place for people to gain the help they need. To rest, and get better. After which they return to their real lives. We are trying to help you, Katherine. We are trying so very hard. And it just seems to me that you resist our every effort.'

'But I'm—'

'What I mean to say,' she continues, 'is that maybe this is not the best environment for you.'

Baboom, goes my heart. My eyes flick to Joyce's face.

'Rhona has fought tooth and nail to keep you here. She wanted you to fill Mary's spot. To become the tenth member of our flock. But you're not the only contender, Katherine. Far from it. There's a waiting list for that spot as long as my

318

arm, and your recent behaviour has convinced me you no longer deserve to be in the running. You're bedridden! You need round-the-clock care. And that is something that—'

'I'm not bedridden! I don't want to be!'

Joyce smiles sadly.

'My dear, I'm afraid that you are. And with the growing cost of your medicine – not to mention your increasingly violent tendencies – I've had no choice but to arrange your transfer to a different institution.'

'No! You can't! Rhona won't—'

'Rhona has already lent her authorisation. We signed the papers this morning.'

'But . . . but . . . Where—'

'Dundee. You leave at the end of the week.'

I can't see Joyce any more. There are too many tears in the way.

'She *wouldn't*!' I squawk. 'I don't believe you!'

'I'd be happy to show you the paperwork. I can bring it up to show you.'

I lower my head into my hands.

'She wouldn't . . . She wouldn't . . .'

'We only want the best for you,' says Joyce crisply. And with those words, she leaves me alone.

#

Caroline brings my pills. She does not mention Rhona, and her behaviour indicates she doesn't know what happened. My body feels stronger somehow. Harder.

'Are you all right?' asks Caroline. 'You seem a little off.'

I look at her, and cannot speak.

'Do you feel hot? Your eyes look different.'

I stiffen as Caroline lays the back of her hand on my forehead, but all she says is, 'Hmm.'

I try to avoid Caroline's eyes. She hands me the red pills, and I put them in my mouth. She hands me the white pills, then the yellow pills, and I put them in too. Then the plastic ones, and a drink of water. When I've finished, she takes my beaker and stands up.

'Have you brushed your teeth?' she asks.

I nod.

'Good.'

I watch as she heads to the door. 'Night, then,' she says, and turns out the light. When she has gone, I lean out of bed and spit the pills into my hand.

30

I think I hear a car when I reach the track, so I change course and veer off into the big field. Here there are no lights at all, but the thick snow throws a ghostly luminescence across the landscape. It scares me, because I don't know how visible this makes me from the track. In summer, the wheat crop might have hidden me. But this is February and the ground is barren.

I crawl through the snow. Trying not to think of Hans. One time I make the mistake of looking over my shoulder and see the house, still so close behind. The porch light remains on, throwing an orange triangle down on the snow. Why hasn't it gone off yet? Did someone follow me? I scan for movement but find nothing. Upstairs, one window is illuminated.

My whole body hurts. Adrenaline is all I have left. Right now, that's more precious than possessions.

Wait . . .

My passport!

I look at the house. A pointed shape against the sky.

I have to go back . . .

This time I really do break down. Squatting on my haunches, shaking uncontrollably. In my mind I see Hans grunting on top of me. His hairy arms thrashing. The sweat and blood and semen. Did I kill him? Am I a killer?

Magnus's face. So beautiful . . .

I love you, he says. *I love you. I can't let you go.*
Wait . . .

I look up.

The upstairs light. Someone turned it off. Does that mean someone's there? Someone besides Lina? I stiffen.

Kolbeinn . . .

No. If Kolbeinn was here I'd have seen his car.

Concentrate.

Any minute now, Hans's friends could return. If I want my passport I must go now. Where did I bury it? Come on. Try to think straight. It was a tree. Under a big tree. Which tree?

I widen my eyes in the direction of the track. The skeletal windbreak, halfway between me and the house. It's under one of the middle ones. That tall, bendy one. I'm sure of it.

I cast my eyes back at the house, but there's no movement. No sound at all. Stealthily, I creep forwards. Heart thumping in my ears, like a slave drum. On I go. On, until the tree looms above me. Then I drop to my knees and claw the ground. Where's the right place? I remember a natural hollow between the roots. And a black triangular stone that I put on top. But that was summertime, and in daylight. There's so much snow here now. Frantically, I rake my fingers round. They're so numb I can barely feel the ground beneath them. Wait. There! I feel a stone!

Using my sleeve, I scrape away some snow. Thank God it's just snow and not ice. I tug the stone out, take it in my hands and use it to dig. Beneath me, a dark shape opens up. The topsoil is looser than I'd feared, but the further I go the harder it gets. How deep did I bury the bag? I can't remember . . .

Just then, the unmistakable squeak of plastic. My heart leaps violently. Breathing hard, I put my hand in the hole. There! Inside the Rimi bag, the hard edges of the passport are unmistakable. I fall back, clutching it to my chest. One deep breath. Two. Then I rise up, and run.

#

The sky is changing. Shades of indigo creeping in to conceal the stars. I lie on my front at the north edge of the field. Listening. Waiting. Not far ahead, I see the lights of the main road. Every so often I unclasp my hands and check my passport's still there. In the bag, I hear the dull jangle of spare change and thank God I didn't just leave it under the tree. My nose is fucked up, and my right eye too. Now I'm closer to the street lights, I see red in the corner of my vision. For a while I close both eyes and concentrate on listening. Nearby, a dog is yodelling. Time drags. The dog sounds like a woman. I wish I had my knife.

Sometimes, I hear footsteps. Hard against the ground. Sharp and fast. The first time I hear them, I freeze. Then I remember the deer. Of course, just deer. Like in summer.

Christ. Summer. All those nights, lying out here on my back. Why didn't I get out then? Before things went this far. Was it because of Magnus? Despite all the pain, I still believed he was the one . . .

Everything has gone wrong . . .

I have to go. I have to go now, before the sun comes up.

Come on . . .

I'm so scared.

Come on!

I climb out of the field and run. A single deer stands in the road. There are no cars. No people. Just us. We flee in the same direction.

Street lights flash over my hands and I see that the wetness

323

is blood. The station. I reach the station. The payphones. Coins. Incredibly, the first number I dial is Magnus's. Then I remember, and put my hand down to break the connection.

Fuck . . .

Holding the receiver to my face, I sob. In front of me, someone has scratched their name and number into the wall, and for a second I consider calling them. Then I think of calling the police, but that idea scares me most of all. The phone line hums. I hang up and sink to my knees. What now? Then Tim's number just drops into my head.

I jam my money into the phone and dial. At first there is no tone, and I panic that I've wasted my last coins. Then I remember the UK dialling code. After six tries, I manage to input this correctly. The British dial tone comes on and I almost weep with relief. But that's where my joy ends. I wait. I listen. But no one picks up. The phone rings and rings and rings. It's an hour earlier over there. He's probably still in bed. But I don't stop calling. I can't. This is my final lifeline. Each time the phone spits my coins out, I feed them back in. Over and over and over and over.

Click.

'Hello?'

'Tim!'

Pause.

'Kathy, is that you?'

A sob blusters out of me.

'Tim. Oh Tim. Thank God!'

#

I wander round the airport like a lost dog. My pockets contain only my passport and boarding pass. I hitched a ride here – not just because I'm penniless, but because Hans's men might have been at the station. Tim bought me my plane ticket. I've been at Gardermoen for four hours.

Everyone has coffee. I want coffee too, but the coffee costs a lot of money. I keep walking past the kiosk, just to smell it. Maybe if I stand here long enough someone will buy one for me. I hang around for a while, but people only scowl, so I give up and return to my drifting. When I get hungry I go to the bathroom and drink tap water. I kill a lot of time this way. People stare at my face. It feels strange to have no luggage. I sit opposite the pizza place, watching all the people eating. Stealing crusts when they've gone. Sometimes I see men who look like Hans, and when this happens I dive into the toilets. Every man I see could be one of his men, or Kolbeinn's. I try to stay in plain sight, so that no one can grab me without causing a scene.

Whenever I close my eyes, I find myself back in the field. Waiting for the sound of footsteps, or men's voices, or sirens. Jumping at every breath of wind. For a moment I'll drift away and the human voices of the airport descend into those horrible, animal vocals last uttered by Hans. At this point my eyes will shoot open, and I leap up to find myself covered in sweat. My fingers scrabble instinctively for my passport, and then relax. By the time my flight comes around, I have taken to clutching it in both hands.

The aeroplane takes off into a spotless sky. Below me, the landscape is intensely beautiful. Tall, serene trees and the fine black soil. Bare mountains shining with lakes. I cast my eyes down and feel nothing but hatred.

#

Tim's smiling face is the most amazing thing I have ever seen. We embrace till my arms go numb. Then we walk to his car and get in. We sit there in the car park until I've managed to stop crying. Finally I look up and see Tim staring grimly out of the window. It feels strange for the driver's seat to be on that side.

'Where are you going to go?' he asks when he sees me looking at him.

'I don't know,' I answer. My voice sounds weak and faraway. It is strange to hear myself speak.

He flicks the keyring that hangs from the ignition. There's a crocheted space invader attached to it, with neon beads for eyes. *Space invader* is Tim's nickname, because he has this habit of standing too close to people. It freaked the hell out of me when I first met him. But it's not his fault. He's just one of those touchy-feely people. Like a big brother. Afterwards, of course, this turned into a joke. Whenever he got too much for me I'd quip, 'Back off, Tim! I'm *sensitive*!'

'Okay, cap'n,' he'd salute, and that would be the end of it. We were daft like that back then.

'Natalie's home,' says Tim flatly.

These are the worst two worst words he could possibly have said, and I know he knows it. I stare at him, knowing exactly what this announcement means. Tim does not meet my eyes. I struggle to construct a reply.

'Can I—'

'What about your family?' asks Tim.

The restraint in his face breaks my heart. I know he cares, but I also know that no matter how much I regard him as one, he is not my brother. He's not blood. And this is one mess he's decided to sidestep . . .

'You can stay on the sofa for one night,' says Tim. 'Natalie's

326

working the night shift. She won't even know you've been there. But that's all I can do.'

'Thank you,' I hear my voice say. And that is where I run out. Silence fills the gap where I should explain that I understand. And I do understand, in a way. But it doesn't make this any easier to swallow. It's hard not to start hitting Tim. Not to scream and cry and step out into the road. Emotions overwhelm me. I gulp and close my eyes. After an eternity, Tim's voice returns.

'You know . . . things aren't good with us right now . . . I can't just . . . I mean . . . There's the baby to think about.'

'She moved back in?' I croak.

'Yeah. A month ago. It's due in August.'

I try not to let my face crumple.

'What about your mother?' asks Tim.

'She . . . um . . . I can't . . . I don't . . . She's . . .'

My lower lip curls. I fight it, but this nosedive is too strong to pull out of. For a moment my face elongates into a freakish, childish mask. Then I snap and the tears stream out. In the corner of my eye the space invader jiggles. Tim does not touch me or say everything will be okay. I close my eyes, feeling the tears leak out of them. Rain bangs on the windscreen.

When the real world returns, the car is moving. I lie with my eyes closed, swaying with the movements of the car. Tim turns on the radio and a British DJ comes on, talking about a band I haven't heard of. The car jogs to the left, then to the right. Tim shifts into a higher gear. The vibrations from the car door tickle my forehead. Soon I have entered a weird state of calm. Visions jostle me. I remember taking my passport photo in Boots while Magnus held my hand under the curtain. Everything had been so perfect that day. If I'd done

327

something differently, maybe things still would be perfect. How did this happen? Why did I trust him for so long?

'I'm taking you north,' says Tim when he sees me looking. 'To your family.'

'What?' I say, sitting up. 'Aren't we going to your house?'

'I really think you should talk to them,' he replies. 'You've been through a lot.'

'But—'

'They're your parents. It's their *job* to look after you!'

'But ... I thought I could help you in the shop tomorrow—'

'Don't be silly. You need to rest.'

Tim lifts a hand from the wheel and squeezes my arm. With his eyes on the road, he smiles at me. A huge signpost flashes past us, with a big white arrow pointing to 'The North'. For reasons I cannot fathom, the Englishness of the sign fills me with rage. Tim changes lanes. I put my feet on the dashboard and try to think. How can I explain about my parents?

'Hey, don't do that,' says Tim as we pull up at the lights.

'What?'

'Your feet ... I don't want to get the police's attention.'

'What police?!'

'No ... There aren't any right now! Just, you know ... in case.'

'Why would the—'

'No insurance,' says Tim. He winks at me. Then the lights turn green and he roars out onto the roundabout.

#

Poor dear Tim.

Everything is going to be all right.

328

I watch his mouth forming the words, before the sound comes. There is conviction in his eyes. I know he means well.

We're nearly at Newcastle airport, and I convince him it's too late in the evening to arrive at my parents' house. No time of day would be good enough to turn up in such a state, right enough. But I convince him to stay the night on the airport floor with me. Just one night, I plead. Tell Natalie it was an emergency. Tomorrow he can take me there.

A matter of life and death.

I try to laugh. I think it fools him. We park the car and go in.

Hunter-gatherer style, Tim finds an empty spot and we lie down. The floor is freezing. I huddle into his shoulder, and he shelters my head. Through his fingers, I spy people walking past. Each time footsteps draw near, my heartbeat rises. But the faces are never ones I recognise.

Everything is going to be all right.

Tim. You have such a perfect family. You were lucky that way. How could you ever understand the type of father I have? Oh God, the shame of telling my parents I've failed. By now I should have a ring on my finger. A perfect house and a perfect husband. To prove the fucker wrong. But look at that. He was right all along.

'You should call them. At least let them know you're coming.'

'Tim, I don't have any money.'

'Here.'

Fuck.

'No, Tim. No. They'll only worry. It's late.'

'Look, I'm taking you there whether you like it or not. I won't leave you in the middle of nowhere in such a state. You need support. Go call them.'

'Tim—'

329

'Now.'

I love you for that fake anger in your voice. I nod and accept the coins you are pushing into my hand. You look happy. Proud to be helping me. And I don't want to rob you of that feeling.

I walk away, feeling vulnerable in the near-deserted check-in area. Behind me, some people are sleeping in front of the desks. I check their faces for a long time before letting you out of my sight. Then, with trembling steps, I follow signposts to the public telephones. Am I really going to do this? Will I just tell you I did? Or . . .

There they are. I approach. My hand is sweaty when I take the coins out of it. They clunk into the slot. I dial.

Click.

'Hello?' says a voice, and instantly I want to hang up.

'Hi Dad.'

'Kathy! Where have y—'

I reel back, stunned by the torrent of words. He does not pause even once. I wait, feeling the words fall over and over me, and more over the top of that. He's angry. Well, he's always angry, but now he's *really* angry . . . I pull at my collar. He keeps shouting.

'. . . hospital . . .'

'. . . come . . .'

'. . . get on a plane . . .'

'. . . hell have you . . .'

'Dad. Wait. Dad.'

'. . . to call you all day . . .'

'Dad! Stop!'

'. . . heard a word I've said?'

'What's happened?' I manage. And he starts again. Only angrier.

330

'. . . Your mum's been knocked down. A hit-and-run . . .'

'What? I . . . When?'

'This morning.'

'Is Mum all right?'

'Get on a plane. Right now.'

'Is she all right?'

'Get on the first possible flight. She's hanging by a thread. She asked for you. She's waiting for you, Kathy.'

'I . . .'

Bastards. Cowards. Just drove off. Foreign number plates. Didn't stand a chance. A Porsche.

My vision swerves and I drop the phone. Dad's voice rattles on, all tinny.

Oh God . . .

'Kathy?'

It was Hans. Oh my God. It was Hans. Or Kolbeinn. Or one of their people. Hans knew my parents' address. *Hans tried to kill my mother.*

Light behind my eyes. Flashing. Blinding. I swoon.

'Get on a plane. Get to the hospital.'

'I can't . . .'

'Why the hell not?'

'I'm . . . too busy . . . My work . . .'

'Well, Miss La-di-da . . . Sorry to interrupt your fantastic new life, but your mother is at death's door—'

'Dad, I can't come . . .'

Kolbeinn might be there. Or Hans.

'This is serious. If you don't come, you're no daughter of mine.'

They've killed her, and now he'll kill me . . .

31

The darkened room glides with shadows. I watch the crack in
the curtains. A slim triangle, swarming with white. Either it's
snowing outside or I'm hallucinating. Rhona's head is bowed,
but I think she is looking at my face. She hasn't moved or
spoken since I noticed her presence. Maybe because she
thinks I'm still drugged. That I'm not really here, though my
eyes appear open. And that's certainly been the case lately.
I've been away with the fairies and no mistake. But today I
feel different. Slowly, so as not to arouse detection, I try flex-
ing my toes beneath the sheets. They bend to my will with
barely a delay.

'Hi,' says Rhona quietly.

Damn. I blur my eyes, hoping to fool her.

'I know you're awake,' she says. Her voice is not angry. I
focus my eyes on her. There's a wide blue burn plaster on her
cheek.

'Why did you come back?' I croak.

'You've been shouting again. In your sleep.'

I stare. Annoyed. The nightmare is still clear in my mind,
and I dread to think which parts Rhona overheard.

'You said Hans killed your mother,' she continues, in the
same steady tone.

I draw in a breath.

'And I suppose he tried to kill you too?'

'What?' I try. But I know it's no good.

'Don't play the fool,' says Rhona. 'I know you remember.'

Her tone is sharp. But in her eyes I see excitement.

'This is what we've been waiting for. We can finally bring this man to justice for—'

'No.'

'Don't you see what a breakthrough this is?'

'No.'

Rhona sighs heavily. I hide my face in my hands.

'Look,' she says. 'There's a lot to sort out. If we start the ball rolling now, this whole matter can be—'

'Yeah. And what then?'

'What do you mean?'

'You're still packing me off to Dundee.'

'Look . . . I've tried to be honest. I've done all I possibly can. But I'm not superwoman. I can't—'

'Is that what Joyce told you to say?' I snap, before I can stop myself.

'Look at me.'

Behind her head, the crack in the curtains swirls. It blisters from left to right, diagonally. It froths in little circles. Then it slows, and the individual flakes become visible. I follow them with my eyes. Trickling softly downwards. Is that snow? What month is this? I must be going mad.

'Dundee is for the best,' she says. 'You'll have the best doctors—'

'Let go of me.'

'You need to talk about him. I know if we just—'

I shake her hands off mine, and she does not try to put them back. There is moisture in her eyes, but I won't let it weaken me. I've been weak for far too long.

'I refuse to give up on you,' says Rhona. 'Sending you to Dundee is my way of doing that. They have better facilities there. They can deal with this far better than us. And Hans will get what's coming to him.'

I shiver to hear her speak Hans's name.

'You don't understand,' I say.

'I'm on your *side*, Kathy! I'm sending you there for your own g—'

'Go on then. Fuck off. Get it over with.'

I turn my head down to hide the tears. Rhona gets to her feet.

'I've tried my best for you,' she says in a very small voice. 'One day you'll understand that. You'll look back and know I did my best.'

As she walks from my side, I force myself to remain silent. The door handle trundles round. A swish of fabric. A gasp. Then the floorboard in the corridor creaks, and she's gone. When I let myself look, the sight of the empty room crushes me.

#

My head is full of horrors. I count my heart as it patters and rises. Towing me into an unknown future. It's the only clock I need now, and the only one to which I will surrender.

Mary, are you there? Can you see me?

I can't see you. But I feel you.

They all left me. Like I knew they would.

The room is cold enough to see my breath. Slowly, I uncurl my legs and test their strength. I feel light-headed, but that's okay because for the first time in ages my limbs are light too. When I try to move my legs, they move.

It's just you and me.

The room is stuffed full of plants. Tall, black, they sway in the breeze. Far above my head, unable to help me. I want to reach for them, to hide myself in them, but nothing will work now. I am the one to run from. The hard, black kernel of evil. Night animals romp and bark, and I laugh in the knowledge that Hans is not amongst them. He's not coming, because he's *dead*.

Over and over, Lina crawls away from me. She roars in the corner like an animal, and roars louder when I try to drag her away. She's more afraid of me than of Hans. *What have you done?* And the look in her eyes reflects my new self back at me. I can't bear to see.

There. The bed is sinking now. Flouncing into the cold. Blackness seeps into the sheets. Rising like mould. Staining away the white.

What have you done?

No one calls my name any more. Not even Coral.

Mary. Please.

And when you respond, my heart cracks with gratitude.

Come down, you say. So I crawl out of bed. Sink a leg in the water and shunt down to take your hand. A beautiful light waits at the bottom, and with your hand in mine we descend at your own pace. I cannot see the last step. It dissolves into whiteness, like underwater snow clouds, and as we step off into them your hand is the last solid thing left. Animals lurch and bolt beside us.

Badumbadumbadumbadumba . . .

Heart so loud. Can they hear it?

Shush. It's all right.

The walls bend into a tunnel, and as we advance the edges open out. I recognise Rhona's desk. The mountain, the noticeboard, the soft corduroy sofa. I drop Mary's hand and sit down.

Can I really do this?

I hug myself and look at Rhona's desk. Heat leaches out of my bones. But you stroke my head and say, *The cold won't last.*

On the noticeboard, I recognise a photograph of me and Rhona wearing paper crowns. Rhona has both arms around me. Kissing me on the cheek and squeezing me so hard that my left eye is squashed out of shape. Rhona looks so strong. So protective. She could almost be my mother in that photograph.

But she can't protect me. She's thrown me to the wolves.

I picture Rhona signing the Dundee papers, and rage propels me to my feet. I fly at the photograph and rip it off the wall. I tear it into bits. I swipe at the in-tray, fill my fists with paper and sling it across the room. I kick the desk, which sends a jolt through the potted yucca plant. In slow motion, I watch it go down.

Kathy!

That plant was Rhona's favourite.

What have you done?

When I look, your hand has disappeared. I cry out.

Mary?

The animals fade from my side, and with a cold shove, I land fully into the room.

Silence, broken only by the ticking of the clock. I crouch forwards, stunned.

Oh God . . .

I fold onto the floor. It takes some time for my shoulders to stop shaking. My tears have stuck a bit of paper to my hand, and when I look down I find a scrap of photograph there. My own face. Dumb and happy in a yellow paper crown. I yearn to rewind to that moment. But there's no one to wear crowns with any more. No one to put their arm around me. Rhona has chosen to put herself first. This day has been coming for a long time.

I want to smash my head into the wall. To return to those empty, painless days. But I have no choice now. Only one future is left open, and that is to run. Because if they send me to Dundee, the newspapers will report it. If the newspapers report it, my mum's killers will find me. And if they find me, I'm as good as dead.

From here, the floor looks like it's made from paper. I rise to my knees and survey the damage. The fan guy's keyring crunches under my hand, and as I sit back to peel it away I see the fob is shaped like a record. Grooved on one side, with a hole in the middle and everything. *Vinyl Vultures!* it says on the little record label. I chuck it back into the carnage. Only then do I notice the manila folder. It's the same file Rhona brought to my room. I gaze at it with dead eyes. Then I crawl forwards and open it. The first thing I see makes me jump in the air.

Dagbladet!

I take a deep breath. It's the front page of a Norwegian newspaper. Or, rather, a photocopy of it. On the edge, someone has written a message in English: *Here is largest 'Hans' story for requested time period. Perhaps this helps? With friendly greetings /Jorunn.*

Horrified, I run my eyes down the page. There are no photographs of his face, but that hardly matters. I'd recognise that wooden house anywhere. *Narkobaron Dødsgåte*, blares the headline in thick black letters. *Drug Lord Death Riddle.* None of the report has been translated yet, though Rhona has jotted several annotations in the margin.

Same Lina as in transcripts?

Blue house(!!!)
20km north of Oslo.

I speed-read the article, without managing to take much in. The date on the newspaper is 13th Mar, 2006.

Suddenly, a peripheral movement catches my eye.

'I can't even . . .' says a voice. Crystal hard.

I turn round. Our eyes lock. Stillness descends.

Rhona's face is ghostly. Verging on blue in the pre-dawn light. Her hands wobble at her sides. Slowly, and with great effort, she waggles a finger in the air.

'Get back upstairs,' she gurgles. 'Before I do something I regret!'

I remain where I am. Stuck to the floor. Rhona's eyes bulge.

'I said MOVE! Right this minute!'

I cannot move. But not out of fear. Inside me, a vast anger is growing. Pushing on my insides. Swelling higher, wider, until it covers everything. I get to my feet. From here, Rhona looks small.

'I'm leaving.'

'What?' coughs Rhona. 'What did you say?'

My throat dries up. Rhona steps forward. I flinch as she grabs my arm.

'Now!'

'No!'

I yank my arm away and Rhona tumbles to her knees. She shoots a hand out and manages to steady herself.

'Traitor!' I hiss.

Rhona's face twists. '*Traitor?* How am I a traitor? I've done *everything* for you!'

'You said you'd look after me, but—'

'For God's sake, Kathy!'

'How long have you had this?' I demand, waving the news-paper extract.

'I've busted a *gut* for you! How *dare* you—'

I move for the door, but Rhona blocks my path.

'You blew your last chance for me to protect you!' she spits. '*No one* will help you if you keep fighting!'

'I'm not fighting!'

'Then testify! Tell the police what Hans—'

'I can't!'

'Why the hell not?!'

'Because he's dead!'

Silence rings out. Rhona looks at the report in my hand.

'So that's him?' she asks.

I nod.

'Well then, what are you so worried about? If someone already killed the guy, there's no way he can hur—'

'*I* killed him.'

Rhona jolts. We stare at each other. I hear her breathing in little short gasps, like sobs.

'What?' she says.

But I can no longer look at her.

'Tell me what you just said!'

She grabs for my arm, but I shove her away. A weight drags on my arm, and I realise Rhona has fallen to the floor. I stand over her, horrified by the look in her eyes.

'Kathy . . .' she starts, and trails off. For a second I see a flash of fear. Then she gets up, and says, 'Please. Just trust me.'

'I'm leaving.'

'No you're not, and we both kn—'

'Get *off*!'

I pull my arm away, but this time she's ready. I gasp as her fingers tighten.

339

'No!' I cry. 'No! No!'

Rhona's face is inches from my own. For the first time I see her tears. They're all over her face.

'I'm sick of it,' she shudders. 'I'm sick of you fighting me.'

I struggle. I flex what muscles I have. I go limp and try to dodge away. But it's no good. She's behind me every step of the way. In desperation, I swing a fist and manage to clip her chin. Rhona inhales.

We sway. Then straighten. Then she has hold of my right arm too.

'Joyce was right!' she thunders. 'You're *never* going to get better!'

These words deliver the death blow. I fold to my knees, tears streaming from my eyes.

'How could you?' I weep. But my words are barely audible. Rhona walks past me, decisively, and with horror I realise she's heading for the panic button. I look up. This is my last chance.

Gathering all my strength, I leap onto Rhona's back. We tumble forwards, through the spilled soil of the yucca plant. Then I lunge again. In a second, I'm on top of her. My left hand comes free. On the floor beside us is Rhona's glass globe. Cold, and solid, and even heavier than I'd imagined. In one swift movement, I bring it down on Rhona's head. She raises an arm. But too late.

#

I'd forgotten about the perimeter gate. I stand on the gravel track, cowed by its silent authority. I am not allowed to go through the perimeter gate. That rule is hardwired through me. The bars are not electrified or anything. I know that. And

340

there aren't any spikes, or cameras. But it's tall. And I am not allowed.

Afraid, I turn back towards Gille Dubh. I can just see its outline against the sky. My home. What am I doing?

The wind musses my hair. Shivering, I grip the beige folder to my chest.

No. That life has gone. I'll never have that again.

My whole body is shaking. I take a breath. Chuck the folder through the bars. Then I tuck my pyjama legs into my socks and start to climb. The hard red rust hurts my palms. As I hoist myself over the top a rough bit catches my sleeve, and I tumble backwards. For a second I dangle by one arm, kicking against the railings. Then the cloth rips. I land on my side in a hail of gravel, and something sharp punches the air from me. I roll and gasp. My hand is sticky with blood. It takes several seconds to compose myself.

How long will it take for them to find Rhona? How long till they sound the alarm?

I hurry down the road we took on Mary's day, legs swaying crazily under my weight. Ahead of me, there's a junction. It's not signposted, but I know which way to go. Downhill, the loch twinkles at me. The place where all of this will end.

Mary, I'm coming back to the place where I should have stayed. I will lower myself, singing, into the surf, and this time they will not drag me out. We will drift away from the world of men. Into the Gulf Stream, into the clouds. And I will sing my song for you.

The sun is rising higher.

How stupid of me to trash Rhona's office! If I hadn't done that, they might not have checked on me until five. I'd have had hours to get away. But now. My God . . . They'll be down here with a *cage*. The papers will have a field day.

341

I run in the middle of the road. My shoes clatter.

Out of nowhere, my heart fills with Tim. The pain is unbearable. I rejected him as I did Rhona, and in return he abandoned me. He never even came to get his car. I never heard a thing about that car, now I come to think of it. It's something even the police seemed to miss. But I can't blame Tim. He has his own life. By now, he'll be a dad.

So many houses. It makes me nervous. I don't remember seeing so many houses the last time. The closer I get to the water, the more houses there are. Each one full of people, with watchful eyes and gossiping mouths. Is it obvious I'm from Gille Dubh? I covered my pyjamas with a cardigan I found in the porch. And these are Rhona's shoes, so I'm not barefoot. But I don't know what kind of clothes the outside people wear. Maybe I'm horribly outdated. Maybe only nutters wear cardigans and leather shoes these days.

Finally I reach the seafront and conceal myself in the shadows beside the inn. To my right, there's a garden edged with palm trees. Downhill, the sea. The beige folder is growing cumbersome and I know I should leave it behind. But the news report is too tantalising, so I kneel on the ground and do my best to read it. Lina's name catches my eye – circled with red pen in several places – and I focus my attention on these parts. This is when I make my discovery.

Lina is missing. That's what that word means, isn't it? I struggle to remember.

Yes. That's definitely right. *Hair stylist Lina Tarasevičiūtė. Concerns for . . . safety. Family . . . reported . . . her missing. Drugs (something) uncovered . . . 100 kilos of cocaine found . . . at property. Fifteen stolen passports found. Suspected (gang?) killing. Police investigating.*

My skin goes cold. I swallow. Desperately, I read

further. But as far as I can make out, there's no mention of me.

Hans is definitely dead.

Killer . . .

A banging sound makes me jump, and I look back to the road. Downhill, a family with three children is getting out of a car. They jabber and shriek. My heart skitters.

What am I doing? Get up!

Leaving the folder, I scrabble to my feet. The family are heading downhill. I wait against the wall till they're out of sight. Then I take a sharp right and bolt along the road. My shoes clomp on the tarmac. I go past the general store. Past the church. Past the guest houses. After the sign with the name of the town, the road narrows to a single lane. A rocky beach opens out to my left, and at the sight of the water my heart stops racing. I go over a stile, stray through some sheep and scale a crumbling wall. Stones tip and clack beneath my feet.

I'm here, Mary. I made it.

Katherine, what are you doing?

I'm coming to be with you.

Are you crazy?

I don't know, Mary. I think I might be. Maybe I am. Yes.

Go back, Katherine.

Please don't make me.

This is madness.

Mary. I've killed Rhona.

The sea flips an' licks around my ankles. Around my thighs.

Go backbackback go back go back. ack. ack.

So cold around my waist. Feet slide on weeds. My hand stings. And I'm sorry. I'm sorry. I'm so sorry.

32

'Are you all right?' asks Tim.

I shake my head.

His feet walk away. Minutes later he returns and delivers a plastic cup into my hands. Hot chocolate. We share this while I get myself together. Then Tim tugs my hand and we're off again. This time we go upstairs and find a spot by a glass wall. We huddle there on the floor till our backs get tired. After that we lie down. My bruises hurt. I'm terrified about tomorrow and don't know how to tell Tim I can't go home. But Tim's already done so much. I can't expect him to babysit me forever.

'Stop it,' murmurs Tim, from behind my ear. I turn over.

'What?'

'Stop thinking.'

I smile. 'Okay.'

'Good. Thank you.'

A black-haired man stops in front of us. I look up and turn rigid. Without thinking, I howl. My hands grab for Tim.

'What the . . . !' says Tim, but I'm already on my feet. I haul him after me by one sleeve, and we stagger across the floor. The half-empty cup rolls behind us, leaving a thick brown trail. I howl again. The black-haired man dances backwards, and our eyes meet. He holds his hands out. I stop.

It's not him. It's not him.

I drop Tim's sleeve.

'Oh God,' I say. 'I'm sorry.'

'I was just lookin' at the screens, mate,' says the man. He looks shaken. 'Honest to God, I didn't—'

I turn away, cupping my face in my hands. Behind me, Tim is apologising. Their voices sound embarrassed. Moments later, a hand appears on my shoulder. I jump, but of course it's Tim. Over his shoulder, the stranger is hurrying away, watched by every single person in the room.

'What the holy fuck . . . ?' demands Tim.

'I thought . . . it was someone else . . .'

'Yeah, I got that. But who?'

'It looked like . . . I'm sorry. It just . . . It just really looked like . . .'

'Looked like *who*? I mean, what the fuck, Kathy!'

I look at Tim. My lip trembles.

'Did something happen?' he asks.

'I told you . . . I left Magnus.'

'No, it's more than that. I can see it in your face.'

I look across his shoulder, but people have stopped staring now. The black-haired man is gone.

'There's someone after me,' I whisper. 'A man.'

'What man?'

I shake my head. 'It doesn't matter.'

'Kathy.'

I grab Tim's hand. 'You have to promise me something. It's very important.'

'Okay,' says Tim. His lips barely move.

'If anyone comes looking for me . . . If some people come . . . Just . . . Never tell anyone my name. I mean, my full name . . .'

I look round, and lower my voice even more.

'Tim . . . They hurt my mum.'

345

'What?!'

'He did it . . . He found out her address. So you see . . . I can't go home . . .'

'Kathy, this is serious! We have to go to the police!'

My eyes widen.

'No! Nononono! It's too dangerous! Promise me!'

'But—'

'Promise me!'

Tim's arms fasten around me. For a long time I huddle into him, staring at the floor. The tiles are so shiny I can see my face in them. My eyes like deep black bowls. I am not real. A cartoon character, constructed from geometric shapes. Across the room, someone drives a floor buffer round. Time drifts. I am almost asleep by the time Tim sighs, 'Okay, cap'n.'

#

I wake from a nightmarish vision of men standing over me. Magnus and Hans, laughing side by side. Behind them, Kolbeinn. Black rainclouds all around, and ice below my knees.

Something cold is pressed to my face. Startled, I roll away. I bump into something. A person. I jump. Then my eyes open fully, and I see that that person is Tim. Thank God. I sit back. Just Tim. He looks peaceful as he sleeps. Angelic, with his tousled golden hair. On top of him, his jacket gently rising and falling. Sitting up, I look round and see strangers lying huddled on benches. Fast asleep beneath coats and travel blankets. Someone nearby is snoring. I turn back to Tim, and my heart turns hollow.

I want to go to my mum. I do, more than anything. But I

346

can't, because I know who'll be waiting there for me. Hanging around, looking to avenge Hans's death. Even in my mind, I'm too afraid to speak his name. But I know, more clearly than anything, that he's out there. Him or his men. My mother is bait, and I daren't fall into the trap.

No daughter of mine . . .

I can't go home. Besides, that house is no longer my home. The only place I've ever truly felt at home is miles away.

Tim's jacket is inside out. I see the car keys hanging out of the pocket. For a long time, I look at them. Rising and falling with Tim's gentle breaths.

I look at the clock: 4.15 a.m.

I'm so sorry . . .

Painfully slowly, I lift Tim's keys. They clink once. The space invader hangs out over my hand. I stare at it. I stare at Tim. Then I edge away. By the time I reach the entrance, my face is pink with tears.

#

I don't listen to the radio. Silence is all I can handle now. My driving skills are rusty, but after Inverness the roads grow simpler. It's mid-afternoon now, and the sun is already on its way down. Browns and lilacs flood in as the landscape grows more ragged, and dark mountains loom in to shelter me. At intervals, rumpled slopes choked with silver birch roll down to meet the road, and ravines widen out into vast straw-coloured plains. Hills erupt into towering, oddly shaped formations, their peaks pocketed with snow, and twice I snatch glimpses along glens to Aegean-blue lochs. The road is twisty here, with many bumps and drops and rises, and I never seem to be driving in the same direction for more than a few seconds. On I go, until Loch Oscaig opens out below me and the road zigzags down to its side. Faced with this familiar scene, I'm tempted to stop. But the fuel gauge is a millimetre shy of empty, and I must reach the farm before the car packs up. So on I go, spewing smoke, till the old post office swings into view. By now, the car has gone into spasms. But it's okay. I'm close. I pull in behind the petrol pumps and rattle to a stop. Already I recognise the roll in the hill. The bank of ash trees that shadows the track. The clouds on the horizon are ruffled, like a womb awaiting my return.

Sighing heavily, I lean my head on the steering wheel. For many minutes I remain this way. The sky is royal blue now. The silence so deafening I can hear my ears whistle.

I don't know what makes me turn the radio on. Fear, maybe. The need to hear a friendly voice. But the first, preset station I find is halfway through the news headlines.

'—was unavailable for comment at this time. Police are appealing for witnesses after a brutal hit-and-run in the Tyneside area yesterday morning. The woman, whose name has still not been released, was rushed to Tyneside General and died from her injuries several hours later . . .'

No . . .

No . . .

I get out of the car. I walk across the ground. I throw up.

The shaking takes some time to subside. I loll on the ground, feeling wind pick through my hair. By the time I uncurl, hours could have passed. Dragging my feet, I go back to the car. Voices twitter quietly from the radio. I turn off the ignition and put my head back on the wheel. Exhaustion finally claims me, and when I open my eyes again I have no idea how long I've been gone. My head feels dull. Injured beyond repair. In my head I see the farm, and this gives me the strength to open the door. I sit here for a long time, listening to the waves. Then I get up, and I go.

The first house I pass is the large one, which belonged to the younger farmer. We stayed there one summer when the McLennans were sick. I remember the bedspread that was too heavy to lift, and the slanted windows in the kitchen. I see myself sitting there, eating Coco Pops from a thick pottery bowl with a spoon that was too big for my mouth. The farmer's wife had painted-on eyebrows, which frightened me, and lipstick the colour of balloons.

Across the road is the field where Coral lived. But the brown caravan is gone now. The grass plush where it once was scraggly. Further down the track, the cattle grid remains, but a polished steel sign now rises behind it, embossed with the words *The Hawthornes – private*. I strain to see further, but the bushes have grown into a jungle and it's hard to make out more than the barn roof. What are The Hawthornes? I cross the grid and continue. The track is curved for the last part of the way, so I walk on the right-hand side, waiting for the full view to greet me. Despite everything, I realise I am smiling. The trees thin out. Behind them only sky. That's strange. I start to run. But all that rushes into sight is more emptiness. Then the track widens and I come out of the trees.

At first I think I might throw up again. The hill is there, where it ought to be. The beck is still there, and the little bridge. But the house is gone. Completely and utterly gone. Dumbstruck, I turn round. Then the biggest shock of all hits me. What I took for the barn was not the barn at all. There, across the car park, stands a modern three-storey building. On the bottom floor I recognise the original barn doorway, but the rest of the building is completely new. Pale pine planks form most of the façade, and on the very top floor the walls are made out of glass. Above the entrance, a stark balcony sits atop steel pillars. The door to the room where Mr McLennan sheared sheep is double-glazed.

I remember the greasy smell of wool and the muscles in Mr McLennan's old arms. I remember feeding the kittens in the hay bales while rain drummed on the roof. I remember the chickens in the rafters, and the games of hide and seek with Coral. But all of that is gone. In the back of my mind, I think I'd expected to find the McLennans here. And if not them, then their children. When I told them who I was, they'd've asked me in for tea. I might have got a job on the farm and lived out my days in safety. Everything would have been all right.

But no. No . . .

I fall to my knees, and like a clap of thunder my composure finally snaps. Fast, fast, it rushes past my ears. All at once, like a hundred slaps in the face.

Oh God . . .

Oh God . . .

Oh God . . .

A squeak draws my attention, and I turn to see a woman leaning through a window. She talks loudly in a posh English accent, and for a moment I think she is talking to me. Then I see the phone in her hand. Wireless Internet, she's talking about. Bandwidth.

'This is my *livelihood*!' she snaps. 'I don't care about the call-out charge . . .'

This can't be happening . . .

Rising, I float back to the road. The trees pass in a blur. Tim's car is still parked at the post office. But I don't stop walking. I can't. I see the rocks and head for them. Past the trees, past the caravans, past everything, till it's just me an' the sea an' the sky. The rocks are brown an' black. Though it's March, the water is shockingly cold. Neon blazes across my vision. Mrs McLennan is singing as she pegs out the washing. Magnus's face outlined in white. I slide downwards, dragging the pain behind me. I think I am screaming. I feel it, all of it, stuffed inside my chest. Too big. Too much. The darkening sky lashes down, and I see it see me. I want to smash that sky and its knowing, patient eyes. I want to break everything. I want it all to end. The water flounces up to my chest, an' as I slip further in my heart gives way to a memory. Magnus, singing to me for comfort. I feel him brush my cheek. One last hug. Then blackness drags my feet away, an' the crashin' folds over my head.

Tiny shapes. Glitter. Sting.

Try not to struggle.

My face pierces the surface. Alive, boilin' water. Mouth tastes of blood. I laugh. Fingers hurt. Noise. Static. I see jellyfish. All around. Floating blancmanges. Welts on my arms. Sea crunches into me, an' I follow it down. Stingin'. Gulpin' acid. Another wave. Hard, like fists. The bubbles blink out, an' down I go.

Oh you silly girl . . .

You fool . . .

33

Acka acka ack ack ikk likk likk lakk

Oh God . . .

What's that? Church bells?

Water is round my face now. I snort out a salty torrent. Bobbled weeds strangle me, like Coral's fancy necklace.

I look up and the sky is electric. With my feet I strain for a foothold. But there's nothing down there. Craning my head round, I look for shore. There. It seems miles away.

Acka acka acka

A wiggling, buzzing purr rises up behind the bells. On and on. Drawing me out of myself. Back to a place I had wanted to leave behind.

'Fucking shut *up*!' I yell. And that is when the speedboat rounds the headland.

I gasp as a wave slams me under. In my head, Rhona's face. Eyes closed, as if sleeping. I start to cry.

Here they come. They're coming to get me.

I claw for the surface. Thrash my arms in slow motion. On my feet, one deathly heavy shoe remains. I kick it off.

On board are three figures. The holes of their mouths blink like eyes.

No . . .

I try to swim for shore, and get nowhere. Stones hit my

knees. Rush sideways. Head stings. When I break the surface
I have lost my bearings.

Acka acka acka acka acka ack ack acka ackaacka ack!

Black triangles fringed with white pull me with them.
Froth smashing in from left and right and behind. Pulling me
away till the slurping of the sea is all I hear. A wave boosts me
high into the air, and from this fleeting vantage point I
glimpse the headland. Blacker and flatter, and impossibly far
away. The boat is nowhere to be seen.

Oh God . . .

Are there islands close by? I can't see. What if there are
none and the tide sweeps me right into the Atlantic? No one
would even find my bones then.

Behind me the horizon whirls. Dark slabs, hiding the land
from me. Then my vision retreats into light and dark, and my
eyes swarm with dots.

#

*On the beach, Dad kicks the football. I run after it, kick, and it
sails into the sea. Stupid little . . . Mum wiping my face, Dad
shouting. From high above, we watch the ball cross the bay. A brilliant white speck, bobbing northwards. In the car we follow it.
Rushing peninsula to peninsula. Running down to the beach, too
late every time. You'll pay for that with your pocket money . . .
Sobbing snottily into my sleeves. Desperately watching the sea from
the back seat. Dad drives fast, but the ball's progress remains faster.
The last beach we reach, it's gone altogether. On its way to Atlantis
now, says Mum, as she wipes my tears.*

*There, I see our house. A red-brick council semi. Dying window
boxes, flaking gate. My room is at the front, above the door. The
curtains, burgundy velvet. I can see them from here. The long,*

sloping street that's exactly four hundred and twelve steps long. The stunted laurel bush across the road, where I hide for hours in the den I made.

#

Nose stinging. I roar into the air. But the image remains. Clearer now, against the sky. Eleven Stainton Street. Is my mother still there, cutting scones in the kitchen? I have to go back. I have to know what happened. But now I might never get a chance.

Stupid girl . . .

I flail uselessly. Craving something solid to grab. But I know I can't go on. My limbs are losing sensation. A wave rushes me upwards, and for a split second I glimpse land. Dull brown.

Oh please . . .

I crash back. Yell out bubbles. A tiny white spot traverses the brown. Close, then far, then close.

Shapes. Black zigzags. The white spot blinks away.

Ee!

'EE!'

I open my eyes. Rocks. Wet. Black. Water crashing. A single figure, high up. White blob . . . a *car*.

'Kathy!' screams the figure.

I'm close to the rocks. The rolling maelstrom where salt water hits stone. I force my legs to kick. Bright patches flood my eyes. The current scoops me backwards, and for some time all I feel is the rushing.

Dark clouds roll across me. A wide brown bay. Twin headlands, rising steadily to a barren skyline. Mountains like a pack of reclining greyhounds. Stubby islands crowned in gold and brown. I've been here before.

354

Concentrate . . .

Was that Rhona's voice? I want to believe it.

Time drags. Thoughts simplify. Waves roughen into scallops of brown. I'm going back out again. Round the next headland. On the land, thousands of white dots dance. Faster than before, and in all directions. Rhona? Arms reach out. Blackness curls high, shunts, and crushes down.

#

Are those my legs? Were they kicking all along? Don't stop. Can't. Must . . .

Concentrate.

Bang my leg. Gasp. Look down. Smash head. Go under.

Bubbles. Hard threads curled around. Whipping.

Seaweed!

Shore . . .

Bellowing, I thrash my legs. Sky opens up and I reach for it. A bulbous formation slams down, curtseys backwards. Blackness. Circling water. Then rocks slam back, and I pile into them. Head goes smash. Elbows scream. Slowwwww. Scrape. Up. Then I'm out in the freezing whiteness, and I weigh a million tons.

#

Warm body, not my own.

'Stay with me.'

A rush of movement dizzies me. Ground. Gravity. Air.

'Kathy! Wake up! Wake up!'

I roll into a grainy surface. Splutter. Hands shaking, burning. Can't feel legs. There's someone . . . Somethin' hap'nin'. Hands. *Focus.* Hands round my own. Movin' fast.

'Whuh . . .'

Wind blasts into me, colder than any wind I've ever felt. I jolt. My whole head is chattering, not just my teeth.

'You're all right, you're all right,' babbles Rhona. In technicolor, her face comes into focus. Red and white and yellow, with that blue plaster still hanging on. I watch her eyebrow, caked in blood.

'Didn't know you could swim,' I mumble.

'Yeah, well. There's lots of things you don't know.'

I stare down the cliff. One of Rhona's shoes is there. Bobbing in the sea like a slice of bread.

My neck is crunched up, like a ton weight has been hanging from it. I bring my eyes in line with hers. Try to let her know I'm all right. But my mouth won't form the words.

'We have to get you to the car,' she blusters. 'Can you walk?'

'Uh . . .'

'You have to walk!'

She drags me up, and seems surprised I stay on my feet. With my arm round her shoulder, we climb. It takes an awfully long time. Halfway, Rhona swears and dumps me in a hollow. I watch her rushing away. By the time she climbs back down, I am laughing like a drain. She shrouds me in a tartan blanket and keeps rubbing my arms and legs.

I'm alive . . .

For a long while, all I can do is laugh. Rhona watches with an alarmed expression.

I'm not dead. I'm not dead. I'm not dead . . .

'We have to get you to the doctor,' she insists.

'No.'

'You'll get hypothermia.'

'No.'

'This is serious! You've been out here for over an hour!'

'I'm all right!'

I wave my arms to prove it. Reluctantly, Rhona deflates. We huddle side by side, getting our breath back. She watches me like a hawk.

'Are you angry?' I ask, when I'm able to speak.

'No. They are. But I'm not.'

'Why did you help me?'

'Katherine . . . I'll *always* help you.'

This statement brings tears to my eyes. I try to scowl them away.

'By sending me away?'

Rhona does not answer. She doesn't even seem to breathe.

'I'm not going to that place,' I tremble. 'I'd rather die.'

Wind blows my hair across my face. I don't bother to pull it away.

'Were you going to kill yourself?' asks Rhona. 'In the water?'

I move my eyes away from hers. When I look back, Rhona is wiping her eyes.

'I thought so,' she hiccups. 'Thank God *someone* did, or your wish might've come true.'

'That boat,' I ask. 'Was that the police?'

'I don't know, but I know they're looking for you on land. They found that file you dropped near the inn.'

'Am I in trouble?'

'I just know what Joyce told me.'

I flinch.

'Don't worry,' says Rhona. 'I left her in the middle of nowhere. It'll be hours before she raises the alarm.'

'What? What happened?'

'She was driving me to the surgery in Invercraig, but I stole the car and drove back.'

'Why?'

'Have you still not got it? I'm on your side! I'm the only one who still is!'

I draw a breath. Flick my eyes up to Rhona's. For a moment I'm so happy I can't speak. Then I remember to be cautious.

'What are you going to do?'

'The only thing I can do. Take you back.'

'You can't!'

'Look, this all rests on me. I'm the one you attacked. As long as I don't press charges—'

'No! They'll find out about Hans!'

Rhona sighs. 'So you meant what you said back there?'

'Yes.'

'That's him, in the newspaper clipping?'

'Yes.'

She leans forward and puts her head in her hands. When she speaks again, her voice is muffled.

'Look. Even if you did do it . . . I'm sure you had a good reason . . . The police will take that into account.'

'They already think I'm crazy. They'll lock me away!'

This time Rhona is quiet for longer. I watch her clasping and unclasping her hands around the back of her head.

'I don't know what to do,' she mumbles.

'Let me go!'

'You know I can't!'

'Say you couldn't find me! Tell them I drowned!'

'You're *sick*! You need help! Can't you see that?!'

'What kind of help? Locking me up, all alone? Drugging me up to the eyeballs?'

'Look, the sedatives were never a permanent solution. I

admit Joyce overreacted. But in Dundee you'll get proper treatment.'

'How do you know that?'

'It's out of my hands! There's protocol to follow.'

'Rhona, I'm scared. It's not just the transfer. It's Hans's . . . *people*.'

'What people?'

'I've seen them do things . . .'

'Who?'

'There's a man, with white hair. I think they killed my mother . . .'

Rhona sits up straight.

'Well, that's even more reason to go to the police!'

Our eyes lock, and for several seconds we just glare at each other. She means well, I know that. If she didn't, she wouldn't have stuck her neck out like this. But I can't go to the police. I'm not ready to officially admit murder. Right now, all I want is to go home. My real home. I must be sure what happened to Mum. To visit her grave, if not her deathbed. I owe her that. And Dad. Despite everything, I have to find him too.

I wrap myself further in the tartan blanket, and take a deep breath.

'Please, let me go.'

'And what would you do then? Where would you go?'

'Home,' I reply, in a small voice.

Rhona whips round and scrutinises my face. Already I see the uncertainty in her. The curiosity. And underneath the rhetoric, the genuine desire to help.

'Which home?' she replies slowly.

'My parents' home.'

'Where is that?'

'I don't know its name, but I think I know the way.'

Rhona's eyes dart across my face. Maybe she thinks I'm lying. But I can see she wants to believe me.

'We drove back from here every summer,' I say. 'It's in England. The east.'

'Do you think anyone's still there?'

'I don't know. I have to find out.'

'You said these men killed your mother . . .'

'Yes. But my dad might still be there . . .'

'Look, I'm sure the police will let you g—'

I glare at Rhona.

'All right,' she says. 'Maybe they won't. But . . . Oh . . .' She hangs her head. Mumbles, 'I don't know what to do . . .'

For a while, the wind blows us around. The blood is drying on Rhona's forehead, leaving dark-brown trails on the side of her face. I scrunch my toes up under the blanket, and wait.

'Is that what you want, to find your father?' asks Rhona, without looking at me.

'Yes.'

'Look, I was all for you finding your mother. But your father . . . He doesn't sound like a nice man.'

'He's still my dad.'

'You said it yourself. Why didn't he come to get you? He must have seen you on the news . . .'

'That's what I need to know.'

'Say you do find him, and he's alive, and he's an arsehole . . . What will you do then?'

'I don't know.'

'There can't be anything else, after this, you know. We can't do a . . . Bonnie and Clyde for the rest of our lives.'

I smile.

'Dundee is the end of the line. There's no escaping that.'

'I know.'

Rhona falls silent. This time for longer. She hugs her knees against the wind. This is it now. I've played my last card.

Finally, Rhona turns to study my face. That old fire is back in her eyes. The one I thought had gone for good. 'I must be mad,' she murmurs. Then, with that smile that's not really a smile, she bows her head and says, 'All right.'

34

For the first hour, Rhona drives like a maniac. Joyce's car's a classic Mini, not even a Mini Cooper, and is really not built to travel at these speeds. When the needle creeps over seventy, the car screeches and a smell like burning dust comes through the air vents. I wrinkle my nose up and clutch my seat belt.

'We'll be on the bigger road soon,' says Rhona, squinting into the rear-view mirror. 'You should lie down in the back seat.'

I nod. That would certainly make more sense.

'Motorbike coming up behind,' says Rhona. Obediently, I get down in the footwell. Rhona slows the car for a short period and the screeching sound slackens off. Then she puts her foot back down and I know it's safe to sit up.

'This is madness,' she says, for the tenth time. But her tone is not accusatory. I undo my seat belt and climb into the back seat.

'Put the blanket over you,' Rhona says over her shoulder.

'We're not on the big road yet.'

'I know, but you need to keep warm. I've got my eye on you. One funny turn and it's straight to the hospital.'

'Aren't you cold too?' I ask, but Rhona makes a dismissive noise with her mouth. 'Was Joyce mad, when you stranded her?' I ask.

'What do you think?'

I giggle. Rhona does not join in, so I stop.

'I told her I had to puke,' says Rhona. 'I really did have to puke. And she got out to comfort me. I hadn't planned it. I just . . . It just happened. I knew what you were likely to do, and Joyce had refused to turn back. The car was still revving . . . I pushed her in the ditch . . .'

'You pushed Joyce in a ditch?!'

I sit up straight on the back seat, overcome with laughter. This time Rhona joins in. Then she says, 'Car!' and I must lie back down.

'You're a bad influence,' says Rhona. I hear the smile in her voice. 'You've brought out the rebel in me.'

'Do you think anyone's picked her up by now?' I ask, and then we both stop laughing. Another car swooshes past us. Rhona makes a nervous sound under her breath. Then her foot goes down on the accelerator and the burning smell comes back.

#

After Inverness we join the big road south. Rhona stops talking to me now, and I know from the sounds she makes that she's nervous. We haven't spoken of what will happen when we reach my town. I don't think either of us knows that. But it's what we'll do afterwards that worries me. Will Rhona just turn me in? I mustn't let my guard down.

'Is it Newcastle?' asks Rhona suddenly. 'That's a big city in the north-east. Does that ring any bells?'

I frown. The name is familiar, but it doesn't sound quite right. It's the closest guess yet though. So far we've ruled out Berwick, Leeds, Middlesbrough and Hull.

'I know that name,' I say. 'Maybe it's close to there.'

'Look, I'm trying to make decisions here! This isn't a day trip to the zoo! I need more than *maybe*s if we're ever going to . . .'

A car flashes past us. Rhona falls silent. Then clears her throat and says, 'Sorry. But I do need to—'

'Head for Newcastle,' I say.

'Are you sure?'

'I think it's near there.'

'You're sure?'

My mind races in the silence that follows.

'I'll know it when I see it,' I say. 'I'll know the road.'

'Right.'

'I'll need to sit up.'

Rhona sighs. 'Okay. When we get closer, we'll figure something out.'

A long-distance bus overtakes us, filled with passengers. I jump and hide my face.

'God, I wish the radio worked,' says Rhona, as if reading my mind.

'Do you think I'm on the news?'

'We'll *both* be on the news after Joyce gets to a phone.'

'Maybe they'll just put it in the *Western Courier*,' I say. 'Then the people down here won't hear about it.'

Rhona's silence does not fill me with confidence.

'Don't you think?' I ask.

Rhona exhales heavily. For a second, she remains quiet. Then she mutters, 'Hon, you're more of a celebrity than you know.'

\#

We stop at a service station to use the toilet. Until now, Rhona had just snapped 'No!' when I asked, but now she needs to go too, so we pull in at South Queensferry services and park on the far edge of the car park. Only when we get out do we remember neither of us have shoes.

'Damn,' says Rhona, and stares at her feet. I look at our reflection in the car window and see what she means. We're going to draw attention.

'What if I go in alone,' says Rhona, 'and bring you back a cup to go in? Or you could go right here, behind the car. I'll stand watch.'

'Are you *joking*?' I splutter. But already the presence of strangers is making me nervous. I can't remember the last time I saw so many cars in one place, and each one belongs to a person I do not know. Though we're on the edge of the car park, the main entrance is in sight and I can see ten, maybe fifteen people from here. Behind us, the Forth bridges rise up like the gateposts to hell. Their monstrous size makes me nervous and I'm anxious to leave them behind.

'I'll go behind the car,' I say, and run round the other side.

Afterwards, I feel much better. Rhona locks me in the back seat and tells me not to open the door for anyone. From the window, I watch her running to the main building. Then, for ten awful minutes, I wait. Twice, people walk past and I have to hide.

Rhona finally emerges, with her face turned down. She wears sunglasses and a pair of pink flip-flops, and in one hand she grips a white plastic carrier bag. I am overwhelmed with relief that she's come back in one piece.

'Put these on,' she says as she chucks the bag into my lap. Immediately she puts the car in reverse, and as she turns to look through the back window I notice how white her face is.

'What's happened?' I ask.

But she just says, 'Put those on and get down.'

In the bag I find sunglasses, pink flip-flops, a scarf and a baseball cap with a picture of a cow on it.

'Make sure you're well covered,' says Rhona as we roar back onto the A1. For the next hour we travel in silence. The movements of the car remain constant now, lulling me into a light sleep, and when Rhona's voice speaks again it comes as a surprise.

'Kathy? You awake?'

'Muh . . .'

I uncurl. My neck aching from being crushed into the corner. Outside, sky rushes past.

'I need to tell you something,' says Rhona. 'A secret.'

'What?'

'There was a phone call. You know, back then.'

I pull the blanket down from my face and stare at the back of Rhona's head.

'He called a few hours after the first news bulletin. You were still in Invercraig then, at the doctor's. When I took on your case, they played me the tape . . .'

Rhona turns slightly and grimaces in the rear-view mirror. Then her eyes go back to the road.

'The first thing he said was that he—'

'Rhona. I know.'

'What?'

'Dr Harrison told me. That's the warning I was talking about.'

Rhona turns round again.

'Oh!' she says. Then, after a moment, 'So that was *him*? The dangerous man?'

'I think so.'

'Everyone thought it was Magnus back then. Even I did. Then I thought it was Hans. But I think you and me have dispelled that myth.'

I shiver. Rhona eases off the accelerator.

'Do you understand the message, then? After the *I'll be waiting* part?'

'I don't know what the last bit was. Dr Harrison just told me about it.'

'So you haven't heard the message?'

'No.'

'Do you want to?'

I stare at Rhona, terrified. I hadn't expected this. I know I should just let her tell me. That I should be in full possession of the facts. But . . .

In my mind I picture Stian howling on the porch steps. Kolbeinn with the tyre iron in his hand. The Duck, the heavy-set, silent man, and all the unknown spies.

'I memorised it,' says Rhona. 'Shall I tell you?'

I close my eyes. I breathe slowly in. Then out.

'Tell me.'

'Right. Please bear with my pronunciation. It's quite short, but I'm not good with languages. He said: Tell her, *Ayoo kaykapp oongh.*'

I sit up straight. Rhona's face appears in the rear-view mirror.

'What does it mean? Do you know?' she asks.

'That's not Norwegian.'

'Well, why would—'

'Say it again!'

Rhona's eyes flick between me and the road. Then she clears her throat and says, '*Ayookay kap pungh.*'

A smile creeps across my face.

'You said you heard the tape?' I say. 'What accent did the guy have?'

'Hard to say. It sounded weird. Mixed up. Like he was—'

'Putting it on.'

'*Yeah.* I mean, his English was perfect. In some sections he sounded sort of southern. You know. Etonian. Like a public schoolboy.'

The truth is undeniable now. Infectious. Flopping back onto the back seat, I start to laugh. The car swerves as Rhona sits up. She takes one hand off the steering wheel and pushes her sunglasses onto her forehead.

'What?!'

'Oh my God . . .'

Darling Tim. All this time, he's been waiting for me.

'You know what it is, don't you?'

Rhona strains high enough in her seat to meet my eyes. Grinning like an idiot, I nod. Her eyes go wide in the rear-view mirror.

'*Tell* me!'

'*Okay, cap'n!* That's the message. It's English.'

'What? What does that mean?'

'It's a private joke. It means he won't tread on my toes. He wants to, but he won't. Not till I give him the go-ahead.'

'You mean . . . It's not from the bad men?'

'No.'

'Who then?'

'Tim! He's my best . . . He's . . .'

Rhona makes a strangled noise.

'Wait . . . Not the Tim you told Susan about? The Tim who lives above the shop?'

My heart jolts again. The record shop . . .

Vinyl Vultures . . . That keyring . . . Oh my God! It was

368

Tim who came over the fence! He *has* been trying to get to me . . .

For a moment I'm so happy that I forget to hide from passing cars. Overjoyed, I stick my legs in the air.

'Hoy,' says Rhona. 'Get those down! We'll be pulled over!'

'Sorry.'

After frowning in the mirror for a bit, Rhona shakes her head. She puts her sunglasses back down and turns her attention back to the road. The sunlight is dim against her face now, but I still see her eyes glint behind her glasses. When cars overtake us, her eyes follow them and her behaviour becomes less settled.

'Are you all right?' I ask.

She doesn't answer. I look at her mouth in the rear-view mirror. Pressed tightly closed.

'What's wrong?'

'In case you didn't know, Katherine, we're fugitives from justice. I'm a bit tense.'

'Did something happen?'

Rhona sighs. 'Sorry. Look . . . I didn't want to worry you before, but . . . I think someone recognised me.'

'What? When?'

'A little girl. In the service station.'

I fall silent.

'A TV was on in the café,' says Rhona. 'We're all over the news. Car registration. Mugshots. Everything.'

Suddenly I feel faint. I wilt into the back seat.

'What did it say?'

'They're saying you've kidnapped me. Ridiculous, I know, but—'

'What?! But . . . why would they think . . .'

'I think Joyce is at the bottom of that wee gem. But that's not important. Right now we need to find this town of yours.'

We continue in silence. Rhona's left hand starts jiggling on the steering wheel.

Tappatappatappatappatappatappatappa . . .

'Get up in the front, she says finally.

'Really?'

'Yeah. It's getting dark out.'

I gather myself together and climb carefully over into the passenger seat.

'Right,' declares Rhona. 'Start recognising!'

'Are we close to Newcastle?'

'Soon.'

As I look out of the window, a tiny cry escapes me. Until now I'd somehow convinced myself we were alone on this road. But that could not be further from the truth. Around us there are more cars than I can count, and everything is moving very, very fast. My eyes grow moist behind my glasses, and I realise with shame that I am shaking. My God, what's wrong with me? Maybe I *am* as sick as they say . . .

A road sign flashes past, declaring Newcastle to be fifteen miles away. I look from left to right, and a sense of déjà vu creeps over me. That curve in the road. That bridge. That bank with the six thin trees on top. Rhona remains silent as I touch a hand to my mouth.

'Not much further. It's before Newcastle,' I tell her in a tiny voice.

Rhona indicates she understands. Another sign flashes past, with a diagram of a junction on it. On we go, into the darkening horizon. Then, just as the sun is slipping away, we reach a very familiar stretch of road. I sit up straight.

'Here,' I say.

'What?' bursts Rhona, looking sideways through the gloom. She's taken her sunglasses off, but I still have mine on.

'This turn-off. Go left here.'

'Thank *God*,' says Rhona, and turns on the indicators. The slip road is mercifully empty as we rattle to a more Mini-friendly speed. At the junction with the new road, we stop, and though there's no traffic to give way to, Rhona takes a moment before continuing.

I look in the wing mirror, just in time to see the sun sink over the horizon. Stillness descends.

We drive more slowly now, along quieter roads, around tree-filled roundabouts. For some stretches there are street-lights, and for others there are not. In places the embankments lining the road sink lower, revealing a flat, rural landscape beyond. The glow on the horizon suggests nearby industry. Sporadically I provide directions, and Rhona obeys. On we go, past public parks, discount car dealerships and dormant leisure centres. Working men's clubs, council estates and high-rises. Chip shops on street corners, flanked by gangs of kids up to no good. All of these scenes should frighten me witless, but as we draw closer to our destination a strange calm descends on me. I look through the window, and remember, and know this is my home. Silently, we progress through town. Then, in the middle of a long, straight road, I touch Rhona's arm.

'Stop here,' I say.

The car creeps to a halt, and with a deep breath, I remove my sunglasses. We sit in the dark, indicators clacking.

Rhona turns to me, the rustle of her jacket amplified by the sudden silence.

'Shall I turn off the engine?' she asks.

I squeeze my hands tight around my sunglasses.

'Go right at the next corner.'

'Stainton Street?' She points to the junction several feet before us.

I nod.

Rhona starts the car and we creep forwards. As we turn into the street where I grew up, I struggle to withhold a whimper. An image flashes through my mind, of the day I left this street for good. Dad shouting at me to get a real job. Mum crying. I swore never to come back. And until now, I'm pretty sure I kept my word.

'Are you all right?'

'Mm hmm.'

'Tell me where to stop.'

'Not yet.'

Slowly, we climb a shallow slope. Sometimes we creep so gently that the car almost rolls back. But Rhona never loses her patience with me. When we reach number eleven, I whisper, 'Stop.'

#

For some time, we sit in the car. My parents' house looks much smaller than I remembered. All of the lights are off, and this detail raises questions I am wholly unprepared to face. There is no car in the driveway.

'Looks like no one's home,' whispers Rhona.

'Give me a minute. I'll go look in a minute.'

'I'll come with you.'

'I'm not scared . . . I just . . .'

My voice trails off. Rhona keeps schtum for a second. Then she says, decisively, 'I'm coming with you.'

We look at the house.

'Seems a nice neighbourhood,' offers Rhona. I don't know if this is meant to be sarcastic or not. Without a word, I click my door open and set a foot on the kerb. The breeze is colder than I'd expected. Behind me, I hear Rhona following.

'You'd better lock it,' I tell her. 'The kids round here are little shits.'

We cross the scrubby front garden. Flip-flopped feet schlopping in unison.

'What time is it?' I ask, just before we reach the door. She looks at her wrist. Makes a face.

'I don't know. My watch stopped working.'

I stare at the door knocker, which is fancier than the one I remember. More curly. Tarnished in a deliberate, shabby-chic way. That must have been my mother's doing. Dad has no taste when it comes to such things.

'It must be nine-ish,' adds Rhona, over my shoulder. 'Do you think he's in bed?'

'No . . . He stays up late . . .'

My stomach twinges. It's not like I'd expected everything to be the same, here. I'd already known my mother wouldn't answer the door. That *something* has happened to my Dad. But now that I'm faced with it, it's a shock. As I stand looking up at the house, I realise how naïve I was to imagine my childhood home would remain the same forever. A hollow feeling burrows into my chest as I realise my father might not even be here. That he might not be alive.

'I feel sick,' I whisper as I raise a hand to knock. The brand-new door knocker is too big a step for me right now. I can't bring myself to even touch it.

Holding our breath, we wait.

Nothing.

Across the road, no one is in sight. I stand back from the house and scan the first-floor windows. No sign of life.

'Hmm,' I say, and go round the house, to the driveway. In the shadows at the end I see the gate that leads into the back yard, and almost automatically, I try the handle. It opens.

'What are you doing?' hisses Rhona. Then we step through, and I close the gate behind us.

'It's okay,' I whisper.

Back here, like the front of the house, the drawn curtains are dark. I tiptoe to the back of the yard and lift up the last, cracked paving stone. There! The back-door key. Some things *don't* change after all.

#

'Dad?' I call as we close the kitchen door behind us. Gingerly, I switch on the light. The first thing I see is my dad's green anorak, draped over a kitchen chair. Then I know for sure we're in the right house. The wallpaper is the same. The beige telephone. The mugs on the shelf. The butter dish in the shape of a cow.

'Dad?' I repeat, feeling dizzy now.

'This feels wrong,' mutters Rhona. Her voice is tense.

I rush past her, through the sliding door into the living room. Through the door to the stairs, up to my parents' bedroom, and turn on the light. Nothing. The bed is perfectly made.

I go back to the landing and look down the stairs. Rhona is in the hall, looking up at me.

'There's no one here,' I say.

'Are you sure?'

'Yeah.'

'But . . . you recognise it?'

'Yeah. All of this stuff is theirs.'

'Maybe he's away?'

I walk across the landing and open the door to my old bedroom. Without meaning to, I give a little cry.

'What?' calls Rhona. As her feet patter upstairs, I remain frozen to the spot. Rhona appears at my shoulder. She looks at me, then at the room, then back at me.

'What?'

'My old room. It's exactly the same.'

'My God, don't scare me like that. I thought you'd—'

'No. I mean *exactly* the same.'

Steadying myself on the door frame, I hobble inside. None of it has altered since the day I left for university. The tiny single bed with its Halloween duvet cover. The shelves of books and *NME*s. The giant poster of Trent Reznor, now faded to beige. The photos of long-gone school friends. My sketches and clippings and study notes still sellotaped to the peeling wallpaper. A nectarine stone wrapped in a tissue by the reading lamp. Scrunched-up receipts and loose change. Even my Lightwater Valley mug with an unwashed coffee stain clinging to the inside rim. Every surface, whether flat or vertical, hard or porous, bears a thick, bluish-grey mantle of dust.

'Why would he keep it the same?' I gasp. 'It's been . . . years . . .'

Rhona pats the duvet cover, sending a grainy cloud into the air. Both of us cough.

'No,' she says. 'It's not just this room. This dust's all over the house.'

Outside, a dog is yapping, and though I know it can't be the same dog that used to yap out there, the memory sends a shiver through me. Behind those curtains, is it still 1998? It feels like I could pick up where I left off. Rewind to a point where I still had choices, and choose a different path.

'Come on,' calls Rhona, from halfway down the stairs. 'It's not good for you to be in there.'

'Wait. I just—'

'Come on,' she repeats. I drift to the top of the landing and look downstairs. The floor below the front door is piled with letters. I descend to Rhona's side and we hover over it.

'Do you think we should open one?' she asks.

I shrug. We start to kneel down. And that's when we hear the footsteps.

35

The door knocker raps loudly and our shoulders leap up to our ears. Rhona is making a face at me that I think means *Don't make a sound.* We hover, semi-hunched, staring at each other. Outside, I hear feet shifting. A rustle of cloth. Then a shadow passes the keyhole and the door knocker raps again.

'I know it's you, Bill,' says a woman's voice. 'I can see the light on.'

My eyes widen. I leap to look through the spyhole, and Rhona leaps after me, making a noise like *f-th-wp-fth-thp!*

'Go round the back!' I hiss.

Rhona's fingers claw my arm. Outside, feet shuffle. A pause. Then, 'Kathy?'

'Go round,' I repeat. Then I free myself from Rhona and slip through the house.

A tiny woman waits at the back door, arms crossed across her massive bosom. She wears a Michael Jackson T-shirt over tracksuit bottoms, and a pair of pink sheepskin slippers. As I approach, she peers through her varifocals.

'It *is* you!' she cries. 'I thought my old ears were playing up.'

'Hi Madge,' I grin. She's the closest thing to family I've seen in a long time.

Rhona comes around the corner then, and Madge jumps at the sight of her.

'Well, haven't *you* been in the wars?' she exclaims. Suddenly

I realise how dishevelled we must look. The cut on Rhona's head has scabbed up, and though we washed our faces earlier with a bottle of water we're still not a pretty sight.

'Kathy, what on earth are you doing here?' Madge asks.

'I came to see Dad. Where is he?'

Madge puts a hand to her mouth. 'I thought you were him,' she says. 'I thought they'd finally let him out . . .'

'Is he away?'

'Do you really not know? Oh . . . Heck . . .'

A tear trickles from her eye and pools along the frame of her glasses. She leans on the wall with one hand and holds her face with the other.

'Your dad's in the hospital, pet. They've had him there since the breakdown . . .'

My stomach lurches. But this is better news than I'd feared.

'What hospital?'

'Lysdon Manor.'

'Where's that?'

'Is that your car out front?'

'Yes,' I reply. Rhona shoots me a look.

'Well, if you'll give me a lift, I can take you. It'll have to be the morning, though. Visiting hours are over.'

I look at Rhona. She frowns.

'I can't believe you didn't know,' says Madge. 'But seriously, pet, why are you here? Your Dad said you were in Norway—'

'I was.'

Rhona clears her throat. I look at her, then say, 'Listen, Madge . . . It's kind of a secret that I'm here.'

'Oh! Well, you know me! Say no more, petal. I wouldn't have anyone to tell anyway.'

'It's really important,' I say. 'That you don't tell anyone.'

'Righto. Well, I'm freezing me cheeks off. I only nipped across for a minute. But I'll come by tomorrow . . . Say, ten o'clock? That should give us plenty of—'

'No,' says Rhona. 'We have to go now.'

Madge stares at her, the light bouncing off her glasses.

'It's after nine,' she replies, in a *does not compute* voice.

I look at Rhona too. She raises her eyebrows.

'Surely it can wait till morning,' adds Madge. Her facial expression suggests she is waiting for the punchline.

'No. It can't.'

'What if they won't let us in?' I say.

'We'll tell them it's an emergency.'

'What kind of emergency?'

'I don't know. But it's the only way. Time is not exactly on our side.'

'Oh dear . . .' murmurs Madge, and rubs her glasses with the back of her hand.

'Can you take us there?' I ask.

'Kathy, love, are you in some kind of trouble?'

Over Madge's shoulder, Rhona gives me a look.

'Yes,' I reply. Rhona does an angry-dance.

Madge's face crunches smaller.

'Don't you watch the news?' I ask.

'Telly's on the blink. Why?'

'We're on it.'

She steps back and looks at me. In the silence that follows, I can almost hear her brain whirring. A cool breeze drifts around us, smelling like vinegary fish 'n' chips.

'Well,' replies Madge, at last. 'We'd best get going, hadn't we?'

\#

379

We wait in the car while Madge fetches her anorak. As the minutes tick away, Rhona's knuckles grow white round the steering wheel.

'She's calling the police. I know it.'

'No. She wouldn't.'

'How do you know? How well do you know her?'

'She's as good as family.'

We drift back into silence. Five minutes later, Madge rushes out, dressed in a dark-green tracksuit. I sit up as she crashes into the passenger seat. But before I can open my mouth, she pants, 'Sorry! Sorry! I didn't have anything black!'

'Why would you need black?'

'We're undercover, aren't we?'

I glance through the front. Her tracksuit bottoms are tucked into a pair of buccaneer boots.

'Sorry!' she says again, and the earnestness in her face makes me want to giggle.

'Right,' says Rhona, and starts the engine. All of us tilt backwards.

The drive to Whitley Bay is tense. Though the roads are smaller now, there's far more traffic, and we're forced to stop at many brightly lit intersections. I slide further and further down in my seat, shielding my face when pedestrians come close. Rhona adheres wordlessly to Madge's directions, but the rhythm of her breathing shows she's scared. At one junction we stop beside a supermarket, and I have a clear view through the doors to the news stand. There, the front page of a newspaper displays a picture of my face. After that, I lie down.

Lysdon Manor lies in private grounds on the northern edge of town. An eighteenth-century mansion house, hidden from the road by a tall stone wall.

'Not NHS, then,' says Rhona as she brings the car to a halt. I sit up and peer through the windscreen. Before us, the gates are closed.

'Come on,' squawks Madge. 'There's a car park at the top of the—'

'No, this is fine right here. Some exercise won't hurt us.'

I shoot a glance at Rhona, but her expression is difficult to decipher.

'How will we get in?' I ask.

But Madge says, 'Don't worry. I know the lass on reception.'

'The gates . . .'

'There's a button,' says Madge. She shoves her door open and disappears.

Rhona tips her seat forwards for me. As I get out I hear Madge on the intercom, saying she has important business.

Madge grumbles about her legs all the way up the driveway. Rhona and I trail behind, and though it's too dark to see each other's faces, she turns her head my way many times. Twice she touches my hand with her own, and I know she is offering me the chance to turn back. But I shake my head and keep walking.

As the driveway curves closer to the house, the sculptured bank to our right flattens out and we catch a glimpse to the garden beyond. Just a featureless black expanse from this distance, though by daylight I'm sure it's impressive. At the back, five spotlights throw circles against an evergreen hedge. Men on a scaffold are threading fairy lights through the branches.

'Doing it up for the Christmas ball, I see,' says Madge.

'Ball?'

'Yeah. For the residents.'

'But it's September—'

'Ach. They do things a bit early here. It's not like anyone will notice.'

I stare at the back of Madge's head. She keeps ambling forwards. Somewhere nearby, a hedge trimmer fires up, buzzes for a minute, then dies. We pass a man in a fleece jacket loading branches onto a pick-up.

'Award-winning gardens, these,' calls Madge.

'Wait. You said this was a hospital.'

'It is. Sort of.'

'Sort of?'

Madge's hand rises, in silhouette, and flutters beside her ear.

'They're all . . . you know . . . a bit doolally,' she says.

#

'Hallo, Margaret, long time no see!' says the girl on reception. Rhona and I hang back, trying to avoid eye contact, while Madge reels off a fantastically long-winded lie about delivering an important letter. 'Got new chauffeurs?' jokes the receptionist, pointing her biro at us. I jump forwards, fearing Madge will spill the beans. But to Madge's credit, she replies, 'No, these are my nieces.'

'Well, I'll need signatures from you all,' says the receptionist, and slaps a dog-eared clipboard onto the desktop. Madge signs her name and hands the pen to me. I pause. But Rhona dives in to take over. Without hesitation, she scrawls *A. McDonald*. Then, in the line below this, *S. McDonald*. We hand back the clipboard and the girl buzzes us through to a buttercup-yellow waiting room.

'He'll be glad to see you,' she calls, before the door closes. 'He's barely had any visitors.'

We sit in silence. We are the only ones here. Cardboard reindeer adorn the back wall, each fastened to the last with yellowing string. Three crimson foil bells hang from the middle of the ceiling, and under the plastic Christmas tree someone has made a manger from a shoebox.

'Madge,' I say. 'Do you mind if I go in alone?'

'No probs, love.'

'What about this letter we're meant to be delivering?' asks Rhona. 'They might ask to see it.'

Madge lifts a carrier bag from her handbag and silently hands it to me. Inside, it's full of envelopes.

'Mostly junk mail,' she says. 'But don't worry. I don't think anyone will ask.'

'Where did you—'

'Off the doormat. I usually sneak it in for him.'

I look at the letters and suddenly feel very sad.

'How long has he been in here?' I ask.

'Let me see . . .' Madge counts on her fingers. 'It was the day after your mum's funeral, if I'm not mistaken. They found him in his pyjamas, near where the ferries go out. Terrible business. He was out of it for weeks. Since the very day she died, if you ask me.'

'What date was that?' asks Rhona.

'Hoo, I dunno . . . March, I think, because of the snow-drops. Such a beautiful ceremony . . .'

'Same time you showed up,' whispers Rhona. 'March 15th.'

My gaze drifts to a pamphlet on the coffee table. *Living with Mental Illness*, it says. And below these words, a picture of a family laughing.

The door buzzes and a different nurse comes through. Younger than the other girl, with an asymmetrical haircut I can only assume is fashionable. She perches herself on the coffee table, clasps her hands together and smiles.

'Okay. I've got some ground rules for you new guys.'

I shrink beneath the girl's gaze, but her eyes keep firm contact with my own.

'We've been in places like this before,' says Rhona.

'Well, I'll go through them anyway. Right. Rule number one – and I can't stress this enough – is that you don't discuss the outside world. No news stories, no TV stuff, no gossip, nothing that would upset him. We try to protect our patients from that as much as possible. All right?'

We nod.

'Second of all, Mr Fenwick is still quite jumpy. He gets anxious easily and is sensitive to sudden movements, loud noises et cetera. So please keep this in mind at all times. Also, we'd thank you not to use any bad language.'

She claps her hands brightly.

'So! Who's first? I'm afraid it's one at a time.'

She looks at Madge, who in turn points at me. My eyes turn moist.

'Youngest first,' says Madge.

'Right,' says the nurse, and without further ado she leads me through the doors.

#

The room I walk into smells of bleach and flowers, with a faint musty tang lingering underneath. I'd expected the place to be dark, or at least look something like my bedroom at Gille Dubh. But I'm south of the border now, and I suppose

384

they do things differently here. The decor is sparse but functional, with a pine writing desk, single bed and easy chair. A cork noticeboard hangs above the desk, devoid of notices or pins, and a giant blue flower has been stencilled onto the woodchip wallpaper. Through the open curtains, the sky is deep black.

A man with steel-coloured hair sits in the chair, hunched almost double over his knees. His hands stick like lollipops through the sleeves of a brown plaid bathrobe, and on his feet there's a pair of matching slippers. As I creep forwards, his head jerks up. Both of us freeze, and draw a breath.

The glasses are new. Thick-rimmed, making his face look gaunter than it already is. Suddenly I feel like I've travelled into the future. That the door behind me is a portal, and stepping through it has somehow, suddenly, stuck a decade onto my father's age. Because it's him. Despite everything, it's him.

The cords in his throat tighten. Then, in a voice like wallpaper paste, he croaks, 'Kathy!'

I want to run. Not through fear. At least, not the same fear I harboured as a child. All the way here, I've been steeling myself to face him. Preparing to unearth the years of pain and bitterness he represented. But the man before me is not the fearsome overlord of my childhood. Not any more. He's a faded photocopy. A ghost.

I feel behind my back for the door handle before remembering there's not one. If I want to leave early, I'll have to attract the camera's attention.

'Katherine,' hiccups the man. 'Is that you?'

I am rooted to the spot.

'Dad?'

A little sound comes from his throat. He stretches out an

arm and holds it there. Then tears start gushing down his face. I blunder forwards and he flings his arms round me.

'I'm back, Dad,' I sob. 'I've come home.'

'I thought I'd never see you again . . .'

For several minutes, neither of us can speak. It's the first time I have ever seen my father cry. Finally, I kneel down on the floor and we search each other's faces. I'd wanted to off-load my anger on him. To demand why he never came to get me. But the answer to that question is crystal clear. He's been as lost from the real world as me. Battling the same demons.

'Your mother . . .' he says, and cannot continue.

I watch until I can stand no more. Then I blurt, 'I know.'

'That she . . . she's . . . ?'

'They told me.'

'She went so quickly. I was with her when . . .'

He looks at me with that awful, shrunken face. Trembling, twitching. Fresh tears bloom from my eyes.

'If I'd driven her to the shops myself,' he wobbles. 'She'd have been nowhere near that road. That bastard would never have . . .'

I sit up straight.

'Did they catch the one who . . . hit her?'

'Oh yes. He's in HMP Durham. And thanks to our joke of a legal system, he'll be out again by spring! Drunken bastard . . . What kind of justice . . .'

'What was his name?' I tremble.

'Jim Wilkinson,' replies my father, with visible hatred. He snorts and puts a hand to his face. With wide eyes, I watch my father wiping his glasses on his bathrobe.

'That's an English name,' I hear myself saying.

'Doing 92 mph when he hit her. Snivelling, boy-racer swine . . .'

'He was English?'

'From Gateshead.'

'But you said . . . on the phone . . . You said the car was foreign . . .'

Dad looks at me. His glasses are back on now, and behind them his eyes are bitter.

'Vanity plates,' he says, with emphasis on the *vanity* bit. Then his mouth snaps shut.

For many moments, this information is too much to get my head around. Is it true? Did Hans have no part in her death? If so, it's a bittersweet victory. My mother is still gone. She still died without me by her side.

'Was Mum hurt,' I tremble, 'that I didn't come?'

Dad shakes his head.

'She was unconscious. She never knew.'

'But *you* were hurt . . .'

He looks at me.

'It was my fault,' he whispers. 'I drove you both away.'

These words have an electrifying effect on me. Frantically, I start patting his back.

'No, Dad! It wasn't your fault!'

'I've been a terrible father . . .'

'Please don't say that!'

I lean back to look him in the face. To convince him it's all right. But his eyes are far away now, and I know my words would not reach him. For some time he cries into his knees and, not knowing what else to do, I keep my hand on his arm.

My father's sobs become quieter, though the trembling never fully stops. I hear him gasping for breath and remove my hand so as not to crowd him.

'Has your husband come with you?' he asks, when he

is able to speak again. I look up from my perch on the armrest.

'No.'

'Where is he, then?'

'Long gone.'

Dad is silent for a moment. Then he murmurs, 'Good. He never did love you.'

A gust of wind jolts the window, stirring the curtains.

'I've been sick,' I say. 'I still am.'

Dad sits back and studies my face. The bags under his eyes are still shiny.

'Sick how?'

'Sick like you.'

The sadness in his eyes is unbearable. Quietly, he asks, 'The gloom?' His pronunciation makes this sound almost comical.

'Yeah.'

'How long's that been going on?'

'Years.'

He looks at the floor, and his face turns hard.

'No wonder you hate me,' he says.

'I don't hate you. Not any more . . .'

As soon as these words leave my mouth, I realise they're true. I forgive him, and always would have. But Dad seems not to have heard.

'I'll make it up to you,' he says. Then his shoulders start shaking again. This time the shaking doesn't stop at all. I see him fighting it. Trying to stop, without success. He removes his glasses and flusters blindly in an attempt to clean them.

'What are we like?' I say when he has slotted them back on his face. And both of us try to smile.

Suddenly I remember the letters.

'Here,' I say. 'Express delivery.'

Dad smiles and accepts the bag. 'Madge?' he asks.

I nod.

'Probably junk,' he says. 'It usually is. They don't want me to have this, you know . . .'

I watch him sorting through it, glad of the distraction. His mouth moves silently as he reads the envelopes. Once or twice he chuckles. Then, without opening anything, he hands the whole lot back.

'Junk,' he confirms. 'But thanks anyway. My hiding place is only big enough for essentials.'

'Do you ever get any real post?' I ask. My father knits his brow.

'There were sympathy cards, in the beginning. But I didn't . . . I couldn't . . . I threw them away.'

I place the envelopes back into the bag and roll it closed.

'Hey!' says my father, suddenly. 'I have a letter for you . . .'

'What? For me?'

'I kept it. In case you ever . . . I mean, just in case you . . .'

With effort, he hauls himself to his feet. He crosses the room to the bed and gets down on his hands and knees.

'Do you need help?' I call.

But he just replies, 'Cameras don't cover this bit. Puh. Might as well be in prison myself.'

'Why don't you go home?'

'I don't know. I could . . .'

He ambles back to my side, deposits a blue envelope in my hands and eases himself back into his chair.

'I suppose I just think . . . what's the point?' he says, and with these words his face darkens.

'It's your *home*.'

'I'm not the same, Kathy. I'm not as strong as—'

389

'What do the doctors say?'

He sighs heavily, and scratches his head. 'They think I'd be okay. But—'

'Well then.'

'Kathy. I'm not normal.'

'Well, neither am I.'

For a moment we stare at each other. My father's eyes dart around my face. Breathing shallowly.

'We have to live our lives,' I say.

Wind buffets the windowpanes. Eventually I look down at the envelope in my hands.

'I've had that for a long while,' says my father.

I turn over the letter and look at the front. The writing is smudged, scrawled in thin blue biro and all crammed into one line.

Kathy, 11 Staiton Street, Northsheel, England.

Suddenly my heart leaps into my mouth. I'd recognise that handwriting anywhere. Jumping up, I hold the letter to the light. The postmark is illegible, but the stamp . . .

'Watch for the cameras!' calls my father.

Norge. Noreg. A.

'Oh my God!'

'What?'

With trembling fingers, I open the envelope. A paper rectangle falls out onto my feet, and I unfold this into a single sheet of college-ruled paper. Huge, messy handwriting fills both sides. I turn to the back, and find what I was looking for.

Love, Lina.

I turn to my father. 'How long?' I demand.

'I don't know. Madge brought it with the first lot.'

My legs are too shaky to raise me off the floor, so I remain on my knees. Silently, I start to read.

390

Deare Kathy,

I do not know how to find you. You are gone one day now. I sat with Hans until I got strength to get out. Then I came here to town in night. I am in the barbars. You are not here like I thought you might. I have not called Stian yet. After I post this letter, I will go. We will run through Sweden. I found my passport in Hans house.

I hope you are okay. I hope Petter and Håvard did not find you. They did not bring Kolbeinn with them back for me, but I am frightend they will come here to barbar so I must go.

Thankyou for helping me. I don't know what had happend if you had not come. I am sorry did not say thankyou, and sorry so much screams. I am hurt. Still blooding.

I want you to know, you did not kill Hans. Maybe you think you did. But I finisht it myself. Put hands round neck before he waked up, and his body stoppt moving. Hans is dead for one day. Now I go. Too scared to go to Politi. If they find me I will not tell of you. It is gift to you, for helping me.

Please be careful for Magnus. Your old boyfriend. He was there yesterday, at dinner. They sign a kind of contract. Heard Magnus say could not find your passport.

I hope you are alive. I hope the letter finds you. Please know I am so thankfull to you, for ever. I will run now. Goodbye Kathy my good friend.

Love,
Lina

36

I rock back on my heels. The wind must be blowing in from the sea, because all I can hear is the hedge trimmer. Blankly, I look to the window, but see nothing.

'Bloody gardeners,' spits my father. 'Every single day!'

I turn back to him, with tears in my eyes, and his face softens.

'Bad news?' he asks, nodding at the letter.

'No,' I sob. 'No, it's good.'

Beyond the high-pitched grinding, I become aware of a different noise. Crackling. Smattering. It stops and starts, growing steadily in volume.

Crackle ackle ackle ackle. CRACKLEACKLEACKLEACKLE!

I stand bolt upright. My chair goes over.

Footsteps, running fast over gravel. There are many now, and growing louder. The letter drops from my hands.

'Oh God,' I say.

'What?'

'They're here.'

A sudden flash of light makes me turn to the door. There, in the square glass panel, I have a partial view of the corridor through which I entered. In it, a person is running forwards. I stand back in alarm. As their torso rushes closer, a door opens behind them. Then Rhona's face slams up to fill the window, and the movement behind her is blocked from view.

Her eyes are panicked. Soundlessly, she shouts words. But the look on her face tells me all I need to know. I see her looking for a door handle, as I did. Then hands appear on her shoulders, and she turns round. A sharp-eyed face looks through the gap, and I recognise the nurse with the fancy haircut. A bleep sounds from this side of the door. Then it springs open and a throng of people bursts in.

I stand back in alarm. Between arms and legs I glimpse a hand grasping a newspaper. *Lullaby Loony Seen on A1*, says the headline.

'Get back! You *morons*!'

That's Rhona's voice. But the others are louder than her now. A hand yanks my wrist, making me lose my balance. Then the floor hits my knees and faces rush in on every side. For a second all I see are Rhona's flip-flops. Then hands drag me sideways and the doorway swings into view. There must be twenty people in here. Legs all clad in the same navy blue.

'Is it her? Is it her?' gabbles the nurse, while Rhona yells, 'You'll hurt her!'

'It's all right now, Mrs McNeill,' a policewoman says to Rhona. 'You're safe now.'

'She's not dangerous!'

'Come away now, let's see to that cut—'

'Let *go*!'

Rhona pushes the policewoman. Some people topple sideways. But there are hands all over my arms now, and their grip is too solid to break. Someone puts my face into the ground.

'It's all right,' I tell Rhona as metal clicks round my wrists. Then a man's voice starts blaring above the others, and as I'm drawn back to my feet his face swings into view.

'Katherine Fenwick, I am arresting you for the attempted murder of Rhona McNeill. You do not have to say any—'

'It's useless,' says a voice. 'She won't understand.'

'—thing, but it may harm your defence if you do not mention, when questioned—'

Through the arms and legs of the throng, I notice my father, standing by the place he hides his letters. Face drained of colour, eyes fixed on mine. In his hand, I see Lina's letter. He signals with his eyes. Then firmly closes his hand over the letter. No one is looking at him.

'—something you later rely on in court. Anything you do say may be given in evidence.'

Bodies close in, cutting my father from view, and again all I see are shoes. Then my captor swings me upright, and all of us move towards the door. We frogmarch through the yellow waiting room, through reception and down the steps to the entrance. My flip-flops have been lost in the tussle and as we step out into the breeze the gravel pricks my feet.

'Didn't they get the van through yet?' asks a voice. Everyone halts.

What's going on? I'd expected helicopters and tear gas and abseiling bloody marines. But there aren't even any police cars. For a moment I'm stumped. Then my gaze shifts down the driveway to the gates. There, I can just see the top of a police van. A crowd of heads struggles behind the gates, and behind them there's something that looks like a satellite dish. A large white floodlight illuminates the scene.

'Jesus Christ,' says one officer. 'When did the cavalry arrive?'

At that moment a door opens and Rhona comes out, escorted by two policewomen.

'Mrs McNeill,' someone says, 'if you're up to it, would you please move your car?'

Suddenly I realise why the police moved in on foot. Joyce's Mini is parked slap bang in front of the gates.

'And let that mob in?' spits Rhona.

I stare at the jumble of strangers. Moving and struggling. Every gap is filled by a face. Arms whip like tarantula legs.

'Kathy! Katherine! Kathy! Kathy!'

'We'll move it for you then.'

'I don't have the keys,' she replies coldly.

'Fuck it. Let's just walk it,' says someone.

'Put something on her head.'

A policewoman drapes me with her jacket. Slowly, we start to move.

I can't see the crowd as it grows nearer, but I can hear them. Old and young, male and female, their voices form a chattering, baying cloud. Some have local accents and some do not. As my breathing speeds up, the air under the jacket grows stuffy. I gulp in breath. People behind me start shouting.

'Move back! Get back!'

'John – watch that camera.'

An arm wraps round my neck. Lights start flashing. Once. Twice. Then continuously, transforming my legs into a glittering disco. Something soft hits my chest, and as I skitter sideways it falls onto my feet. A small blue teddy bear, with a gift tag full of writing.

'Kathy! Kathy! Can you give us a comment?'

'Look at her feet! Sid, get a shot of her feet. Quick!'

An extra-big flash. I look down and see my own grimy legs lit in white.

Something hits me again.

'For fuck's sake, John. Watch her head.'

'Clear a path!'

'Lunatic!'

'—be locked up!'

'—love you!'

'—wasted good money on your treatment. Can you explain why you saw fit—'

'Mrs McNeill, how bad are your injuries? Can you comment on your ordeal?'

Somewhere nearby, I feel a struggle going on.

'Kathy, do you have anything to say to the Lullaby Girl Foundation?'

'Vultures!'

Was that Rhona's voice? A scuffle breaks out, and for several seconds the voices cut off. Shoes scrabble. A hand hits the tarmac, palm down, and a woman cries out in pain. Strong hands yank me backwards. Then the lights swing away from my feet and I hear them clicking in a different place.

'BBC News, Kathy. Can you tell us why you turned on the people who—'

'Get her through the other side! Get her through!'

'Move back!'

'—say to all the people you've let down?'

The bodies around me press closer. I can feel them breathing now, pressed close into me. I stumble.

'Fucking pigs!' shouts a man. A hand claws my arm. Fingers pull my clothes. Then, quite suddenly, the jacket over my head becomes taut. Everything jolts to a stop. I feel hands fighting above me.

'Get back!' yells a voice. Then the jacket whirls away and I am unveiled to a ceiling of eyes. Collectively, the crowd inhale. Several feet away, a woman in a pale suit holds a microphone, and I realise with shock that I recognise her.

She's the one Joyce was so mad at that day after the thunderstorm. Her microphone has a strip of metal embossed with the words *Daily Post*. Over her right shoulder, a huge camera lens is pointed at me.

She lunges.

'Kathy, how do you justify your blasé attitude towards the Lullaby Girl Foundation? Don't you think your supporters deserve some payback for all the—'

'So *that's* what you are,' I exclaim.

'Yes. I spearheaded the campaign which evolved into the Lullaby Girl Foundation. Until your lawyer shut us down, our readers raised over eighteen thousand pounds for your treatment. Aren't you grateful for—'

'You broke into our house. You said you were from the church.'

A hush falls. The woman in the suit looks shocked but recovers quickly.

'We've invested so much in you. Don't you think you owe us for that? Photographs? An interview? Some indication that you *appreciate*—'

'I never asked for your help,' I say. 'Why did you help?'

'Because we *care*.'

I look at the *Daily Post* woman. At the camera.

'No. I don't think you do,' I say quietly.

The newspaper woman's mouth opens and anger flashes through her eyes. Around us, I notice the mood shifting. The shouting has turned into whispering, but on the whole people seem taken aback. As though they've discovered a talking chihuahua and are figuring out what to do about it.

The policeman beside me has recovered the jacket now and tries to put it back on my head. But I duck away and say, 'Wait.'

'So you *are* ungrateful,' snaps the woman with the microphone.

'No. I just need some privacy, like anyone else.'

'She's mad,' says someone. 'She doesn't know what she's saying.'

'I am not mad.'

'You're a public figure! People are interested in you!'

'Why? What do you want?'

'We want to know what happened!'

'Why?'

'We just do!'

I glance around the crowd. Some faces are kind, some are not, but the thing that unifies them all is the hunger in their eyes. Every single person is dying to hear me speak again. For a moment, I wonder if I do, indeed, belong to them. And regardless of the reasons behind their interest, I find this concept oddly comforting.

'Well, maybe I'll tell you one day,' I say. 'But not here. Not like this. We'll do it my way.'

'Let's move, people!' yells a police officer, and to my amazement people clear a path. But there's a commotion at one side. Behind a row of police, one man is struggling like crazy. I see an elbow. A fist. A flash of blond hair.

'Katherine!' shouts a voice.

I freeze. A face slots through a gap and is shoved back through. People stumble. Arms and legs squashed tight, with the police line leaning on them. I'm running back to them now, but my captors intercept me. I slither to the tarmac. Look up. Struggle forwards. Look for the blond man.

'Tim!' I yell.

People gasp. A hand stretches through and holds my face. Then a gap opens up, and I see him. Slightly battered but grinning like a maniac. Tears spring into my eyes. His hair's longer than when I last saw him. And someone appears to have smacked him in the nose recently. But it's him. Alive and well and right here. Our eyes clamp together. Then more bodies barge between us and strong arms scoop me backwards. My heart is beating hard. But I'm happy. So happy. Stumbling, I am shepherded away.

At the van, Rhona catches up to me. Her face is flushed as they bundle me through the doors.

'The police won't let me go with you,' she says. 'But don't be scared. I won't press charges.'

'I'm not scared.'

'Everything's going to be okay,' she says.

'I know.'

The doors close, leaving Rhona on the pavement. She waves as the van rumbles to life, and I'd have waved back if it wasn't for my handcuffs. Camera bulbs flash through the darkened windows, and amidst this light show her silhouette fades from view. This ought to have been my worst nightmare. But instead I feel quite fine. My heartbeat slackens as the van whisks me smoothly away.

Everything *is* going to be okay. It is. Because finally I know what to do . . .

How many months have I carried this fear in my belly? Protecting it from those who sought to extract it. Kidding myself while it fed on me and grew fat. I've had enough of that parasite, and the time has come to purge it. Into the open air, into the ears of the police. I'll tell them about Hans, about Kolbeinn and Magnus. About what they did to me, and what I did in return. God knows, Hans's house was full of evidence. It might be enough to send Kolbeinn down, if they haven't weeded him out already. Maybe Magnus too.

But not Lina. The news that she got away hit my heart like sunshine, and I refuse to drag her back into this. Maybe that'll mean prison for me. Maybe Dundee. But I'm ready for those things. Only by letting go will I free myself. Only then can the clock start to tick again.

Through the windows of the van, dark shapes whirr past. There are no flashing lights now, and no shouting voices. Just the rushing of the northern wind. Cold and crisp, laced with the scent of the sea. It's the last thing the Lullaby Girl will ever smell, before returning to Mary's side. My pale twin, born of despair. Tonight I hand the baton back, and reclaim my rightful place. My name is Katherine. I came from the waves. And at long last, I am awake.

Acknowledgements

I'm very grateful to Zoe King, Liz Bonsor and Caroline Hardman for their invaluable feedback on my early manuscript. Also to Nina for her endless positivity, and for nudging me in the right direction. Thank you Sandra for the secret-keeping, lussebullar and Malmö japery. Thank you Ulrika, my Oslo partner-in-crime. Thank you Clara, Kevin, Douglas, Maija, Lynsey, Jon, Dougie, Davie and all my early readers for your support. Thank you to Mike for looking out for me back in the day, and to Astrid for the crazy years. Thanks to Paul and Sarah, Anna on Scoraig, and Dot and Brenda for your kind hospitality during the many edits of this book. Sorry to Kolbeinn for stealing your awesome name and turning you into a baddie! Thank you Bård for opening my eyes to the autumn leaves. Thank you to my fabulous family, and to all the musicians and writers who turned me into me. Thank you to Sim, who was there through the dark times, and without whom I would surely have given up. Father Dougal mittens to you!

Last of all, I'm immensely grateful to Janne, Kristen, Karyn, Laura, Alison and everyone at Black & White. Your professionalism, attention to detail and feedback have been amazing. Thank you for believing in me, and for making my dream come true.